D0436476

Where you are, believe it or not, is at the very center of life. It is precious beyond your recognition. Cherish it. Be more careful than you have these past days. Really.

APRIL DELANEY

The Magic Journey
by John Nichols

Sisters
OF THE Dream

A Novel by
MARY
SOJOURNER

Northland Publishing

While many of the geographic settings in this book are real,
all characters and events are the products of the author's imagination.
Any resemblance to persons living or dead is purely coincidental.

FIRST EDITION
Library of Congress Catalog Card Number 88-43551
Manufactured in the United States of America
Library of Congress Cataloging-in-Publication Data

Sojourner, Mary.
    Sisters of the dream : a novel / by Mary Sojourner. — 1st ed.
       p.   cm.
    ISBN 0-87358-486-4 : $19.95
    1. Hopi Indians—Fiction. I. Title.
PS3569.045S57 1989   88-43551
813'.54—dc20   CIP

Quote from *The Magic Journey* used with permission of John Nichols.

Text designed by Lisa Brownfield
Typeset by LSK Computype

5K/3-89/0184

For solitude
for Light,
for joy in life;
for Joyce Dubrin, who taught me
to celebrate all three.

Acknowledgments

TALASI MAY HAVE LIVED IN NORTHERN ARIZONA in the twelfth and thirteenth centuries, a time neither as mysterious nor "primitive" as we have been taught. I have let Hopi history tell me about the life and perseverance of Talasi and her people. In respect for the great Hopi overthrow of the Spanish Catholic missionaries in 1680, I have used no Spanish terms in the dream narratives. The most obvious examples are the Hopi terms *tuukwi* for mesa, and *tupqa* for canyon.

Though gold and silver were not present at Black Sands in those centuries, I have used them as adjectives because they most accurately convey our Southwestern light. I tried to avoid terms unknown to the early Hopi. Of course, to adhere strictly to that courtesy would have been to write the book in Hopi. That is for someone else to do, and it will be a different story.

I have used non-traditional accounts, adapted to fit Talasi's view, for the major Hopi ceremonials and histories: Frank Waters' *Book of the Hopi*, for the migration history; Helen Sekaquaptewa/Louise Udall's *Me and Mine* and Polingaysi Qoyawayma/Vada Carlson's *No Turning Back* for Talasi's initiation ceremony. Talasi's last song was adopted from two Ghost Dance songs in *In the Trail of the Wind*, edited by John Bierhorst.

I moved aspects of the Magician's Burial from its original site to Black Sands. May Toho's spirit forgive me.

Tenderhome resembles no nursing home in northern Arizona. It is a composite of places I staffed and visited in the late seventies. I pray that the description is out-moded.

Finally, I thank Violet Laban, of Second Mesa, whose friendship, wisdom and patience far exceed her *nok qui vi* . . . as wonderful as it is. I thank my editor, Susan McDonald, of Northland, especially for saying: "How many pages? As many as it takes to tell the story!" I thank the Mammosser Foundation for their generous support during the summer of '88. I thank Sam, Jae, Matt and Tasha for being exactly who they are. I thank Nick for leaving and Deena, Eva, Lynette and my other sisters for staying. I thank Portly S., with his unflinching honesty, playfulness and steady warmth, for appearing in my life. I thank Paul Shaughnessy . . . and Black Sands.

If I could sing, I would sing in gratitude to Goddess, Dreamweaver, Spider Grandmother, Morgana Le Fay and all the stories of our Mother Earth, waiting to be told.

MARY SOJOURNER
near Flagstaff, 1988

Invitation

THE OLDEST WOMAN SPEAKS:
"How good it is to be in this circle, my kin, and to see your faces, you women, you men, you children and old ones. You are all colors and you are beautiful; your eyes of sky, of water, of earth, all shining in the firelight that illuminates this longest night, this brief story, this dream.

"My name is Cerridwen, or perhaps Hecate, or Acca; or is it Tlatentli or Tiamat or Kohkyangwwuhti? I am very old. Time blurs, and names. You have given me so many, as you have named the stars, the flowers, the birds and snakes and mountains. I am Dreamweaver. As are you.

"Imagine this, my kin, that dreams are only pathways through time and trails through possibility. Imagine that some may be strong enough to travel these pathways, with fear and courage. Were you so strong, where would you travel?

"And this, dear children, imagine this: some might be blessed, unseeking, with this double gift of time and possibility. Were you so blessed, where would you find yourself?

"I am both strong and blessed. As you may be. Tonight, in this dream, in this bright darkness, I travel long ago and far ahead. In this circle, in this story, listening and dreaming, you may travel with me. We begin.

"This is a dream of five women, five sisters, as there might be five strands of fine cotton, as there are five directions on this earth, north, west, south, east and the ever-shifting pathway of the heart. One woman is the copper of high desert canyons, another the pale olive of fresh-split juniper, the third is mountain snow at sunset; the fourth, sea-foam; the last cinnamon, warm and scented, not brown, not red, but both.

1

"These sisters are the daughters of one Mother. They worked and danced and sang together, weaving their lives as they would strong cloth. Then, as most sisters, as most women, they were parted. They learned to shun their Mother and adore their Father. They learned to fear their joy, to hide their true faces, to dread the dance alone. They learned the cutting blade of gossip and how that wound does not heal. Alone and never alone, they learned to give away their greatest treasure: Time.

"They learned to live in a waking sleep, a sleep without dreams; to wait, wait, through sunrise and sunset, snow and violets, thunder and blue October air, to wake into life, to wake to their hearts' return. The fine cloth of their sisterhood frayed and the threads of their lives were cast on the wind. To drift."

The Oldest Woman set juniper on the fire and waited for the strong, thin smoke to rise. Her kin were silent. Not even the tiniest baby made a sound.

"Somewhere in Time, One is weaving, as She always has and always will, as He always has and always will. Sometimes, She is called Penelope and She weaves and waits; sometimes, She is called Xochiquetzal and weaves with marigolds a thousand lovers' snares; sometimes, He is called Kwaayo or Toho or Shadow and He weaves the bride's robe and her shroud; sometimes, One is called Spider Woman and weaves the unfinished web of Creation.

"The weaving continues . . ."

To you, reader: This dream is twice Anglo told. I have no Native American blood. I have used Anglo re-tellings of Hopi, Navajo and Meso-American spiritual tales and history. Some secrets have been withheld, some joys left to the imagination. Fill those silences with your own secrets and joys.

To you, dreamer: All dreams spin out from the same web.

Setting Out

HER FIRST CRY WOULD BE THE MOST SACRED SOUND; more holy than the elders' songs, more holy than the whisper of rain on parched fields, more holy than the rattle of cornstalks at harvest. She was to be first daughter, most treasured child, bearer of her mother's clan. She would carry the Parrot clan forward, through her daughters and their daughters; as had her mother, her grandmother, her great-grandmother, as had all those women, who, though they might be no more than wisps of Spirit or heroines in stories told by firelight, embodied her lineage, passing it on, labor by labor, birth by birth, blessing by blessing, in a strong web of women's lives.

Her mother, Choovio, named for the dark eyes of the antelope, was alone in the birthing room. They had covered the roof-hole with a thick cotton shawl and piled juniper near the fire-pit. Smoke trailed through the room and up the air shaft; it was the smoke of healing, the sweet blue smoke of life. Choovio squatted over a patch of warm sand. She was tired and more than a little afraid. She had been at her first labor since Third Dawn. It seemed the longest she had ever been alone. Only her mother, Gray Bird, had entered to bring her hot teas, to renew the warm sand.

There were juniper-bark pads close at hand. They would protect the birth opening once the work was done. The tea she drank was juniper. It would deepen the work and hasten it. The juniper was like an older sister, sustaining, comforting and yet reminding that one was woman, one *was* work. Choovio welcomed the steady power of the pains in her strong body. She thanked the juniper and the silence and the pain. She was nearly Mother and she was fourteen winters old.

The fire cast its shadows on the stone walls, she dozed, grateful to be in the dreaming world. It seemed to her that her dead grandmother, Sihu, spoke with her from the other side. It was beautiful there, all cool green mist, the color of the *sohovi* leaves. The mist cleared and the old woman crouched at Choovio's side. She was dressed in a new cotton robe; strings of turquoise and shells hung round her neck. She moved easily, though Choovio knew Sihu had died from the sickness that twists the body.

"My granddaughter, my sister," Sihu said, "I bring you strength and happiness for this hard work."

She smiled and her dark eyes were sad. Choovio knew the sorrow was all women's sadness for the birthing pain, for the sharp spasms that not only cut through the belly, but severed a woman from her childhood. To be wife was playing; to be mother was the real work.

There was a greater sadness, cruel to imagine, and that was the sadness of the woman who could not bear children, for then the web of the clan was torn and weakened. Choovio turned her thoughts from that sorrow and gazed up into Sihu's eyes. There was rest there, and comfort—she felt as though she could float in them, as in a pool left in the pocked sandstone of the mesas after a summer storm. She sighed.

And Sihu was gone, the vision shattered in a burst of white light, in the thrust of pain that cut through Choovio's belly. For an instant she tensed and cried out, then, remembering the joy of this time, she gripped her ankles and breathed deep into her work. Time and pain and breath melted into each other. Choovio was time. She was pain. She was breath. She found herself trembling as though chilled by Powamuya's winds. Heat poured up from her belly.

And then, all work, all breath, all pain gathered into one final, timeless bearing down, she felt herself released, the child released; and she gathered into her arms, the wet, wobbly, gasping bundle of her daughter.

"Welcome," she whispered. "I am so happy you are here."

"Eveline, push down," the voices said. They came from far away, they came from in her head, somewhere behind her eyes, somewhere in the bones of her skull.

"Don't fight us," they droned. "You must push down."

Someone had given her a drug. She could remember the cold prick of the needle. It was the miracle labor drug of the '40s; a blessing, a gift, her doctor had called it Twilight Sleep. Twilight, yes, light sinking, winter, deep cold, voices coming from far away, from within, as though one lay freezing to death at twilight; not sleeping, no, only suspended.

"Pusshhhhhh . . ." Faces, shifting, staring down at her out of their great eyes, the voices echoing, a masked creature, two, three, all of them screaming at her, their voices echoing. She was bound, ankles and wrists, to a cold metal table. There were hands on her, in her. She had forgotten how to breathe, to scream, to obey. White light blinded her. She longed to roll over, to escape the light and eyes and voices, to crouch on hands and knees, to arch her back, to scream, to breathe.

"Be a good girl," a woman said. "That noise doesn't help. You need your strength to push. Help doctor deliver this baby. You're making his job harder. Hush. Work."

There was no silence. These was no sweet, warm and quiet space to occupy, no room to work. The words became foreign. She had never heard such sounds and she was so cold, so naked. Pain ripped through her. She had forgotten why she was there and was astonished to feel herself begin to split open. With gratitude, she gave one long howl and went into the blackness.

Some time later, she could not guess how long, she came awake and they brought her the baby. It was wrapped tight in pink flannel. It was screaming, its tiny bruised face twisted in rage. She looked down at it, and knew it hated her.

"Mother Morrigan," the nurse said, "meet your daughter." Eveline had never held a baby. She rolled on her side and touched its face. It jerked its head away. She knew without doubt that she would never be enough for this child, this furious stranger. Still, she began to unwrap it so that it might wave its arms and legs. She wished it had been a boy. Then, once she had got through the first few years, it would have its father to teach it, to give it what it could not take from her. But it was not *it*. It was not a boy. It was a girl. The nurse rushed back to her side.

"No, Mother," she said. "You don't want to do that. She'll just get more agitated. They need lots of security at this age. She likes the wrapping. You'll keep her on schedule—she needs that routine."

"I'm sorry," Eveline said. She looked up into the nurse's kind face. Her eyes felt thick with tears and she thought she might begin to cry. "Does she have a name?" she asked. The nurse smiled. She cranked up the bed and settled the baby in Eveline's arms.

"Of course she does," she said. "Elizabeth. Elizabeth Margaret Morrigan, a happy compromise, your husband said." She held out a baby bottle. "Here," she said, "it's time for you to start being a mother."

Eveline held the bottle to the baby's mouth. In her terrible hunger, the baby jerked her head frantically from side to side, the nipple lost, found and lost again. Eveline's hand trembled.

"I'm sorry," she said again. "I'm not very good at this." The tears began to slip from her eyes. "I'm tired," she said. The nurse hesitated.

"Relax, Mother," she said. "You new mothers are always nervous at first." She studied Eveline's face and sighed. "Tell you what," she said. "I'll take baby Elizabeth back to the nursery and give her a proper breakfast." She smiled. "She's just excited by this new world." Eveline held the baby up. The nurse briskly gathered in the screaming child.

"You have a nice cry, dear," she said cheerfully. "It'll do you a world of good."

Eveline watched them leave. She pulled the blankets up under her chin. All she wanted was sleep, silence and her own dead mother and the turning back of time.

"Lizzie," she whispered and turned her wet face to the window and the dawn shimmering there.

The child clung to her mother's skirt. Though she was well-wrapped in rabbit skins, her plump legs trembled with the winter cold. It was Kelmuya, the Respected Moon. It was Soyala, the Time of Least Light. The child was three winters old. They had named her Talasi, pollen, for on her naming day, the wind had scattered corn pollen in a golden cloud. For a time, there had been other names: Masichuvio, for the gray deer seen by her cousin on the morning of her birth; Sakapa, for the pines climbing Two-Color Mountain; Muha, for the milkweed's silk. Those names blew away, frail as *muha* on the wind. And, Talasi was said so often and she was so light on her little feet, that all knew the name was hers.

Every *Soyal*, Choovio had brought her girl to the plaza, first in her belly, then in her arms and now, standing on her own. They waited with the others of the village, the old ones and women and children of Place of Water, for the return of the Kachinas, the holy Spirits from Neavatukaovi, the indigo, snow-crested mountains to the far South.

It was late in the day of the shortest light. The plaza was silent. Cold and hungry and restless as she felt, Talasi made no sound. Tiny flakes of dry snow sifted over the People. The light began to fade. Silent as the snow, silent as the pale light, He appeared. White, all white, robed in white, masked in white, His eyes black slits, bright feathers on His helmet and in His hand, Soyal Kachina staggered into the plaza.

"See," Choovio whispered, "He is like a baby. Or an old man, tired from His long journey. He brings us prayer feathers and blessing." The words were nearly a chant on her lips; she had said them even when the child was in her belly. Talasi clung to her mother's fur-wrapped legs. Slowly, steadily, the Spirit gained His strength. He circled the plaza and it was the Peoples' welcome that flowed into His legs, His back, holding Him up, carrying Him forward. He stopped four times, once to scatter cornmeal on an outside wall, next at the entrance to the place Talasi was never to go, then, to the center of the plaza, to sing, and, to another forbidden place, where He placed four prayer feathers.

Prayer feathers were not to be touched. It was hard to obey that teaching. They were so beautiful, white and downy, slender and striped, shuddering in the wind, nodding and trembling over the earth, the waters they blessed. Talasi watched the old Spirit receive welcome from the gray-haired Soyal chief. She wondered what it was to be old, how it was to be Spirit, a grandmother, a priest. Everything she saw became a question in her heart, and there was so much to see. Sometimes her mother joked that they should have named her Mongwau, for the bird with big eyes.

The Soyal chief gave the Spirit cornmeal and prayer feathers. Above the empty houses of the Old Ones on Juniper Tuukwi, the gray sun descended. Soyal Kachina bowed His thanks. The chief bowed his. The Great Cycle swung foward, time renewed, life renewed, the seasons, once again, set in motion. The Spirit circled the plaza, as time would swing in its great life-giving dance, and, slowly, silently, as the days would grow longer and the nights wane, he walked out of sight into the deepening dusk.

Choovio gathered Talasi in her arms and climbed the steep path to their home. She had built the rooms herself, working with her family, mixing the *tsoqa* from earth and water, patting it into place, setting the soft red stones she had carried up the trail from the wash below the village, the wash where the milkweed grew. Her home seemed to melt into her mother's. On warm evenings, they sat together on the roofs, hulling corn, sewing, mending, talking and talking, their laughter soft on the nightwind.

Choovio built up the fire, warmed cornmeal soup and fed them both, grateful for the shadows flickering on the walls, for the food in their bellies. Nuuva, her husband, was gone with the other men. It would be many sunrises before he would return, back from the dark mysteries of the kiva, back from that unknown, round room beneath the earth, where hidden away from the women, he and the other men did the sacred work of Soyal.

She sat for a time with Talasi, smiling down at the round sleeping face. Then she turned to her grinding stones and ground corn far into the night, corn for the ceremonies, corn for the feasts, sacred corn for the sacred work of Soyal. Talasi, drifting in and out of dreams, heard the rasp of her mother's work, the music of the grinding, the music of her mother's songs and saw, behind her closed owl eyes, the Spirits dancing high above, laughing and playing, bounding from star to star.

Lizzie couldn't move. The big glass door closed behind her mother. The room was full of strange children. A red-haired lady stepped forward and smiled at her. There were paper flowers in the windows and letters, bright letters, strung across the blackboard. She knew those letters. They were the alphabet and they made words. The red-haired lady took her hand and gently tugged her forward, into the big room.

"Lizzie," she said, "I'm Miss Carlson. I'm your teacher." She pointed to the children. Some of them were giggling. "These are your classmates," the lady said. "There are your new friends." She turned to the class. "Children," she said, "this is Lizzie Morrigan. She was sick when school started, so she is joining us now. I know you will make her welcome."

Lizzie looked back through the glass door. Her mother was not there.

She looked at the children. They were all watching her. She didn't know what to do. The red-haired lady, the teacher, smiled again. It was a funny smile, not like her mother's smile.

"Your mother will be back soon to get you," the teacher said. "She must be very proud of you. You are a big girl now, you are in kindergarten."

Lizzie felt sick to her stomach. It wouldn't be good to throw up. She remembered her mother talking about school—it was going to be fun and she would make friends. She looked up at the teacher. Miss Carlson saw the misery welling in Lizzie's gray eyes, she had seen it before. And she had seen the same blind terror. A kind woman, she had found it best to bring these new little ones into some activity. Sometimes they forgot their fears. She guided Lizzie to a desk.

"We're going to take out our crayons," she said, "and make some pictures now. Would you like to join us?"

Lizzie nodded. She loved to draw and she loved the colors in the crayon box. She always put them in rainbow order. Her mother had taught her to do that. Miss Carlson gave her a brand-new box of crayons. She saw Lizzie glance wistfully at the classroom door, and, with a sigh, open the crayon box.

For a few minutes, the room was peaceful. Then, with a look of pure shame, Lizzie was violently sick, over herself, over her desk, over the just-begun picture. Miss Carlson led her to the bathroom. Someone giggled. Someone whispered. Lizzie held her picture over face, sobbing into it.

"I want my mother," she whispered. "I want her now."

Talasi crouched near the roof-hole of her home. Gray clouds raced across the last glow of the setting sun. It had been an eerie, yellowish afternoon and a blood-red sunset. She wondered if Taiwa was angry, to be so dark and hot as that. She piled some pebbles carefully into little houses, knocked them down and began again. She felt strange and sad. Many aunts and grandmothers were in the house with her mother. Her father had gone to the kiva, the place she must not go, not ever, not even if she was very frightened. She had never been alone before. It was nearly dark and she wanted her supper, her rabbit blanket, her mother's face, the smell of her, the touch.

There was a rustle at the roof-hole and Great-aunt Hopaqa scurried up carrying a pile of wet bark in her broad hands. She glanced down at the silent girl.

"Child," she said, "why are you hiding here alone? Your mother is resting. Run to Rupi's house for supper. You will sleep there tonight. We are with your mother. All will be as it should."

Talasi pressed her cheek to her aunt's hand. The bark smelled sharp and spicy, her aunt's skin of juniper smoke.

"Go," Hopaqa said, "go fill your belly."

Talasi climbed the wood ladder to the path below. Her father had made the ladder, felling and trimming the pine poles, lashing them together with strong yucca rope. He had let her pull away the bark and sniff the clean white wood beneath. She stepped down onto the packed sand. Rupi's house was only a little way down the path. Their village lay in a broad wash, between black cinder hills and sunset-red *tuukwi*, upon whose flat tops little pine and twisted juniper grew.

In the center of that rock and light and sand, the village was safe: from flood, from storm, from the sudden terrifying appearance of the raiders who swept in from the north. There were two clusters of rooms, three stories high. Below them lay the plaza, the place of talk and ceremony; and, more and more, the games of the bone dice, the stalks, the games women hated and men loved. To the northeast was the ballcourt, a great open-ended oval, like a huge open mouth in the earth. The men played there. Talasi was afraid of that place . . . the sound, the silence.

Not many steps west of the ballcourt was her favorite place. There, from a small hole in the earth, the Spirits drew breath at night and breathed out by day. She could go there, but only in prayer, only with offerings and only in the company of a grown-up. Sometimes, the women left flowers and pollen and salt. She was not afraid. There was a peace there, and welcome. The Spirit's breath was comfort, hushed and steady as the rasp of grinding.

Forbidden, deep in the earth, were the kivas, great round rooms, from whose smoke-holes rose the sound of laughter and chanting, the sound of men, the sound of the sacred work. She was not sure what they did down there, her father and the other men. Once she had asked her mother and her mother said,

"They do the Spirit's work, as I grind corn, as Aunt Pamosi shapes clay into bowls and paints her dreams on them." She had smiled. "And," she said, "as you watch with your big eyes and ask your big questions." Talasi wanted her mother. She did not want to wait till morning, to sleep in Rupi's bed. She stood outside the roof-hole. The sky was black and great Hotomqam hung in the sky, the stars shiny on his hero's helmet.

Rupi's mother looked up to see a small frightened face in the roof-hole. She climbed the ladder and carried Talasi down. The child trembled in her arms. She had closed her eyes and did not open them, even when Rupi spoke to her. The girls were best friends and more than that, they were cousins, daughters of the Parrot clan. Talasi burrowed deeper into Owasi's bosom. Owasi patted her thin shoulders.

It was no wonder the child was terrified. Choovio had been in labor for nearly two days, her pains so deep that she was ashen beneath her warm brown skin. Choovio was a brave woman, strong enough to have lost a second son to the summer fever and, only a little later, welcomed this new soul into her belly. There were many deaths of the babies and children. One summer every family in the village had lost at least one child. Summer fever was evil—it drained the child, bent it double with cramps, left it burning bright-eyed and silent. During those long dry months, Place of Water had been Place of Sadness. Children were precious: sons were hunters and farmers and priests, daughters the lifeline of the clans. This one, this little Parrot, clung to her as Choovio clung to life. Gently, Owasi set the child down.

"Come," she said, "come and sit with us, Talasi." Owasi smiled to herself. At any other time, Talasi would have scarcely needed the invitation. Rupi was friend and cousin, and the children of the village wandered freely from home to home, always sure of welcome, of food and blanket and place to sleep. And, when needed, a lesson, a story, a reminder of the Peoples' ways.

Talasi stood silent, her thumb in her mouth, her eyes shut tight. Owasi picked her up. This night, she needed more than stew or *piki* or cuddling with Rupi under rabbit robes while Grandmother told the old stories of coyote and bluebird and badger. Talasi buried her face in Owasi's neck. There, in the good smell of sun and cooking and smoke, was safety. There was mother, there, against warm skin, there in the soft dark.

Owasi was silent. The family chattered over their food. There was nothing to say to the child; it would be foolish to make promises. Choovio was very weakened. It could happen that a woman grew so tired she could not do the work of giving birth. Sometimes, the baby was turned the wrong way. Sometimes, the lifecord became the deathcord, tightening around the baby's neck, sending the little soul back into the dark as the sacred eagles were sent on their journey to the Spirits. Sometimes, there was nothing to do and both mother and child would die.

Talasi was too small to be told of Masau'u, He who watched over life and death, whose appearance to the dying was a blessing, whose hands eased the going-over, whose touch might be the greatest joy. All Talasi could know, should this labor take Choovio, was that Mother, Source, all-comfort, was gone. Owasi stopped her thoughts. They would not help. They were out-of-balance. They were *qahopi*, not of the Way. There was enough doubt in the village, enough gossip, enough of the games in the plaza.

She settled herself and Talasi into a pile of robes and began to sing. It was a song to Father Sun, a song to Mother Earth, to She who gave and received all beings, all juniper and corn and pine, all eagles and snakes, all children, all Old Ones, all life, who watched over Place of Water, who cradled all of Black Sands.

At First Dawn's purple light, an eerie sound filled the village. It was sharper than a hawk's cry, falling and soaring on the harsh wind of the Hawk's Moon. It was the cry of death. The women, from rooftops, from pathways, on the cold sand and cinders, were mourning. Choovio stirred in her blankets. The pain was gone. She felt empty, lightened, as though water ran through her meat and bones. She ran her hands over her body. Her breasts were swollen and sore, her belly flat. The smoky air seemed a weight on her eyes. She closed them and heard a voice.

"It is dawn," Hopaqa said. "You have been given another day."

Choovio looked, and saw, in a circle around her, the women of her clan. Their heads were bowed. Near her left hand lay a cradleboard, holding a carefully wrapped bundle. She turned towards the tiny thing, tears running into her sweat-salt hair. There was a touch on her brow, another on her arm, on her hair, on her shoulder. With each touch, the tears ran more quickly. She set her hand on her empty belly and felt a hand on hers. Someone held her head up and tilted a mug of warm tea to her lips. She swallowed past the lump of sorrow in her throat.

"It is time for prayer," Hopaqa said.

"Again," Choovio whispered.

Hopaqa set her finger on her dry lips. "Hush, child," she said. "He needs our prayers."

Choovio sighed. As the breath left her body, she felt the gift again, of breath, of life, of another day. A prayer began to form in her heart. She knew she need not say the words. Her grandmother had taught her that. Old Sihu, in pain beyond words, her eyes clear, her spirit shining there.

"She hears our prayers before we know them," she had said. So Choovio drew in breath and let the prayer drift up from her heart: that the baby might have a good journey, that it might return to her belly, that it might know breath . . . and life. How welcome that would be. She stroked the little bundle. Soon, they would tuck the child in its earthen bed in a near *tuukwi*, a parrot at its feet, the wide sky above and the baby, son of the Parrot clan, would sleep till his next journey.

"I have treasured you," she said. "Blessed be."

"Your daughter is here," Hopaqa said.

'Oh yes," Choovio said and held out her arms. Talasi moved into them and lay, pressed close to her mother's breast and belly, Choovio's heart beating against her cheek.

"Rest," Hopaqa whispered.

Only Choovio, slipping into that warm dark, knew and noted the tiny seed of bitterness that had lodged sharp in her aching heart. Talasi's hand rested on the place, and for that moment, it was comfort enough.

Silence lay beyond the locked door. Lizzie rang the bell again. There was nothing but silence. She knew her mother was there. It was right after school and her mother was always there right after school. Always. Except for the time, and her father had promised it would be the only time, when Lizzie was almost a baby and sick in bed and her mother was out in the kitchen, singing, talking to herself, singing a song Lizzie didn't know, a song that had no words. Then, the ambulance had come and taken her mother away.

A strange woman had come and cooked strange food. She had braided Lizzie's hair so tight that it seemed as if her brains would be pulled out. Her mother had been gone a long time. Her father had said that Mom was sick, but that she was feeling better and would be home soon. He had said that every day for a long time, till Lizzie had stopped asking.

Then, and it had been worse than the absence, her mother, or someone like her mother, had come home on weekends. She sat in the living-room, hour after hour, turning the pages of magazines. There was a terrible smell about her, like the taste of metal. When she talked again, she told Lizzie it was the medicine that helped her sleep. After a while, she was mother again and came home for good. The smell was gone and her face was pretty and music poured out of the old dark piano and when she made cookies, they were exactly perfect. Lizzie had almost forgotten about the bad time.

She rang the bell again. There was only silence. She knocked. After all, the bell could be broken. Sometimes the landlord didn't get around to fix things as quickly as he should. She knocked again. There was the other family behind the door across the hall, but she wasn't to bother them. Her father was at work. The baby was with her mother. She decided to walk around the hall twenty times, say twenty Hail Marys maybe, then knock again. If her mother didn't answer, she would just do it again. Sometimes, you would get very worried about something and just do something ordinary and suddenly everything would be fine. Besides, fear was a sin. The Sisters said that.

Lizzie walked past the ugly table, the picture of the ocean, the gold light, the neighbors' door, the head of the stairs; she walked the circle twenty times. She had trouble concentrating on the prayer. The Sisters said it wasn't good, really, to ask for anything when you prayed. It was much better to just pray and, sometimes, when you were afraid, you could make yourself stronger by offering your fear up to God.

"I offer my fear to You," Lizzie whispered, and she went up to the door and knocked as hard as she could with both fists. There was nothing. She could walk and pray again. Circling slowly, her hands clasped in front of her, she closed her eyes and tried to picture God. It didn't work; it never did. All she ever saw was the terrible hurt body hanging above the altar, the blood, the closed eyes. She opened her eyes and saw the glint of the gold picture frame, the splintered rainbows cast through the prisms in the door at the bottom of the stairs. The other, the Great Comfort, the Great Judge, she could not see.

Again, Lizzie knocked. And again. Her heart banged against her ribs. She was crying. That was bad. That was losing faith. That was asking for attention. She knocked again. Nothing. She kicked the door. Nothing.

By the time her father found her, she was crouched in the fading light at the bottom of the stairs, reading. She looked up at him.

"I can't get in," she said. Without a word, he raced up the stairs and threw his solid body against the door. It burst open. Lizzie slowly climbed the stairs. He was on the phone. There was a casserole on the kitchen table, chocolate pudding in the cold oven, the baby screaming in his crib and her mother, pale and quiet, in the big double bed. Lizzie looked once in through the bedroom door.

"I'm sorry," she whispered.

She put the casserole in the oven. She knew how to light the flame. She knew how to be careful. Danny sobbed in their bedroom. She picked him up and fed him some of the chocolate pudding. When the ambulance men came, she carried him back into the bedroom so she wouldn't have to see the men or what they were carrying. She was glad when they were gone. Her father made some phone calls. Then the casserole was done and they all sat down to eat. When her father said grace, she couldn't keep her eyes closed. She was afraid she would see, in the dark, something terrible.

One

AUGUST BURNED IN, WET, AIRLESS, TROUBLESOME as a bad promise. Lizzie and Ben decided to drive the three kids to California. Ben's folks were there, in the pink trailer near the highway. They would leave the kids there and they would, for a while, go their separate ways. It could help. It couldn't hurt.

About an hour after the Arizona/New Mexico border, Ben and the kids fell asleep in the back of the van. Alone in the front, her ears humming with fatigue and silence, Lizzie drove. It was pure glory. The silence, the solitude, the halos of light that move ahead of a car in moonless dark on an empty desert road. They led and illuminated and slipped away, picking out great moths and skeletal bushes and the quick, gorgeous glitter of beer cans and broken glass.

Drunk on the quiet, Liz let go the wheel. The van rolled on. Inside, the dashboard shone pale green, the gauges, the radio dial, the tiny fluorescing skull Jenny had bought at the last trading post. Everything else was blurred and wan, as though something inside and out had sucked up the light. She guessed there were stars. Now and again, glowing clouds, like worn nap on velvet, trembled above the unknown foothills. The van swerved. Liz set her hands firm on the wheel.

She was a solid woman, a real Earth Mother, Ben said. Everyone said. Her wild auburn hair was tied up in a blue bandana, her olive skin had burned brown in the desert sun. By the dashlights, her Navajo bracelet and the silver in her gray eyes were twin ghost-glints in the rear-view mirror. She felt spooky, beautiful. She brushed wisps of hair away from her eyes. She was not in fashion—those days, it was Guinevere who was queen, and Twiggy, and Mama Michelle. Those were the cool, blonde,

14

magic ladies; they were the distant fantasies for the California wet-dreamin'. It was the Lizzies, the big mamas who kept the whole thing moving, who kept the cool dudes awake and on their feet.

Keith, the smallest boy, whimpered in his sleep. She could hear the four of them, snoring and rustling, Ben and the babies safe in her hands. She could drive through till morning, whenever that was. They would sleep. She would be alone. The radio pulled in fading snatches of rock and roll. "Be my baby," somebody sang, the music wavering, the voice spooky, as though the sound warped in the night air, ricocheting off mountains, sailing down on desert thermals.

Arizona was a dream beyond the headlights' burn, the road cutting straight through nothing, gas stations and trading posts leaping up like debris in space. Liz would not have been surprised to drive into some twist in time and find herself back home, dreaming on the bed by the lakeside window, breathing in that wet and rose-sweet air. It seemed reasonable that phantoms might appear or will-o-wisps or luminous sagebrush. Moths burst on the windshield.

She imagined how the sky might be, the stars, how dawn would melt in over the far hills, how somewhere a waitress was serving coffee, workers were stumbling in off the late shift, somewhere a hundred miles down the road, a thousand.

The air pouring in the van window was alien; there was nothing familiar in it. A week ago, less, she had been able to smell the wild roses, rain coming, the lake, pungent as an animal; change, leaves into mould, mould into dirt, dirt into flowers. This air held no life. Liz needed to touch something out there, to break a twig from one of those bony bushes and see that it had, indeed, grown. She needed to turn over a rock and see something living, no matter how pale, how grotesque. She needed to see the flash of something escaping, something going home. There had been no more than five cars on the road in the last hour. Gently, she braked and pulled the van to the side of the road. Her family stirred, then settled back into sleep. She stepped down onto the sand.

The air was cooler than she expected. Above, the stars blazed across endless sky, not just the constellations, but powderings and pastel washes of stardust. The desert seemed to phosphoresce. She bent and placed her palms flat against the sand, letting the ache in her back release. The earth was smooth and warm as flesh. Ben's voice floated on the air.

"Anything wrong?" he whispered.

"Nothing," she said quietly.

He was silent. The van seemed a distant planet, its occupants of no concern or kinship. She walked a few yards from the car, down into a little wash and sat on the sand. In the soft breeze, the bushes rattled like bone wind-chimes. Beyond, the greater silence broke into tiny rustlings, faint bird cries, a fading howl; within, her pulse sounded in her ears. Delicate tracks laced the sand. By daylight, the great desert spaces had been unsettling, but in starlight, with the glowing hills coiled around, she felt quite safe. She understood how a woman or man might simply start walking and never stop.

She and Lazar had started fighting the moment they left the house. It was a wonderful house, airy, tall, her room on the third floor like a nest, her windows looking out across a shimmering carpet of treetops, toward the city lights, toward dawn and sunset. Her marriage to Ben was long gone—the children were with him for the night. She was Liz Lazar. Her opponent had given that, the name, only that, no ceremony, no promise. He was a little famous, a research scientist of behavior, of the quick and precarious mysteries of the brain. They were fighting about marriage, the two of them, polite, tricky. She wanted marriage. He needed "space" and he still needed her.

The children horrified him. She had begun to be horrifying, too, with her demands, her hunger for his promise. His elegant face was pinched, feral—he, who worked with laboratory animals, with rats and monkeys and electric shock. The kids hated him. They were in their teens, the three of them, Keith, Jen, Steve, and they were funny and cruel.

She and Lazar were going to a dinner party. She and *Dr.* Lazar, La-ZAR. He liked people to call him that. It went with his sweep of silver hair and his small elegance. He had a first name. No one knew it, only that it began with S. The kids had been only too glad to fill in the rest.

The dinner party was at his mentor's, in a huge, old, mansion on a cliff above the lake, the lake of wild roses. Their hostess, a Peruvian surgeon, had seated Lazar and Liz across from each other, separated by ivory tapers and a silver bowl filled with late magnolias. There was a pale yellow wine in big goblets, and séviche, and platters of empañadas. Liz watched Lazar watch her eat. She was the thinnest she had ever been. He wanted her thinner. For her own good. Clara poured them more wine.

Liz knew she and Lazar were drinking too much. His fine-planed face thickened. His speech became more eloquent and his brown eyes seemed to shrink. She felt the dilute winey blood pound in her wrists. He sniped at her, flirted with the woman next to him. Liz felt she could easily kill him—she could take the little antique fruit knife off her plate and draw the blade slowly, raggedly across his tan throat. She sipped her coffee.

Clara led them into the living-room. A massive couch and soft chairs faced the huge window-wall that overlooked the lake. The black lawn was frosted with moonlight. Liz watched the waves tremble onto an unseen beach at the cliff's base. The room was very noisy. Lazar had disappeared. She was too warm, too grouchy, too spooked to keep standing there, smiling, nodding, agreeing about the charm of the view and the perfection of Clara's parties.

She glanced at Clara and moved towards the archway. Clara gestured to the hall. Liz slipped away and walked slowly down the dim corridor, trying one door after another; she felt like Alice in Wonderland. There was, at the very end, a small, quiet room, its walls lined with books, its one window looking out over the lake.

She sat in the dark. Moonlit waves rippled in over the ebony water. It seemed to her that they were chains, rolling in, again and again, taming that black water, with beauty, and dreadful in that. She thought of the first nights with Lazar, his lean body above hers, those dark eyes sweeping over her, his tireless passion. She remembered embroidering violets on a white cotton shirt and evolving an elaborate scheme to present it to him at an office birthday party . . . in full view of his wife. Friends had warned her. They had repeated the old, old wisdom about unfaithful husbands, and she had known it would be different. He loved her. He took her big body in his hands and he made her beautiful. And now, while she sat here, gorgeously drunk, he was sitting somewhere else, gazing into someone's wife's adoring eyes and that woman was knowing, for the first time in years, that she too was beautiful.

"There you are."

Liz turned. Clara stood in the doorway, her hair silvered in the dim light. She hesitated.

"Elizabeth," she said. "I did not mean to disturb you. Lazar wondered where you were and sent me hunting." She laughed.

Liz smiled. He would do that, conspire with Clara's charm and his, to make a small intriguing drama of her "mood swings."

"I'm fine," she said. "I drank that wonderful wine too fast. I needed some quiet."

Clara nodded. "I will leave you to recover," she said. "There are some interesting books on the desk. You will find the light switch behind the curtain. I will tell Lazar that you are mysteriously disappeared." Liz walked over to her and surprised them both by kissing Clara's cool cheek. Clara smiled.

"Yes," she said. "Even with my husband, but especially with a man like Lazar, we women need to have our little mysteries." She gently tapped Liz's face. "Go explore," she said.

Liz turned on the light. Under its circle, the desk was cluttered. There were ivory netsukes and cloissoné boxes and a very old Japanese writing set. She wanted one of the netsukes more than she'd wanted anything in a long time. It was a tiny bat with jade eyes. On its back rode a water spirit, grinning, a little fiendish, foam streaming off its lizard head. There were two German photography books, one on bats, the other a mystery. On the cover were golden toppled walls and light and, in great black letters the word, *Anasaziche*. She opened the book into mystery and more, into memory and brief regret; then, each page turned more beautiful than the last, into a bright and opening wonder.

She thought of a vacation with Lazar in England, of the Great Barrow and Avebury and a monk's beehive cell on Wales' most western point and how they had argued over every ruin. She had seen magic; he, science and the triumph of mind. It would be years before she would know they had both been right. She turned the pages to deserts and burning blue skies and a red sandstone ruin held in a shadowed hollow in a red sandstone cliff, all of it washed in copper light. There were doorways within doorways within doorways, the light flooding, the shadows black and sharp as obsidian. There was a tower, dark against a dawn sky, a crescent moon pale and clean above it. She felt her heart stir. It seemed to her just then that, more than the netsuke, more than Lazar's promise, she wanted to stand in the sun and shadow of those ruined walls. She wanted to enter the doorways. She wanted to set her hands on that warm stone.

Clara tapped on the door.

"Are you feeling a little more steady?" she asked. Liz nodded and held up the book.

"Where is this?" she said.

"Here," Clara said, "In your country . . . in mine."

"Here?" Liz said.

"Yes," Clara said. "Marco and I visited some of those places last year when he taught in Albuquerque. Anasazi, that's what the anthropologists call them. They were the early people. Their descendents still live here, and in my country. There is so much mystery about those places. That one, the city in the cave, they lived there only fifty years and moved on, without a trace, without a clue. You must persuade Lazar to take you there someday." She tapped the picture of the great cave. "This one . . . it's in northern Arizona, in the high desert. You must go."

Liz closed the book. For an instant, the banshee rock-and-roll radio came back, the low hills, the incandescent moths, the road slicing into the desert night.

"Thank you, Clara," she said. "For the quiet, for the book. I must find a copy."

"There is an English version," Clara said. She wrote down the name and slipped the paper into Liz's evening bag. "Lazar is ready to go home," she said. "He asked me to tell you."

They stood by the window. The waves were gone and the lake a perfect sheet of black glass. The moon was mirrored there, cool, full, working its power where it could, on water, on the tides of heart and brain; and, to the west, washing over that warm red rock.

Months later, moving clothes into the extra closet in Lazar's empty room, Liz found Clara's note. Lazar was gone, full gone, the final betrayal and release coming in the sound of a young woman's voice on the phone at dawn. "My first real love," he said for the fourth time in six years, and was gone by noon.

A week later, Liz found a package bound with braided silk on the front hall table. She undid the cord and saw the book, in English; Clara's elegant script slanted across the title page.

"Find something beautiful," Clara wrote, "to hang from this cord . . . and wear it. Every time you touch or see it, know that I wish you a whole heart and adventure. Perhaps you could take yourself to these miraculous places? Clara"

The silver rabbit was icy between Liz's breasts, the braided silk the perfect length. The little charm touched and swung free, blessing her with Clara's wishes, still warm after eight years and across two thousand miles, warm even in the December air pouring in through the car window. It was mountain air, black-cold, dry, the hint of woodsmoke weaving through. Liz had opened her window and jacket for the drive through the dark pines to the hilltop observatory that overlooked her new home, the observatory that drew in, through miracles of glass and connection, the divine glitter of the Arizona heavens.

She had wandered the observatory grounds by daylight. There had been the massive old library, its doors locked, its stone chimneys cold. There had been the founder's tomb, tucked in the shadow of the old observatory dome. It was stone and round and its ceiling was a stained-glass star.

He was, Liz guessed, curious, tempermental, a seer who loved, above all miracles, the slow dance of the planets and the never-mastered lessons of the night. He might have wished to return, as the great Haley's Comet returned, to the future, to black December, 1985, to icy dark and dry air, to the stuff of perfect visibility. He would have treasured, this imagined man, watching the ancient thing of dust and vapor and fire, in a near-century-old building, through equipment so stunningly new it seemed nearly science fiction. He would have not been surprised, this man who wrote, "to see into the beyond requires purity, and the securing it makes him perforce a hermit from his kind," to know that some would come there, to the sight, to the terror of the dark and the reassurance of the light, as they might come, unwitting, to a healing, would come alone.

Liz drove up the steep road, the city lights swirling away behind her. It was nearly Christmas. She was alone, Lazar eight years gone, her name re-taken, home and children and true, true love two thousand miles away. This last was Nicholas, dark one, whose leaving had left her heart a numb thing. She had just signed a one-year lease on a cabin in the pines south of town. Saturday night's downtown glitter flickered in and out of the trees, the sky opening out, thick with stars and stardust. It was the longest night of the shortest day. It was a time of turning.

She was nearly forty-five years old. She was very tired—that was the simple way to say it. She needed some miracle of light, something beyond explanation, something kin to meteors and dawns and the shuddering fox-fire of the Northern Lights. She needed to see something that would not remind her of Nick. The comet might serve. It might be a terror, something out of an ancient Japanese woodcut, half light, half beast, its tail a dragon's breath, its alien beauty enough to knock her senseless. She was too chicken to die, and amnesia seemed the next best thing.

The observatory parking lot was full, families straggling in from campers and pick-up trucks. Liz pulled off onto the roadside and walked up the driveway; she was breathing hard. The air was dry and fragrant, so thin one paid attention to breath. The library was set like a stone jewel in the pines' shadow. She opened the heavy door into a big, dim room whose walls curved up into the domed ceiling. People, still bundled against the cold, sat silent in front of a movie screen.

She took a seat and watched. The room was very quiet. Pictures flashed quick and frail as dreams. There was her dragon and sleek rockets and birds with burning tails; formulae that filled the screen and woodcut crowds standing, gape-mouthed, in some early Flemish morning; there were ice-clouds and rock carvings, and then the thing itself, an old dandelion, blowing through space.

A hand-hewn log platform ran half the room's circumference, wrought-iron staircases coiling up at either end. You could climb up there and walk slowly along the rows and rows of books, Liz thought. You could stop and take one in your hand. The cover would be leather and there would be the smell of age. The lower walls were filled with sepia photos and framed manuscripts. There were portraits, wonderfully serious young men in stiff dark clothes, a woman in a black jumper, hair drawn back in a perfect twist, her eye pressed to a telescope. In cases set into the stone walls, there were cracked wooden models of Mars, the canals etched in, the deserts scrawled with Latin in the old astronomer's young, spidery hand.

The screen went blinding bright. A pleasant woman guided them all outside and pointed out the path to the hilltop observatory. The lamps were faint, the moon new; only starlight shone on the faces of the people climbing with her. Liz studied them. No one walked alone. No one returned her gaze. They were in couples, in families, in groups. She sensed that she had a kind of invisibility.

The dome hovered above them. She climbed the rough stone steps and leaned against the iron railing a minute, letting the others brush by. She imagined the astronomers, plotting coordinates, typing numbers into their computers, getting numbers back, messages sent and received, day after day, night after night. Once, she had stood in Chaco Canyon, Clara's gift new round her neck. She had imagined astronomers, those Anasazi priests watching the holy sun's emergence above the mesas, the waxing and waning of the constant moon. They too would have kept careful track, using the fixed profile of butte or pinnacle, that steady rock, to gauge the floating miracle of the season, for weather, for planting, for prediction and survival. She wondered what miracles chattered in and out of the new astronomers' computers, what hope.

A bearded man gestured from the doorway. She walked in, into nothing. There was no light, no visible boundaries, only black cold. People whispered. Someone waved a red light to move her forward. She took a step, felt the floor vanish, grabbed an icy metal rail and stepped down. Her eyes began to adjust. The telescope seemed a giant insect, poised, barely seen against a thin wedge of indigo sky high above. Liz tied her wool scarf tight and shoved her gloved hands deep in her pockets. It did no good. Dark and cold fed each other. Someone bumped her from behind. She stumbled forward into a warm back and realized she was standing in line.

They waited a long time. The dark thinned. She wondered if amputation was going to be required for her feet. It was as though they stood on a sheet of black ice. Shadows, like the scenery changers in Japanese theater, moved the people forward, the platform up and down, the scope's eyepiece into place. They wore dark bulky clothes and they barely spoke. A touch on her elbow sent her smoothly through the last curve of the line to the platform ladder. She began to climb, the metal burning through her gloves. A parka-shrouded man slid the viewing piece to her eye. She heard the rustle and whisper of the people below . . . and went deaf with wonder.

She could have been floating in a black tunnel; at its end, the comet burned modestly. "A piece of cosmic lint," some guy in the crowd had whispered. That it was, and more. No dragon, no flaming bird, no terror, no messenger: it was light, pure, white, unearthly round and vaporous. It *was* an aged dandelion, a cool blossom of light. It was impossible and ordinary. It was a miracle.

"There are people waiting," the man said and gently swung the scope away. Liz looked out into the dark room. It was then, imagining the couples huddled in the cold, that she resumed thinking of Nick, of his absolute absence in her life. He would have loved the place, the fine old woodworking, the craft of the iron on the massive doors. He would have loved that leap out into space and back. The man in the parka touched her arm gently.

"You'll have to climb down," he said softly. She set her foot on the top rung and was abruptly afraid. It had been like that since the moment she had known Nick was not coming back. She would relax for a while. She would get lost in something. He would be gone from her thoughts as thoroughly as he was from her life. Then, she would smell woodsmoke or see some tall guy in bluejeans or a Ford pick-up or a goofy dog and it would start all over again. She would feel bitter with grief and aging. He had believed her young, demanded it, and that way, they had held time at bay. It took two. She couldn't do it alone; alone she was emphatically middle-aged. Alone she felt invisible. Alone she was most ordinary, alone, no miracle at all.

She moved easily through the dark and stepped out into the air. The solstice sky was luminous, brilliant with light, sequins and gems and washes of light. Looking through the eyepiece, it had seemed less complex, the black deeper, the light utterly without color. Liz walked to the parking lot and stopped. She wasn't ready to go home. Since she had found the cabin and occupied it, she could hardly wait to get home, to pull into the pine grove and see the place, small and separate against the trees. It was new to walk into her home and find no one there. For twenty years or more, she had come home to children or man or both, to their demands and her own, to a failure of privacy that had been lulling, then deadening, then deadly. Her new solitude, this unknown companion, was both resisted and received.

There was a sadness to the comet, to its journey; a fragility, a silence, an isolation that made her crave human noise. She knew no one. She watched families troop back to their cars and two lovers unclasp long enough to climb into their truck. Five blithe girls in thick jackets and skin-tight pants, their hair spiky around their smooth faces, half-danced down the hill. One of the girls, her hair a raven's ruffled helmet, spun round and round the parking lot, her arms outflung to the stars, her voice high and clear. "Let's go," she cried. "Let's go, go, go!"

She saw Liz. "Hey," she said and blew her a kiss. "Come dancing with us, sweetie-pie. You know how to dance. I can tell 'cause you got that Camaro caliente." She waited for Liz to do something. "Really," she said. "Juniper . . . on Butler . . . you'll love it."

"I could do that," Liz said. The girl shot her a thumbs-up and bounced into the back seat of a beat-to-death Monte Carlo parked nearby. They peeled out of the parking lot. Liz climbed in the Camaro. She studied her eyes in the rear-view mirror. It had been years since she had bounced like that, years since she'd invited strangers to gala occasions, years since she'd walked into a bar alone.

She started the engine and turned on the heater. The windows fogged. The girl had been right about her car. It was hot, it was cool, it was the perfect mix of hot and cool, the perfect car to hold age at bay. It had reminded her, the first summer night she'd seen it in the dealer's lot, of high school and lust and jazz and the way they moved together. It moved like the music, those hard changes, the scotch-on-the-rocks racing burn of it.

Gerry Mulligan, Anita O'Day, Dakota Station, Bird. They'd been saints to her long before Camaros had existed. She'd been seventeen. She'd outlined her gray eyes with black, painted her young mouth, shoved her feet into brutally pointed four-inch heels and taken herself—illegal, terrified, ecstatic—to the only jazz club in town. Somehow, she'd survived. She'd been too innocent to get hurt.

One night, long after closing, she'd sat with a pale man more than twice her age while he clung to her hand and begged her to stay with him till he could feel sleepy. She had looked past his thin shoulder to the puddle of light where his horn lay. It had been that dramatic, as though the make-up table was an altar, the saxophone some shining relic. She had wondered what might happen to her. She was a virgin. She had told him that. He raised his death's head face to hers and kissed her gently.

"Don't worry," he said. "I can't do anything. I just want to sit with you." He cracked open a Benzedrex inhaler and swallowed the cotton inside. She'd heard about that. Speed, how it kept you going, how it made things sharp and clear. He bent over her hand and traced the lines in her palm.

"You're so young," he said. "I can't sleep much anymore," he said. "My wife's in New York. I miss her."

"I have to go home," Liz said. She didn't want to leave. His sadness, the clean set of the bones in his face, his feral eyes, the memory of the music curling up through the smoke.

"We could drive out to the lake," she said. "It's beautiful there. Quiet. You could just sit. I can drive. I have a permit." He dropped the rental keys in her hand.

"I'd like that," he said.

At water's edge, he pulled her close to him, resting his chin on her hair. He talked about how it was to need to play, how strange it was to be a little famous.

"I'd play for free," he said. "It keeps me alive."

They had sat on a low stone wall, watching the water, till sunrise melted like opal on the far horizon. Lizzie drove him to her parents' house. He held her carefully for a minute and when she walked up the steps, tooted the horn gently and drove away.

A few months later, she had found her first boyfriend. They became part of a crowd of couples. She stopped going to the clubs alone. He didn't really like jazz, but he adored her. They learned to make love, and, somehow, the clubs, the music, the scotch smoking off the ice became only excuses for later on, for later on when his tongue touched hers or his big hand cupped her breast or she felt him hard against her belly. Then, she would come awake; the club and the jazz would seem only a half-dream. Sometimes, hovering over that first lover, she thought of the musician and of how the music had taken him, had gone through him, and it would seem to her that sex was like that. She was freed and taken and she would have to make love to stay alive.

The car, which had stalled and then stopped, grew cold. The parking lot was empty. She restarted the engine and headed down the curving road, driving hard, letting herself slide out toward the slick edges of the turns, accelerating through them. Nick had taught her that and he would have thought she was a fool for driving that way. It didn't matter; it made her feel alive. It made her feel she just might be able to walk alone into a room filled with music and strangers.

The bar she considered was not Juniper. It was an old bar, in the old downtown. There were no plants in the window, though there was glass, in a town where serious bars had board windows. She couldn't drink in those places anymore. She came down off the icy hill and drove through the dark streets. The old part of the town was fighting to hold its own. The bright lights, the money were moving, year after year, out into the northeast suburbs.

She parked in the alley, paid the two-dollar cover, had her hand stamped with a smudged grace note and walked to the end of the bar. There was a blues band of white boys and a dance floor jammed with college kids. Liz ordered a ceremonial scotch on the rocks and wished she still liked cigarettes. The boys lurched into "Got my Mojo Workin," and she set the drink aside and ordered club soda. If she started drinking and the music didn't get any better, she was going to have to drink enough for alchemy, for strong magic, and if she drank that much, she was going to start seeing that comet hanging there, alone and delicate in zero space. And then she was going to know she could not sleep alone one more damn night and she was going to find a man, any man, and settle right back into that wired, sweet ride that curved out and up, then in on itself, till all that survived was the ride itself and no stars at all.

The band stopped. The jukebox whined in. Next to her, a couple leaned towards each other. The woman gazed up at the man, who was big, who was drunk, who was spitting a little as he talked, who assured the woman that he and a friend had concluded that man was the mos' sophisicaded mutation so far. The woman nodded and played with the man's fingers. He beamed down at her. The woman's slim foot jiggled steadily. The rest of her was strung-tight motionless. Liz wanted to touch her. It would be like soothing a spooked cat.

The boys stumbled back on the bandstand. They were adorable, more of that shiny-clean, spiky hair, those smooth faces, the bodies like reeds. The drummer wore a tweed sportcoat encrusted with glittering dime-store brooches. The guitarist's t-shirt had been ripped till it was no more than a shoulder strap. His thin arms were white as mist. A mahogany-haired girl handed him his guitar. He smiled and trailed his bony fingers across the strings.

They were different, the boys, from the haggard middle-aged men in dark suits who had played past closing at the jazz club. They were anything but cool. The singer, a chubby, olive-skinned boy with a great beak of a nose, tripped on the stage-steps and collapsed in laughter. Somebody in the audience hooted and the guitarist said, "Whoa, Jamie, you're so coooool!" One by one, they picked up their instruments and settled into the music. They found the music. They let it go. The set was fast and loud and solid. The dance floor was full. Most of the college kids had gone home, except for all the sweet misfits. A big Mexican kid danced on the pool table, roaring, his eyes closed, sweat running off his long hair.

When she turned back to the bar, the couple was gone. She dropped a tip near her empty glass and walked out through all the enormous young men, through all that baying and lurching and wacky laughter. The street smelled like late Saturday night; somebody had urinated in the phone booth, more than once, and the air was fumy with cheap wine and woodsmoke, the sky rhinestone bright. She stood on the corner, waiting for the light to change. Behind her, the old building throbbed with the blues, ahead, the street was empty.

Driving home, the last song beat in her blood. She felt better than she had in months. Orion lay above the horizon. She had loved him for a long time, his wide shoulders and hunter's easy lope. He would never fool his prey. He was sharp as danger in that chaos of stars; he was of stars, his dagger of stars, his belt of stars, Betelgeuse, Bellatrix, Alnilam, Rigel, Alnitak, Mintaka, and Saiph, as though he were made, god himself, of the luminous bodies of sacred cousins. In that family of stars, in that desert, that forest of stars, the man of stars prowled faithfully. At his shining feet crouched Lepus the Hare, barely seen, perfectly still, sheltered, free from the terror of the hounded. The star-hunter seemed to have forgotten the little creature. He seemed gone beyond memory, beyond the kill, his great face turned to limitless dark, on about his business forever.

She had looked for Orion in lovers, for something essential and incandescent, something of silence, something urgent and ancient, something that would loose him from her arms and bring him back, again and again. She thought she had found him in Nick. She had been wrong, not about the incandescence nor the silence, but about the return.

She turned onto the dirt road, clattered over the cattle guard and pulled into the parking space above the cabins. A sudden gust shook the pines, a fine sift of snow shimmered in the air. She stood for a minute at the edge of the meadow behind the cabin. The air was icy, the snow glowing in the starlight. The stars were doing their trick of seeming to be within hand's reach. Across the meadow somebody had a fire going, burning juniper. Liz took a deep breath and went into the cabin.

She threw an extra quilt over the sleeping bag and crawled in, jeans and all. It was bone-rattling cold. She felt as though she'd sucked the indigo chill of the observatory into her cells and she hadn't really been warm since Nick left; five years of his absence burned like dry ice.

Star shadows played against the raw wood walls. The big pines creaked in the wind. By her side, the new cat, the silver gray, settled in to nurse its tail and purr. Bob, the old cat, was out about his stalking, a tiger shadow in the snow. Liz turned on her side. She turned away from the east, from Nick's direction, from the thought of him. Five years. Two thousand, two hundred miles; she no longer had to look or not look for his truck. This town's streets were new streets. Empty. Neutral and leading straight back to his ghost.

She flopped on her back. Five years of sleeping alone and she was still tense with it. She had tried to read a book right after he left, something called *Sixty Days to Letting Go*. The authors, whose earnest faces yearned out from the cover, said that you could "let go" in sixty days if you just learned to love yourself enough. They had convinced her that she was not a modern woman. Five years and twenty-two hundred miles and she lay under her sleeping bag, with her privacy and her beautiful cabin and that comet overhead and wished for him to burst through the door and take it all.

Sleep was holding out for something special. She tensed her body and let it go. The *Sixty Days* couple had said that would work. She counted her breaths. She thought of old riddles and made up new ones. Nothing worked. Through the east window she saw the black pine trunks. She tried to think of their beauty, of the snow thin and sparkling on them, of the perfect curve of the observatory, of Orion, of Bob the cat, all stripes and bulk and shadows, hunting by starlight. There had been the comet, the fuzzy cloud of it. Behind her closed lids, she fixed that perfect circle, that shimmer, absolute white against absolute black. She breathed into it, submerged, felt herself soar out, slip away, let go, come back, again and again, to that circle of light, that circle . . .

. . . of gray chipped into the black cliff-face. The air was very hot. She was, as always, very hungry, very dry. That circle was a mystery. She thought her head might burst with it, with the questions she always had, with the heat, with the slow, slow steps of Aunt Hopaqa. Talasi stared up at the circle. It wasn't a journey sign, like the one her uncle had pecked near her cousin's house; nor was it a sun sign or water sign. They were sharp and clear. Aunt Hopaqa tugged gently on Talasi's dusty hair.

"Come along, Talasi," she said patiently. "That is nothing, just a picture one of those lazy men put there. These men. They could be hunting or planting or carrying wood. Instead, they go off together, just like little boys, and mark up the rocks. I think they never grow up!" She sighed and settled her water jug more firmly in its sling.

"But what is it?" Talasi said. Hopaqa stopped.

"What a *mongwu* you are," she laughed. "Those big eyes of yours, those questions." She resettled Talasi's small jug and smoothed the twisted head-strap.

"Those old fools," she said, "they say there was a big star that came for a while, then went over. It was after Two-Color Mountain spat fire and rocks, long ago. They say it returned, the big star, when I was a little girl, no bigger than you. I did not see it."

"Why?" Talasi asked.

"Why?" Hopaqa parroted. "Because we women do not have time for star-gazing, you know that. That is for the men, that foolishness."

Talasi looked around her, saw four young junipers almost in a row across the wash, saw the big boulder beside her, now this path curved three times between the star sign and the trail up from the spring; how, from this place, near some firerock, she could see the Sacred Mountains, small and sharp, below the sky. She saw those things . . .

. . . Liz came slowly awake. The dream drifted hot and golden, was gone, returned, and gone again. She saw an August sun slip behind a thunderhead, reached out to draw it back and was awake and thirsty. It was three-fifteen and it was going to be one of those hard mornings. There had been too many vanished dreams and sudden wakings, waking to hear her heart gone crazy in her chest, to salt on her lips and no tears, waking to longing, thinking of Nick, his lean body, his wit.

She pulled on the heavy wool shirt he had left behind that long-gone last morning, crouched in front of the woodstove and built a fire. There was comfort in that, if not peace. There was the smell of fresh-split juniper, the sound of the fire catching and taking hold. She crawled back into bed. The fire cast slivers of orange on the ceiling, bright against the trail of cool starlight from the west window. Liz let herself float in and out of that haze that is not quite sleep; the dream teased. She let it be. She had spent years working in dreams, unravelling, all of it in a way of *un*-dreaming, a way out of mystery, a way, perhaps, out of the gift.

She could smell spicy perfume. She stepped on something that gave way beneath her feet so that walking was work. The fire burned low. She wondered whether to add wood, but it would be so hard to walk all that long way to the stove. Wondering, she fell asleep.

NORTH

For the Disir, our divine and ancient Grandmothers,
from whom the gods learned true magic.

Two

LIZ STRUGGLED UP FROM DREAMLESS SLEEP. It was a surfacing from bad water with a body that had forgotten how to swim and a spirit that would have settled for drowning. The fire was out. Truck lights from the far highway flickered in the east window. Dawn was hanging back. She pulled the sleeping bag tight around her chin and imagined the drivers on that last leg into town. They'd be wired, sleepy, looking forward to coffee at the cafe by the underpass.

She remembered riding next to Nick in the old blue pick-up one October dawn, through rose light, on their way to bad coffee and home-made doughnuts in a tiny place in a dying upstate town. The goofy dog had bounced in the truck-bed. Its name was Sock, Sock R. Tees, and it was out of its mind with the thousand scents rushing up its nose. The hills had seemed to glow, a pale fury of maple and oak and elm.

She hated dark mornings. Winter's shrinking light tugged at her heart. And yet in the cabin, under the dark pines, it was easier than it had been. The first few years after Nick left, absolutely left, she had jolted awake hours before dawn. She would sit in the dim kitchen, drinking coffee and waiting for first light. There had been a shaky peace in those early hours, in the refrigerator hum, the clang of the furnace catching, the deep creaking in the old house when the lake winds were harsh. That first cup of strong coffee, rich with cream, had been the last pleasure of the day.

Then, her work as a therapist had been a mirror of her loneliness. She still did not quite understand how it was that she had been able to sit, hour after hour, story after story, with wounded people and be good for them. There was nothing, no fear, no horror, no shame, no rage, no despair she couldn't sit with. Sometimes she raged at it, at the unfairness, the cruelty, the bad genetic luck, and her clients raged with her. Sometimes, as she left the room, she expected to look back and see the air foul with anger, yellow with pain.

She had made some big mistakes; she had occasionally seen miracles. But most hours, most stories, she had done that which all work and witness require: one's faulty best. The work had insisted on being done till she was done with it. The room had become her grandchild's bedroom, its air renewed. There Jen and the baby lived, in the big house, near the black lake, under the winter light already beginning to open out. Jen ran the house and when a stray call came in, told the person that Liz was gone, that they had reached her old number and that no new number was to be given out. The baby was a girl. Her name was Tina.

The east window shimmered into translucence. Pink-washed light lifted above the treetops. Liz scattered pine needles and cones on the cold fire, then breathed on them till the flames came up. Again, that reliable joy, that touch of warmth on her cold skin. The room brightened, the pink flared gold. She fed kindling to the fire and set a fat log of alligator juniper on the flames. A piece of bark broke off in her fingers. She sniffed it—it was scented, sharp and musky as the forest floor. In her hand, it could have been the skin of some ancient reptile: dragon juniper a better name.

Liz stretched out on top of the quilts. The fire roared and crackled. Just enough smoke drifted through the room. There was, beyond the fire-song, a wonderful silence to the place. She closed her eyes. Sometimes in early morning, on the path, she heard the hiss of traffic on the highway beyond the trees, but, in the cabin, there was always a hush. She dozed, half-hearing the whisper of the fire, feeling its perfect warmth along her side . . .

. . . Talasi leaned on the boulder. The spring sun had warmed the pocked basalt. No more than a woman's height below, a hawk crouched on a rabbit. The bird could not see her, she was sure of that. She had been watching for a long while, watching what happened down there where the *tuukwi* crumbled away to the sand. She studied the hawk, the way her tail was marked, reddish above, light below. As it had swooped down, it had screamed sharp and high. The rabbit had gone still.

She had watched the boys play at hunting, some the rabbits, some the hawks. They would try to stand very still, to be so quiet that they were no more than shadows. Sometimes if she breathed slowly she could do it, holding shadow-still, the only movement her heart beneath her breast. But this rabbit was better. It had gone as still as one gone over. Its big black eyes had seemed to dull. The hawk had not been fooled. She had struck once and the rabbit had flopped to its side, its long back legs twitching. The hawk danced on the rabbit's back, her great talons digging into the bloody fur. Talasi felt the hawk's joy. Though she was barely five winters old, her belly had too often been empty. There was little more wonderful than a feast.

Her carrying sling hung over the boulder, her waterpot was near her feet. She knew she should finish her trip to the spring. Slowly, quiet as shadow, she leaned away from the rock and stood up. The hawk raised her head, her copper eyes fixed on Talasi. As the girl bent for the jug, the hawk jerked her head and flew off, rising easily on the warm wind.

Talasi watched her go. She was a story, that hawk, more than just a dark speck against Father Sun. She was a spirit-hawk carrying someone's prayers to the Cloud People; she was a mother hawk, carrying rabbit to her baby; she was a girl hawk, carrying nothing but her wild sweet joy, laughing at Talasi, so slow and unwinged on the dusty trail.

Talasi stopped to look at the rabbit. Its eyes were truly dull. A white bone stuck through the meat. Where the hawk had torn away fur and skin, Talasi could see how the meat lay in long strips. She bent and felt the back of her leg. The same. She and the rabbit, alike. She steadied the carrying sling and trudged on down towards the spring . . .

. . . Liz opened her eyes. The woodstove was roaring. She opened the front door to icy light and damped the fire. A drift of juniper smoke stirred a memory and was gone. She was still sleepy. Nick had called her a bear—she went slow and grumpy and quiet in the winter and ate chocolate the way a bear would honey. Ravens screamed outside the door. She tossed them some bread, poured cream and cocoa in her coffee and went out to sit on the cold stoop. The heat poured out from the cabin over her back. There was a lemon sun and ice in the light-dappled pine boughs. She had wash to do, groceries to buy, water to haul.

Bob the cat nudged her ankle with his nose. She went in, fed him and dressed. She pulled on jeans; they were just right, worn to that fleeting stage of comfort just before self-destruct. She was still wearing Nick's shirts; he'd left a few behind. Work shirts, corduroy, a shredded turtleneck, every one of them blue. She was surprised he'd let her get away with them, cheap and spooky as he was.

She pulled onto the main highway and cracked the window. The air whistled, rich and thin, all burning juniper and pine oils steaming up from the ponderosa, and that cold crystalline breath off the peaks. Ahead, the mountains flashed in the sun; some believed they were sacred. She could believe that, especially at sunset, especially under this strong sun, their flanks purple, the snow on their tops blue-white and blinding.

A log truck heaved directly in front of her. She slowed and rode his diesel wake all the way into town, into the clutter of shopping centers squatting on the outskirts, past a raw, red hillside, its pines chain-logged into tinder. You couldn't miss what was happening, the torn earth, the clear-cuts, the hand-printed posters all over downtown that warned of uranium mining threatening the Grand Canyon's forested rim.

She made herself see those things. Nick had taught her well.

"There's more than human misery, shrink," he'd said. "Give up on 'em. People don't change. Bring on the Ice Age," he'd said. That late spring afternoon, they'd searched for a place to roll logs down a hillside. He pointed out rabbit burrows, nests in dead snags, the frail marks of invisible watercourses.

"Leave nothing behind," he said. She knew he was talking about more than the woods; she knew he lived what he talked. She looked where he pointed and saw more than a beautiful hunk of scenery. She saw the web of life, the network in which she had no place, that living connection that was insensible to her, unless she was careless or greedy, or both. And she saw him leaving—she saw what he would leave.

The North Country web was torn, the network in the high desert broken. There was carelessness. There was greed. They moved together over the earth, through the pines; there were broken hillsides, meadows bladed and gone, silence shattered by the sound of helicopters and heavy equipment and profit. A terrible nothing was left behind; it had the color and stink of rot.

"Preach on," she muttered to herself and pulled into the parking lot next to the laundromat. She could hear Nick, she could hear the kids, "You can't save the world." Right there, as she sat in the front seat of a Camaro Caliente, roasting coffee fumes drifting on the air, the sun hot on her skin, it didn't seem to need any rescue operation. She took her wash in and got it started. The coffee fumes seduced. She followed them.

As she got to the door of the cafe, the scent deepened. There were undertones of cinnamon, chocolate, apricot and rum. Liz stopped in front of the big window; it was jammed with posters: You could experience natural-light healing for thirty dollars. There was a dance concert by the multi-ethnic, multi-gender group, Heart of Datura. Five reggae groups were playing "inna Hopiland." You could become part of a living process of change by going to a rally on Nicaragua. And they were still planning to mine uranium on the Canyon's South Rim.

She remembered the first time . . . standing on a filthy street on Chicago's South Side, handing out leaflets, urging people to shop elsewhere so that Negroes could buy a bad hamburger in a luncheonette in Georgia. The women had worn skirts and high heels; the men suits and ties. It had been August and the air gray with packing-house soot. She had been so afraid that she didn't notice till she got home that her sweat-stinking blouse was on backwards, so exhilarated that it was twenty years before she stopped believing that witness and resistance and sweat worked.

She took a hard look at herself in the glass door. Mirrored in the painted glass were the lines, the circles of fatigue under her eyes, the gray hairs in her crazy mane. Fine. She pushed open the door and went in, thinking of the women of her mother's generation, all those long-suffering souls, giving and giving, scorching their hair, yanking out their eyebrows, painting new ones in, painting out age, painting out change, so their men could come home to the girls of their dreams; and when that failed, mothering and mothering and mothering, so that their boys could be boys.

"They can kiss that goodbye."—she'd seen that on a t-shirt. So there was gray in her still-wild hair, no gloss on her lips. There were lines and exhaustion and two bitter creases on either side of her mouth and, unseen, undisguised, there was new caution. She was more than willing to have an affair with coffee, to surrender to chocolate or pine vapor or the bold desert sun. For the rest of it, the t-shirt said it all.

It was a sweet little cafe, half-empty, the walls hung with Viennese posters, vintage psychedelia and shelves of porcelain doo-dads. A long smoky mirror reflected the room. A rangy boy was reading Carlos Casta-ñeda and there were three girls in bold black-and-white checks and stripes and what appeared to be their fathers' undershorts over dance tights. One wore a torn leather vest; another had pulled lacy socks over her scarlet hose. The young women were very serious, sipping their coffee slowly and watching each others' faces as they spoke. Liz walked up to the pastry case and looked in. Seduction would not be necessary. There were fist-sized blueberry muffins studded with almonds, slabs of eggy apple cake, scones as big as a brick. When she looked up, the waitress handed some-one an enormous coffee mug brimming with whipped cream.

It was too much. She felt something tighten in her, something mean-spirited. A skinny man in those ugly German sandals said, "Go for it!" and nudged her forward. She wanted to punch him. She wanted to grab a bucket of gray paint and play High Plains Drifter over everybody and everything. It was all just so incredibly cheerful. She bought plain coffee to go and walked out.

She sat down on a splintered bench in front of the window and breathed in the fine, austere smell of the coffee. From inside, she could hear the happy chug of Creedence Clearwater. She looked down at her bare hands. All her rings were gone, the garnet and gold, the silver badger for healing, the little lizard whose head was moonstone, whose tail was held gently in its jaws. Continuity, the promise of return, of letting go and holding on, everything the little lizard had meant to her was gone, vapor-ized as thoroughly as gold tossed in the crucible: a reverse alchemy.

Getting older in a time when cycles were unseen, when straight ahead and up were the only ways to go, when the moon's teaching was unknown. She was a relic.

She had packed the rings away the week before she moved. Then she had mixed a double gin and soda, dropped in half a lime for vitamin C, turned out the lights and leaned up against a stack of pillows on her double bed in the silent attic room. She had looked out the window across the bare tree tops to the sparkle of downtown and she had thought about a way to get old. It would be very quiet. She would let go and let go. She would fade away. She had once said to her students, "If we see ourselves solely through men's eyes, then every one of us in this room will disappear before she dies." That's how she could do it. Disappear. Be very careful to want nothing, to desire no thing. She had felt serene. She had been forty-four and her thoughts had seemed neither unusual nor extreme.

She set the empty coffee mug on the table and shook her head. It hadn't quite worked that way. There were those hungry wakings, the nightmares that brought Nick to her and took him away, the day-dreams that drifted in. She made herself look around. It was, after all, at least nineteen hundred days to letting go and she hadn't made it to anger, much less sadness and acceptance. Every day, every night, she expected Nick to suddenly appear.

The only man on the sidewalk was an old guy in a filthy ski hat. He swept the sidewalk in front of the laundromat, over and over, muttering to himself and shaking his fist at the customers who stepped gingerly past him. Down the block, Goodwill was having a "two for the price of one" sale. The red-stockinged girl burst out of its door, waving a glittering string of something in her hand.

"Look," she cried to Liz. "Aren't they great?" She turned to the old guy, who was grinning wildly, and patted his arm.

"Victor, *mi amor*," she said, "you want a coffee?" He nodded and bowed her in through the cafe door. Her dark perfume lingered behind. He sniffed it appreciatively and smiled at Liz.

"Good girl," he said. "Nice tee-tas."

Liz shook her head.

"Beetch," he said cheerfully. She nodded and ducked into the laundromat.

The Star Empress video game shrieked; the kid playing it hit Liz up for a quarter. She shook her head and walked over to the dryers.

"I hate that," a woman said. Liz turned. The woman was bending into the next dryer. She was big, she was tan, she was solid and muscled and dressed to show it. "I hate it when kids beg," she said, still half into the dryer. "Damn doors," she said as she extracted herself and slammed the dryer door shut. She had thick honey hair pulled into a pony-tail and wore a t-shirt that said "Cause I'm the Mom, That's Why!" She lit a cigarette and smiled.

"I mean," she said, "what are you supposed to do? If you hold out, they hate you; if you give in, they know you're a sucker. Right?"

"I guess," Liz said and ducked into the dryer. It was quiet in there, and warm and simple. She did not have a chat in mind, and she could tell from the shiny cherry-pink tights and the very long eyelashes that if they did chat, any second it would turn into the failure-of-the-planet-to-hold-any-good-men conversation. She plunged her hands into the warm clothes. Dark and warm, it was beginning to be a direction.

"Hey," the woman said, "you okay?" Liz backed out. The woman grinned at her.

"I'm sorry," she said, "it's the curse of the working mom. You start talking to yourself . . . or anybody over three feet tall." Liz dropped her wash in the metal cart.

"Too well I know," she said. She looked up. The woman was still grinning. She had sea-blue eyes. "You're new," she said. "What's that accent?"

"Very," Liz said. "Upstate New York, the worst of two worlds, a cross between Chicago and Long Island." She was in it. She was going for the chat.

"Well, then," the woman said. "California . . . pure. My name's Deena." She held out her hand. Liz shook it. No soft handshakes here, they both had that New Woman grip.

"I'm Liz Morrigan," she said.

Deena watched while Liz folded her wash. "Got time for coffee?" she asked.

"Next door?" Liz said.

"Where else?" Deena patted her solid butt. "Built for comfort, not for speed. I ought to sue that place."

"I never met a muffin I didn't like," Liz said. "Let's do it."

"My treat," Deena said. "Christmas bonus." She tugged leg-warmers up over her tights and checked her face in her compact. "I don't know who I'm doing this for," she said. "The cowboys out here just graduated from heifers and their right hands." She sighed. Liz hefted her wash up over her shoulder and they marched out.

"Okay," Deena said. "I'm nosy. What brought you here?"

"You first," Liz said. "Why did you talk to me?" They had brought their food back to one of the little tables. Liz had allowed herself to be swayed. She had a slab of apple cake, Deena a chunk of pear braid. Whipped cream melted off both their Mocha Espresso Ultimos. She watched butter soak into the molten cinnamon sugar glistening on the cake. It was almost as pretty as sunset.

"Who knows?" Deena said. "We single broads just sort of cry out to each other." She laughed. "Am I right?"

"You are," Liz said. Deena held out a forkful of pear braid.

"Try this," she said. "What *is* that spice? They will *not* give out their secrets."

Liz hesitated. Nobody had offered her food in a long time. She was the cook, the feast-maker. There was a power there, in the elaborate dinners for Lazar and his colleagues, all those men talking through the good food about their research, about the effects of major tranquilizers on the nervous systems of rhesus monkeys, about convulsions and toxic dosage and how so many milligrams produced brain damage and so many didn't. She had listened and made knowing comments, made sure the wine was uncorked at a decent interval before pouring, made sure no one smoked and, when she could, gathered up the remains of the paella or couscous or gumbo and fled to the kitchen, to the fine quiet of washing dishes. Women weren't fools. Once you caught on to professor-speak, you welcomed exile.

For Nick, for his friends, she had put out enchiladas and home-made bread and good beer and wines they'd never heard of. They had talked dope and bikes and dope and television and dope and more dope. She'd stayed put right next to him, given up solitude, given up that power. Rebel-speak had seemed less deadly.

"Earth to Liz," Deena said. "Want some?"

"I do," Liz said. She swallowed. "It's cardamom."

Deena looked delighted. "Welcome back," she said. "Let's talk."

"I'm out of practice," Liz said.

"Hey," Deena said. "I am the separated mother of a four-year-old kid. *You're* out of practice?!"

"Let's start with the Cookie Monster," Liz said.

"You got it," Deena grinned, "or why that lady is so fat or why that man's nose is so big or why does Daddy hate you."

"You go first," Liz said.

"You just heard it," Deena said. "Your turn."

"I am here, in Arizona," Liz said, "for all the usual reasons. A fresh start. The light. The rocks. I ran away, mostly, from a man."

"Why this town?" Deena said.

"It's a long story," Liz said.

"Fine," Deena said. She loosened the waistband on her tights, lit a cigarette and leaned back. "It's non-custody weekend. I do not date. I have cleaned the cat litter, done the wash and run out of excuses to be in the house. I'm a free woman."

"Fine," Liz said. "I came to be near the ruins."

"Indian?" Deena asked.

"Exactly," Liz said, "and moving myself as far as I could from Nick, the man, without having to worry every day about the great earthquake that will cast Los Angeles into the sea."

"I pray for it," Deena said. "So does everybody else in Arizona."

"Four years ago," Liz said, "Cockney Davie talked me into going to the Grand Canyon. I had a book on the Anasazi; a wonderful woman had given it to me. I fell in love with the ruins, I fell in love with where they were.

"We saw Mesa Verde first, then White House at Canyon de Chelly." We stopped up at Hopi, saw a dance. I was, for once, struck dumb. I bought this turquoise bracelet to bring me back." She held up her wrist and the plain beads caught the light. "I did *not* want to move on, to see that hole in the ground, that tourist trap, but he was driving."

"Never let 'em drive," Deena said. "That was our first mistake. After we got that wheel roughed out, we should have taken off on it."

"You're good," Liz said.

"Bitter," Deena commented, "you know?"

"I do." Liz said. "Anyway, I let him drive. We swung down from Tuba City in the July glare, not a cloud in sight. I complained till the Desert View parking lot. I'm good at finding everything wrong with a moment, a place, whatever." She stopped.

"I read this article the other day," Deena said, "in one of my modern woman magazines." She smiled and lit another cigarette. "It was about power breakfasts and we are both doing it all wrong: a) Never smoke cigarettes; b) Never wear spandex; c) Never reveal too much."

"Yeah," Liz said. "What is *it?* Maybe I'm not cut out for the hermit life."

"Go ahead," Deena said. "It's my Active Listening. They taught us how to do it during divorce mediation. Note my eye contact. Note how I mirror your gestures."

"I used to teach that stuff," Liz said. "I *believed* in it."

"So do I," Deena said, "I'm free of the SOB. That's good enough for me." She leaned forward. "So, then what . . ."

"Well," Liz said, "we stopped in the Desert View parking lot. Davie told me to close my eyes. He led me up a path that seemed endless. I smelled some plant, spicy, a little dusty. I could hear other tourists. There was a strong, warm breeze. Then he told me to open my eyes."

"And?"

"I stood there, burned-out, messed-up, one hundred fifty percent cynical and, right there, with all those nice people in bermuda shorts and weird hats, my spirit opened right up. I didn't even know I had one till that moment."

"That's how it is," Deena said.

"We drove on into the park and walked and walked and walked," Liz said. "I couldn't get enough. I did *not* want to go back. There wasn't much left there anyhow: work that was chewing me up and spitting me out, kids who needed to leave home and weren't, a city that's second in the country for sunless days and, Nick—or not-Nick most of the time—seeing him, not-seeing him, his damn truck, his damn dog."

"Yes," Deena said. "My old man lives six blocks away. We exchange the kid. There he is. He makes sure I see him."

"I cried for half a day on the way back," Liz said. "Spent a year homesick for a place I barely knew and came back on my first solo vacation. I don't fly in planes. So, I took the train and this town is the Santa Fe stop in the middle of most of the ruins. About ten-thirty one night, I climbed down from the train steps into this beautiful air. Next morning, I ate a great breakfast in some diner out on the highway—food will factor big in this story. I took off and after about an hour of being scared, I loved it. Being alone. I actually loved it. And, after a while, I was up by Tuba and I saw that the place wasn't ugly and it was far from empty. There were mountains and striped cliffs and jackrabbits and old ladies on horseback and miles of broken glass."

"And fry bread," Deena added.

"Well, yes," Liz grinned. "Fry bread, of course. Between the fry bread and driving back from Chaco Canyon, up in those northwest mountains in New Mexico, in full sunlight, with black thunderheads and lightning in the ranges on either side of me, when I knew I was as free as a woman could be, kids grown, work almost done, body strong, brain hanging on by a thread, I decided to cut loose."

"I like that idea," Deena sighed. "I'd give anything to grab Deej and just cut loose."

"Your daughter?" Liz asked. "Deej?" Deena nodded. She closed her eyes for a second.

"Short for Deborah Jean," she said. "She hates Deborah Jean, so she says D.J. D for Deena, J for Jerk . . . I mean Jack. Jack's idea. He likes to keep everything family sewed up tight. If I'd had a boy, it would have been Jack David, Jr. He was not pleased that we produced a girl."

"Produced?" Liz said.

"Produced!" Deena said. " 'we'; I always appreciated his team approach. 'What's mine is mine, what's yours is mine,' except when it came to that last stage of labor."

"What happened to all that progress we women have been making?" Liz asked.

"Ha!" Deena said. "This is northern Arizona. How'd you get from northwest New Mexico to here?"

"Miracles," Liz said. "I went back and the only thing that kept me alive was knowing out here was out here. I'd feel that death-in-life fog and I'd get out my maps and trail guides and Ed Abbey's book, the one about the desert, and I'd come alive."

Deena was quiet for a moment. She stubbed out her cigarette and drained the last foam from her coffee.

"That must have taken guts," she said. "To say goodbye to everything you knew. To your kids."

"No," Liz said. "Courage had nothing to do with it. I would have died if I'd stayed there, and my kids would have gotten stuck."

"All right," Deena said. "That's how it was with the marriage. I would have died. I was dying." She thumped her cup down on the table. "No more," she said.

"Cut loose," Deena said fiercely. She shook her head. "Well, we certainly have moved right along here, haven't we?" she said. "It's like that out here. People talk slow and move fast." She poked around in her big baggy purse. "Here," she said, "they're about to kick us out." Liz looked up. They were the only customers in the place and the counter-girl was wiping down the glass counter. She waved to them.

"Hey," she said, "no prob. Really. Like, take your time." Somebody cranked up the sound system. The Grateful Dead roller-coasted full volume.

"Hey," Deena mouthed. "no prob. We're outta here." She handed Liz a slip of paper. "My phone," she said. "Call. Anytime. Really. I know how three in the morning can be sometimes."

"It might be a while," Liz said. "I need a lot of time alone still." She wondered why she was saying those words. It felt like an old useless caution. Still, she said them and looked up at Deena.

Deena smiled. "My old dad says, 'Never apologize, never explain.' Just use the number when you want."

"Thanks," Liz said. "I'll do that." They walked out into the sun-dazzled cold. Liz looked down at those cherry-pink, shining legs. They looked like hard candy in the sunlight. They were fluorescing a little. Deena caught her glance.

"Jack's influence," she said. "He never let me wear shorts or low-cut blouses or anything that would 'drive men crazy.' So now . . ."

"You wear them well," Liz said. Deena climbed into a beat-up Blazer. She opened the window and leaned out.

"Call," she said.

"Thanks," Liz said. "Really."

"No problem," Deena grinned. "My pleasure." She raced the engine. "Hey," she yelled, "once a California Girl, forever. No Problem!" She backed out of the parking lot and swerved onto the street.

Liz loaded her stuff into the car and headed home. No problem. No prob. She wondered if Arizona was the big state Time had left behind.

She folded the clean wash and put it away. There was that quiet peace again and a beauty in the colors, the touch of good cotton, the memories. Nick's workshirt was fading badly, cuffs frayed beyond repair. She folded it and set it in the top drawer. Cut loose she was not. She was hanging by a

slender and most tenacious thread. "Dangling," as the playwright Nto-
zake Shange had put it, "from a string of personal carelessness."

She poured a glass of grapefruit juice and carried it to the lawn chair at
the edge of the meadow. Sun flooded. She could hear a jay scolding
somewhere. She had seen them; they were turquoise and had black
pointed heads and bright bead eyes like tiny dots of obsidian. They were
also discovering how to drive the cats crazy. She sipped the juice. It was
perfect, bitter and cold. It washed the taste of carelessness from her
throat.

She closed her eyes. The jay went silent. She could hear the cats
slipping through the dry grass. Sun beat on her face, burning in behind
her bones, her eyelids; rose-red, steady. Her hands were stretched out
along her thighs. They felt thin and delicate and strong. She thought of
untying knots, of cutting loose and then, kids in the laundromat, their old
eyes, the smooth masks of their faces. . . .

. . . there was a visitor. He had come to the village just after Third Dawn,
as though he had walked by night. His sandals were frayed and dirty, his
goods-sack bulging. He had been greeted eagerly by some of the men,
by the ones who gathered in the plaza every day to gossip and play the bone
dice game. Kunya was there. He was always there. He cried out to his wife to
bring some food. She hurried out with corncakes and a jug of water. The man
ate and drank without stopping to give thanks.

Talasi had seen all of this from the ledge behind her house. She was
supposed to be with the other girls, playing dolls and scaring the robber ravens
from the fields, but she had complained of belly pains and run home. And got
this far, where she could watch, where she could see things.

The men were laughing. They pointed to the sack. Kunya called again to his
wife. Again the greediness. Again no thanks. Kunya's wife cast a sharp glance
at the man and climbed the steps to her house.

Kunya laughed. He pulled the bone dice from his pouch and held them
to the stranger. The man nodded and set the sack carefully on the sand.
From its mouth spilled something terribly beautiful, something, perhaps,
magical, something shiny blue and yellow and red. Talasi started to creep
forward and stopped.

She didn't dare be seen. Any second, her mother might look down from her
grinding stone on the roof and see her. She was not to run off alone. Ever. She
had been told that time and again. As her mother's only daughter, she was very
precious. If anything happened to her, and Grandmother was very careful to
explain each of these dreadful things, if she fell from one of the steep *tuukwi*, if
she was tasted by snake or spider, if *she* tasted the white flower of the *tsimona*,
their clan would cease in their family.

She decided to go into the house, to tell her mother she wanted to come home. She might be allowed to stay and, once her mother knew about the stranger from the east, she would be curious and they would go to see. She climbed the ladder to the roof. Choovio looked up from the grinding stone and kept on grinding. Talasi thought it was pretty as a dance, the smooth rock and flow of her mother's round body, the push-push of her strong arms. She could hardly wait to be taught, to have her own stone, her own grinding.

"Daughter," Choovio said gently, "why are you here? You were to go with Grandmother today to watch the corn. You have been told, again and again." She sighed.

"My mother," Talasi said softly, "I wanted to see you. I . . . I had a pain in my belly. I am afraid of the summer sickness." She looked down at the floor. It was not a lie. There was a pain there, not big, actually very little. Choovio sighed and rocked back on her heels. She did not want to remember that it was the season of the sickness, the sickness that struck harshly at the smallest and the old, bending them double with terrible pain and bowels that ran and ran. They could not eat. They could not sleep. They could not swallow water. Their eyes would begin to shine with an awful brightness and the flesh would melt from their bones. She looked at Talasi.

"Look at me," she said. "You do not look sick. You may stay with me, but you must tell the truth. To tell a false story is to set things out of balance. You know that."

Talasi crouched near her mother. "It was a very small pain," she said. "It could have gotten bigger." She lay her head in her mother's lap.

"There is a stranger in the plaza," she whispered. "He came from the Sun's house. He brought a big sack with him. He and Kunya are going to play with the bone dice. He did not say thanks for food. Or water. He . . ."

. . . Liz jolted awake. A cold wind had come up. Clouds dimmed the setting sun. She felt the dream hover, as real and elusive as the scudding clouds. There had been scent to it and sound. The clouds shifted and the red sun descended behind the pine, glittering through the black branches. She pulled on her sweater. The cold moved in, mountain cold, fifty degrees in the fading light, thirty in the shadows. She waited and watched. The dream was gone. She was grateful just to have the time to dream. There had been so little.

Once, back in that other life, she had taken her dinner to the backyard, at the edge of the little garden and sat, breathing the green twilight air, watching silver moths appear against the dark snap-pea vines and disappear into the pale evening sky. She had sat a long time, slowly eating kasha and mushrooms and sour cream. It had seemed to her at that magic hour as if the air took up the green from the lilac bushes and early lettuce and drooping willow.

Jen had called from the back porch. The work-room light had blazed. There was welcome there, and insistence. Liz had climbed the steps slowly. Behind her, the garden had become black and gray, and where the last band of pale blue hugged the horizon, there were crows, rising from the treetops, rising together.

Three

BY THE TIME LIZ FINISHED SUPPER, delicate snowflakes sifted through the window cracks. The night was blue-black, lapping in the corners of the cabin, at the dim forest and meadow beyond the cabin light. When the wind roared through the pines, when the snow shushed against the windows, it seemed the cabin was a houseboat and the North Country the ocean it had once been.

She set more juniper on the fire and found herself thinking of Deena, of that easy warmth, of her own quick thaw. She wondered if there really were *Westerners*, a new hospitality, an ease. It could be that in the sun, in this sudden and ephemeral weather, people didn't freeze. They weren't bundled against the gray, protected from that ancient seasonal failure of the light. Back home—it still was home—there had been so much gray. She had heard her people described as cold, as slow to thaw, slow to welcome. She had heard they matched the weather. And worse.

The cabin was silent except for the fire's roar. She washed her dishes; it was a good, slow ritual. The cabin had no running water, only a sink and drain. A few hundred feet from her door was a shower-house and spigot. She carried water in gallon jugs, walking slow so that she could see Orion, breathing deep to taste the air. Back in the cabin, she heated water and went to work. Back home, there would not have been the time.

The water was warm on her hands, the meadow black beyond the gilded arc of light outside the window. Snow hissed on the glass. A cup, a bowl steamed in the rack; one fork, a pan. She sloshed boiling water over them and reached up to turn out the light. She had hung an ivory paper lantern over the bare bulb. It reminded her of other days, of North Beach and huge airy rooms, nearly bare, the ocean seen from tall windows, the light off fuchsias hanging there, the teak floor cool and polished under her bare feet. She poured a glass of cider and went into the living room, a journey of five steps. Living in one big room required imagination; it required fantasy walls and real clutter and the ability to hang a paper lantern and remember sea-gray California light.

She sat in the rocker that had once occupied her office. The old chair was part of her gift for hearing; when the stories had been particularly bleak, when the air had gone dense with pain, and rage threatened to rise up and smash, she had rocked steadily, the motion a quiet comfort. In the silence of the cabin, with the fire-glow warm on her face, the rocking was a way to memory. As some dance, as others chant, she rocked. It was an old woman's work. A child's.

In the perfect silence, she thought of *her* child, of Keith and his music. Before his movies, there had been the guitar. Hours, days, months, he had played and played. Toward the end, when she knew her leaving would not be postponed and she knew that to leave one must say goodbye, she had taken the rocker every night to her room in the attic. There, she would sit, the old house finally quiet, a candle burning or not, and she would listen to Keith's music drifting up from his room next door. He played Villa Lobos, he played Bach, and, on those nights when his young face was tense and pale, he played rock and roll. He played the Stones and Clapton and, more than any others, he played The Who. On his wonderful, hand-made, acoustic, gleaming wood guitar, he made the new music sound old, the anger burn, the sadness melt away. She missed him. She missed the music.

He was very far away. His music had become movies, his anger spoken, his sadness transformed into light and dark, silence and sound, still after still, Kurosawa his master, Cocteau his god. He had stood on the porch as she drove away, his thin face grinning, his eyes gray-green and wet as hers. She poked the fire. That was the joy of a fire. There was always something to do with it—it always responded with beauty. That was the joy of music. *That*, she had; she had brought hundreds of tapes west with her.

She got up and slipped The Who's *Quadrophenia* in the deck. There was the hush-hush of the North Atlantic, the sound of surf on a chill Brighton beach, then a voice crying. As the music began to swell, she thought of the story, of the moody kid growing up poor, working as an office boy in the '60s, in his tight Mod suit, with his bad haircut and his pale, pitted face, his great beak of a nose, his thin hands and his longing. Holidays found him, the kid, Jimmy, on those Brighton beaches, caught in the epoch teen battles between the Mods and the Rockers, their pipers the white-boy bands, the piping a new electric rip and whine.

The music was raging. She thought of those days, of other battles and she wondered at the kinship she felt. It was as though some wild girl in her had never died. She thought of Sunny, her best friend in the Chicago days, before Ben, before Steve and Jen and Keith, before Lazar. There had been a brief first marriage, a son. She had abandoned both. Erased. When she thought of those days, they blurred. Only the nights had stayed with her, the nights when she and Sunny, twenty-one, lucky with youth and looks; babies and husbands tucked safely at home, had swung through the deadly early-morning streets, from after-hours bar to chicken shack to rent party. The point of it, the reason, had been the music. In those smoky places, crazy, truly crazy white boys and Detroit-born and bred, Black men played the Blues. She and Sunny had danced through the smoke, the wail, even the desire, the hot eyes and nasty words, immune, somehow, in their skin-tight jeans, with jacket collars turned up in mimicry, cigarettes dangling from their lips.

One late night, much later, gazing up at Nick, at his body above her, his face closing in on her, she had told him about those early mornings, had told him about Sunny. She had excited them both with the story, with the danger. They had barely touched, the two of them, just thighs, lips and lips, and her words, floating between them. He had been silent, drifting in her, coming without a sound. Weeks later, he had remembered and asked her to dress that way.

"The way you did then," he said. "You and Sunny."

"It wasn't so different," she said. "I am a creature of habit." And lining her eyes in black, turning up her collar, feeling sentimental and very middle-aged, she took his cigarette and let it dangle from her lips. She put on his dark glasses and grinned.

"Your husband was a fool," he said. "I would have killed you first." He had held her against him and when they made love, she had felt the killing in him.

The music ended. There was a sob, a scream. Liz sat a minute in the silence, then got up and shut off the machine. Her bones ached. Too often, they ached with a deep dim pain. The wild girl, Sunny's friend, she could not have danced through this one.

There had been something about the time with Deena, as though she'd already started coming back from that wan, awful peace she'd settled for. She knew what to do with uneasiness. She knew what to do with pain. And she knew what to do with missing the people she loved. No matter what, she could walk it off. She could walk right through it.

She buttoned her heavy sweater, wrapped her purple scarf—the one with stars, the one Jen had knitted—around her neck and pulled on her mittens. The fire was working, flame and ash and coal in perfect balance. She set a big juniper log on top and closed down the damper. She left a light burning. It still seemed a little miracle that she didn't have to lock the cabin. She closed the door and stepped out.

Fresh snow powdered the path from the cabin to the road, everything luminous and still, the sky a starred black arch. She felt a little high. As she walked, it seemed to her that her steps resonated, as though she stepped on the taut surface of a great drum. The night was strange, off-key, in that way of new places, in that way of old memories still so vivid they are half-dreams, so that place and memory interweave imperfectly, and jar. She remembered, unwilling, other cold skies, a meteor seaming a chill midnight, dawns over mist, iced opal on the horizon, and, her body warm, her spirit and flesh and wild thoughts gone into Nick's hands, under the weight of him, soaring. She'd been fearless in those strange long-gone nights.

The snow muffled her footsteps. Up the white road, horses stamped and snorted in a hillside paddock, their breath pouring silver from their dark muzzles. The snow slid off the pines, so light and dry it felt like feathers on her face. There was a little clump of houses to the right; their lights burned yellow between the thick trunks of the trees. The road twisted ahead and disappeared. She stopped, the music still whispering in her. She spun in a slow circle, looked up and saw Orion, turning with her.

Something rustled in the pine needles under the trees. She saw shadows where the snow had barely fallen. She froze. Wild creatures lived here. She had seen their tracks, seen the bones of their meals, the scattered feathers and bright splashes of blood. Something moved slowly toward the road, its passage barely heard, its motion more a shudder in the air. She turned slowly toward the presence and lowered her eyes, ready to look away if she met the creature's stare.

"Wild things," Nick had said, "don't want to see your eyes." He'd held her face in his hands so she couldn't look away. "Even your eyes," he'd said. "Even these pretty eyes."

There was nothing. Twigs rattled against each other, then a shadow twined low on a pine trunk, curved up, then flowed down the tree and across the road. It emerged into the starlight. Liz laughed and shook herself. As she recognized the new cat, the gray kitten, she thought of other walks, other friends. The cat purred steadily. It sniffed her boots and curled around her ankle. She thought of Lynette, her dear friend, the woman of a hundred cats, the woman of stubborn loyalty. She picked the kitten up and cuddled it close to her body. It was not much more than a solid cloud of shivering silvery fluff. She thought of Lynette, her tall, slim body, her slim arms cradling. She thought of their midnight walks, how the two of them would stomp out of her house and brave the dark city park between their front doors. They had been angry a lot, Lynette a painter with no time to paint, Liz a worker who had not yet found her work.

The kitten struggled in her arms. She wanted to go on, to walk with her memories of Lynette, but she had to take the kitten back to the cabin's safety. There were coyotes. There was the cutting cold. The kitten hadn't learned yet where it belonged. It tore at her thick mittens with its needle claws. She laughed again and walked back up the road, Lynette in her mind, the kitten in her arms. It was a relief to remember that love, a joy to picture that face, and, a greater joy to think of someone other than Nick.

The cabin was still warm. She fed the cats and added another log to the fire. Lynette would love the place and she would hate it. She was visible in her work, a woman of many treasures, dried flowers and sequins and a quote or two, a photo, sepia, tucked in. The quotes were about mothers and work, about war and betrayal. She would love the light of the place and hate the inconvenience. She would hate the idea that others bathed where she did. There was a cool privacy in her and a terrible need to surround herself with people and tasks.

Liz watched the light. She had brought a task with her. It was work that only she could begin, only she could see through. Thinking of Lynette, of her colláges, the faded mauves and purples, the sudden glint of mylar or mirror, she saw as she had seen before how much she and the other women of her generation were patchwork girls. Bits and pieces, a hundred different lives in a hundred different locations, they had been the bright ones, the bad ones, the Beats and Hippies and Libbers. She and Ben had moved eleven times in the first year of their marriage, from smoky Chinese hotel to a redwood cabin a hundred feet above the Pacific to basement hole in Chicago's South Side. She had worked at a hundred jobs.

It was warm by the fire and she had no reason to wake early. There was as much silence as she needed. The work would not go away. It was a weaving, that much she knew, as though she had begun a hundred different shawls on a hundred different looms and finished none, started a hundred different stories, a hundred different loves and left each one, all hundreds incomplete; threads, tales, people frayed and useless, tied-up, good for nothing but nostalgia.

Her grandfather's old bathrobe hung near the stove. He was a story, but the thread of it was indistinct. She had salvaged the robe, a woolen one, from his house before the auctioneer arrived. The robe was faded and pilled, but still thick; its stripes orange, its background brown and gray and black. He had told her it was an Indian blanket. He had held her on his lap and pulled a feather from the pocket. He was the last man she had trusted. He had loved her and wanted nothing.

She wrapped herself in the robe and stretched out on the narrow bed. Before the weaving, unravelling was required. She lay half-awake, half-dreaming, till early morning. It was clear that the unravelling had more than begun . . .

 . . . a shadow filled the roof-hole, a shadow with heavy steps. Choovio looked up. Talasi ran to her father as he appeared on the sunny rooftop. He swung her up in his arms, then hurried to a basket near a neatly rolled sleeping mat.

"A trader from the Sun's home is here. He has brought shells and tools and more."

"Yes," Choovio said, "and those bone dice." Talasi was surprised to hear something cold and harsh in her mother's voice.

"Yes, those too, but much more, wife," Nuuva replied evenly. He knew how most of the wives felt about the bone dice and he didn't want to take time to argue with Choovio, who had turned her back to him and was grinding corn with renewed vigor.

"If a man comes from the east, carrying bone dice to our village, nothing else he does is of interest to me," Choovio said.

Talasi hugged her knees, as though she could hold onto all the questions that wanted to spill from her. It would be improper for her to ask when her mother seemed so disinterested. Nuuva smiled down at her.

"Perhaps the little owl wants to know, she is very quiet and she is looking up at me with those big, round eyes."

Choovio said nothing.

"Very well, then, Talasi may come with me to see for herself the wonderful things the man has brought." Nuuva said calmly.

"As it suits you, husband," Choovio murmured.

Talasi felt a little thump in her belly. She had never heard her mother and father speak this way before. Nuuva was smiling, but she could feel something tight in the air, as though the rabbit crouched silent beneath the *tuuve'e*, the little pine, so still, while a shadow of something hovered over it.

Nuuva picked up his daughter and set her on his lean shoulders.

When they reached the ladder, he said in his sternest voice, "My daughter, why are you not in the fields with Grandmother and the others?"

"I was wanting to be at home with my mother," Talasi whispered, "I was worried I might get a belly ache, so I came home."

Nuuva laughed. He could not be angry with this treasure of his, this bright-eyed girl who so often was where she ought not be. He squeezed her ankle.

"So, little one, now we go to see what treasures this stranger has brought," he said gently.

He bounced down the path to the plaza, Talasi giggling and squealing, hanging on to his thick hair with both fists. He stopped at the edge of the cluster of men and crouched so she could swing down off his back. There were no other children present, no women, except for Tsohtsona, whose bold, black eyes studied the stranger.

Talasi thought Tsohtsona was very beautiful. Many strings of stones and shells hung around her neck. Her plump wrists were thick with shell bracelets. She stood a little apart from the men, smiling to herself, fingering a painted skin bag that hung from her sash. Talasi crept close to her. She wondered why the women of the village whispered when Tsohtsona walked by. Tsohtsona reached down and stroked Talasi's shining hair.

Nuuva disappeared into the circle. Talasi quietly wriggled through the crowd, till she stood within view of the trader. He had emptied his sack onto the hard-packed plaza floor. Talasi held her breath at the beauty of his wares: purple-striped shells; many *qalahayni;* flat shell pendants; copper bells from the south; cotton sashes, tightly woven and hung with clay beads and cotton tassels; gourds, halved and carved in strange designs; black-on-white bowls, some painted with animals Talasi had never seen—three-headed rabbits, birds with lizard heads, men with skyfire shooting from their fingers. But as exciting and beautiful as these things were, something even finer spilled from the sack. It lay on a brown and white mat like a spirit from a dream. It was a bird, with a thick, shiny bill, its eyes glazed in death, its feathers the color of sky and sunset and sunrise, as though dawn and noon and evening had all come at the same time. Talasi knew *kwaayo* the hawk, she knew *tsooro* the bluebird and *kwaahu* the eagle. She knew *kyaaro,* the red and green parrots that were kept in small pens behind the village. But she had never seen anything like this bird. She thought for a moment that it might have been made by some clever grandmother, but she knew that even with all the plants and powders of the high desert, the women had never been able to make a paint or dye that was as bright as this creature.

The trader picked the bird up by its feet. Tsohtsona pushed her way to the front of the crowd.

"Stranger, what is that creature?" she said.

The stranger appeared startled. He stared boldly at Tsohtsona.

"Woman, what are you doing here? Why are you not in your house or in the fields? This is man's business," he said coldly.

Tsohtsona held up the fringed bag. She looked straight into the trader's eyes.

"I am a widow. I have come to play the game. These men are my clan-mates. They know me," she said with perfect calm.

The stranger laughed uneasily.

"Forgive me. With my people, the women do not place themselves in a men's circle. I see it is different here." Tsohtsona nodded.

Talasi made herself as small as possible. She did not want the stranger to notice her. She did not know how she would answer him. She thought Tsohtsona was very brave and somehow different. She had heard something of *powaqa,* witches, those two-hearted ones, and she had heard the wives whisper, but she saw Tsohtsona standing straight and proud and she thought *powaqa* would not be like this, so strong in her words.

"This bird," the stranger said, "is from the lands far to the south. It is sacred to us. I bring it to show my friendship and good will, for I have been told that the people of Black Sands value beauty. He who wins the game will take with his winnings this bird of fire." He paused. "Or she."

Each gazed at the dazzling bird, its broad wings, the way the feathers were tipped with black, how the sunlight danced off their shining. Each saw the beauty and wanted it; each felt a little ashamed of the wanting, but wanted nonetheless.

Talasi crept forward, her shyness overcome by her hunger to touch the bird. The trader glanced down at her and laughed.

"Even this little one knows this is a prize," he said. "Touch it."

She petted the scarlet head. The feathers were sleek and soft under her trembling fingers. She looked up at the man.

"I thought it might burn," she whispered. "But it is cool and so soft."

The circle of men burst into laughter. Talasi fled through them, up the steep path and into the dark, quiet safety of her house. Choovio turned. Her face was a mask. Talasi saw no curiosity there, no questions, and that seemed odd.

"Bring me more corn," Choovio said. "There is so much to do. It seems that more and more falls to us, the women." She sighed. It was not good to dwell on these complaints. Perhaps it had always been so, the men busy with prayers and ceremonials, the weaving, the hunting. But it seemed lately that there had been more . . . the dice . . . the rude laughter. To think of the imbalance, to honor it with thought . . . that might be a deep betrayal, a meddling with the flow of the days, the work, the dreams, the sunrise and sunset, the smooth path of the seasons, the coming of the rain, the arrivals and farewells of the Kachinas, the great wheeling circle of life itself.

Still, Choovio thought, it is my husband who has begun to go more and more to the circle of men in the plaza. It is he who sometimes forgets his duties. It is he who played with the dice and lost two of the three rabbits that were his in the last hunt. It is not me.

Talasi stood at her side, holding the rough bowl filled with dried, shelled corn.

"Shall I pour some in for you?" she asked.

Choovio slipped her arm around her daughter's round waist.

"Yes, my owl," she said. "My good helper. Forget my other words. Your father is a good man, a hard worker. I am a little tired today."

Talasi scattered two handfuls of corn in the shallow stone trough. She didn't know why, but she felt scared. She pushed the fear aside with happy thoughts of the day that she would be big enough to learn to grind, of the day she would grind at her *own* metate, with her daughter at her side. Those were the thoughts that always made the fear or sadness go away . . .

Four

NAVAJO WOMEN WEAVE A SPIRIT LINE INTO THEIR WORK, a few plain threads that run straight from the rug's heart to its outside edge. It guarantees that the woman will not become trapped in her work. As Liz awoke, she wondered how you did that with a weaving so frayed, so torn and stained. There had been another dream, one without a spirit line. The dream was gone with the dreaming. She wondered how to weave that path out, how to weave it free from memory.

Bob was bumping his dish around. He was a thorough nag, headed for some dubious world record for girth. Against her better judgement, she fed him and sat, shivering, in the old rocker. Every joint in her body ached. Her brain felt sandpapered. It was the hangover of nostalgia. So she warmed some milk, drank it with a double splash of rum and went back to sleep . . .

. . . her belly ached. It was no story. Choovio brewed tea of juniper and sage. Talasi felt it warm the pain but then it was as though she had swallowed burning coals. She screamed. Her father appeared in the hearth-fire's light. She could not see his face. He seemed very tall, black, black as an ogre, black as something she had once known. She screamed again.

"There is only one thing to do," Choovio said. Her voice was calm. She sponged cold water on Talasi's forehead. "Get Kunya," she said, "make yourself ready, my husband. There is juniper water there. Wash yourself. She must go where she will be safe.". . .

. . . The windows were lace agate, black and frost, glittering. Liz shivered. Where was safety? There was no running any more, no haven. She wrapped the quilt around her shoulders and stood up. The cold was deep—sometimes it seemed almost solid, as though she could reach out and touch a sheet of ice, of stone. She started the coffee heating and built a fire on the ashes of the night before.

Her hands ached. She looked down at them. In the dim light, you could not see the veins, the dry skin. They had been one of her best points. Not pretty, no, not that, but strong, as was her face, as was her touch. There had been moments caressing some man, when she had realized that it was not his flesh that excited her. It was the sight of her fingers moving; they seemed to take on a kind of power. He could have been invisible. He could have been canvas or paper or stone.

She poured out coffee. The warm cup felt wonderful. She needed heat, she needed light flooding and sun on her face. For an instant, the coffee jolted back a scrap of dream: a bird, iridescent, scarlet and blue, lying on cinnamon sand in copper light. There had been wonder and fear. She jotted the words on the telephone book cover. Bird, scarlet, blue, luminous, cinnamon sand, wonder and fear; a story-teller could weave them easily. They told of Qumavi Tuuwa, the ruins to the north of town, the ruins in the second chapter of the Anasazi book; she once again blessed Clara for that particular gift. The black and cinnamon sands. The light. She would find warmth there . . . and perhaps, blessing.

Driving down the curving road from the old cinder cone, its peak burnt-orange in the late morning light, she felt the ache in her hands ease. The sun beat in through the windshield. Ponderosa gave way to piñon, lava to cinders, piñon to juniper. Ahead stretched miles of dappled sand, of olive brush and, a hundred miles away, the lilac and peach and cool yellow of the Painted Desert. The air warmed and began to carry the sharp scent of juniper. She rolled the window all the way down.

There was a turn-out right before the road dropped into the desert; there was a redwood table and bench; she pulled off. To her left, the Sacred Mountains seemed to float above the trees. To her right, mesas squatted on the horizon. She unpacked her lunch, took off her boots and socks and stretched her naked feet and hands to the beautiful sun. The black cinders were hot under her toes. The place was silent. Far out, beyond the sand, that ribbon of rock went brilliant, then gaudy, then unearthly in the shifting light.

By the time she picked up her sandwich, the bread had begun to dry and the cheese was warm. She poured grapefruit juice from her thermos. As the strong, sour taste cleared her throat, she began to cry. The wind dried her tears as fast as they fell—there was salt on her lips. She licked it off and felt like an animal, wise, almost at peace.

She sat a long time, sipping juice, crying, smiling to herself, watching the light and shadows shift, and praying that no one came along. When she finally packed up and climbed back into the car, she realized that it was Christmas Eve. She drove out from the long shadows of afternoon, down the two-lane road, past stands of juniper and a cattle stockade and the winter bones of a cottonwood and the place where the black sand brightened into red-brown. The sun began to throw up shafts of rosy light. The warm, scented wind dried her tears. There might be healing like that, impersonal, unprescribed, nothing more or less than light and wind and their blessedly inhuman touch.

She'd heard solitude could drive you mad. If this was madness, this curving road, the scent of juniper, that double kiss on her wet face, she welcomed it. She thought of her children—she could hear Steve.

"Mom's losing it again," he would say. He would pick her up and spin her around, all five feet six inches of her, until she laughed or cried or wacked him so hard he yelped. "Little Mom," he would say. "She's so excitable."

"Mom," Jen would say, "you really need to . . . Seek Professional Help!" They would all crack open a beer or make popcorn or send out for pizza. Tina would do something charming and the madness would have cleared. She blew her nose. She would have given anything to round one of the curves and find them there.

At the bottom of the last slope, she saw a sign. There was a little Kokopelli, the ancient lover with his flute and the words, "East-Rising House, 3 mi." She turned and drove on, through a sand-drifted landscape, sprinkled with sage and pale gold grass. Behind her, the sun melted steadily down toward the Sacred Mountains. She wasn't sure what she was looking for.

Till she saw it. Then, it was perfectly clear. Deep orange in the setting sun, a jagged tower lofted toward the pale sky. She stopped the car in the middle of the road and stepped out. She looked so hard that her vision blurred. The tower was built on a huge boulder, both of the same stone, a stone the color of apricots, as was the sand beneath her feet.

It was the most beautiful place she had ever seen; it grew from the rock, the rock became the tower and all—tower, rock, ruined walls—were eroding back to the glowing sand. She walked up the road, her shadow moving ahead of her. A jackrabbit, its ears translucent in the light, bounded away. She followed his track toward the ruin. In the perfect silence a car horn blared.

She turned around. There was a faded truck behind her car. A sandy-haired man leaned out of the driver's window. He wore a NPS truck hat and he was smiling.

"I hate to tell you," he said. His voice was twangy, more Midwest than Old West. "You've got to move your car," he said.

"Oh," Liz said. Her voice cracked. She turned around to look for the rabbit. It was gone.

"There's a parking lot right up there," the man said. He laughed and pointed. "You can see the curb from here," he said. "It's painted tasteful desert pink."

"Nice," she said and started to walk toward the car. Each step required thought. She wondered if she was dehydrated. She felt foreign to herself.

"I'm sorry," she said. "I wasn't thinking."

"It's okay." He was bearded, his hair rough, sandy-red, his light eyes amused. "It gets to you, out here," he said. "I've been here five years and it still gets to me." She nodded

"Just drive up there and park," he said. He hesitated. "Listen," he said, "I didn't tell you this, but there's a beautiful small canyon out behind the ruin. Go take a look at it."

"Thanks," she said. "I thought I might just curl up and spend the rest of my life up in that tower. They were geniuses."

"Could have been genius," he said. "Could have been defense. Could have been water. That's my standard spiel. But I can't believe we were the first folks to think of beauty." He started the truck, leaned out the window and touched his hat brim. "I'm Paul Shaughnessy," he said. "I'm supposed to manage resources out here. Give me a call sometime." He slid the truck through a perfect reverse K-turn and drove away.

She pulled up into the parking lot. There was an asphalt path and the tasteful curb and three tasteful garbage cans. She saw a greasy Jack-in-the-Box wrapper blowing across the sand. We might not have been the first folks to think beauty, but we do hold the record for ugly, Liz thought. She locked the car and started up the path. The late sun was warm on her shoulders. She could have been walking in any afternoon, any time, one hundred, two hundred, nine hundred years ago. The path spiralled up the boulder to the ruin. She walked up into the indigo shadows. To her left, the boulder top formed a small plaza. They had walled it, just high enough to keep children from tumbling to the desert below.

The wall curved in a half-circle. If you stood in the outmost bow, you faced the Sacred Mountains. She set her hand on the wall's top. It was still warm. In the distance, the mountains went scarlet. She turned and looked back at the ruin. It glowed as though lit from within. As the light faded, the walls became dark, as coals go cold and black; they soared against the pale evening sky.

She crouched at a low door. The room on the other side was unroofed, the stones gray, the warmth leached out of them. She scraped through, then again through the doorway into the tower. Last light illuminated the upper story. There were three tiny windows just below her eye level, one above. From the most western, she saw the silvery twilight desert. Cold seemed to pour up from the hard-packed floor, from the walls.

She moved to the north window, steadying herself on the walls, and raised her face to the opening. A rush of icy air poured past her. She leaned into it, looked past it. The bony bushes were not moving, the sparse grasses were still. It seemed a wind of time. She closed her eyes and took a breath. It carried more than desert air; there was the smell of burning juniper, of wet animal fur, of corn roasting, of dye brewing, sharp and pungent. She saw, in the pressure of the wind against her closed eyelids, an old man, sitting before a loom, weaving white cloth. He was naked above a breech-clout, his skin deep brown and finely wrinkled. His broad hands moved firmly over the weft, beating down the fine thread, weaving it through, over and over. As he wove, he sang. He was weaving for a bride; for her wedding and for her burial.

Liz stepped back from the window and stood in the center of the dim room, her arms wrapped around herself. She was afraid. It had taken years and more will than she had known she had, to bring herself away from the ghetto apartment of her early twenties, from the men, the drugs and visions and imaginings. Her children had been the only fixed stars in that darkness, and they were gone. Nick, her failed Orion, was gone. She had only herself to steer by. There was no room for imagining, for a ghost horizon. She pressed her hands down on the rough sill of the east window until her palms hurt. The pain brought her back.

She bent and pushed through the first door, then the next and came out, scraped and shaking, into the plaza. The mountains were black, the snow on their peaks like fire. She made herself stand still and ran her finger over the mortar between the stones. There were fingerprints there. She had read that the women had been part of the building. They had done the patchwork, the preservation. For beauty, for shelter, for safety. She decided to stay awhile; the nightmare days could be over. And running never worked.

She sat on the stoop outside the little door. The stone was still warm. It had been worn smooth. She thought how good it was to be alone. If she went mean or crazy or low, there was no one close to be hurt by it. If she looked up, there was a sliver of moon. If she looked right, the peaks glimmered softly. She felt the changes in the air, a pulse of warmth, a chill, a howl, so faint, so far-away that it was nothing more than a ripple along her cheekbones. Behind her, solid and dark, the ruin sheltered her from the deepening cold.

She crawled back into the tower, and put her face again to the wind. There was sound, fire crackling, a whisper, a scraping, as though stone on stone. Then, nothing came. She stayed at the space, cheeks burning in the cold, eyes closed. When she finally opened them, it was brighter, the pale blue starlight washing in through all four windows. She turned and saw her shadow. And, in the west window's sill, something glittering, something bright as polished silver.

It was the edge of a steel support rod. She touched it. It was grooved. It had been worked by tools of this century. The tower was fake. It had been re-built. The fingerprints in the mortar were not nine hundred years old. They were not women's. She stood in an exquisite reconstruction, a guess. What she had found, those women had not left behind.

She was grateful that the car started on the first try, that the heater worked and that the road curved empty and black up away from that beautiful, false place. A few miles after the turn, she pulled off and looked back. The tower could not be seen. There was little but starlight, a frail crescent of moon, drifts of sand, the ebony of small canyons, and shadows that might be anything, saltbush, coyote, failed mystery.

She descended the long hill into town. The east side of town blazed, bright lights, holiday money. The big shopping center was cookin', its parking lot packed with cars. Hungry, she pulled in. It would be good to celebrate, to eat something special, to call home. She'd always liked holiday eves the best, that sense that something wonderful was coming.

It was the first Christmas she hadn't sent a gift to Nick. Un-saint Nick. He hated holidays, all holidays. Still, once a year, every year till this one, she had mailed a gift, first with hope, then with sadness, then with the same spirit with which the Japanese float burning poems to ancestors down twilight rivers. She wondered if he would notice there was no gift and thank her. She finally understood that. Still, she wore the plain silver bracelet he had given her. Without it, her wrist felt alien. Without it, she did not know herself.

The supermarket was a cathedral of jittering color. There were bright green lights over the produce section. The broccoli and lettuce fluoresced. A vinyl Christmas tree sparkled near the bananas and carols jangled overhead. A chill mist touched her skin. She jumped. A dark stocky man in immaculate coveralls sprayed the vegetables. He stopped and smiled.

"Did I get you?" he asked. "I'm sorry."

"No," she said. "You surprised me, that's all."

"Can I help you?" he asked. "Do you want something you don't see?"

"No," she said. "You just surprised me. Really." He waited.

"It's so bright in here," she said. She felt that same rush of friendliness she'd felt with Deena. "I just drove in from the desert."

"Oh my," he said pleasantly. His face was pock-marked, his eyes warm brown. "It must seem pretty wild in here," he said. Liz wanted them to both pull up a couple orange crates and have a nice chat. It seemed perfectly reasonable and it seemed logical that the old weaver had been his great-great-grandfather.

"Well, yes," she said. "I'm new here. Everything seems pretty wild, strange, I mean. But this place, I mean we have them at home and it seems the strangest."

He laughed. "I'm old here and this place seems pretty strange to me. When I was little, we ate what my dad and grandpa grew. Peaches, beans, corn, squash, stuff like that. Whatever canned goods you could get." He gazed at the produce.

"Imagine," he said, "eating melons and strawberries in December. When I was little, that would have seemed like magic." He started to move down the aisle, leaving glittering drops of water on the strawberries, the melons, the clouds of cauliflower. He stopped and turned back.

"Welcome," he said. Liz smiled. "Thanks," she said. She watched him move on, saw his broad back, his thick body and wide hands.

Orion sailed above her on the drive home. She was the only one on the highway. There was a thin film of snow on the dirt road. One of her neighbors had strung tiny white lights around his window. His car was gone. As she looked around, she realized that all the other cabins were dark.

She carried her groceries in, started the fire and set candles around the room. Their pale circles of fire reflected in the black windows, light on light, flame on flame. She took off her sweater and unpacked the groceries. The woodstove warmed the cabin in minutes. She remembered lying in her big bed on the third floor of the house back home, waiting for the furnace to do its work, listening to the banshee wind plucking at the shutters. Her fuel bill had been three hundred dollars a month and she had still never been warm. She poured a glass of wine and toasted the stack of juniper.

She was coming back to cooking. The last few years, she and the kids had lived on spaghetti and nachos and Chinese take-out. She hadn't had the heart or energy to cook. That gift had run out. Here, alone, no strings attached, she made meals for herself and ate them in silence and felt satisfied. She fried garlic and mushrooms in butter, boiled eggs and set rice to steam. The wine was clear gold on her tongue. She chopped apples and green onions and tossed them in the pan, stirred curry powder and fresh-ground pepper into sour cream and spooned it into the vegetables. Spices for cold, cream for comfort.

There were a few gifts on the bookcase. She would save them for morning. She had carried home a curved pine bough, a windfall from the meadow's edge. She tacked it to the wall and hung *milagros* and Tina's paper snowflakes along its base. With bronze pheasant feathers from an upstate New York meadow tucked into its branches and tiny clear lights shining along the perfect curve of it, it was just right. She settled back in the rocker and stretched her hands to the fire. The morning ache was gone.

When she tried to call home, the lines were jammed. The kids, Tina— she could see them at her folks' house, eating some astonishing feast her mom had put together, perched like grown-ups on the couch in the living-room, till the spirit got them and they tore into their gifts; Tina, the bearer, her round face rosy with joy. They had always had that, every Christmas Eve, without fail, through horror-show depression, betrayals, pain; they had managed that brief reprieve. She could no longer manage it. She could no longer summon the spirit.

She served herself food, rice and eggs and curry in a deep gray bowl a friend had made. With her big, square hands and her delicate mind, Jo had shaped it and painted it. The fire of her kiln had fixed it forever. A trio of shadow rabbits leaped along the rim of the bowl. Liz had dreamed it, Jo had made it real. She refilled her wineglass and settled back in the chair. Wine and spice and woodsmoke melted into each other. She felt hazy and smug. She knew she ought to be lonely, might feel guilt, but the food, the candles' cool light, the fire, the pine branch casting shadows on the wall and the wine, hanging like a bell of light in her glass, were more than enough.

Much later, as the fire went to coals and the crescent moon appeared in the skylight, she pulled the quilts up over her body and whispered into them, "I'd like a dream, a gift, and to remember. . ."

. . . They had carried her to her aunt's house, an hour's walk to the East. There was so much illness at Place of Water. It was not safe for her, who burned with fever, to stay there and heal. No chance could be taken with her life. Kunya and her father carried the litter carefully, trying not to jar her as they trudged over the hot sand.

"There is your Aunt Pamosi's house," her father said in his most gentle voice, "You will be safe there. Aunt has plenty of water and her children are grown so she will be able to care for you through the day and night."

Talasi tried to raise her head, but when she looked the tall red house on its boulder doubled and blurred.

"Stop, father," she cried. "I see many houses. My aunt's house is many and the great rock is sliding into the ground." She threw her arms up over her eyes.

Nuuva motioned to Kunya to stop. They set Talasi carefully on the sand, in the shade of a piñon.

"Oh, it is burning," she screamed. "It is terrible. Carry me on the wind again, on the cool wind."

Nuuva dipped a scrap of cloth in the water jug that hung from his shoulders. Tenderly, he wiped Talasi's face, then held the cloth to her lips.

"You do not have to swallow," he said. "Wet your lips. We are nearly at your aunt's. Kunya and I will move very carefully. Soon you will be in a cool dark room. One of the boys ran ahead to tell her we are bringing you. There will be tea for the pain in your belly."

Kunya studied his friend. Nuuva looked away. Kunya knew what tragedy might fall from Talasi's illness . . . her belly pain, the terrible fever, the way her eyes glittered . . . summer sickness. He had lost two daughters and a son to that curse.

"There is hope," he said quietly. "She does not have the running of the bowels. She can keep water in her body."

"Ah," Nuuva said, "but she grows weaker every morning. It is those dice . . . I know it . . . it is those dice and the game . . . they have me. I pray they do not take my daughter."

Kunya bent and picked up the litter poles. Prayer feathers had been tied to them, and the feathers fluttered in the wind.

"We will talk later," he said. They moved forward. Talasi closed her eyes. She could hear the *pahos* singing.

By the time they climbed the path to the top of the great rock, Talasi had fallen into a restless sleep. Pamosi stood in the plaza, watching them approach. Nuuva stared; his wife's sister was dressed in her best robe. She had painted her face red and purple and wrapped an embroidered sash around her waist. Her hair was freshly washed, wound into the coils of the married woman. Strings of *tsorposi,* the precious blue-green stone from the East, hung round her neck. She had strung mosaic earrings of *tsorposi* and the red stone from the great water in her ears. She smiled and blessed them with corn meal.

"Sister," Nuuva said, "why are you dressed so? This is not a celebration."

Pamosi smiled again. Her eyes were warm. "You bring my favorite niece to visit," she said calmly. "I can only celebrate. Should her pain be caused by some evil-doing or *qahopi* wishes, those who might be two-hearted will see that I celebrate the child's visit. They will see that my wish for good is stronger than their wish for evil."

Nuuva bowed his head. His wife's sister frightened him.

"Take the child inside," she said, "where it is cooler. Do not speak her name while you are here. They might be listening." She smiled again. "I have made fresh *piki* to tempt her."

Step by slow step, the men climbed to the tower roof. Carefully, they descended the wooden ladder into Pamosi's home. They lowered Talasi to a pile of rabbit-fur blankets near the hearth. She opened her eyes. Again, it was terrible. Her father, not-her-father stared down at her. He was grinning. He held a bone knife in his hand. He would skin her. She knew that. She screamed and rolled into the corner.

Nuuva jumped back. He, too, was terrified. His beloved child, his first-born, she whose name he must not speak, lay huddled under her robe, silent, eyes shut against the sight of him. He knew not to touch her. Pamosi's shadow crossed the light.

"It would be well if you left, my brother," she said gently. "I will send word when you and Choovio may come for her. I have sent for Toho. He will be here when the sun rises. Till then, I will give her teas and keep her safe."

Nuuva bowed again to Pamosi. She nodded. He climbed the ladder and left. Only then did Pamosi permit herself to sink to the floor near the child, and bow her head into her hands. She sat awhile in sadness and prayer, then turned to the child. She was startled to see Talasi gazing at her with clear eyes. The flush had faded from her cheeks. She reached out her small hand.

"Why are you sad, my aunt?" she asked. "I am here to visit." Then, as suddenly as the fever had left, it returned. Her eyes glazed and she gave out a little moan.

"*Iis'ana, iis'ana* . . . I hurt, I hurt."

Pamosi raised her arms to the scrap of sky and sun in the roof-hole.

"*Taawa,* Father Sun . . . *Kohkyangwwuhti,* Spider Woman . . . hear my prayer, guide me. She is bearer of the clan. There have been no more daughters for my sister. If it is this child's path, let her live. You hear the prayer of my heart. I am your will."

She unrolled a bundle of skin. In its center was a faded yellow and blue striped bag, made from the full bodies of three lizards, their heads clustered at the bottom like a bright-eyed, three-pointed star. Pamosi poured out a handful of bones and pebbles. She hesitated, then picked up a round, clear stone and set it aside. She lit a sprig of sage from the fire, blew out the flame and carried the smoking herb to all four directions, *kwiningya,* north; *tavangw,* west; *tatkya,* south; and *hoopo,* east. She sat in silence, then held the crystal to her eye, sunlight from the roof-hole streaming through it. Her hand began to tremble. She sighed. The sun shifted slowly across the roof-hole. Its passage was pain. At last, she lowered her hand and sat motionless. Only the slow rise and fall of her breathing showed that she lived; only the whisper of air in and out of her body, in and out of the child's breast, broke the silence.

Swiftly, Pamosi stood. Bones and pebbles spilled from her lap. Her dark eyes were flat as stone. She stripped Talasi's cotton shift from her body and stretched her flat on the floor, arms outspread, face up to the roof-hole. She scooped water from the *wikoro,* smoothed a film of it over Talasi's still face, watched it dry and smoothed it again, over and over. Talasi pulled away, then moved up into the touch, her lips parted, her breathing deep and slow. Behind her thin eyelids, her eyes stopped roving. Pamosi crouched over her, bent to the task. She felt, she saw nothing but the girl. She was nothing more than clay, pliable in the Spirit's hands. The healing moved through her, cool and strong. What she did was as wonderful and impossible as flight . . .

Five

SNOW POWDERED LIZ'S FACE. The sill was heaped with tiny crystals. She lay quiet and warm, skin tingling from the snowmelt. During the night, the world had become blue-white and formless. Trees and meadow and woodpile shimmered. The Camaro was buried. She pulled a sweater over her nightgown, boots over her long-johns and trudged up to the outhouse. On her way back, she noticed that the cats had already been scouting—the snow was criss-crossed with their delicate trails, intersecting, winding together, then unravelling and straggling away. She stepped carefully between the paw-prints, warm sun on her face, a sweet lonesomeness in her heart.

She had left the cabin door open, and sunlight poured like honey over the sill. She built a fire and turned on the tiny Christmas lights. She pulled the rocker out to the stoop and sat in the morning light, coffee-grinder in her lap, grinding, breathing in pine vapor and fresh-ground French Roast beans. There were medieval carols on the radio, the singers' voices thin and clear. She thought of her mother, of the old music books on the piano, her mother's hands sure on the keys; she thought of how her mother had taught her the old, old songs, the songs of Light and holly and mistletoe, the songs that still celebrate a masqued and ancient holiday. They were the songs in praise of a Mother. She imagined the Yule Log. She imagined those greater fires and the dancing there and the people's joy that the dark had, once more, been turned around.

She looked down. The grinding was done. She could hear the kettle whistling in the kitchen, shrill above the carols, the carols to the Light. She saw how her Dark had been gray, how her infernal busyness, her constant motion, her endless caretaking and bargains had leached out light and sound and scent. She saw that any woman raising children alone, without partner, without any form of support, would have to live that way. Rushed, vigilant, bossy and bitter; anyone would want only to get through the days. The luxuries here—splitting juniper; grinding coffee beans; washing dishes in four gallons of water, pouring that water on the plants, scrubbing the floor with it; taking time; taking care; wasting nothing because garbage had to be hauled to town; building a fire perfectly, because without its steady heat there was no heat—were solitude's privilege. If she'd had to take care of anyone other than herself, those luxuries would have been burdens.

She spooned the coffee into the pot, poured water over and waited. A quick wind slammed the door; she pulled in the rocker, gathered up coffee and gifts and sat in front of the stove. The phone rang. It was a wrong number. She tried to call home, but the lines were still useless. An electronic voice wished her a Happy Holiday and thanked her for using AT&T. She set the phone near her feet and began to open the gifts.

Eva, her last friend from the crazy days, had sent burgundy silk socks and turquoise bikini pants. There were binoculars from her parents, rosemary shampoo from Jen, good coffee from Steve and an ivory mother-and-baby goat netsuke from Keith. Lynette had sent a tiny collage, cool gray and silver and gold, and a box of butterscotch. Still, the lonesomeness, ungrateful, deepened.

Liz tried the phone again. The computer wished her "Season's Greetings" and urged her to try later. She looked at Lynette's hand-painted card, two linked gilt swirls on magenta paper. She sucked on a butterscotch. Through the binoculars she could see the younger cat sleeping in the window.

"You need a name," she said. She dialed again and hung up before the voice got past, "Due to the volume of holiday calls . . ." She set the binoculars back to her eyes. To the west, she saw every detail of the empty bottle of Finger Lakes wine that held a Solitary Vireo's nest Nick had handed her one drizzly November day. The lonesomeness kicked hard. She took it. Gifts, the luxuries of juniper and fire and time, meant less than nothing. She wanted a call from Him who never called, who was probably passed out somewhere on a friend's couch or in front of his desk, Scrooge in jeans and blue turtleneck, un-shaven, stinking of whatever got him through the Eve before. That was the gift she wanted more than anything, a call from a man who never called.

"Piss on Christmas," she said. The old cat, sleeping near the fire, opened one eye and glared at her. "You, too," she said, "You're as useless as all of them. I feed you, I brush your fur, I pay your vet bills and you give me the evil eye!" He blinked. The younger cat uncoiled and climbed up in Liz's lap. She began purring. "Hey, Sugar," Liz said and laughed. The cat was named.

She glanced at the clock. It was nine. She tried again to call and, frustrated, slammed the phone down. Solitude's privilege was looming large and gray and empty. She flipped open her address book and turned to Deena's number. She started to dial, then stopped. They'd be opening presents, Deena and the kid. She stood up and saw the guy across the way pull up in his truck, the back full of kids. He ran in the house, came back with a shopping bag of presents and took off. She put water to boil for the dishes and started to cry.

"When you run out of ways to run," Eva had said, "be quiet and wait." She was a Buddhist. She would burst into Liz's house, her clothes scented with incense, the "stink of wall-gazing," as she called it; she would drag Liz out of the gray, to the park, to the lakeshore, to some club where, between the rock-and-roll rant and the people screaming to be heard, there was nowhere to run. They would drink beer and dance. They got called every name and kept on dancing.

Liz turned off the water. The dishes would wait, and she could do that too. She took the binoculars and stood on the stoop. Ravens flashed from pine to pine. A little silver plane whined up from the airport. She carried a bag of bread-crumbs out to the space between the cabins, stamped the snow hard and scattered the crumbs. By the time she walked back to the stoop, the ravens were screaming over them, the light off their feathers blue as an oil slick. She watched them awhile. When she went back to the phone, it was close to ten.

Deena answered on the second ring.

"It's me, Liz," she said, "the lady from the laundromat."

"Hey you!" Deena said.

"I don't want to intrude," Liz said carefully, "but I've been trying to call home and I don't think I can listen to another electronic voice wishing me a happy holiday, so I thought I'd just call and say Merry Christmas or some other cheery thing like that."

Deena sighed.

"I am so glad to hear your voice," she said. "There's nothing for you to intrude into, sweetie. Jack took Deej yesterday. I got loaded, woke up this morning to no brain cells and I've been sitting here thinking about doing it all over again."

"Piss on Christmas," Liz said.

"Doubled," Deena said. "Got any destructive ideas for the rest of the day?"

"Doughnuts," Liz said. "Coffee. You tell me where to drive. We go there and sit in the sun."

"Twist my arm," Deena said. "Fifteen minutes, I'll be ready. Here's how you get here."

They picked up coffee and a dozen assorted-to-go at the doughnut shop.

"Are we going to eat all of these?" Deena asked.

"It's a dirty job," Liz said. "But . . ."

"Somebody's gotta do it."

Through brilliant sunlight on empty roads, the Sacred Mountains bright behind them, they drove to one of the manmade lakes south of town. There was a family camped on the shoreline; the guy was working on the engine of a rusted-out van, the woman frying something. The kids bounced up and down in the cold, darting down to the shore-ice in their sneakers, scooting back to the fire.

"Hey," the woman yelled. "Are y'all from town?"

"Sure are," Deena yelled. The woman set her skillet on the side of the fire and walked over. She was red-faced, her hair pulled back into a ponytail that hung to her waist.

"My God," Deena said. "Where'd you get that hair?"

"Grew it," the woman laughed. "Since I was twelve." She shook Deena's hand.

"Is there a kitchen in town?" she asked.

"A kitchen?" Deena said and looked puzzled. The woman's face went redder.

"A soup kitchen," she said. "You know." Deena nodded. "It's for the kids," the woman said. "Me and my old man. We make it on our own. But the kids . . ."

"Sunbeam House," Deena said. "They'll preach at you, but they serve lunch and dinner, and I think, for a buck, you can get showers if you want 'em."

"Thanks," the woman said. "Hey," she said, "Merry Christmas." She walked away. Deena and Liz looked at each other.

"What the hell," Liz said. She took two doughnuts and held the box out to Deena. "Catholic guilt," she said. Deena took a raspberry and a crunch and closed the box. She called out to the kids. They came running and the doughnuts were gone.

"Saved," Liz said. They sat on the warm hood of the car, eating doughnuts and drinking strong coffee.

"I haven't done this since I was a girl," Deena said.

"Me neither," Liz said. "You know that Springsteen song about bare-foot girls?" Deena nodded.

"It makes me cry," Liz said. "I want to run back home, back to 1957. There was a little swamp of a lake, just like this one. We'd get somebody to buy us beer and we'd turn on the car radios and dance and smoke cigarettes and do everything our folks were scared we were doing."

"1967," Deena said. "Surf up, cool breeze, hot sun, hot boys, necking like crazy. It was heaven. Of course, I was a good girl, so nobody knew but me and the boy. The boy was Jack, can you stand it? I lived, breathed and dreamed for him. Now," she said dryly, "he roars into the drive, slams the car door, beeps so Deej will know it's him, picks her up and leaves without a word." She lit a cigarette and blew a perfect smoke ring. "Nice?" she said. "He taught me to do that."

They sat quietly, watching a breeze ruffle the dark water.

"Surf's up," Deena said. Liz unzipped her parka and opened her shirt collar. The sun melted across her throat, warm and gold as honey. She could hear the kids laughing. The engine roared. She looked over. The woman was packing up. The man had stepped away from the van and was showing the kids how to skip stones into the rippled water.

"Well," Deena said. "This is pretty painless."

"It's better than last year," Liz said. "Last year, I cancelled Christmas and told the kids that if they wanted to do it, it was theirs."

"Did they?" Deena asked. "Encourage me. Tell me all about it."

"They did," Liz said. "Steve made dinner, Beef Wellington and asparagus with hollandaise and chocolate killer mousse pie. Jen and Tina got the tree and made decorations. Keith played a half-hour of Spanish guitar and then filmed us opening presents. It was right out of *Ladies Home Journal*. Afterwards, I went up to my room and drank three brandies and stared out over the rooftops to Nick's house."

"It's like that, isn't it?" Deena said.

"I felt so guilty," Liz said, "that I went downstairs and picked a major fight. Good old Mom. I doubt I'll ever be able to make up for it. This Christmas was better. In fact, last night was fine. I even liked sleeping alone. That's a first."

Deena nodded. "I sure know that one," she said. "Not having that ice-man next to me, poking at me, grabbing me. How could somebody be so hot and so cold at the same time?"

"That was Lazar," Liz said. "We screwed every night and that's exactly what it was, mechanical. It got the job done."

"Who was he?" Deena asked.

"The tenth, the eleventh," Liz said. "Doesn't matter."

"Sometimes I get so scared," Deena said. "I get scared I'll get so *nothing* matters." They went quiet. There was pale dried grass at the water's edge. It caught the breeze and light. Slabs of ice broke away from the shoreline and floated out into the muddy water.

"See that ice," Deena said. "That's how I feel a lot. I miss Deej so much it's like drowning. And if I think about going back, there's no way. Sometimes when she's with me and I think, for a second, that I could stand it, I could stand lying next to him just to have her with me all the time, I feel like I'll choke to death. I have to grab her up and go for a walk. She loves it. It's almost bedtime and here's crazy Mommy bundling her up and the two of us zooming around the block."

"Lucky kid," Liz said.

"I hope so," Deena said. "Jeez, these are crazy days!" Liz poured out the last of the coffee. Deena raised her cup.

"Here's to us," she said. "To whatever this is we're doing."

"I'll drink to that," Liz said. "Whatever it is."

"I've got an idea," Deena said. "It's real corny."

"Yeah?" Liz said.

"One of my neighbors got put in the nursing home," she said. "Let's go see her." Liz stared at her.

"Well," Deena said. "What?"

"I worked in nursing homes," Liz said. "Are you sure you want to go there?"

"I'm sure," Deena said. "This lady's great. You'll like her. She's got stories."

"Have mercy," Liz said. "Let's go."

Tenderhome was very clean. The parking lot was clean. The sidewalk was clean. The concrete blocks were clean and the landscaping was clean. The immaculate lobby, though, smelled like lamb fat and urine and disinfectant. A Christmas tree sparkled near the empty Greetings desk. Paper angels fluttered overhead.

"She's in the infirmary," Deena said. "Let's try this hallway."

They walked into the silence, down a hall lined with closed doors. Liz looked straight ahead. If a door *was* open, she didn't want to see it. It would be better to die than to sit, visible to strangers, seeing some unknown face peer in and vanish, as though one had been hurt in an accident and looked up into a ring of curious, unfamiliar faces, faces that gawked and were gone.

"I hate this," Deena hissed. "There's just fifty years between us and this."

"Forty," Liz said quietly. "Some of us have an edge." The french doors at the end of the hall were closed. Deena opened them and walked through. There was a crash and Deena crouched low. A magazine flew past her head, and she heard metal clash on metal and the muffled voices of people struggling in silence.

"Are you all right?" Liz whispered.

"Come on," Deena said, and pulled her forward. They stepped into what was certainly called the solarium. Plastic plants flourished there. Three very old people, tied into wheelchairs, stared out through the glass at the Sacred Mountains. A television flickered at the end of the room and there was a ping-pong table near the nurses' station. Three nurses held onto a white-haired woman who was wailing like a banshee and whacking the daylights out of the ping-pong table with a bent pole-lamp. The net was shredded, the paint gone. Liz grinned.

"Can we help?" Deena said and stepped toward the fight. One of the nurses turned and silently gestured them away. Her eyes were near-black and wet. Deena kept moving.

"It's okay," the male nurse said. "We're trying to calm her. It takes a minute for the stuff to take hold. You better get back—insurance won't cover you." He took hold of the old woman's wrist and tried to look in her eyes. She spit at him.

"Mrs. Latham," he said. "Mrs. Latham, it's okay. We're trying to help you. Harriet, Mrs. Latham, please, look at me." She went dead still, but not limp; shaking with fury, she looked him straight in the eyes.

"My name is Hatt," she said clearly. "My husband, Mr. Latham, is dead and you will call me Hatt." Just then, the third nurse slipped the point of the syringe into her upper arm and the dark-eyed nurse grabbed her other wrist. The lamp fell from Hatt's hand.

"You *will* let me go," the old woman said and slumped to the clean tiles.

"Please leave," the dark-eyed nurse said. "There's nothing left to do."

"We go," Deena said. Liz looked back. The nurses were bent over the woman; the other patients were still staring out at the Peaks.

Liz left Deena gossiping with her friend and wandered out to the nursing station. The guy was working on his notes. He looked very tired. She tapped on the glass.

"I was here earlier," she said. "You know? When you were calming that woman down."

"Hatt!" he said and smiled. "I hate this job," he said cheerfully.

"I used to work these places," Liz said. "Forget the holidays."

"Believe it!" he said. "No big deal, though. She was just surprised to find herself here. Happens all the time."

"Didn't she know she was being admitted?" Liz asked. His face went wary.

"No can tell," he said. "Did you want something?"

"Sorry," she said. "I'm professionally nosy."

He grinned. "What were you?" he asked. "A social worker?"

"Close," she said. "You probably won't tell me, but I'll ask anyway. What meds is she on? I saw a lady get like that once on one of those big-gun tranqs."

"I'll tell," he said, "if you won't. You're right. We gave her some when she first got here because she nutted out so bad. That stuff hit her just like speed. She had the strength of a football team and she was just as wired." He shook his head.

"Those paradoxical reactions," Liz said. "You never know." He laughed.

"You gotta love this business," he said. "Or, take me, be nuts yourself.

That night, Liz dreamed of Hatt Latham. It was a simple dream. Hatt lay subdued and silent in her bed. Liz bent over her, pleading with her to get up, to fight, to talk, to destroy the ping-pong table. Behind beige curtains, a window shattered. Foul water oozed into the room. Liz climbed up on the bed. The water rose. She held Hatt's head up and away from the water. It kept rising. It stained the sheets, her thighs; it rose to Hatt's throat. She pressed the old woman's face to her breasts, as though there were air there. And woke.

The cabin was ordinary. There was no storm, no open window, no cat warm on her breasts. She set a log on the glowing coals and went back to sleep . . .

. . . the fire hissed. Talasi woke. The room was dark. It was both familiar and strange. She was alone. One dark-red coal glowed in the hearth. She was naked, wrapped tight in fur blankets. She was thirsty. She was pretty sure she hadn't died. Her belly hurt too much for her to be dead; it was as if fire-snakes coiled there.

The burning coal began to move. It drifted up, higher and higher, then floated towards her. The snakes began to uncoil. She could barely breathe, from pain, from fear. The snakes began to writhe. If she moved, they would bite her, but the pain was so great, so burning. She tried to cry out, but no sound came from her lips. The glowing coal hovered and she saw it clearly. It was the deep-burning eye of some thing, some black and ragged shape.

Smoke rose off the being. The flesh around the burning eye was charred; there was only a crater where the other should have been. The eye could see the snakes. It could summon them. She knew that. The snakes and the eye became one: a fiery eye in her belly, a being with an eye of blazing snakes. In all her fear, she wondered how.

The fire-snakes danced in the air. The being faded back into the darkness, then drifted forward. Now he was a beautiful man, his face round and full, his eyes soft and clear, like dew on brown stone, his hair shining soft. The snakes were not snakes at all; they were the brilliant feathers of the bird from the South, woven through his hair. He held his broad hands out to Talasi in blessing. She had never seen such kindness in a person's face. He touched her belly and, though the rabbit-fur lay warm and heavy over her, it was his naked hand on her naked belly. He called out the snakes. Ribbons of fire swirled up and away from her body and mingled with the fire's smoke. The room filled with the smell of rain on piñon and juniper. The pain was gone.

He dripped the sweet rain from his hands to her lips. Talasi tasted corn meal and red berries and baked squash fresh from the fields. He raised his arms and smoke, whiter than cotton, trailed from his fingers. He danced for her and wove the smoke into a robe, softer than fur and stitched with teardrops, red as the blood of womanhood. Tassels and breath feathers drifted from its hem. It was her marriage robe; it was her shroud, for the women of her clan were wed and buried in the same snowy robes. Talasi tried to work her arms free from the blankets, to take the robe, to hold it. The movement seemed to take forever;

she had to stop and gasp for breath. But she wanted the robe, she ached for the robe. As she freed her arms, she heard a voice, neither woman's nor man's, neither human nor animal, a voice of wind, of water, and the voice rose from her breast and flew from her lips, whispering.

"No. Not yet." She drew back her hand.

The beautiful man lowered his arms. The robe melted into smoke and rose as a veil in front of him. He moved forward and was revealed. Changed. With a gentle brown eye and an eye glowing red; with a soft smile and a twisted frown; with her grandfather's voice and an unearthly hiss, the being stood before her and held out his two hands, palm up, one hand charred black, the other lined with hard work.

"These are your gifts," it said in its double voice.

Her heart answered.

"I accept."

She watched as the being set upon her belly a charred seed. That last pain was so terrible that she screamed, then the scream and the pain faded away. The being turned sideways and she saw only the beautiful man. He held out to her a shimmering seed of light; it trembled and melted and re-formed, perhaps scarlet, perhaps purple as the far desert, perhaps blue, perhaps green as the new shoots of spring. Talasi reached out. The man spoke.

"If you take this gift, beloved sister, it will light your way. Should you waver in your path or forget to teach others, the light will begin to fade. Should you use your power without thought of your Mother and Grandmother and all they have given you, the light will be gone forever."

Talasi looked up into the man's eye. There she saw all that had ever been, the people climbing up out of Mother Earth; the witches and their two-hearts; the Twins parting, one to the North, one to the South, the people walking and walking, the mountain spewing fire, the great star, her mother crouched in a darkened room. She saw all that would be, the bone dice rolling, rolling, growing so big they swept the people away, crushing them, leaving the earth stripped and barren, the great trees toppled. She saw a huge cave in a light-washed cliff, all rosy sandstone, and the people building there and leaving; *tuukwi* and pine and gray caves, and the people building there and leaving; three sun-burnt *tuukwi* high above the desert, and the people building there. . . . Here the vision blurred, then leaped, sharp and terrible, into clarity, and Talasi saw things not of the world, unimaginable, unholy . . . pictures made of colored light, old people in front of them, dying alone, girl children having babies, arrows with flaming tails, moon-bright birds that dove to earth and burst into fire, villages, burning, burning. She saw the earth, Mother Earth, scarred and dead and smoking. She thought her heart would burst.

"Do not despair," the being said. "You are not alone." He turned again and in the center of that black, charred socket, she saw a faint shining figure running, stumbling, struggling towards her. The darkness grew and grew, till it became the world around and she saw that the running creature was a woman. It beckoned to her and she went forward. When she saw Her eyes, she knew the woman for Herself, reflected as bright and clear as though she saw Her in the calm waters of East-Rising Spring. She held out her hands. The woman Talasi smiled and set in the girl's palm a shimmering seed. It was cool as rain. The woman began to shrink and fade. Talasi lay still, looking straight into Her beautiful eyes. They were filled with sadness and love. And were gone. Only the dark socket remained. The being turned and, he, too, slowly disappeared, his dreadful, wonderful face drifting away into smoke.

Talasi woke, covered with a clean cotton robe. She looked around the room, Pamosi's room. It was Qøyangwnuptu, First Dawn. Pale purple light filled the roof-hole. She licked her lips. They were soft and damp. The pain in her belly was gone. She rolled cautiously to her side. The pain stayed away. Aunt Pamosi lay beside her, not sleeping, saying nothing, just watching.

"Greetings, my niece," she said. "Have you slept well?"

Talasi found she couldn't speak. She had just enough strength to smile. Pamosi stroked her hair. From somewhere in the room, a thin, old, deep voice spoke.

"Do not say anything," the voice said. "You are healing. That is quiet work."

An old man bent over her. His hair was thick and gray, and he was as wrinkled as a slab of dried squash. Behind his withered lids, his eyes were golden-brown. He smiled sweetly. His teeth were strong and white. You did not see that in the old ones; years and tough corn wore down their teeth. Sometimes, terrible pain took them. When he smiled, he was a young man.

"I am Toho," he said, "the old lion." He held out his thin, twisted hands. "I do not look like a lion, do I?" he said. "As you can see, I have no claws."

Talasi touched his finger. He stroked the back of her hand. She played with a string of shells tied around his wrist. He was dressed for a ceremony, strings of *tsorposi* and shell round his neck, a scarlet feather thrust through his top-knot. Talasi pulled back. Her eyes went wide. She pointed to the feather.

"It is from a bird from the South," he said. "I will have your aunt put it outside if it troubles you."

Talasi remembered the seed of light. It gave her courage. She looked straight at the scarlet; it was just a feather.

"No," she whispered. "It is harmless."

"Then," Toho said, "I think we will eat together. It is morning. I have thanked Taawa for this day. Will you do so too?"

Talasi nodded. Though her lips were weak, her heart was strong with thanks. Pamosi brought corn meal porridge, rolls of fresh *piki,* three mugs of dark tea. She and Toho propped the child up against a soft pile of turkey feather robes. Talasi bowed her thanks and began to sip the tea.

"How good this is!" she said. "How delicious, Aunt. I am so hungry." Her voice was a whisper.

The old man and Pamosi looked at each other. Talasi gulped down the last of the tea. Toho watched her carefully.

"You must drink slowly, little one," Pamosi said. "Your belly has been empty a long while. You mustn't surprise it."

The old man smiled. "She will be eating stew by night-fall," he said. "The pain is gone." He glanced at Talasi. She nodded. Toho looked away. When he looked back, his eyes were sad. He spoke directly to the girl. She listened carefully.

"You have been very ill," he said. She watched his eyes. "It was not the summer sickness," he said. "You do not have the gray skin. Your eyes do not burn." He smoothed her matted hair. "I have questions," he said. "Will you answer them? We must know what fever burned in you."

"It was the fire-snakes," she said clearly. Toho rocked back on his heels.

"You know this?" he said.

"Yes," she said. "It was the fire-snakes and the being that is terrible and beautiful made them go away and gave me two seeds. I am not to despair."

Toho bowed his head. Pamosi brought more tea. Her face was pale.

"Child," Toho said. "May I pass my hands over your belly and learn if there is anything left behind by the fire-snakes? May I do that?"

"Yes, Uncle," Talasi said. "But there is only charred seed."

"That may be," he said. "I must know." He settled beside her. Pamosi moved through the room carrying smoking juniper, the thin blue smoke weaving its work in the air. Toho raised his arms to the morning light. He asked for help, for patience, for knowledge. Talasi closed her eyes. Pamosi's prayers rang out in the smoky room. The old man lowered his arms and held his hand, palm down, in the air over Talasi's belly. His face darkened and his breathing slowed. Talasi felt nothing. She was calm under his hand. He sighed deeply, then rocked back and gently shook his hand, as though he shook off water.

Pamosi was silent. Talasi opened her eyes. She saw the question in Pamosi's face. She saw the patience. Toho took both their hands in his. Talasi gazed up into his golden eyes. They were mirrors. She remembered a mask she had once seen, a mask brought by a trader from the South, a mask that glittered on the plaza sand.

"You have survived this sickness," he said, "but there is a wound that will not heal. The fire burned shut the passage for life." His gold eyes shimmered. Pamosi bowed her head. "You will not bear children," Toho said. "You will never be mother nor wife nor grandmother."

Pamosi set her hand on Talasi's belly. She gave thanks that her niece lived. Bitterness rose in her throat and she prayed past it. Talasi was too sleepy to think about what the old healer had said. It was *qahopi*, she knew that. It was sad, but the being had warned against despair. He had taken away and he had given. She stretched out her left hand and unfolded her fingers.

"What of this?" she asked. "What does this tell you?"

Toho and Pamosi looked down. In Talasi's palm lay a stone like starlight, round as the full moon, cool, perfect. It was not a seeing stone nor pale *tsorposi*. This stone was milky white and when Talasi held it to the sunlight streaming through the roof-hole, it flashed with many colors. Talasi laughed.

"It is my delight," she said. "It is the guiding-stone for my path. The being said so. I will carry it with me a long time." She closed her fingers. When she opened them, the stone was gone.

"This is her mystery," Toho said. He smiled at Pamosi. "We will say nothing. It is her secret."

Six

ONE WARM MORNING IN MID-JANUARY, Liz called Tenderhome. The day had dawned soft, and she'd sat on the stoop and smelled damp earth and fool's Spring. Half-dreaming, she'd suddenly thought of Hatt in that dead building. The social worker took her call and assured her that they would welcome a visiting friend for Mrs. Latham.

"Oh," the social worker said, "do call her Hatt."

She greeted Liz in the lobby and took her to an office that seemed to be covered wall to ceiling with posters and plaques. One was reminded that God did not make junk, that smiles take less effort than frowns and that today was the first day of the rest of one's life.

"Good," Liz said, pointing to the last. A misty rainbow arced over a unicorn. The social worker smiled politely. She was very young, neatly pulled together in off-white cotton skirt and blouse, her hair cut in the same shape as a famous ice-skater's.

"Beg pardon?" she said.

"The rest of my life," Liz said. "Today is my forty-fifth birthday. The rest of my life."

"You're kidding," the social worker said. Liz gritted her teeth. She knew what was coming. "You don't *look* forty-five," the woman said.

"This is how forty-five looks," Liz said brightly.

"Yes," the social worker said, "yes, I guess it does." She nodded firmly. "Age *is* all in the mind, isn't it?" Liz nodded.

"Well," the woman said, "I *am* delighted to meet you, Ms. Morrigan. Hatt has received *no* visitors since admission." She kept her face very still. There was something in the set of her mouth that said that although judgement was forbidden, she sure had one.

"What's the story?" Liz said. The social worker looked down at a pale blue folder on her desk. "I'm afraid that's confidential," she said. "But it's not a very nice one."

Liz nodded.

"Parent-child conflict," the social worker said.

"Look," Liz said, "what's your name? We went right past that."

"Cindy," the social worker said, "my name is Cindy Clayton. Call me Cindy. Please."

"Well, Cindy," Liz said, "I'm here and I'm ready to start today. What's the plan?"

"Just visits," Cindy said. "She's still heavily medicated. Just your visits count. You see, visitor contact is very important for our people. You'll see. She'll begin to orient more and more toward reality. She'll relearn those lost social skills."

"Lost?" Liz said. She remembered the fire in Hatt's eyes.

Cindy flipped through the folder. "Oh yes," she said, "the adjustment phase is almost always a very confusing time."

"Well," Liz said, "let's get started."

Hatt Latham was gray. She was slumped in a fine old oak rocker, her back to the door, her face turned to an expanse of beige curtain. Her head shook. Cindy stood directly in front of her, squatted, crooked her head and said carefully,

"Hatt, you have a visitor." There was no response. Cindy smiled at Liz.

"Come in," she said. "Come in and meet Hatt." Liz walked up to the chair. Hatt stared at a corner of a faded Navajo rug. Cindy gently eased her upright.

"Reshaping," she whispered to Liz. "It helps to get those messages moving again."

"Messages?" Liz said.

"From the brain to the body," Cindy said.

"Right," Liz said. "I could use a little reshaping myself."

"Couldn't we all!" Cindy said and grinned.

"Liz," she said, "please meet Hatt." Liz took Hatt's limp hand in hers. "Hatt," Cindy said brightly, "this is Liz Morrigan. She's going to be visiting you." Hatt began to slip down in the chair. Cindy propped her up. She was still smiling and there were little sweat circles in the armpits of her nice outfit. "Oh dear," she said.

"We'll be fine," Liz said and sat on the edge of the bed.

"There you go," Cindy said. "You two have fun."

"Right," Liz said.

"Really," Cindy said. "This can be a fun experience. You'll see." She backed out the door and closed it.

"Fun, Hatt," Liz said. "I can hardly wait. How about you?" They hadn't brought much to Hatt's new home: an oak bed, an old, stained glass lamp, all violets and emerald leaves, an oak dresser, the rug and a matching blanket folded at the foot of the bed. They were Two Grey Hills and they both carried the Spirit Line.

"Do you mind if I open the curtains?" Liz asked. "It's a beautiful day outside." There was no answer. She opened the curtains half-way. Hatt stared down at the floor, a muscle in the corner of her mouth twitching. She was very pale, her skin wrinkled from a lifetime of Southwest sun. She was clean enough. They had washed her and dressed her and combed her silver-blonde hair into a neat bun. A silk rose was pinned at the throat of her dress. Her hands were twisted as bare cedar roots, her pulse leaped under the papery skin. She sighed.

"I'd like to sit here a while," Liz said. "I'm new in town. I could use some company." She crossed her fingers against the lie. If Hatt was whole in there, in the fog of medicine, Liz was going to have some fancy talking to do later.

Hatt shifted in the rocker. Liz pulled up one of the Tenderhome standard-issue chairs. It was classic institutional, chrome, and there was no way to sit in it in comfort. The light behind the curtains went from beige to pale gold. Liz opened the curtains. There wasn't much to see, the back parking lot, a few scrubby juniper and, if you could raise your head, the dull hump of Mt. Elden. It was truly restful.

Liz checked her watch. She'd been there in that silence watching the light, hearing Hatt's slow breathing, for over an hour. She touched Hatt's wrist. It felt like the skin of a snake, warm, a little rough.

"Thank you," she said. "For your company." She stood up. In the light, Hatt's hair was a shining helmet. "I'll be back," Liz said. "In two days." She drew the curtains and rang the buzzer for the nurse. "Hatt," she said. "Your hair is like silver. It really is."

That night, sleep moved into her easily, as though earned, as natural as breath, as welcome as a dear, familiar lover . . .

. . . Talasi lay awake. She could hear her mother and father talking softly. Most nights, the gentle rise and fall of their voices was a song to sleep by. She could ride on the gentle waves, letting herself slip deeper and deeper into her dreaming. But this night, there were long silences. She seemed to see her father's voice. His words were darts, stinging and sharp. She fought against sleep; she tried to feel the pathstone in her left hand. She felt she was being dragged from her path by her parents' words and silence.

"Help me," she whispered. She felt the stone, cool and smooth; it seemed to float through her arm, through her sore heart, to rest in the mysterious place behind her eyes.

"You can do nothing," it filled her head with comfort. "You must sleep. You will need to be strong tomorrow."

She woke before dawn and crept past her sleeping parents to the roof. There was that melting above the dark hills to the east; it was Qøyangwnuptu, the purple dawn-dusk, when one could first see clearly the black shape of the pueblo against the sky. Talasi crouched on the cold roof, waiting through the pale yellow light of second dawn, Sikangnuqa, when she could see her breath before her as a white cloud. Then came Talawva, the third dawn that brought the red sun up above the edge of the world. She stood and gave thanks for the new day and asked that she would know her path and follow it well and happily. It was the first prayer she had learned, the prayer she and the People repeated every day. Smoke began to thread up from the smoke-hole. She heard her mother and father moving below. Her stomach tightened. It was then she realized she was frightened to go into her mother's house. That seemed very bad. It was *qahopi,* that fear. She tried to quiet the warning in her head.

"Stay away," the words said, "stay away from your mother's house." They were terrible words. They were as awful as the Monster Kachina, So'yo'kwuti. They seemed to have the same terrible yellow eyes. They found her with those awful eyes. They chased each other in her head, those words, and never turned their yellow eyes from hers. She turned her face up to the sun and asked for courage. The sun's warmth melted the monster-words away and she climbed down the ladder into her mother's house.

Below, all seemed well. Her father left for his morning run to the spring, where he would bathe and say his prayers. Choovio followed him to the roof-top and quickly returned to stir the porridge. Talasi helped with the meal. She filled a smaller jug from the brimming *wikoro.* It was her favorite jug— Pamosi had made it. At the top of the handle there was a little dimple, the perfect spot for Talasi's thumb. Choovio watched her daughter. She was so serious. There was a grace to her, and sometimes a silence.

"Today," Choovio said, "you are to go to the fields." She smiled. "And you are to stay there."

Talasi nodded. She had turned her face away.

"Look at me," Choovio said. "You will want to go today. The birds have settled just outside the field near the spring and you will have to make lots of noise to chase them off." Talasi looked up. "You may take my rattle," Choovio said, "you will be as noisy as the boys." Talasi laughed.

That would be good. The big boys had their *umukpi,* the bones they swung around their head. Those bones would begin to buzz in the air, louder and louder, till it sounded as though one of the little *to'tsa* had grown huge and was humming from cornstalk to cornstalk, sticking its needle bill into the plants, hunting for something sweet to suck. Her mother's rattle was big and noisy. It was more snake than hummingbird.

"What are the birds?" she asked.

"Angwusi," Choovio said. "The greedy things."

"I like them," Talasi said. Her mother stared at her.

"They are so noisy," she said, "and black, so black that there are colors in their feathers."

Choovio laughed. Talasi wondered why her mother laughed at her so often. She had sat a long time watching one of the birds, watching the light change on its great wings. She set the water jug on the eating mat. Her mother poured out the porridge.

"Today," Choovio said, "you will chase those beautiful birds away. They eat our corn. They take the porridge right out of your mouth. Remember that."

She opened a basket as tall as Talasi, a basket woven in black and yellow and white, a striped lizard coiled on the lid by the weaver's dreaming fingers, and took out the rattle. It was egg-shaped, made from a big gourd, and it was carved with clown ravens with great open mouths and tiny eyes. Tall corn plants stretched from top to bottom as though the birds played between them. The colors had faded, red and yellow and black, and the handle was smooth from the touch of many hands, Choovio's, her mother's and her grandmother's.

Talasi gave it a strong shake. It was filled with the tiny pebbles a child could find outside an ants' hill. They filled the room with an angry clatter. Choovio laughed.

"Enough," she said. "Take that to the ravens." She brushed a lock of hair back from Talasi's forehead and straightened the shoulder of her dress. The child was so restless, so quick to move, to dance, to run off, that her clothing was always disarranged, her long hair tangled and wild. She gave Talasi a pouch with *piki* and dried berries and sent her up the ladder.

Rupi ran up the path. She saw Talasi and shook her rattle at the sky. She was a little taller than Talasi, a little thinner, though her face was just as full. That was good. The girls with the roundest faces and the roundest arms were the most chosen. They were the ones the boys would begin to notice after the big rabbit hunt. Rupi bounced on the path, her *manta* slipping from her little shoulder. Her black eyes snapped with excitement.

"Cousin," she cried. "Hurry! The birds are there! The boys will be there . . . from East-Rising House, too, those boys! That squirrel boy, that Sakuna! And," she stopped for breath, "my grandmother has made me a new family of dolls!"

Talasi joined Rupi in her bouncing. They danced back and forth across the path. They could not leave before Rupi's grandmother, Tuvumsi, came for them and they could not hurry her along. They thought the sun would set before they saw the old woman finally emerge on the roof, her broad face opened out into a huge smile. She treasured the girls. They were her favorites, Talasi, so curious, so restless, Rupi, a chatterbox, as she had been. They greeted her, settled their carrying slings on their shoulders and began to descend the trail in the brilliant sun.

They hurried past the ball-court. Talasi's belly tightened. The place was quiet. There were flowers growing in the wall's cracks. She made herself look. They had, as always, smoothed the earth of the playing field. All she saw was stone and yellow flowers and the unmarked, unblemished oval of pale sand. And yet there was something wrong about the place. There were no shadows.

"Come *on!*" Rupi hissed. Talasi turned her face to the trail and ran to catch up.

"Why were you looking at that place?" Rupi whispered. "There is nothing there for us." Tuvumsi moved steadily ahead. Her broad back, her firm steps were comfort to see. "Why are there no shadows there?" Talasi asked and it was as though the morning breeze ate her words. Rupi gave no sign she had heard. Tuvumsi marched steadily on. Talasi looked over her shoulder. Someone had left corn cakes at the opening of the Spirit's breath-hole. There was a painted jar of water and a bunch of *tumi,* pink against the rough black rock.

A handful of women and twice as many children gathered at the field. The boys from East-Rising House were racing around shrieking, their *umukpi* and rattles roaring and buzzing and clattering. Many years ago, the women had dragged boulders into long rows to guide the men's hands in planting, and built a stone shelter, roofing it with brush. A guiding channel led from the nearby spring to the fields where the young corn grew in thick clumps, its pale leaves swaying in the morning air. In late summer, daily thunderstorms flooded the earth, filling the spring to overflowing; only the women's stonework caught the water, held it and fed it, as milk to a baby, to the growing plants. Tuvumsi taught the girls these lessons again and again, with each stone they carried to keep the dam and channel whole.

The women stood in a circle at the south end of the field. Tuvumsi joined them. Even Tsohtsona waited, her necklaces left at home, her arms bare. She smiled at Talasi. Two others, women of Nest House, whispered and turned away. Three girls ran to greet the newcomers, while the boys kept on running in crazy circles, shaking their rattles at nothing and throwing stones at invisible birds.

Pamosi stood back from the circle of women, staring eastward, shading her eyes against the sun. Her face was solemn. She stepped back into the circle.

"You might stop your chatter," she said quietly. "It would be well if the *angwusi* do not fly in from the east. Gossip draws them to us from that direction." Tuvumsi glared at her.

"Woman," she said, "you are always seeing witches. Leave that for your husband. It is his people who believe *angwusi* to be witches. We of Parrot Clan think that is foolish."

Pamosi continued to stare east. Talasi stepped away from the cluster of girls and stood at her aunt's side. Black specks appeared. Like bits of ash caught on the wind, they wheeled and floated toward them.

"They are coming," Pamosi said.

"My aunt," Talasi whispered. She tugged at Pamosi's *manta.* "Is it true what you say? About *angwusi* and *powaqa?* How could that be? How could those beautiful birds have two-hearts?" Pamosi smiled down at her. Talasi kept tugging at the robe.

"Is that like two faces?" she asked. "How could that be? A bird with two faces could not see to fly. It would fly forward and backward at once. How could this be?" She stopped to take a breath. Pamosi ruffled her hair.

"I see," Pamosi said, "that you are thinking very hard about things. You will tire your great owl eyes and your great owl brain if you think so hard." Talasi backed away from her touch.

"I am not foolish," she said. "I am not funny."

"I did not say you were foolish," Pamosi said. "That is a *qahopi* word. You should not have to hear it." She pulled Talasi close. "What you say is true," she said. "If there are witches, they most certainly fly forward and backward at once. That is how they cause so much mischief. They are always ahead of and behind themselves, never right now, where we could stop them."

Talasi looked hard at her aunt. "But then . . ." she said. Pamosi set her cool fingers over the child's mouth.

"Enough," she said. "The ravens are here and we have work to do."

The brilliant sky was patched with birds, sun-dazzle in their wings, their screams piercing. Talasi shook her rattle once. The noise that had been so loud, so angry in her mother's house was a whisper against their cries. The older boys ran at the birds, whirling the humming bones around their heads, yelling terrible threats; they crashed together, tumbled to the ground and leaped to their feet. The *angwusi* wheeled calmly above. Rupi darted into the mass of boys. The squirrel boy bumped her hard. She sat down on the hot sand and jumped up, shrieking. Talasi watched her. She did not know how to do that. She did not know why a girl would want to.

She did know that they could not drive the ravens away. For all their noise, for all their wild dancing, they could only keep the ravens aloft. It was the ravens who made the game. It was the ravens who taught the rules. She ran toward the other children. She was seeing something very clearly and it made her heart leap. It caught her breath in her throat and made the tears ache behind her eyes. The ravens were going to come again. They would never go away. All the people had were their bodies, their sound, their stubborn presence in the fields. They would never win.

"Talasi," Rupi screamed. "Come here. Help us." Talasi ran into the jumble of children. She shrieked. She shook the great rattle. She waved her round arms in the air till they ached. They began to sing a loud and rude song. Above, the ravens screamed back and kept up their smooth circling. They did not land.

One boy held back. He was frowning. His arms were crossed in front of his chest. He was very dirty, smudged with soot, his breech-clout frayed and unmended. Talasi bounced up to him and shook the rattle in his face.

"Are you a friend of the ravens?" she cried. He glared at her.

"Go away," he said calmly. Quickly, easily, unnoticed in the dust and tumult, he began to walk backwards, slipped into the juniper's shadow and disappeared. Talasi was fascinated. It was not like one of the older boys to leave the crowd. She sidled over to the bush and found the boy crouched in its shade, winding the thong tight around the *umukpi.* He glanced up.

"Go away," he hissed. He did not sound so calm now. Talasi stared at him. He was a big boy, taller than the others, and very thin. His hair was coarse and badly cut. It hadn't been washed or brushed in a long while. She noticed his hands. They were long and covered with little scars. Though he was only a few winters older than she, it seemed that all his childhood softness had melted from those long fingers. He was, she decided, quite ugly and most interesting.

"Go away, stupid girl," he said. "I would scream at you but that is not a man's way." He flushed red. "Besides, then they would know where we were."

Talasi suddenly wanted very much to stay. No one had ever told her to go away before. She crouched beside him and smiled.

"Why did you leave?" she whispered. "Why did you stand so still? Don't you want to scare the ravens, so we will have corn in the cold time?"

"Will you go away?" he cried. "Stupid, stupid, stubborn girl. They will see us and I will have to go back to that child's game. Leave me alone."

"But you *are* a child," Talasi said reasonably. "I am eight winters old and I am a child and you are not much older than I."

"Stupid girl," he screamed. "Go away. I will hurt you."

Talasi stared straight into his eyes. She did not see evil there, only something like the look in the eyes of the red-and-green parrots locked in reed cages behind the *kikmongwi*'s house. He was a puzzle. She sighed. As she stood to obey him, he pushed her hard. She fell out of the juniper's shadow into the blinding sun. He bent over her. He was nothing but shadow against the light, huge, dark. He shoved something in her hand. It was the *umukpi.*

"You are *qahopi!*" she hissed. She scrambled to her feet and stared into his face. "They should hang you by your heels over smoke," she cried and slapped his thin arm. They glared at each other.

"I will not forget this," she said. She held out the toy. "I don't want your bribe," she said.

"Keep it," he said, "girl-who-is-a-boy. When you look at it, tell yourself that you need to learn how to be a proper girl, to stay away from boys, to keep your mouth shut." He put his fingertips on her shoulders. It was a feather touch. She felt his fingers burning there.

"Go back," he said. He turned her gently around and, with the smallest push, set her moving toward the others. She ran. And, without thought, found herself twirling the *umukpi* over her head. Tuvumsi stopped her.

"Where did you get that?" she said sternly. "That is for boys."

"I found it over there," Talasi said. She pointed to the juniper. There was nothing there but shadow. "It was lying there," she said. Tuvumsi took it from her hand and gave it to one of the boys. Talasi looked back toward the juniper and saw the shadow shift and elongate. Then, it was gone . . .

Seven

LIZ WOKE, ABRUPTLY LONELY. The air was bitter: the fire out, the stove's iron icy and searing. She pulled on mittens and made a fire, wrapped herself in her grandpa's robe and sat in the rocker, staring at the orange light in the chinks of the stove. She had dreamed, a good long one, one with a story, one that had been perfectly clear in the dreaming and, in waking, was only scraps.

Through the east window, she saw the black tips of the pines against a pale dawn. In the west, scattered clouds reflected silver; the dream was as distant, as shifting. The windows glowed, lilac to lemon to the dazzle of sun on snow. She wondered if Hatt Latham woke early, from half-sleep to half-waking, and lay in the big oak bed watching the curtains come alight. She wondered if young Hatt had watched these slow, luxurious winter sunrises from her marriage bed. She half-saw, half-dreamed that young ghost turning to her husband, bringing him into the slow warm melt of her body; and pushed the vision away, because the woman was not Hatt and the man was no stranger.

She needed to move away from that wondering, from the fire's heat and the sudden ache in her body. She pulled a heavy sweater over her robe and went out. Frost glittered on the pine needles. She sat on the old stump and watched the soft morning lights blink on in the houses across the meadow. She wondered who lived there and if they guessed that she sat so near, watching them wake, breathing in the smoke of their morning fires. She remembered waking next to Nick in his battered little house that always smelled of pine smoke and northeast damp, of motor oil and his dusty pack-rat loot. She would throw together breakfast in his messy kitchen and take it to his bed, and herself to his warm body.

One morning he had pulled the covers up under her chin and stumbled into the kitchen. She had heard him, like a coon in a campsite, muttering and groaning, making disastrous sounds with metal and glass. He had padded back to bed with cheese, crackers and coffee, beer and a bag of chocolate chip cookies. Around three, they had dressed, kissed and gone back to bed. Much later, she had read a magazine article on "The New Lover," and had laughed and cried, because he had never been "new" and because he was gone, and in the leaving, somehow ancient.

Tears rolled down her cold cheeks. She thought of Hatt, of abandonment. A raven screamed from her roof. She wiped her eyes on her bathrobe sleeve and looked up. It was a huge bird. She was always a little afraid of them. They had a spooky way about them, a way of cocking their big heads and staring, yellow eye to yours, appraising, a little contemptuous. This one stretched out its glossy, ragged wing. For an instant, she saw colors bright as oil slick, iridescent, shifting from red to green to blue to gone. The bird bent its head to its feathers, then froze. Liz heard a "scrawk" from the grove near the bathhouse. The raven looked up and took off directly above her, the beat, beat of its wings ruffling her hair; it cried once again and was answered.

She shivered. The bird had flown northeast. That seemed a good direction, but she did not know why. Something about the dream lay that way. She had driven that direction in early January, to southern Utah, courting amnesia and focus, the sloughing-off that driving for hours on straight roads always induced. It had worked. She had gone to the rock with stories of nostalgia and longing; the rock, in its silence, had talked back.

That rock had told her to find out what was important. It had said, in those canyonlands, in those networks of light and stone and air, that she had to learn to pay attention. She had to learn to let go. And she had best learn to take hold. Out there, in burnt-orange arroyos, from a ledge that opened onto a pale red, soaring sandstone arch, she felt the scarred fibers of her heart begin to soften. She began to think of Place in the way she had once thought of Passion.

The earth-gifts were everywhere, their giving endless. At the Grand Canyon, she had stood in fog and watched the sun burn through, patch by patch, beauty revealed in cameos: spire and mesa and North Rim, umber butte and gray-green river, one, two, five thousand feet away; the brown leather leaves of gambel oak, two feet below her; empty sky miles above. The sun persisted. The cameos melted into one great jewel and she had stood looking down at the shining foam of Unkar Rapids a mile below. The fog had left prisms of water on everything, juniper and red rock sequinned, shuddering in the breeze, tossing light back to the sun.

A ranger had walked up to her. She turned and the woman's face was as beautiful as everything else she saw. They were both crying.

Liz laughed.

"It's special effects, right?" she said. The ranger nodded. "Takes hours to get that ready," she said. As quickly as the fog had burned off, the dew was gone. Clouds scudded in from the north. The light went gray.

"What's next?" Liz asked.

"Hard to say," the ranger said. "The script writes itself . . . I think it drinks a little."

"I want to thank somebody," Liz said.

"What's stopping you?" the ranger said. "We're understaffed, over-worked, all the parks are that way. Maybe you can figure something out." She touched the brim of her hat and covered her name tag with her other hand. "I didn't say that," she said. "Must have been another special effect." She shook Liz's hand. Liz thought of Paul Shaughnessy.

"What about Qumavi Tuuwa?" Liz said.

"One of the worst," the ranger said. "Their resource guy is up to his eyebrows in radioactive water, pot thieves and well-meaning wannabes who think it's groovy to sleep in the ruins."

"What's a wannabe?" Liz asked.

"Wanna be Indians," the ranger said. "They think they're beyond the rules." She walked back to her truck and climbed in.

"Thanks," Liz called out. "I needed that."

"Call Shaughnessy . . . you guys were made for each other!" the ranger yelled back.

Liz stood up slowly. The ravens were long gone. She carried water back to the cabin. Her breakfast took ten minutes. Back in the crazy days, the days that ran from six A.M. to midnight, she'd perfected quick food. Now, home-made apple-plum sauce with yogurt and an indecent number of cashews and she was ready to get on with it.

The highway was clear, the sun strong. She drove in from the north entrance, past spotted cattle and black cinder cones. There was a flash of light on the flank of the red mesa. Two pronghorn antelope sniffed the air, bounded toward her and leaped across the road—lofted, dreamily intent. She slammed on the brakes. They neither swerved nor turned their heads, and suddenly, were gone.

Paul met her at the door. He had a day-pack slung over one shoulder and an army canteen hung from his belt; he was not smiling. Liz climbed out of the car. The warm, dry air rose off the sand. She could smell plants, things growing, something astringent and clean.

"Bad day?" she asked. He grinned.

"Welcome," he said. "I was afraid you might be somebody else. Let's go before they show up." He hustled her to the green truck. "I got a call yesterday," he said as he started the engine, "from somebody named Coyote who wanted to talk to me about House-of-Tragedy. Seems she's been remembering when she died there two thousand years ago."

"Mmmm," Liz said.

"My time's tight as a tick," he said, "but I just can't say no."

"Say more," Liz said.

"Well, shit," he said, "a.), these ruins have only been here nine hundred years, and b.), you don't talk "coyote" out here. The Navajos have ideas about them—they're dark animals to them."

They rode in silence for a while. He turned off the asphalt onto a rough road that faded fast to tire tracks straggling across the sand. Liz rolled down the window. A big buck jackrabbit leaped straight up a little ahead of the truck.

"There he is again." Liz said.

"Dime a dozen," Paul said.

"No way," she said. "Never. Look at those ears. Look at those moves."

"Oh, spare me," Paul groaned. "I can't take anymore. You're gonna tell me about the relationship of everything to everything and Mother Earth and holy rocks. Right? Why me?" He glared at her and tugged his cap lower on his forehead. Liz slouched down in her seat.

"Yeah," he said, "just like me, just like Susie up at the Canyon. Let me tell you, the Yewnited States Park Service isn't going to like this one bit. Another one, another busy-body bleeding-heart tree-hugger. Just like the ones that hung that fake crack on Glen Canyon National Dam. And those commies that keep nagging about uranium near the Canyon. Two of us. In the same park. Thank Bureaucracy for the 1985 Paper Reduction Act or I'd be buried in the blizzard of memos that's about to fly. Up Top isn't going to like this, whoever Up Top is. I've never known."

"Are you done?" Liz said. He grinned and looked over at her.

"Lady," he said, "I'd *have* to be a dreamer to do this, chasing down radioactive tailings, reminding nice people day after day not to pick up arrow points and bones and nine-hundred-year-old pottery pieces and put them in their hundred-dollar backpacks, picking up broken beer bottles after college kids have driven their pig-tired, belch-engined, off-road vehicles over the beeweed. With*out* bucks and with*out* back-up." He jerked off his cap and threw it on the seat. "Now I'm done," he said cheerfully.

"I swear," Liz said, "my fantasy of the strong and silent rugged ranger is dying. Did Ed Abbey lie?"

"It's the park service," he said glumly. "We join up with some high-minded idea of protecting national treasures and we end up telling people two crucial facts." He paused.

"Which are?"

"The location of the john," he said, "and whether the thousand-foot walk to the main ruin is worth it."

"Well," Liz said, "here I am. What are you going to do with me?"

"What brought you here?" he asked.

"Gratitude," she said. "I write, I walk, I type, I can read. I can count. All I ask is that I not have to talk to people."

"Good enough for me," he said and pulled the truck off onto a slab of rock. "Here," he said. "Carry the water. I've got some mapping to do. There's some prairie dog villages that used to be out here. The guys that graze their cattle out here don't like 'em much, so I need to make sure they haven't been wiped out." He pointed to a little mesa to the south. "We'll climb up that talus slope."

"Hey," Liz said, "look at this!" She held up a piece of pottery. It was bone-white, its black design perfectly balanced, clear as though the potter's brush had moved over its surface the day before.

"I saw a design like this," she said, "on a Chinese jug in an art museum. The same. Really. It's a perfect spiderweb. I love it!"

"You know," Paul said, "your problem is lack of enthusiasm. I can tell."

"How old *is* this?" Liz asked.

"Eight hundred years," he said. "Looks like Flagstaff-Black-on-White. There're lots of 'em around here. The People had their garbage dumps at the foot of these mesas. Sometimes they buried their dead here, sometimes in unused rooms. There is a theory they smashed pots as offerings to go with the dead . . . journey supplies, you know?"

"I better put it back then," she said.

"Nice instincts," he said.

"No big deal," she said. "I was raised Catholic. I believe in curses." She set the sherd back near a black pebble. When she stood up, Paul seemed very far away. She shook her head.

"You okay?" he asked.

"The vapors," she said. "That's what my dear old Aunt Mary used to call them." She bent and put her head down. She could feel the sun hot on her neck. "I'm okay," she said. "Let's go."

They climbed up over basalt boulders to the mesa top. Paul raised his binoculars and looked out over the desert below. He held the glasses out to her.

"Look there," he said. "Those mounds of dirt. That's prairie dog Manhattan. They're down there trading pine-nut futures."

"And there?" she asked. A broken wall outlined a near mesa.

"House of Tragedy," he said. "The early archeologists found a woman's skeleton huddled near the ventilation shaft. Behind her, crouched near her body, were three smaller ones, two kids and a baby. They guess the shaft plugged up or somebody plugged it and the family asphyxiated."

She handed him the glasses.

"That much for early utopia," she said.

"You bet. They died from accidents and lung disease and tooth infections and malnutrition. I'd like to take some of these earnest idealists and let them live out here for a few years."

"We'd die," she said. He nodded.

"We tried to grow Hopi corn up near the visitor center," he said. "It took constant attention."

"Did you sing?" Liz asked.

"I did," he laughed. "That's why it died." He hoisted his pack on his shoulders. "I'm going up to the end of the mesa," he said. "Take a little time here alone. It's different that way." He walked away, sure-footed as the pronghorn. She walked along the mesa edge, through pale-gold grasses, crushed sage perfuming her way, to its southern tip. A basalt-rimmed circle of bare earth lay in front of her, a rusted metal rod thrust into its center. She sat on one of the boulders. Paul had become a tiny figure on the mesa rim.

She rolled up her sleeves and stretched her arms out to the sun. A jet trail seamed the sky. In the perfect silence, she heard the plane's fading whine. There was a chill along her bare arms. She pulled down her sleeves. A quick shudder of air slipped across her face, and she smelled something long decayed. She wanted it to be some rabbit carcass, left half-eaten by one of those coyotes. All she saw was rock and sand and withered vines and gray-green saltbush. The chill slid down her spine.

She jumped up and stumbled away from the rock ring. A pebble clattered at her feet. She closed her eyes. There was only dark behind her lids. When she opened them, Paul's head and shoulders emerged above the mesa rim. He hauled himself up and ambled towards her, but she was having trouble seeing him. She took off her glasses and squinted. He was still out of focus. The mesa was blurred, the desert below just a shimmer of light. It was as though she looked through a pane of ice. She remembered playing near a creek, in December twilight, lifting a sheet of ice from the black water to her eye and seeing dried grasses like plumes of light and the horizon as a blurred brushstroke of fire.

"Sorry I was gone so long," Paul said. "I found something I've been looking for." She looked up. Everything was clear.

"You getting funny again?" he asked. He handed her the canteen. "Take a drink." The water was awful, warm and brackish. "That's the real thing," he said, "straight from Cottonwood Spring. You're tasting what they tasted."

"No wonder they left," she said,

"You sound shaky," Paul said. "What happened?"

"Nothing," she said. "Just a chill. I have a vivid imagination."

"Look," he said. "If you ever feel funny out here, just go away from the place. The Navajo won't go near these ruins. They won't go near anything associated with death. If one of their own dies in a hogan, they'll seal the place right up and abandon it. They think we *biilagaana* are nuts."

"They're probably right," she said.

"Come on," he said, "I'll take you back to the visitor center. We'll sit right under those nice fluorescent lights and you can fill out forms and drink bad coffee."

"I feel safer already," she said.

Driving home through a thin purple dusk, she still felt shaky. She hadn't wanted a drink in a long time and all she wanted was hot brandy and lemon. It might thaw the ice. When she reached the cabin, even it seemed changed. She built up the fire, got it too hot, opened the door and sat half-way between heat and cold. She was terribly thirsty. The flat mineral taste of the canteen water came back. They must have been thirsty all the time. She wondered what it took to get enough of even that water for their lives, for soup and stew and tea, for crops, for cleansing and ceremony.

On her desk was a tall crystal tumbler, a gift from Nick's dad. She hadn't used it much. When it broke, another link would be gone. She filled it with ice and water and pressed its surface to her hot forehead. There wasn't much left: a few worn shirts, an unopened pack of Camels, her silver bracelet, the bird's nest and this glass, cool in her hand and against her skin. She refilled it with water and set it on the windowsill above her bed.

The wind beat against the north wall. She started to move into sleep and jerked awake, out-of-breath, trying to brush something from her face. She finished the water and turned on her side. There was snowlight through the crystal tumbler, blue-white, splintered, fragile . . .

. . . Choovio sat motionless at her grinding stone, though it was mid-morning, though it was just before Niman, the time when the people would need *piki* and stew and *qa'ǫvala* for the celebration. Talasi knelt by her side at her own small stone. She was growing stronger at grinding, her arms and shoulders beginning to show a woman's strength under a child softness. She pushed the heavy grinder into the cracked corn and tried to sing, but fear swallowed the song. Her mother sat with her hands idle and her head bowed.

Choovio was not praying. She had sat this way the day before, but not so long. This day, the sun had moved from one side of the roof-hole to the middle and still she sat. Even her shadow, so still across the grinding stone, was frightening. Talasi stopped grinding and rocked back on her heels. The silence was cold, even in the warm room. That, too, was strange. Choovio did not want to go to the roof, where the other women ground in the cool air. Talasi touched her mother's wrist.

"My mother," she said, "Have I done something wrong?"

"No, my daughter," Choovio said. "You are, in all ways, the child I prayed for. I am trying to find the words to tell you something."

Talasi shivered. Her mother was easy with words. She could make a story out of anything, dust dancing in sunrays, clouds gathering above the mesa, the way a rabbit darted from *suwvi* to *suwvi*, crouching in their shade, stopping to nibble at the dry leaves.

"Do you remember," Choovio said softly, "when you were taken to your aunt's house?"

"I remember."

"Do you remember that your pains were not summer sickness?"

"Yes," Talasi whispered.

"Your aunt has told me that the old uncle told you that you would not bear children," Choovio said. Talasi looked down at the grinding stone.

"He told me that," she said. "I did not know that there was such a thing."

"There is," Choovio said.

"Will I have my bleeding?" Talasi said.

Choovio smiled. "How do you know about that?" she asked.

"The big girls talk," Talasi said. "They whisper about the red dots on the marriage robe. I look when I relieve myself, but it has not come."

"You are too young," Choovio said. "It is not for *me* to tell you more."

"But will *they* tell me?" Talasi said. "Will I go through the lessons?"

"I do not know."

"How did this happen?" Talasi said. She started to tell her mother about the beautiful, terrible man and felt something cool in her left palm. She bowed her head. If her mother saw her eyes, she would ask. And she was not to tell.

"Why do you ask 'how'?" Choovio said. "You always ask 'how'."

Talasi looked up. "I know why," she said. "It is the bone dice. It is to pay for the bone dice, for my father."

Choovio stared at her.

"They said so," Talasi said. "When they carried me, my father and Kunya."

"That one," Choovio hissed. Talasi pushed the grinder over the corn. She could feel a heat in her belly, in her face. She waited.

"*Mongwi*," Choovio said. "I cannot answer your questions. They are too big for me. I do not know."

Talasi rocked over her grinding, the sound, the motion calming her only a little.

"I am afraid," Talasi said. Choovio bent over her stone, picked up the grinder, and began to sing. "Sing with me," she said. Their voices wove together, sad and high, over the steady rhythm of the work . . .

. . . Liz turned in her sleep. Sugar patted at her cheek with her cool paw and settled into the curve of her arm . . .

. . . Talasi sat on a ruined wall high on the west mesa. She had left her mother grinding corn and she was, as usual, supposed to be somewhere other than where she was. She picked up a pebble from the trail and pressed it to her cheek. It was cool. She tasted it; it tasted of tears and dust. She held it in her palm and watched it dry in the late afternoon sun, its pink gone red. Below, the people of the village were tiny and unknown. Someone carried water up from the spring. A man checked the cloudless sky. A woman sat on her roof, stripping yucca with a gesture so familiar that distance could not fool the watcher. A few men were bent over the bone dice in the far curve of the plaza.

She thought about her mother's words and remembered the sadness in Toho's eyes. All her life was preparation for motherhood, even the parts she ran from. Playing with dolls, watching her mother make *piki*, grinding at her child's stone, they were of themselves and they were of her future. And the corn, all the work with the corn, from the first planting to screaming at ravens to grinding her first handful of kernels; that work was nothing if she would not be mother, if no child would be nourished by her work.

She tucked the stone in her pouch and took out her twig doll. Her mother had given her a scrap of worn cloth for its dress. Talasi held the doll close. Sometimes she felt sorry for it, poor nameless thing. The other girls carried their dolls with them everywhere. They made pretty dresses. Rupi had strung a set of tiny necklaces for her favorite one. Talasi's doll was more often neglected, most often left behind.

"I will not bear babies," Talasi whispered to the doll. "I do not know what that means, to not have babies." She tried to think of women who were not mothers or grandmothers and she could not think of anyone. Even those whose babies had died, and there were many, had carried the babies in their bellies, had given birth, had fed the little ones. Even Tsohtsona, who played dice with the men and was so bold that some said she was a man, was the mother of that boy, the juniper-shadow boy. Pamosi's children were gone, one from summer sickness, one disappeared, two sons gone to live with wives. But Pamosi cared for her husband, and her children came to visit and brought their children.

She thumped her heels against the crumbling wall. Who would she be if she were not mother? Would she be wife? She remembered that Pamosi helped care for her and that some of the other women in the village helped raise their sisters' children. But she had no sister. Her brother would live with his wife. That could be in a village far away. She wished for the cool light of the path stone and it did not come.

A lizard, yellow-green with a pulsing blue throat, darted along the wall and faced her, its tiny head bobbing fiercely. It was male. She could tell by the way his color was as bright in shadow as sun. It was always so, even with the Kachinas. Scales, feathers, robes and paint, always the male was brighter than the female. That was wise. The female body was precious. It held the babies. Gray and brown and gentle blue, the female could hide. If the male died, the female would find another. Children could not be replaced, nor could mothers.

"*Manangya,*" Talasi said, "what is to become of me?"

The lizard yawned. Talasi looked into his mouth. His tongue was pale brown; there were no teeth. As Talasi leaned forward, the lizard bobbed more quickly. When she leaned back, he went still, save for his lightning-quick eyelids. Her doll fell to the sand. She watched the lizard's breath. So quick, almost a flutter in his throat; she tried to breathe with him and got dizzy. A shadow fell across the wall. With a flick of his delicate tail, the lizard vanished.

"It is you, stupid girl," someone mocked. "What are you doing here when you should be home with your mother grinding?" Talasi clenched her fists. Without turning, she made an ugly face. It was the juniper-shadow boy.

"And who are you, dirty boy?" she said, "to come and chase away my lizard?"

He stepped in front of her. His skin was smudged with soot. Sweat ran in trickles through the grime.

"I am Kihsi!" he announced. Talasi stared at him. She shaded her eyes with her hand, as though he stood against the sun.

"Kihsi," she said, "shadow boy. I can hardly see you." He sat on the wall.

"Kihsi," she said. "Is that the shadow that all run from and never lose? Or the shadow who hides the rock that trips the careless boy? Or the shadow that hides in alleys and looks like dirt?" She could hear her mother's voice in hers; and she knew how words could chill the air.

"I am Kihsi," he said quickly, "the shadow who works from sunrise to sunset. I am the shadow who moves the sun." Talasi nodded.

"Yes," she said, "and who might wish that Masau'u is not listening."

"I do not fear Masau'u," he said. "I work for him." He held out his thin hands.

"We have been moving very big boulders to help the women channel more water into the fields," he said. "The men. That is who have been doing this, the men and me. Without my help, the others would still be working. That is the kind of shadow I am."

"I see," Talasi said politely, "and did my father or Tsoki or the *kikmongwi* say this to you? Will the crier shout to all of us tonight about your wonderful strength?"

"I do not need their words," the boy said. "I need no crier, as though I were some braggart. I know this to be true."

Talasi became interested in a broken piece of jug near her feet. Kihsi talked on.

"There was one huge rock," he said, "one of the gray ones that are rough and cut the hands and I went right at it and rolled it all the way to the field . . . the far field. My hands were bleeding and my shoulders ached. That is the way of hard work for a man."

Talasi bent and picked up the piece of pottery. She nodded.

"I can teach you more of this," the boy said. "If you want."

She turned the pot piece in her hand. It was simple, one of the old kind, gray, with the marks of its coils.

"I think," she said, "that this is very old. A woman made this, or maybe a little girl, learning. She dug earth from a special place far away and carried the earth to her workplace. Then she dried the earth and put it through a screen and ground it; many, many baskets of earth to make so little clay. She mixed it with water, water she carried from the spring . . . on her back. She pounded and twisted that clay with all her strength to get out the bits of twig and stone. Then, she rolled it with her hands into coils and made a bowl or a jug. This was a jug, I think." She paused. Kihsi glared at her. She smiled and went on, speaking very slowly.

"It was not done. No, she dug a pit and made a fire and piled her bowls and jugs and cups in the pit. She covered it with deer dung, which she had carried on her back in a large basket—which another woman had taken many days to make—from the grasses that grow a day's walk to the west."

She waved her hand toward the setting sun.

"I know that direction," Kihsi said through his teeth.

"Good," Talasi said. "You have been so busy doing so much work . . . and then, this girl, this woman, set fire to the dung and tended it while it burned. Carefully, carefully, she scraped away the ashes. She was happy and she was sad, because some of the pots were perfect and many were broken. Shall I tell you how she carried her pots back to her house and cleaned them and cooked food in them and fed the food to her family and, after eating, ah . . . and cleaning the dishes, went to the grinding stone and ground, while the men worked so hard, as you say?"

She smiled sweetly at the boy. He turned away.

"No," he said. "You do not need to tell me this. I have a mother. She does these things." She saw the back of his neck go red. "You mock me," he said. 'Who are you to mock me?"

"I am Talasi."

He turned around. His face was red. His eyes were narrow and mean.

"Are you Talasi," he said, "who is blown this way and that on the wind? Are you Talasi, pollen who blows to the boys' side, who falls too soon to the ground, where she is useless? Are you Talasi, who, who . . ." He scowled. "Or, are you Talasi, who . . ." He stammered and stopped. She was quiet. "Bold girl," he said, "you are better with words than I am." He held out his hands. "These are my gift," he said. "Not my words. You win this game."

They fell silent. She wished he would go away. The lizard, the Bright One, returned. She remembered that some called it the messenger. Lulled by their stillness, it crept close to a sunpatch near Kihsi and settled down. Neither boy nor lizard seemed to breathe. Talasi studied its markings. There were red dots, dark as the stone of Pamosi's house, along its throat. Kihsi shifted. The lizard's black bead eyes flicked open. It braced itself squarely on its legs and began fiercely bobbing.

"See," Kihsi whispered, "he is bowing to me."

"Be still, braggart," Talasi snapped. The lizard stood still. Kihsi bowed his head and the lizard climbed up on his leg. Talasi looked up.

"And this game?" she said. She smiled. He smiled back. She looked into his eyes and saw fear there. He had the darkest eyes she had ever seen and his nose was thin and sharp, almost like Kiisa's beak.

"Your name is wrong," she said. "It should be Kiisa."

"Your name is good," he said. "I have seen you move."

They did not leave the wall till long shadows stretched across the sand. The lizard had darted off. They talked of its markings and its messages, of the scorpion and how Tsorosi had been bitten and nearly died, of the bobcat's track and the drawings on the great rock north of the village. They talked of the Old Ones and the Tall Ones and the Dark One and the White One in the East. They talked of the ball-court, of the sounds, of the silence. They did not talk of the bone dice.

From the houses, smoke rose thin and blue against the fading light. As they walked back, Kihsi told Talasi of a place where eagles flew above the basalt cliffs.

"It is near the mark of the great star," she said. "I have been there, long ago."

He stopped and studied her face.

"How do you know all these things?" he said. "You are a girl-who-is-a-boy. How is this?"

Talasi laughed. He ducked his head. "No," she said, "I am not mocking you. You are like me. You ask 'how?', not 'why?'" She would have touched his arm, but that was not done. She felt very old, old as Pamosi. He raised his head and looked at her.

"I have thought about these things," Talasi said. "I am away from my woman's path. I do not always stay with the others. When we play dolls, I think of other things. I go alone. That is qahopi. I watch how the hawk kills and how the sand is marked by waving grass, different every day. I am too curious. I am too bold. Once, my cousins and I went far out on this mesa and I fell. My dress caught on a big rock and they pulled me back. That is a secret." He nodded.

"They say I am qahopi," he said. "They say I will not walk the child path. That is so. In my mother's house, someone must be a man." He shrugged his thin shoulders. "Do not tell this," he said. "Sometimes, when she is away, I make my own food."

"You have my secret and I have yours," Talasi said. She wondered why men were so ashamed of women's work.

"If we are so wicked," Kihsi said, "you may as well come with me someday. I know hidden places, where the eagles are, where a mother bobcat keeps her babies, where there are seeing stones in the earth."

"I will go with you," Talasi said. "I can teach you some things, too. I know a place where the Old Ones left messages. I can tell you some other things. Stories. Puzzles."

"Soon," Kihsi said, "I will leave the field again." His cheeks went red. "If you can follow me," he said, "you may." He clenched his fists. "One thing, girl," he said harshly, "you are never to say anything about my mother. She is very beautiful and very good."

"I have seen this," Talasi said quietly . . .

. . . the children, the path, the violet shadows were gone and Liz stood in blackness. There was no sound. There was nothing but her breath, her heartbeat and the cold floor under her bare feet. She knew she was dreaming. She knew it would be easy to wake. Cold air, musky with the scent of damp earth and herbs, washed over her. She dropped to her knees and crawled forward.

She was on hard-packed dirt. She crawled slowly till she felt a change in the air, stopped and reached up. Under her hand, a rough slab projected out from a wall of the same stone. She reached further and slowly rose to her feet. There was nothing above her head. Knees bent, back to the wall, she slid to her left, inch by inch, and stopped. She pulled off her shirt, tied it in a knot and left it on the slab. The air felt cool on her naked breasts. She had an idea where she was and she wondered that she was allowed there.

The bench ended and she was able to press flat against the wall. She kept moving. With that uncanny sense-sight, she knew there was something only inches from her face. It was a thick wood column, surface still shaggy with bark. Now and again, there was space behind her neck, as though there were deep niches in the wall. She moved carefully. The wall was built from thick slabs, chinked with sandy mortar.

She struck another projection, slid along it and found her knotted shirt. The room was a great circle. She covered herself with the shirt and sat on the bench. Breath burned in her throat. She knew, again, that she could end the dream if she wanted. There seemed nothing to do but breathe and sit and wait.

The air wavered. She remembered that first trip West, the velvet desert sky and the light reflecting from some far-away town. She remembered the fading wail of the radio, the way the bushes had seemed to phosphoresce. The blackness began to crack; a light, like those glowing skeletal bushes, flickered before her eyes. She stared into it. Pink blossomed at its center, deepened to rose, then scarlet. Her eyes ached. The light began to gather in on itself. Her hands had gone numb. She unclenched them and felt her spine melting, supple as a column of mercury. She began to cry.

The light's core radiated, red melting into blue, blue to violet, violet, with a dazzle, into white, the white of the sun's heart. She could have been at the center of the earth, witness to fire and mystery. The light steadied and she saw that she was in a room. Every beam, every niche, every bone and pebble and scrap of pottery were fully revealed. A thin band of wonderfully matched gray-green stone ran the full circumference of the walls. The wooden bench on which she sat was carved with parrots and ears of corn and clouds. She ran her finger over the parrot's tail; the wood was smooth and smelled of cedar.

A whisper filled the room, not human; it could have been a small river speaking, a waterfall. She looked up and saw light streaming through a hole in the roof. It puddled on the floor near her feet, without warmth, without color, without smoke. She reached down and plunged her hand into the center of the stream. Her skin became translucent; the bones glowed orange. She turned her palm up and saw the light fracture and flow downward.

One side burned pure white, the other black, and between were all the colors and possibilities of color that could ever be. She thrust her arms into the light and watched it pour twin cascades of coral and violet and the iridescence of feathers and yellow of bruises and wet rose of desire. She heard a voice.

"This is how it is to see with the heart."

She looked away. She knew she had looked through an icy lens for a long time. She turned back and looked up into a face both hideous and beautiful.

"I will stay this time," she said.

"Not yet," the being said, and laughed softly. "You have always been in such a hurry."

"Don't make me go back," she said, and tears filled her eyes. She knew she could wake herself. The being moved closer. From the heart of the light came a breath of air, so cold that she thought she might die. She did not. She held to the light. As she watched through frozen tears, she saw the light vanish. A column of black and white vapor rose toward the roof, black into white, white into black, till only smoke drifted out of the roof hole . . .

. . . Liz choked and came awake. She padded across the icy tiles, threw open the door, stepped out and breathed in the dawn, clean and cold. Her dream was as lucid, as sharp and mysterious and yet ordinary as the scrawks of the ravens sitting on the bathhouse roof. She closed the door and poked the fire and watched the room fill with orange light. In its glow, she went back to bed, back to the territory of her dreams.

Eight

"I CAN'T REMEMBER THE OTHER DREAMS," Liz said, "just this one."

"Write it down," Deena said. "You're supposed to be the expert. Maybe it'll trigger something."

Liz cradled the phone on her shoulder. Deena's call-waiting shrilled.

"I hate that thing," Liz said. She heard Deena snort.

"Some of us have to work for a living," she said. "Be right back." Liz stirred her coffee. At the sound of spoon on dish, Bob lumbered across the floor. She rubbed the white M between his eyes. He looked disgusted.

"Hel-looo," Deena trilled.

"Your boss is there," Liz said..

"Sure enough," Deena said.

"Should I hang up?"

"Uh uh."

"So, I should write these dreams down," Liz said, "except the second I wake up they're gone. It pisses me off. I feel like I'm living two lives and can't remember one."

"Call me," Deena said. "The second you wake up. Tell me."

"Are you crazy?"

"Hey, nine nights out of ten I'm awake till two. It's no big deal."

"I can try," Liz said.

"Do it," Deena said. "You might be having the time of your life!" She laughed.

"Oops," she said, "gotta run. Call me later." She was gone. Liz hung up. Deena was right. She hadn't touched her journal in weeks. She'd found a book in the library and it had shamed her. It had been the diary of a pioneer woman. She was faithful, no dates blank; her words were sparse and cautiously hopeful, the record of plantings, births and deaths, moon phases, illnesses, recipes and medicines. Only rarely was there self-pity . . . or a wish or anger or dream.

Sugar jumped into her lap. Bob had gone grumbling into the closet. He had his place there, in a welter of old socks. Liz opened the desk drawer and took out the journal. She had no plantings, no births or deaths, no illnesses; forget recipes, and there was no medicine for what ailed her. Sugar stretched and jumped down. Her lap felt cold. She opened the book.

"How could you bring yourself to me and take yourself away?" the last entry read. Even there, even in *her* journal, were letters to Nick, unsent, pitiful, stubborn and sentimental. They made her sister to every woman, every girl who'd clung to something that didn't want her. She wrote down the date, January 15: "Moon: near-full. Sugar is pregnant. In three months, I'll buy peat pots and start peppers and tomatoes and rosemary. Eva will be doing the same thing two thousand miles away. I'll haul manure from the stable across the road and dig rocks out of the old garden at the back of the cabin. I had strong dreams last night. I don't remember them, only scraps of color and longing. They tug on me. I would sleep twelve hours a day if I could."

The day dragged on. She felt thick and jittery and ungrateful for the time that she knew was nothing but a gift. She cooked chili and put it aside, called Steve and got his answering machine. "Leave a message and send money," it said cheerfully.

Bundled against the damp cold, she plodded out for a walk, saw the horses shivering on their hillside and turned back. She tried Eva's trick, stayed put, and it didn't work. As gray afternoon drifted into gray evening, she thought of Hatt. She remembered nursing home nights, the thick silence, the awful, incomplete privacy.

The road was clear. Pewter clouds, dense with snow, lumbered in from the north, wreathing Mt. Agassiz, obliterating Mt. Elden. The farmers would be happy; snowmelt would swell the deep underground waters that were being steadily leached out by Phoenix and Tucson. Wells on the Navajo Reservation were going dry. Contaminants were seeping into the precious reserves and hanging there like deadly clouds, like Hatt's medicine, that poison fog in the clear fluids of her brain. There were deep currents there, old, irreplaceable. Lazar had given Rhesus monkeys the same drug they were giving Hatt. Liz had seen the animals trembling with fear, with the garbled messages from their dying brains; brain and aquifer—once wounded, neither could repair itself, once abused, gone beyond human control.

Hatt faced the pale curtains. She was motionless, except for the fine trembling of her hands and head. Her fingers fluttered on the rocker arm.

She wore a turquoise ring on her left hand, the veined green stone set between silver ears of corn. Liz touched it and let her hand rest on Hatt's.

"Your ring is wonderful," she said. "I'm jealous." There was a sound behind them. Near the door, half-shadowed, the dark nurse stood watching. She smiled.

"Good evening," she said. Her voice was soft, the words precise; there was a lisp and a singing in her speech.

"Hatt," she said. "I see you have company." She nodded to Liz. "I am Rose Willard. I'm Hatt's primary nurse."

"I'm Liz Morrigan. I remember you . . . from Christmas Day?"

Rose set her finger against her lips. Her dark eyes cautioned.

"Welcome," she said. "We always welcome friends."

"Thank you," Liz said. "I've just begun my visit."

"Shall I turn on the light?" Rose asked.

"No," Liz said, "there's enough through the curtains."

"I'll be back," Rose said. "I need to give Hatt her meds."

"Would you shut the door?" Liz said. "It's better that way."

"No problem," Rose said. She slipped out. The room's hush, its shadows and shapes, floated in the dim light.

Liz could see the glint of Hatt's eyes beneath her drooping lids. She half-closed her own, heard the supply cart down the hall, the muted drone of televisions. She thought of the cabin, of the silence there, and the ocean of wind roaring through the pines, the raven's cries. She pressed Hatt's fingers. The old woman's eyes flew open.

"I'm sorry," Liz said.

"I don't need sympathy," Hatt said, and closed her eyes. They sat together a long while.

The door opened. "You are still here," Rose said. She wheeled in the cart. Liz stood up. Hatt gave no notice.

"I'm on my way," Liz said. "What are your visiting hours?"

"Whenever you like," Rose said. "Do you have time to talk for a few minutes?"

"Sure."

"Good. Meet me in the solarium." Rose turned and bent over Hatt's arm. Liz wanted to step forward, to stop her. She watched. One could bear witness. People had once believed that there was power in that. The scent of alcohol drifted in the air. Hatt didn't move. Rose took her arm and led her to the bed, speaking to her as though she were alert, as though she were making choices.

Liz sat at one of the bridge tables. Its top was a little slippery. The rag and disinfectant had not quite done their job. It was supposed to feel like leather, as the coffee table was supposed to look like wood and the centerpiece like flowers. She hoped she'd hang onto just enough clarity and strength, before it came to this, to go out to the black sand, swallow what would do the job and give some coyote lunch. Rose sank into the chair next to her and wiggled her feet out of her spotless sneakers.

"It's so peaceful," she sighed.

"Yes," Liz said, "the sleep of the dead." Rose looked at her. "Ever tactful," Liz said. Rose rubbed her forehead.

"You're right," she said. "We give them medicine to wake them up, to make them eat, to make them cheerful, to calm them down, to help them sleep, to keep their tired old selves going."

"How'd you get into this business?" Liz asked.

"It *is* a business, isn't it?" Rose laughed. "I didn't choose this. I'm in school, master's degree in drug rehab. I've got two kids and no money. I got my LPN during my marriage, so this seemed like the best choice. I get mornings with the kids; the money's barely enough, but it's better than nothing." She smiled. "There's the old people. I was taught to respect them."

She shook her head. "What has happened? I'm Hopi. I grew up in town, but I used to visit my old grandma up on Second Mesa. The old people stayed with their families. If they got sick, they drank teas; if they got sicker, they either got well or died. Their family was with them and they died. People said good-bye, told them how they would be missed . . ." She paused and looked over her shoulder, down the dim hallway.

"I shouldn't be saying these things." She sighed. "We're taking this in-service in 'Dysfunctional Communication,' you know. Gossip, back-biting, competition, complaining, those sorts of things."

"Complaining," Liz said, "keeps you from killing each other . . . or the patients. It's the backbone of staff morale."

Rose laughed. "You *know* these places!"

"I worked in a few back East," Liz said. "Twenty years ago. Nothing changes. The smell. The noises. The dead air."

"I think," Rose said, "that the worst part would be being thrown into no privacy and constant isolation at the same time."

"And drugged," Liz said.

"Can you imagine?"

"I don't have to imagine," Liz said. "I came close."

"That's my husband," Rose said. "Drugs." She closed her eyes. "I am talking too much." She shoved her feet into her sneakers and bent to lace them.

"Wait," Liz said. "Can we talk about Hatt for a minute?"

"I can only say a little," Rose said. "We are not supposed to discuss patients with anybody other than family."

"She's so drugged," Liz said, "that there's no way to tell whether she's sick. There's a spirit in her. She snapped at me a little while ago. She told me not to pity her."

Rose smiled. "I'm glad to hear that," she said. "There's somebody in there. You saw it. She put that ping-pong table in the repair shop."

"I don't think there's anything wrong with her," Liz said.

"I keep thinking about my grandma," Rose said softly. "She'd come for supper and sit at the table like an old mummy. That's not very respectful, but that's what me and my cousins thought. She was quiet as a stone. Sometimes I'd peek to make sure she was still breathing. Then, all of a sudden, she'd open her toothless mouth and say something so sharp, so critical you'd know she'd been listening all the time. We used to call her So'at angwusi, Grandmother Crow. She looked just like one. She had that sharp tongue and those bright black eyes." She laughed. "Sometimes, I get the feeling that she's listening now."

"Pretend I'm Hatt's daughter," Liz said.

"Okay."

"Tell me what meds she's on, please," Liz said.

"Easol. Lots." Rose stopped. "Listen, Hatt's daughter," she said fiercely, "don't mess me up. I've got two kids. I've got a husband who's a junkie. I'm *it* for this family. I need this job."

"I used to be a shrink," Liz said. "I've got a hundred lifetimes of secrets in my head and my heart that will never be told. I promise you, we'll do this clean."

"Okay," Rose said. She dropped her voice to a whisper. "Here's the story. She's the widow of a trader. They had a post out on the res, near Shonto. Her husband, John, made a lot of money. When things started to change out here, about thirty years ago, they closed the post. John died. Heartbreak, some say. Hatt lived there alone for a while, then moved down near Kayenta. Something happened right before Christmas. I couldn't get a clear story from the son, something about being scared she'd start a fire or fall down or get sick. She's eighty-three. He brought her here and hasn't shown his face since. You saw the rest of it. She was shocked when she realized where she was. The family doc had given her enough tranqs to kill a horse. She lost it, Rich gave her one of the 'zines' and she really let loose." She shook her head. "They had told her she was going to a nice hotel down here for the Christmas holidays." She stood up. "I've got to get back to work. I'm on Monday through Friday, three to eleven. Call. We'll talk some more."

"Wait," Liz said. "Her medication. I wonder what she'd be like on less."

Rose held up her hand. Rich pushed through the french doors and dropped onto the couch near the television. He glanced at Rose and Liz.

"Do you girls mind if I turn up the sound?" he asked.

"No problem," Rose said. She shook Liz's hand. "Your mother's prescription is p.r.n., as needed. I'll tell the doctor we'd like to start adjusting the dosage."

"Thank you," Liz said. "I *am* concerned. And do let me know about that ping-pong table." She heard Rich snort.

Liz scattered dry sage on the woodstove top and breathed deep. It smelled like summer on the South Rim of the Canyon. She thought of that great stony light and of the people, how they were struck silent as they came upon it. She thought of the surrounding forests, of Red Butte and the giant ponderosa that grew there, around meadows of lupine and sweet clover and sage. "Thank you," she whispered and stretched her body under the warm quilts for sleep . . .

. . . Talasi trembled under her robes, shuddering into dreams, waking again and again, her heart cold as stone in her breast . . .

. . . *Kihsi pulled her over the* tuukwi *edge. The air was thick with eagles, sunlight pouring through their copper feathers. Lizards filled the* tuukwi, *brilliant green, dull brown, collared with blue, spotted with stone red, shining. Eagle shadows drifted and circled. Kihsi stood an arm's length away. She turned to him. He held his finger to his lips and gestured to the sky. One after another, swift as falling stars, the eagles dropped toward them. Around her, above, eagles swooped and pounced, took the lizards in their talons and carried them off, every one. The birds circled higher and higher, till they were no bigger than black cinders, then sand, then vanished. The sky was clear, the* tuukwi *barren, Kihsi gone and she was tiny as a baby* . . .

. . . She woke. The room was black. She heard her mother turn in her sleep, her father cough. She wanted to wake them, to tell them the dream, but sleep silenced her . . .

. . . *She was alone. It was night and bitter cold, the* tuukwi *powdered with snow. She was a grown woman, her breasts full under a winter* manta, *a strange* manta, *not black, not white, but woven from both colors. Around her neck hung a string of antelope backbones and from each bone hung a hawk feather, pale gray, striped and tipped with brown. She felt very light, as though her flesh was woven on twisted fiber, as though she were no more than a robe.*
She walked to the end of the tuukwi. *There was a tumbled circle of rough black stones, its center a shaft, straighter than the finest throwing stick. She touched it. It burned with a terrible cold; it was* lay'ta, *dangerous. She began to back away, caught her sandal in her skirt and fell to the cold ground so hard that the breath left her body. The stars blurred. She fought to breathe, to see clearly and saw walking to her something not of her world. It was not Kachina. It was not human. It might have*

been a woman, but its hair was as pale as hawk's down, its skin the color of one who is in pain. When it looked down at her, the eyes were terrible. They were gray-green, the eyes of a ghost. It sank to a boulder and seemed to be watching for something at the tuukwi edge.

Talasi lay motionless. From far below, up through the earth, from some ancient sounding cavern, a voice roared in her bones.

"There may be no women here. Be gone." She rose to her feet, not knowing how she moved, will-less as the dolls traders brought from the north. She tried to breathe and choked on the stench of the voice, as though its words were things dead, things rotting.

"Be gone," it howled. Talasi ran. She did not look back. At the tuukwi edge, without fear, without hesitation, she ran out onto the air and kept running, through the night, through the cold, through the stars, away from the voice, from icy rock and the pahaana crouching there . . .

. . . Choovio turned to Nuuva. He moved away, as though in sleep.

"There is something wrong," she said. "Talasi is breathing so fast. She cried out."

"She is dreaming," he said. "You fear for her too much. Sleep." She closed her eyes. She wanted him to turn to her, to wrap her in his arms, but he snored. She folded her arms across her breasts and lay very still.

Talasi woke from dream into dream into vision. It was dawn and the sun burned blue-white. She took Kihsi's hand and led him to the tuukwi above the village edge. He turned his face away from what he saw. She stepped behind him and held his head in her hands so that he must look at their home.

The paths were untended, the Spirit's breath-hole clogged with broken wood and bones. No smoke rose from the houses. There were no people. The bones of the sacred eagles lay tethered on the rooftops, the village and black hills seemed no more than breath. They could see through them to the fields beyond, where the corn lay dead. Badger Spring was dry, piles of cinders blocking its flow.

Masau'u rose before them, his face charred, his eyes red with sorrow. Tears streamed down his smoking skin. Kihsi trembled under her hands.

"I am sorry," he said. Masau'u faded.

"Do you see?" Talasi whispered. "Do you see how it might be?" Kihsi bowed his head. She felt his tears running through her fingers. The village began to crumble. They saw before them the ghosts of the gamblers. Then, four shrunken corn kernels, blue, white, yellow and red; then, bright as blood, the scarlet feathers of the bird from the south; and, then, the People, running, walking, falling . . .

. . . Liz cried out in her sleep and woke to the sound, her breath dry in her throat. She burrowed into the pillows and touched Nick's bracelet. If he were there, she would ask him to hold her; she would ask him to stroke her hair, to soothe her back into the dream, to help her dream the girl out of that ruined place. He had understood that sort of work.

Drifting, she saw the word "girl" as though it had been written in old-fashioned script. She moved the bracelet from her left wrist to her right. It would remind her. She smiled. Nick would have liked that, for his gift to be useful, not sentimental, not magical; nothing more than what it was, a plain circle of silver, a sign for craft.

She remembered a blackboard, a teacher, shy and careful, pointing to a diagram of the dreaming brain. She said the words in her soft way, as though they were a spell for sleep: locus coeruleus, Raphé, serotonin, waves rising, falling. It was so simple, so delicate, the tides, the fluids achemized into music and nightmare and bliss. Take away dream time and the brain was in agony. Hallucinations shimmered in full daylight. Voices carried messages from nowhere. And in the outback, in the Dream Time, the messages shimmered and echoed, the dreams dying, the brain a howl . . .

. . . Talasi woke. She started to cry out and set her hand over her mouth. The pathstone was there. She felt it cool against her lips. When she uncurled her fingers, it glowed bluegreen. She pressed it to her heart, to her eyes, the light as soothing as water.

"Help me see," she whispered. "Help me see what is to happen to us. Help me see my path. Help me be happy and patient. I am so afraid."

She waited. There was no voice, no comfort. The stone was gone. She crept out of the robes and brought her doll back to bed. It was so little, so thin, so still.

"What am I to do?" she whispered. "I am only a child. I am the only one to see these things. My mothers says nothing. Aunt Pamosi says nothing. The people go on as though nothing were wrong. What am I to do with all of this?"

She watched the starlight through the roof-hole. It was too early to step out for prayer. Girls did not go out before light. There were dangers from many places, raiders from the roaming tribes, witches wandering in search of greedy souls; even a twisted ankle from an unseen pebble was serious. If one could not walk, one could not work and without work, there was no joy. Talasi turned on her back, then left, then right, then on her belly. No way was right.

The sky began to pale, the stars fade. She crept up the ladder, sat on the roof-edge and looked out over the village. The ball-court was a clot of shadows, the plaza still and gray. She lay back and gazed up at the last stars. The Kachinas were dancing there. They sang and watched and listened.

"I am so little," she whispered to them. "In two sunrises, you go home to your kiva on Neuvatukaovi. You have much to do to bring us rain. I am afraid we are giving you too much to do. Some of the men, some of the women, they are spending all their time with the bone dice. They have more food than they can use, more salt, more *tsorposi* than they can wear. They trade these things, even the salt that the men bring from Suukotupqa." She shivered. That place, Suukotupqa, that great, deep place in the earth, was so powerful that even to think of it was fearful.

"I am impatient. I do not stay at the fields. I do not pay attention when my mother teaches me things. I go with Kihsi. I wish you had made me a boy. I ask your forgiveness, but I cannot stop thinking these things, I cannot stop watching. I will not."

Through her tears she saw a star leap and fall to earth. She let her tears go with it, back to earth, back to Mother, and peace moved into her. She sat up and looked out over the desert. It seemed to her that she could see a long way. Each bush and grass blade and lizard's eye stood out against the silver sand. She could feel First Dawn melting in behind her.

Far below the rooftop, unseen, a gray figure drifted in and out of the alleys. Kihsi, the shadow that moves as light, in silence, slipped through the village, never taking his eyes from the girl perched above him. He settled into a narrow alley and watched Second Dawn shine off her hair. He wondered why she sat there, what she saw, how it was she seemed, even at that distance, so fierce and proud. He hugged his knees and watched till she climbed down from the rooftop.

Talasi walked down the path, skirted the ball-court and stopped where the trail curved into a broad wash. Third Dawn burned in. She shaded her eyes and watched the sun move up into the East. All to the East, the sun, the bone dice, the ravens, the stories of great cities, of the *pahaana*. How could such beauty and such evil come from the same direction? She thought of Pamosi's husband. He was from an Eastern clan. He had taught her how to chip atlatl points. She had been very clumsy and his voice had stayed soft, his hands patient. She thought of the misty woman in her dream. She had been ugly, but she had brought no harm. She had been near-white, the white of the East.

Once a trader from that direction had brought a wonderful painted bird to the village. It had been small, a parrot, the feathers painted blue and yellow, each plume so perfect one thought it would flutter in the wind. There were those painters, and elders who could use the sun and moon for planting, and women who made bowls and pots; perhaps there was even a girl, qahopi, too much like a boy, who stood in a broad wash, gazing westward, and wondering.

She turned and set out for the far cinder cones. Rabbits leaped away from her step. A lizard scuttled into the sun. She thought she heard the rush of wings and knew it was only juniper whispering in the dawn breeze. Behind her, smoke began to rise from the housetops. Kihsi stood boldly on the ball-court wall, watching her melt into the morning shadows.

Nine

"GREATER LOVE HATH NO FRIEND . . ." Deena said, and opened her door wide.

"You told me 'anytime'," Liz said. "Besides, you need somebody to admire that nightgown." Deena dumped coffee in the pot and turned around. Her skin was pure cream against the maroon satin, the ivory lace. She looked down at her bare feet.

"All I need is a pair of those pom-pom slippers," she said. "You know, with no backs and five-inch heels."

Liz grinned. "Lynette used to call 'em 'Take-me' shoes. Our daughters trotted out in them and short-shorts and tube tops. I wanted to kill the little tarts!"

"It's too early," Deena said. "I need coffee. I can't think about young bodies or sex or kids or Deej as a teen queen."

"I'll tell you the dream," Liz said. "All you have to do is listen."

Deena sat up on the countertop. "I'm ready," she said.

"There was desert," Liz said, "and adobe houses. I was watching it all and, sometimes, I was this little girl. There was a grubby kid, a boy. He came and went. At one point, the girl was a woman. She was on a mesa. I think I know that mesa. I think she saw me, but that part gets fuzzy. I always remember the trivial stuff."

"Like what?" Deena asked. She lit a cigarette and narrowed her eyes against the smoke.

"Like colors, or a necklace. I'd sell my Camaro for that necklace. It was made out of bones and feathers and it was more than beautiful. It felt just right around my neck. I hate having things around my throat, but this felt perfect."

"What else?"

"I saw the boy crouched between two stone houses. He was grubby. His hair was a mess and his knees were all banged up and scarred. He was watching me . . . the girl."

"What was she doing?"

"Just sitting," Liz said. "Then she walked past a plaza or something, you know, like a central square. Except it was a circle. There were circles everywhere, the plaza, a playing field, the way some boulders were set in the sand."

"Oh, wow," Deena said.

"I know," Liz laughed. "Sym-*bolic!*"

"Hey," Deena said. "What do we know?"

"I hate all this sloppy New Age semi-mysticism," Liz said.

"I don't know enough to hate it," Deena said. "But if it helps people get along, what's the harm?"

"It's careless," Liz said. She stopped. "You know?" she said, "Lazar said the same thing to me one time. We were at Stonehenge. I was considering Druids. He was sure of Science."

"Want to know why I bought myself this nightgown?" Deena asked. Liz nodded.

"I bought this nightgown," Deena said slowly, "because I was feeling so bad last week that I bought a book at the grocery store right from the self-help section. It had a little girl on the cover who reminded me of Deej. In that stupid book, it said that if you acted as if something were true, and you did it long enough, it would come true." She lit another cigarette.

"Well, I feel ugly," she said.

"Right," Liz said. "It's rough being a blue-eyed blonde."

"Hey," Deena said. "I said *I* feel ugly. That's how *I* feel."

"Go ahead," Liz said. "My Active Listening must have died."

"So I decided to buy something that nobody else would see. And I decided to wear it. And I decided to look at myself in the mirror *and* feel how I fit inside it *and* how it felt to me."

"And?"

"And I don't know yet, but I do know that this careless book got me off my self-pitying ass."

"You win," Liz said. "I wish I could do that. I truly do."

Deena stood up and left the room. When she came back, the night-gown was draped across her arm. She held it out.

"So, do it," she said. "Go in my room. Close the door. I'll make breakfast."

"Deena," Liz said, "right this second, there's some poor son-of-a-bitch waking up in a cardboard refrigerator carton behind the depot. Three people disappeared in El Salvador. A nine-year-old in the South Bronx just sold his first crack. You know?"

Deena nodded.

"So, does thinking you're ugly help those people?" she asked. "You're scared. I see that." She started breaking eggs into a bowl. "You're not fooling me."

Liz couldn't look till she had slipped the gown over her naked shoulders. She didn't want to see her body in the morning light. There are no shadows that way, no softening of the lines, no hiding the thickness. The mirror seemed huge. She turned and looked. The satin flowed over her body. Its touch was cool and fluid. "How it felt to her," Deena had said. The last time she had worn a gown like this, that hadn't mattered. What *had* were Nick's eyes on her, his sure response, his touch, neither cool nor fluid.

She made herself see the body in the mirror. There was a smooth curve of belly, the jut of her breasts against the lace, the good line of her legs. Her arms were heavy, her wrists delicate, her ankles terrific. The face was no big deal. Her jaw was heavy, her nose broad. She had a thin upper lip that could go mean and tight. And the eyes, her eyes, were sage green. "It's your eyes," Nick had said. "It's those damn eyes." He had held her face in his hands and looked at her. She had hated it, and loved him for doing it. She looked straight into those eyes. They were nothing but haunted, nothing but shamed. She closed them, and felt the slip of the satin along her flesh. Under its touch, she was smooth and supple and ageless. And in that, she was alone.

"Well?" Deena said. She was buttering toast.
"Bearable," Liz said. "I can live with it."
"Why didn't you leave it on?" Deena asked.
"I liked it too much."
"Can't have that," Deena said.
"No," Liz said. "Makes you want more."
"Right."
Liz grinned. "Thank you, my friend," she said.
"No problem," Deena said. "Next week, dancing. In public."
"Wrong," Liz said.
"We'll see."
That night, she went to sleep as to a lover. The dream came quickly . . .

. . . Talasi choked. There was a flood of water in her mouth, something cool on her skin. Through her eyelids, she saw a red light, shadows moving in it. A voice tugged at her.

"Do not speak," the voice said. She felt her heart leap against the cage of her breast bones. Her lips hurt. When she opened her mouth to spit out water, she felt them crack.

"I am sorry," the voice said. Talasi turned her head and let the water run out. She felt wet cloth on her lips, sucked at the cloth and felt her throat tighten.

"Be slow." There were cool hands on her arms, her legs, her brow. She opened her eyes. The shadow bent closer and became her aunt.

"Don't move," Pamosi said. "Rest. There is no hurry."

"Aunt," Talasi whispered. "I dreamed you saw me. You were looking through the stone. I was lost. How did you find me?"

"I see now," Pamosi said, "that you need a new name." She laughed. "We might better have named you Iisaw. You are just like that foolish one, wandering off, sticking your coyote nose into things that bite back, causing mischief." She tapped Talasi's cheek.

"You be still. The others are coming. We will carry you to my home." Talasi swallowed the questions that were in her throat. She felt them settle in her heart. They rested there, as her breath slowed under Pamosi's touch and she moved into sleep.

Within a sunrise, she sat at her aunt's side, quietly watching her work. Her skin was sore, her lips slowly healing. Pamosi bent over a long strip of clay. Quickly, surely, she shaped it up and around, into a shallow bowl and set it aside. Her tools were at her feet: little pots of colored powder, made from ground beeweed cake, from powdered earth, from ground aasa stems mixed with minerals; yucca leaves, their ends chewed to brush points; mortar stones, stained with red or black or yellow. Talasi watched her aunt work the clay until that magic instant when she held in her hands, not a pinched coil but a bowl. It was as though Spirit moved through her arms and hands into the bowl's shape, and through her dreams into the clouds and feathers and stars she painted on the smooth surface. Spirit did not always enter, and those pots were broken, their jagged pieces ground back to clay.

"So Iisaw-girl," Pamosi smiled, "tell me how you came to that cave."

Talasi took a mortar in her hand and began to grind aasa. Pamosi did not look up from the line she had begun to trace on a finished jug.

"Why do you ask me?" Talasi said. "You saw me. I saw you watch me through the seeing-stone. That is why I was not afraid. That is how I walked so far."

Pamosi laughed. "Mongwi-Iisaw," she said. "I cannot hide from those great eyes. I only saw you as you walked away from the south trail, and then not till you stumbled into the cave and fell. I can only see what I am given."

Talasi set the powder near her aunt's hand. She had once tried to make a pot. Spirit had laughed. She rolled a scrap of clay between her hands.

"Will you make another snake?" Pamosi said. "I have a hundred of them now."

"I could put legs on it," Talasi said. "It would be a lizard."

"And a hundred lizards," Pamosi laughed. "Tell your story. Your gift is with words, not clay."

"Nor soup," Talasi said, remembering their burnt supper the night before. She folded her hands in her lap and smiled.

"*Aliksa'i,*" she said. It was how a story always began. "There was a girl," she said, "who was afraid. She had terrible dreams about her village. And there were terrible wakings, *qahopi* words and silences between her mother and father. This girl went out walking to find an answer to her fears, a path for her feet and heart."

"I know that walking," Pamosi said. She turned the jug in her hands, her brush spinning a perfect web across its curve. "Go on."

"This girl was walking along the mesa edge, trying to think what to do. All the trouble was not just from the outside. This girl was impatient. She wished, always, to be away from the fire, away from the grinding stone, away from the boring games with dolls." Talasi glanced sideways at her aunt. Pamosi did not look up. There was something missing from the jug. The dream had told her more. She picked up her brush.

"And?" she said calmly.

"This impatient girl started down the trail from the mesa. She did not know where she would go. A shadow flew across her path and hovered there. It was the shadow of a *palakwayo,* one of the big hawks, and then it was Palakwayo herself, ahead of the girl, flying low above the trail. Under a ledge was half a rabbit she had been eating. That girl hurried past. She did not want the hawk to be angry with her. The hawk turned in a great circle, in no time at all, in the time it took the girl to take four steps, and flew toward the girl's face. She looked into the girl's eyes and she said, 'Follow me.'"

"And did that girl follow the hawk?" Pamosi said.

"She did. That hawk played with that girl. She would circle too high to be seen and the girl would stumble from watching her. Then, when that girl was angry, the hawk would glide down and hover over her head.

"That must have been a *mongwi*-girl," Pamosi said. "All ruffled feathers and grouchy face."

"Like this," Talasi said. She made her eyes very wide. "That girl looked just like that. The hawk led her to a canyon she had never seen. Someday, we shall go there, Aunt."

"That would be good," Pamosi said, "if that girl would take us there."

"She saw many flowers," Talasi said, "not like our flowers, but ones that hung from tall trees and were colors we do not know, purple-green and yellow-blue and red shining as though the sun were in the heart of the blossom. There were flowers bigger than the girl and leaves smaller than her baby fingernail. There were rainbow birds and little furry people that swung from the trees and threw fruit at each other.

"Everything was green, more green than that girl had ever known. Rising from the trees and bushes and flowers was a tall, tall village, taller than your house *and* its rock. The village was made of steps as high as me. As the girl. She was the same height as I am."

"I think I understand that," Pamosi said. "About that girl."

"Good. Those steps were carved on every surface, with funny square people and coiled snakes and sun-spirals like our own. The hawk circled the village four times and flew off to the north. The girl stood at the bottom of the steps and waited. She was afraid and she was too curious to leave."

"This girl would be a good friend for you," Pamosi said. "You could walk with her and the gossips would not talk about the *qahopi* girl who goes off with the witch-woman's son." She watched Talasi carefully.

"If the gossips were quiet," Talasi said, "they might have the silence to hear the troubles murmuring."

"This girl," Pamosi said, "what did this wise girl see?"

"A stairway had been cut through the middle of the village. A woman and man walked down the steps. The man was much like our men, though his nose was curved like a beak, like the nose of that *qahopi* boy that takes bad girls out to see eagles and baby bobcats and the messages the Old Ones left." Pamosi laughed.

"He wore a big ear plug that was carved with leaves and there were white feathers in his hair. The woman wore a *pitkuna,* as our men do. Her breasts were bare, but she was not bold with that. She, too, had a hawk nose. Around her neck was a string of pale green shells. You could see the light through them and they made a sound like bells when she moved." Talasi stopped. "Guess what the best was?" she said.

"You were the girl?" Pamosi said.

"The next best," Talasi said, "was that there was a thick pad on the woman's shoulder and riding on the pad was a bird. It was more beautiful than the bird from the South. It had a fuzzy head and big black eyes and its tail feathers were like black water reflecting rainbows. They hung to the ground. The woman had fruit in a pouch at her waist and she fed the bird. It was very gentle. It blinked its great eyes." She paused. "It said that girl's name."

Pamosi set the jug on the rooftop. Black dots, to be seen as baby spiders, lived on the web. She took more clay in her hands and began to roll it.

"What color were these people?" she asked.

"They were people color," Talasi asked. "What other color could they be?" She paused and gazed away from her aunt.

"Yes?" Pamosi said quietly.

"There *is* another color," Talasi said. "In a dream, I saw a woman, very ugly, tall, *qahopi* hair and her skin was the color of mushrooms. She did not seem evil, but I felt sorry for her to be so ugly."

"I have heard of that one," Pamosi said. "There are old stories of a *pahaana,* a white brother, but she is not that one."

"Who is she?" Talasi asked.

"There are more than one," Pamosi said. "Some have hair the color of sunset, some pale as clouds. Others have seen them in dreams. They can be cruel."

"This one was afraid as I," Talasi said.

"Was she as curious?" Pamosi smiled. "Tell me more."

"I *was* the girl," Talasi said.

"Good," Pamosi said. "It would be a shame to waste such a story on some other girl, some girl who would have run away."

"The man greeted me by my name and the woman said, 'You are also called Mongwi and you are the daughter of Choovio and Nuuva. Greet us as Aunt and Uncle.' They sat on either side of me. The aunt let me feed the parrot. Oh, and she let me taste the fruit . . . some was bright pink . . . some was light green and if I held it up to the sun, I could see through it.

"Then, the uncle said I was to pay close attention and that they would help me see things about my path. I was so happy, Aunt, because I have seen so many things I did not understand.

"The aunt said that I would always try to look too far and what I was seeking was close to home. When I tried to tell her that I have big owl eyes and cannot help looking, she said that was good and a gift and that I must learn to use it. The uncle took my left hand and he told me to look in my palm. The pathstone was there. He said I was to tell the fire-snakes dream to myself every day. The woman took my right hand and said it was time for me to know my teachers and that they were both inside and outside my woman's work. Then, heat passed from the uncle's touch through my body to the aunt's touch, and I saw the canyon melt away. They were gone. I heard their voices, as one voice, say, 'Remember your Mother.'

"I felt very sleepy, but before I slept . . . I do not want to say this part . . . I saw a very big pine tree, like the trees the men cut for roof-beams. A terrible wind began to blow; it tore the tree up by the roots and carried it and the cinders and the fields and our village away, everything away."

Pamosi said nothing. She had begun painting a dream-bird on a bowl. She had finished with the black paint made from ground *tumi*. Carefully, she touched the fine point of a yucca twig to the corners of each feather, leaving a dot of bright red. Talasi waited while she ground more of the red pigment in the stone mortar.

"*Aliksa'i*," Pamosi said. "You have heard many times our People's story of Parrot Clan, of First World, of Taawa, the Creator, of the two Hurung Wuhti, she of the East and her sister of the West, those keepers of precious things, of *tsorposi* and *tsihpu*, the shells from the biggest waters; and how these Ones and Spider Woman created all living beings, men and women and animals alike. You know how our People forgot to keep the Creator's word and had to leave."

"You know of the People's emergence into the Second World. As we have, they began to have more than they needed and to trade with each other. Moment by moment, trade by trade, they drew further away from praise for the Creator and closer to worship of things. It makes me sad to tell of this, for they began to cheat each other, to lie and fight.

"A few good People, women and men and children, kept singing their songs, but the laughter of the wicked ones drowned them out. Again, the world was destroyed and the People moved on." Pamosi set the finished jug next to the bowl.

"What could happen next?" she asked.

"I know," Talasi said. "I can tell it."

Pamosi nodded. It was good for storytellers to begin as children, as it had been good for her to hold in her small hands the coils of her first pot. The telling, the shaping . . . they fixed the story and the bowl in the heart. Once the joy of the work was learned, the teller, the potter, could come back to it again and again. It would not fail the heart or hands.

Talasi sat as straight as she could. She half-closed her eyes, and the old story rose up in her.

"Our People gave thanks. 'You may enter this Third World,' they were told, 'but not before your hearts know these lessons: first, respect the Creators and respect one another; second, sing in harmony from your villages and hilltops and *tuukwi*. When we no longer hear your song, we will know that you have gone again to evil ways.'

"The People climbed out into the Third World, where the way became even harder. *Again!* they had to move on, only the good People, only those who remembered Spider Woman and were thankful to her. She gave them a good-bye gift, a secret: to keep their heads and hearts open and they would find their way.

"I like this part, Aunt—they came to the Sipapu, and they climbed up, just like that. Well, some birds helped them, and a reed carried them, but *they* did it! When they looked around, they saw rock walls stretching high as the sky. There was a big, deep river and the sun was burning hot. Sotuknang spoke to them and told them their Way would be very hard from then on . . ." Talasi stopped and looked at Pamosi. "I think it was hard already, don't you?" she asked.

"I think all true Ways are hard," Pamosi said.

"Shall I go on?" Talasi asked. "I *can* do it." Pamosi nodded.

"So here they were in the Fourth World, where there are places so high you feel dizzy, and dark places so deep you think you will never come out. There was burning heat and freezing cold, beauty and emptiness. I would have been scared, but those People were good-hearted and strong. Sotuknang told them that they would have a helper who was both hard and soft, who would give and take. His name was Masau'u.

"The People looked around the hot, beautiful, empty place and they saw a man, a man whose face was scarred and burned. He told them he was Masau'u and that they still weren't home! They listened hard. He told them they would find their true home. He said 'If you are bad again . . . if you forget to sing your prayers and praise, I WILL TAKE OVER THIS EARTH FROM YOU!' And, hard as it was, they soon learned that something bad had followed them from the Third World." She paused. "Powaqa," she whispered. "They are still with us."

"Go on," Pamosi said quietly.

"'North, *kwiningya* . . . that is the Back Door to this land. If you come through that door, you come without my permission. Go now and find your land, this land of the Fourth World,' Masau'u said.

"So Masau'u told our People that they must travel to the ends of the land, the places where the land meets great water in each of the four directions. Only when they did that could they come back together. They were given four sacred stones and water jugs that filled up all by themselves. There was a clan, Fire Clan, and Masau'u gave to them a special stone. He said that after they reached their final home, there would be some terrible times and, then, they would be overcome by a strange people. They, I mean we, were not to fight back, but we were to wait for our lost white brother and his companions, a man and a woman, who would bring back a broken corner of the special stone. The good-hearted People . . . us . . . we would work with those pahaanas to heal our world.

"So, we People of this Fourth World have been on our migrations, some stopping too soon, some moving on, some of us are here, at Place of Water and East-Rising House and Place of Beauty and Nest House. Along the way, groups of People saw different things and were given names for them. Our clan, Parrot, came from the South. Our first Grandmother and Grandfather met a beautiful lady who told them to lay their right hands on a nest of colored eggs. Those old ones prayed for the blessing of many babies and felt something move inside the eggs. The Goddess, that's who the Lady was, told them the eggs were parrot eggs. She told the old ones that they were Parrot Clan, Kyarmungwa, and they were Yumuteatoa, Mother People. Other clans would ask them for help, so that many babies could be born. They were never to refuse that help.

"The old ones went back to their clan with this blessing and they travelled on, multiplying as they went. They went north through Pusivi, turned west and came to a great, great water. Then, they went east, stopping at Parrot Spring in the wide *tupqa* to the north. They stopped at Sawyava, the Bat Cave in Double Tupqa to the south and turned northwest, passing homes of earlier clans and travelling over wide, flat places with waving grasses. They went up the east side of great mountains, towards the Back Door, then stopped and came down the west side of those mountains. They stopped at Tuwi'i, Wenima, Pavi'ovi and Chosovi.

"We, for Parrot Clan is our clan, stopped again at Double Tupqa, and then came here. We were here when the mountain exploded. Some died and others ran, only to come back. As I have been told our story, I tell you. This is not hearsay. This is our truth."

"You will be a *tuwutsmoki*," Pamosi said. "Do you know this word?"

"A bag of stories," Talasi said. She took a brush and trailed a line of black paint along her wrist.

"There is more," she said.

Pamosi paused in her cleaning. "Tell me."

"I do not know if this is our true home," Talasi said. "In a dream, I saw the village empty, the walls crumbling, the Spirit's breath-hole clogged with weeds and broken things. As hard as I looked—and I could look through hills and *tuukwi*—I saw no people. I saw only broken things. We were gone."

Pamosi set the paint pots one within each other and wrapped them in a piece of deerskin. She handed Talasi a small bowl of water and a rag.

"Drink," she said, "then wash the paint from your arm. They will be gossiping that I teach you to paint yourself, to wear the signs that are only meant for ceremonies." She patted the mat next to her.

"When you are clean, come sit by me. You have told our story well. That last I have only half-known. I fear it. I think it is time for you to know who I am and what I might be to you."

WEST

For the Dakīnī: Sky Dancer and lover without motive.

Ten

HATT SLEPT. ROSE LEANED AGAINST THE DOOR-jamb and studied the shadowed face. It was two hours into her shift and she felt she could stand there forever, just she and the old woman, resting in perfect silence. Peach light glowed through the curtains. Hatt's hair was bronze in that light, her skin rosy. Rose saw how beautiful she had been, how beautiful she was. The dinner-cart clattered to the room next door and stopped. Rose stepped into the room and put on the bedside light.

"Hatt," she said, "it is supper time. It is time to wake up." She watched Hatt turn in her sleep. It seemed to Rose a kind of swimming, as though the room were filled with air so heavy it was fluid. She touched Hatt's wrist.

"Your supper is here," Rose said. Hatt came awake. She stared up at Rose, her eyes clear, the tranquilizer fog drifted away.

"Well," she said, "who are *you*? And how do you know my name?"

Rose bowed her head. She moved to the chair at the side of the bed. She dreaded this task. It fell to her too often, the truth-telling, the graceless revelation.

"You are just super at 'orienting,' the social worker had said. "I want to thank you on behalf of the families." Throw money, Rose had thought, and felt ashamed.

"Where am I?" Hatt said. "Have I been injured, was there an accident?" Her hands and face went bone-white. She closed her eyes.

Rose remembered standing at the mesa edge at dawn with her cousins. *They* had prayed, their words, their gestures as natural as breath. She had pretended, her heart a knot, her prayers gone from her. This was the same. Always, she was unprepared. She folded her hands in her lap.

116

"I am Rose Willard," she said. "You are in a nursing home. I am your evening nurse and it is a little before five o'clock."

Hatt looked up, then away. She straightened the sheet over her breast. Rose waited. Hatt pulled herself up against the pillows and looked into Rose's eyes.

"Tell me the truth," she said. "Have I gone senile?"

"No," Rose said.

"Then why am I here? Nursing homes are for sick people, for senile people. I don't understand."

"Your children and your doctor felt it would be better for you to be here," Rose said. "They were worried about accidents, illness. You've been here about a month."

"That's nonsense," Hatt said. "I don't get sick. I haven't had an accident since before John died. I drive my own car. I have my work." Tears welled in her eyes. She snatched a tissue from the bed-stand, wiped the tears away and began to shred the tissue. "No one asked me," she said and turned away from Rose.

There was a thump at the door. "Come back later," Rose called out. The dinner-cart rattled down the hall.

"There has been a mistake," Hatt said firmly. Rose waited. She thought of her grandmother, wrapped in shawls against the cold, her face turned to the thin December sunlight, watching for the feeble Soyal Kachina to take its first halting steps into the plaza. She thought of her own children and her future, the borderland they occupied, the betrayals that waited there.

Hatt turned back. "There has been a terrible mistake," she said. "It must have been my daughter. She worries about me." She opened the bed-stand drawer and began to rummage through it. "My purse must be here," she said.

"It is locked in the safe," Rose said. "I will get it for you."

"No," Hatt said. "Thank you. I have what I need." She took the Care Kit pen and wrote a number. "Please, call this. It's my son's. He can straighten this out. He's calmer than Jeannie. He will tell you there has been a mistake."

Rose took the slip of paper. This was the worst part. She would call. She would let Hatt have a few hours of hope, perhaps a few days. She would take the lie into her own heart. She reached cautiously for Hatt's hand. The same touch that could comfort, could wound pride. Hatt clutched at her hand.

"You must do something," she said. Someone knocked. Rose patted Hatt's hand and stood up. "I will call," she said. "It is still early."

"Please see who that is," Hatt said. "Perhaps they've come for me." She paused. "How *long* have I been here?"

"A month," Rose said. Hatt's eyes on hers were focused and terrible.

"They often go on vacation over the holidays," Hatt said. "This is holiday-time, isn't it?" Rose nodded. "That could be," she said.

"Shall I bring your supper?" Rose asked.

"Thank you," Hatt said. "I expect I'll need to get my strength back." There was another knock and Liz leaned in.

"Oh," she said, "I'm sorry. Do you want me to wait?"

"I'll be out in a minute," Rose said.

"Who was that woman?" Hatt said.

"Her name is Liz Morrigan," Rose said. "She has been visiting you."

"Oh yes," Hatt said, "we used to visit my Aunt May in one of these places. I understand." She touched her hair. "I'm a mess. Would you please give me my hairbrush and my sweater?" She looked down at her hands. "My ring is here," she said. Her eyes widened. "But my bracelet, where is my bracelet?" She circled her left wrist with her fingers. "I always wear a silver bracelet. Where is it?"

"I don't know," Rose said. "That ring is the only jewelry you wore when they brought you in. I'll call right now. Perhaps your son will know." Hatt looked cautiously around the dim room.

"It's hard to see in here," she said. "Please turn up the light. And send that woman in. Just give me a minute to fix my hair."

Rose handed Hatt the Care Kit brush, An ally, she thought. She is going for an ally. Good.

"Where is *my* hairbrush?" Hatt asked. "It has a bone handle." She ran her hand over the nightstand top. Rose opened the dresser drawer. She knew what she would not find.

"That's all right," Hatt said. "They must have forgotten to pack it. Jeannie has a lot on her mind." She smiled and began to work on her tangled hair. "I shall do what I can to remove myself from her list of worries." She frowned. "This is a mess." She looked at the brush and shook her head. "Please, Miss Willard," she said, "call my son."

"Right now," Rose said.

"Thank you," Hatt said calmly. "He'll be here. As soon as he knows." She smiled again. "Heads will roll."

Rose walked slowly to the nursing station. She wanted to grab her coat and leave. Her hands were shaking with rage. Her heart slammed against her ribs. Her eyes burned. She was shocked by the force of her feelings. She had been warned about it, about the terrible power of anger. Again and again, her mother, her aunts had cautioned against it. Anger was out-of-balance and most ugly in a woman. She was to be cheerful, to smooth the way. When she had gone to her grandfather to learn what lay beneath the warnings, she had been turned away. All she had were the dead words, the sing-song sayings, the lessons without heart . . . and this anger rattling her bones.

She pushed open the door and leaned against the desk. The station was empty, but Rich's cigarette still smoldered in the ashtray. She looked up at her kids' picture tacked to the message board. Some days they were all she had, their small bodies, their curious eyes, their questions and hugs and demands. She was scared to death for them. Their lessons came from television and computer screens and their grandma's stale words. They'd both been sick that morning. It had taken all her stubborn will to walk away from their flushed and grouchy faces. Her mother had parked them in front of the television with bowls of cereal.

On the long drive to school, the fan-belt had begun to whine. The professor had popped a quiz on them. She'd torn her pantyhose on something, stopped to buy a fresh pair and been late for work. She pressed her hands to her swollen belly. Her period was due and she felt the tide of longing that rose in her every month. She remembered stories of places where the women went at the time of their bleeding and she thought of pouring herself a cup of coffee and curling up under the desk, where it was dark, where it was silent, where, if she was lucky, someone would find her and put her in seclusion.

She thought again of her cousins on the bright mesa edge, casting drops of water and scattering pinches of cornmeal, thanking something, someone, for a new day. The fluorescent light above her head was beginning to give out—it jittered over the report she was supposed to read. Heat washed up from the baseboard. The air was dead. She couldn't leave till Rich got back and she thought she'd die if she didn't get, damn quick, a chocolate peanut butter cup and a breath of clean, live air.

"So, Spirit," she whispered to the computer, "what could I thank *you* for?" The screen stayed gray. "For one room in my mother's house, for the noise of her country-western music station, for the silence in my aunt's house when I enter because I am from town, for a pretty husband who loves dope more than his children, for this work, carrying terrible messages to old white people?" She turned the computer on.

"Here," she said, "here is your story." She picked up Hatt's chart and slammed it on the desk and began to enter her report. The computer gave a "ping" and went down.

"Let the son deal with this," she hissed and picked up the phone. Her belly hurt. It wasn't hormones; it was a twist of shame. She knew better. She was a professional. She had been trained. She knew why the aging children behaved the way they did, why they abandoned the old ones, why they avoided. She put down the phone.

And that Liz, that *pahaana*, she would watch that one. She had seen that before, too, the well-meaning white people. Liz would visit for a while, who knew why, until Hatt became confused or smelly or began to shrivel into a silent reminder of what *it was*; to be old, to be a woman. Then, there would be phone calls and broken appointments and sweet excuses. She had seen it. The computer chimed at her and brightened. The screen flashed its report. Everything she had entered was gone. She shut the machine down and lit what was left of Rich's cigarette.

There would be more with that *pahaana*. She would be interested in Rose for a while, till she found out that Rose was not full of exotic secrets about her people, about the Old Way and the prophecies and the hope. She rummaged through the desk drawer. Sometimes the day nurse left chocolate kisses in with the paperclips, but tonight there was nothing. She slammed the drawer shut. There had been that good-looking anthropology student, the one with earring and ponytail, who had pestered her for lunch and "getting to know each other." She'd thought with her body on that one. She'd stolen precious time from a frantic week and it had been as she knew it would be. She told him immediately that she had been raised outside her tradition. He had changed the subject and spent the rest of the lunch watching every long-legged young woman that walked past their table. He had not even bothered to hide his disinterest. She had never heard from him again.

She lit one of her own cigarettes and watched the smoke drift in front of her. So, that Liz with her silver bracelet and her turquoise earrings and her sincere way, she could just keep her distance. Rose could hear her mother's sayings. "Be fair. Don't judge. We are all alike." All those dead words. No true teaching. It was a pretty house built with rotten stone, a Kachina doll molded in plastic. She glared at Hatt's chart. She could see her face in the window. She was fat and ugly and cold-looking. Hopeless. That was the worst, to feel self-hatred, to give up hope. That was the real sin. She opened Hatt's chart and picked up the phone.

"Mrs. Latham," Liz said. Hatt reached up and clasped her hand firmly. Her eyes were clear, her gaze steady.

"You are?" Hatt asked.

"Liz Morrigan. I've been visiting you for a while," Liz said.

"Well, Liz Morrigan, I don't know you from Adam, I must admit."

"I'm not surprised. You were drugged to the teeth."

"That was to keep me from having an accident or getting sick," Hatt said. "It didn't prevent the worst hangover I've ever had."

"That's hardly just," Liz said. Hatt smiled.

"Ah," she said, "the muscles still work. When I began to come out of this I thought I'd had a stroke. My face felt frozen. Dreadful." She studied Liz. "Sit," she said. "What brings you here? I haven't seen anything but this room and I know I hate the whole shebang." She shivered. "It smells awful."

"I miss my favorite aunt," Liz said. "I'm new in town. Alone. I need to stay out of trouble. That's about it."

"It's good enough for me," Hatt said. "I'm scarcely in a position to object."

"I see that," Liz said.

"You're blunt," Hatt said.

"Life's short," Liz replied. Hatt nodded. "Did they tell you why I'm here?"

Liz hesitated. "You first," she said. "I don't know much."

"There's been a mistake," Hatt said. "A strange and terrible mistake. I think my daughter, who worries about everything and can't bear messes, decided I needed to be taken care of." She swung her legs over the side of the bed and went pale. "That damn stuff's made me dizzy," she said. She leaned forward and dropped her head between her knees.

"Want a hand?" Liz said. Hatt sat up and leaned on her arm. Her thin fingers were a feather touch, as though a small bird perched there.

"Thank you," Hatt said. They got her to the bathroom door. She leaned against the wall. "How odd," she said, "it's like walking through sand, or in a high wind." She looked around the room, "How very odd. Some of my furniture is here, but there's so much missing." She stepped into the bathroom and closed the door.

Liz took off her coat. The dinner-cart reappeared and an aide left a tray of sandwich, tea and jello on the bed-stand. Hatt emerged from the bathroom and smiled. Liz guided her back to the bed and realized Hatt was beaming at her.

"My dear," she said. "What a delightful surprise to see you. It's been such a long time. I've wondered about the children." Her face went still. "Dear, there's been a terrible mistake, but now that you're here, we can get it sorted out."

Liz kept quiet and helped her settle into the rocking chair.

"Jeannie," Hatt said firmly. She peered at Liz. "Oh. Excuse me, this light is dim. You're not Jeannie. Of course you're not Jeannie." She gripped the rocker arms. "I am going senile, aren't I?" She stared at Liz. "Please. Tell me your name again. This is dreadful. I'm sorry."

"You're not senile," Liz said. "The main symptom of going senile is that you don't know it."

"Crazy?"

"No."

The color flooded back into Hatt's face. "Can you imagine how embarrassing this is?" she asked.

"Yes," Liz said. "By tomorrow, Saturday, February seventeenth, you will no longer be confused. It's my guess that you will be scared and mad as hell, but you won't be confused."

"By tomorrow, February seventeenth," Hatt said, "my son, Roger, will have removed me from this place. He is going to be furious when he hears about this." She stared out the window. "It's my daughter, I know it's her meddling ways." She turned to Liz. "Do you have children?"

"I do."

"Tell me about them," Hatt smiled. "And, be very, very careful about how you raise them."

"It's too late for that," Liz said. "They're full-grown and beyond hope. My daughter, Jen, is twenty-three, mouthy, opinionated, afflicted with a fatal sense of justice. I am proud of her beyond words. She's putting herself through school and she has a daughter, Tina. They are in much better shape at four and twenty-three than Jen and I were at those same ages. Steve is twenty-four. He's in Boston, studying corporation law and worrying about me. He is large and solid and huge of heart."

"Sounds like a tree," Hatt grinned.

"Close," Liz said, "but funnier. Then, there's Keith. He lives in Chicago. He plays guitar, waits tables and makes movies."

"We had a lot of those," Hatt said vaguely.

"Those?"

"Movies," Hatt smiled. "Those movie crews! We were terribly pictur-esque, you see. I met some of the great ones. We'll talk about it someday." She touched Liz's arm. "Do you think you could call that nurse? She was going to contact my son."

"Of course," Liz said.

"I'm being rude," Hatt said gently, "but I'm more and more worried. I'd like to be out of here before bedtime."

"I'll get the nurse," Liz said. "And I'll leave you my phone number. If you want anything, call me. Anytime."

Hatt clasped her hand in hers. "When I'm free," she said, "you must come and visit me. My home is in Kayenta. It's beautiful. Different from anything you've ever seen. Bring pictures of those children. That grandbaby. I'll make you Navajo mutton stew and fry bread."

"I would love all of that," Liz said.

"Good," Hatt said. "The next time we meet will be up there."

"Soon," Liz said. "I'll send the nurse in."

"I think your aunt must miss you, too," Hatt said.

Liz tapped on the nursing station window. Rose glanced up and slid the glass open.

"What is it?" she said. Liz glanced at her set face, at her red-rimmed eyes. Rose looked away.

"You asked me to come by?" Liz asked.

"Oh, yes," Rose said. She bit her lip and looked down at the charts scattered on the desk. "I just wanted to tell you not to be alarmed by Hatt. She'll drift in and out for a while till the drugs clear out." She picked up her pen and began writing.

"Thanks," Liz said. "She thinks some mistake's been made." Rose said nothing. "I suppose you know that." Liz continued.

"Yes, it's not uncommon." Liz ran her finger over the window frame.

She wanted to ask Rose what was wrong and she didn't seem to be able to.

"You have my phone number," she said. "So does Hatt. If she needs anything, let me know. I'll be back Sunday." She couldn't stop talking. "I'd like to bring some food, fruit, salad, something she doesn't get here?" Rose kept writing. "Is that okay? The food?" She wanted to touch Rose, to stop her pen's steady flow.

"Sure," Rose said. "No problem. Just use your judgement." She glanced up. "Excuse me, I've got to get these notes done before evening rounds. I'll see you." Liz nodded, raised her hand in good-bye and turned to leave.

"Wait," Rose said.

"What?" Liz asked. "Is anything wrong?"

"No," Rose said stiffly. "I just wanted to say good-bye. Really, that's all. I'm sorry."

"For what?" Liz asked.

"Nothing," Rose said. "Never mind. It's not you. It's me."

"Do you want me to come in? We could talk, have coffee, something?"

"No!" Rose said. "Just, thank you. Good-bye. I'll get out of this." She shrugged. Liz stepped forward. Rose closed the window and bent over her papers. When she looked up, Liz was gone. Rich turned away from the locked meds cabinet. He grinned.

"You could use a little something," he said. She glared at him.

"Don't be stupid," she said. He reached in his pocket.

"I don't do that stuff," she said. She'd seen him after he'd done whatever it was that he did—coke, crystal, pot. He'd come alive. His grin would eat up his face. He held out his hand.

"Come on, sweetheart," he said, "I ain't a bad guy once you get to know me." A cluster of M&Ms lay in his palm. She picked out the brown ones. She felt herself smile. It hurt.

"Damn," she said. "I am so damn tired."

"Chemicals," he said. He poured her a cup of coffee. "I keep telling you, Rose, better living through chemistry."

"I don't trust that woman," she said. "She means well."

"They're the worst kind," he said and popped the rest of the candy in his mouth.

Eleven

BY THE TIME LIZ HIT DOWNTOWN, Friday night was rolling. It had rained and the streets glittered. There were pick-ups and four-wheel-drives and black motorcycles and one El Dorado, shining in the bar lights like rain forest beetles. Liz drove slowly between them in that iridescent dark, the Camaro a mask, a fool-the-eye. Teenage guys cruised by, beeped, saw her face and sped on. Everybody was speeding on: gussied-up might-be cowboys in levis and leather jackets; Navajo men with hair-buns tied in white cotton; wild boys yelping at the moon, their shaved heads pastel in the cool light; broad-shouldered, skinny-hipped Navajo women in tight jeans and cowboy boots; Dead-heads and white-kid Rastafarians; a lone boy on a skateboard, his raven hair plastered to his head like a helmet, a skull blue-white on his dark jacket.

The newsdealer pulled the paper racks in. The dim lights of the little shops blinked out. The traffic signal was taking forever to change. She wanted to be back at the cabin. She nearly wanted to be home, back east, back where she knew how to go gray, how to not see all this razzle-dazzle, hot, got something for you, baby, shiny-cool, buzz that was cruising by her closed windows . . . and how to not want it.

A skinny girl, her spine dancer-straight, tossed back her long chestnut hair and sashayed into a board-window bar. The light changed, and Liz drove on. Beyond the railroad underpass, downtown was abruptly gone, the parade of gas stations and fast food huts began. She passed the last lights and turned off onto the highway south. Rose's face, Hatt's eyes, her own fingers jittering on the nursing station window frame, drifted in her mind's eye.

She opened the vents. Wet pine air poured in. Orion floated frozen just above the horizon. Liz thought of Hatt and what she couldn't yet see, of Rose and what she couldn't say. She thought of her fingers tracing that cold chrome window rim, how they couldn't reach out, how they couldn't take leave. And Lepur, safe at his captor's feet, mute, barely seen, free from the terror of pursuit, free from the joy of flight. She thought of sleep, peaceful, and how it had become a door and she drove toward it . . .

. . . Hotomqam strode the horizon, the hero, wearing three jewel-stars in his great helmet. Talasi saw him appear in the roof-hole and be gone. She shivered under her rabbit robes. In the hearth, embers glowed bright as stars, and the room was warm. It made no difference. She was cold with fear and excitement. It was the eve of Kachinvaki, the eve of her initiation into the Kachina mysteries. Morning would bring her to the foot of the ladder that led to the kiva roof; her heart would bring her to the secrets within.

She moved through sleep and half-waking. Sometimes the shivering would rouse her, sometimes the chattering of her teeth or the hiss of the fire or the sound of feet on the roof above. She folded her fingers across her palm and pretended that the pathstone lay there. The robes felt heavy, the sleeping mat too thin to shield her from the cold floor. She knew that in other rooms, on other mats, her friends lay awake. No child slept well on Kachinvaki Eve. She crept from her robes and crouched by the fire. She was thirsty, but water was forbidden.

The fire was nearly dead, the last coals scarlet. She stared into their heart, her eyelids heavy, her body hollow, her head, her hair too much weight for her neck. A shape began to form in the fire-glow. She rested her head on her knees and watched. Pamosi's face took form, her smile calm, her eyes loving. Talasi moved back into her sleeping robes, her eyes never leaving the fire, never leaving those eyes, for they were pathstones, deep as earth, calm as still water. Pamosi was Spirit Mother, earthly teacher and guide, friend and sister. Talasi whispered the words and charmed, fell asleep.

She slept without dreams and woke to a day that moved even more slowly than the night before. Choovio, without a word, wrapped Talasi's waist and hips with thick cloth and drew her best *manta* down over her body. Talasi stood quiet and still while her mother combed her long hair. Choovio smiled. She remembered her own solemn excitement, her own terror on that day. For Talasi to be motionless under the pull of the yucca brush was, in itself, a mystery.

The sun dawdled along the floor. It touched and gilded the old harvest basket, the big turkey-feather robe and the sandstone hearth where Talasi sat. She folded her hands in her lap and tried to soften the harsh thump of her heart. She was thirsty and hungry and she had gone to the back of the village three times to relieve herself since noon.

The sun touched the wall and was gone; in the roof-hole, the sky was ice-blue. She watched wisps of cloud float by. The roof-hole darkened, a shadow fell and Pamosi's eldest son, Aala, peered in. His face was solemn. Talasi shivered. She had never seen him without a welcoming smile. He and Pamosi climbed down the ladder and nodded silently to Talasi. They took her icy hands and helped her to her feet. Without a word, all three climbed the ladder.

It was last light. Watch over me, Talasi's heart whispered. She had to relieve herself again, and it was too late. She kept her eyes on the path. Pamosi handed her an ear of corn.

"Hold tight to it," she said quietly, "all through the ceremony." Nothing else was said. At the kiva entrance, Talasi took a deep breath. With a last wistful look at the clouds threading the dark horizon, she stepped firmly on the top rung and descended. It was like sinking into a deep pool after one of the summer cloudbursts. A man sat in the dim light at the foot of the ladder. His face was covered and he held a big hoop. Without a word, he pointed to the center of the hoop and she stepped in. He raised and lowered it around her four times. She felt very little. There was only the whisper of air slipping over her body, one, two, three, four times, the holy number, the holy directions.

She bowed her thanks and joined Pamosi and Aala on a low bench along the wall. She saw, as she might see shadows, the prayer feathers, the smoke from a small fire, the shifting forms of things that might be masks or skulls or bowls. She sat with her feet drawn up, as she had been told, as young eagles perch. Near her, around the great room, she saw the faces of other children. They were her friends, they were strangers. There was Rupi, her smile gone; Ahqawu, trembling in the kiva's warmth; Kihsi, a thin shadow in the shadows. Even in that dark, his eyes were shining.

The girls wore their robes and shawls, the boys only blankets. Talasi wondered about this. A question began to bubble in her mind. She closed her eyes. She was not to speak. The question tickled in her throat. She coughed and felt Pamosi's elbow jab her side. She bit her lip and stared at the floor. There was only dust there. Her mind began to clear.

The silence deepened. A thud sounded at the roof-hole, and the ladder trembled. Out of the fading light, down into the darkness, into the fire-glow, slowly, steadily, without a sound, came an old man. He wore only a breech-cloth. The firelight played on his face and was gone. He was familiar and then shadow.

"Aliksa'i." It was a sigh, a breath. The story began. In his old, high voice he sang the Kachina story. Talasi was no longer afraid. With her ears, with her heart, with her bones, she listened. His cracked voice wavered and she trembled with the sound. His breath was hers; he breathed the story out and she took in every word, every silence, swallowing it, every step, every arrival, every leave-taking, every song, every mistake.

As he chanted, little Koyemsi, mud-head clowns, came out from the shadows four times. Their bodies were red-brown with mud, their heads, fat balls of clay. They stared at everything with their bulging eyes. Glowing in the firelight, they moved silently toward each child, offering an ear of corn and prayer feathers. Gifts received, they disappeared.

The storyteller finished and it was quiet, more deeply quiet than before. Even the fire had gone to silent coals. Talasi felt grateful for the warm bodies next to her. She looked up. Kihsi's eyes were closed. The storyteller spoke, his words sharp as a slap.

"They come closer," he said. "Closer. Closer." He paused. Talasi imagined that she could feel the great stones of the kiva tremble. "They are here!"

The roof-hole seemed to burst with the thunder of running feet, with a terrible whistling as though the very air were being slashed by cries, neither human nor animal. Talasi stared up. The roof-hole was ragged with the shifting light and the menacing forms that hovered there. Then it went black. She forced herself to breathe. The blackness shattered and two Kachinas raced down the ladder. Their feet were a blur on the ladder rungs, their cry pierced her ears.

"Hu . . . hu . . . hu-u-u-u-u," they cried, their call not quite the high moan of the owl, not quite a hawk's scream, not, and yet very nearly, the ghost-wail of the lion. The Kachinas were black, spotted with white circles. Their huge eyes bulged horribly and great horns coiled from their brows. Sharp, white teeth filled their grinning mouths and fox-skin circled their necks, as though they had swallowed the animals' insides whole. She forced her gaze to their upraised arms. In their black hands, they carried many-bladed yucca whips. They were the Hu Kachinas; they were the Whipping Ones.

They stood one on either side, at the foot of the ladder. The firelight shone on their fangs, on the spines of their whips. Talasi sat straight. She willed her eyes to stay open, to look up. There was a whisper at the roof-hole. Gathering night, as she might a great cape, Crow Mother began her descent. Talasi felt a rush of fear and joy in her throat. Crow Mother held a bundle of yucca blades in Her white arms. Her stern face was turquoise, Her eyes white circles, and the place where Her mouth might have been, a black triangle. She wore the woman's black *manta*, embroidered in red and green, and a long white cape.

Talasi saw Her in the gloom as clearly as in daylight. White eagle down fluttered over Her brow and shining above Her face rose great raven wings, each feather perfect, each spine a shaft of light. She raised that gleaming head and looked at each child. Rupi began to whimper. Kihsi's shoulders trembled under his thin blanket. Talasi bit the inside of her mouth; the pain drew away the fear. She raised her head and looked straight into Her face.

Crow Mother stepped to the corner of a sacred painting that lay half-hidden in the shadows across the kiva floor. The Hu Kachinas moved to Her side. A small boy was led forward by his sponsors. He was naked. He raised one trembling hand above his head and held the other over his budding penis. The Hu Kachina raised his green whip and struck the child three times. On the fourth, boy's godfather thrust out his own leg and took the blow.

Talasi hugged her knees. She could see that the blows were not so dreadful, but she felt something unknown, something worse than fear. It was *qahopi*. It was shame. She did not want to stand naked in front of everyone, and she did not know why. She had splashed naked in the rain puddles for years, playing with all the others at being lizards and rabbits and fish.

Only when Kihsi walked toward the Hu Kachinas did she understand. As they pulled off his blanket, her eyelids fluttered down. She felt her cheeks burn. She clenched her fists on her knees and stared at the far edge of the sacred painting. Its border danced in the light, its creatures and moons and corn plants burning bright, going dark. When she looked up, the beating was done. Kihsi sat, covered, straight-backed and still-faced, on the stone bench. Pamosi and Aala nudged her forward.

She stepped to her spot. Aala pulled the shawl from her shoulders. She was the first girl to stand before the shadow figures. The Hu Kachina seemed to fill the room. His big hand moved towards her. She forced herself to stand still, to keep her eyes on Crow Mother's still face, to hold her body straight and proud. She felt the Hu Kachina's warm hand on her shoulder. She had thought his touch would be cold and wet, as when one passes through fog. He moved her forward and released her.

The yucca lash curled round her waist, round the thick folds of her robe and the cloth beneath. There were three more strokes and it was over. She barely felt them, though she made herself take in their touch, as she took in the blind eyes of the Hu Kachinas and the harsh voice of Crow Mother, as she took in her friends' shadowed faces and the comfort of Aala's hand on her shoulder. In all that taking, her heart went still and calm and she knew, without question, the secret the Kachinas carried. Kihsi's eyes met hers. He smiled and she wished she, too, had been naked, had been given the chance to show her courage and spirit as the boys had.

The initiation drew to its close. After all the children had stepped before the Kachinas, the Hu Kachinas lashed each other, then Crow Mother Herself. Their blows were not punishment; they were blessing and reminder. All were kin in the pain and knowledge. The old storyteller stepped quietly forward and blessed the Kachinas with *pahos* and cornmeal. They bowed their thanks and were gone, vanished in less than a breath. As noisy and terrible as their coming had been, their leave-taking was without sound.

The kiva seemed to shrink, as though the Kachinas had brought the night sky with them, its vastness, its cold and light. With their leaving, the kiva was itself, a warm, dim room of earth. The storyteller smiled.

"*Aliksa'i,*" he said and spun out, in his soft voice, the web of secrets that now held them fast . . . and safe. For to follow the teachings and keep the secrets was the Hopi way, to stray, to carelessly spill the secrets to a stranger or an uninitiated child was *qahopi* and it was the way to destruction, of land, of people, of future. Again, the old man smiled.

"May you be blessed," he said and climbed slowly up the ladder. The children looked at each other, saw what they had always known and more. Talasi stretched out her legs and waited for feeling to sting its way back in. She had never sat so still for so long. Kihsi bent over his long legs, rubbing the cramps from his ankles. She smiled at him. He laughed and rubbed his buttocks. Pamosi nudged her in the ribs.

"Behave yourself," she said. "It is not finished till we walk out into the air." Talasi stepped down to the cold floor. The room seemed to spin. There was a buzz, like *Tsuu'a*'s angry rattle, like the hum of the *umukpi*. She touched Pamosi's outstretched arm and felt her balance return.

"Look down," Pamosi whispered. "You have been given a gift."

At Talasi's feet lay a great black feather . . .

. . . Liz came half-awake. It was barely dawn. Saturday. Saturdays were too long. They were a little out-of-time, a no-woman's land that should and did not stretch into tender evening. She wondered if American women ever got over it as date night, if they didn't always feel—married, unmarried, coupled or single—a little disappointment in Saturday, in Saturnight.

She shivered. The door of sleep lay half-open. She turned from the day that lay ahead and went through . . .

. . . Talasi and Pomosi set out for the spring just after Third Dawn, Pamosi leading, water pots heavy on her back. She carried the weight easily, her feet sure on the well-worn trail. She did not turn to keep track of her niece. Talasi was healthy and smart. It was her task to keep up.

The old steps to the spring were worn smooth. The sun had just cleared the horizon; its light was cool and soft, shining on the spring, and the overflow puddled at the foot of the huge cottonwood. Little creatures skittered along the gray surface of the water; silvery leaves turned in its depths. Pamosi set down her jugs, Talasi hers. In the silence and dappled light, they scattered drops of water to Father Sun and splashed their faces. The place was empty. Pamosi sighed.

"What a gift to be alone," she said.

Talasi watched a many-legged bug dart across the still water. She saw how silver bubbles clung to the dark bottom leaves. That was part of the cottonwood's magic, how the leaves could be green, silver, then gold, then black. Pamosi sat against the far side of the tree, her face raised to the sun's touch. Talasi trailed her hand in the water and felt, for an instant, the pathstone. She heard Pamosi singing softly. The song and the stone were the same, a light, a shining, a way to see.

It had been five seasons since Pamosi had named herself as Spirit Mother. When Choovio and Nuuva stopped speaking and their silence hung in the rooms like Powamuya's fog, Talasi thought of Pamosi, of the warmth in her rooms, in her teaching. The lessons came in little pieces: sometimes a day or two at Pamosi's side, sometimes nothing more than a stern glance. The singing stopped. Talasi tried to slide a leaf under the bug. The bug was not interested.

"Perhaps you have some questions for me," Pamosi said.

Talasi stepped round the thick cottonwood trunk and crouched at her aunt's side. She poked the wet sand. There was a question. She had carried it a long while, waiting with it, dreaming with it, looking to find the answer in the shadows or the clouds or the hawk's high scream. The answer had not come.

"It is time again for the Kachinas to go home," she said. "Since they came, I have been thinking of the hawk-faced Ones, of the woman's words, 'Both inside and outside my woman's work.'" Talasi stared down at the canal she was digging in the sand. "Those words are not an answer. You know how I am, that I cannot wait to finish the grinding, almost before I have begun; that I go with Kihsi whenever I can steal away; that I spoil the soup whenever I am told to watch and stir it, and stir it, and stir it. I do not even like the taste of that soup anymore! When we play dolls, I think of other things. Why should I think of babies or families or love?" She let her hair fall over her face. Pamosi was silent.

"Aunt," Talasi said, "I find many teachers outside my woman's work. You are there. I have Kihsi; I have the rabbits and parrots and clouds and rocks. When Rupi is not giggling about boys, we go to the old walls and find beads and bowls and, once, a basket, half-eaten by mice. Sometimes I feel so full of those lessons that I think I might burst. But, *inside* my woman's work, in the grinding and stirring and mending and sweeping and watching and waiting, what lessons are there? When you pull a bowl from the fire, it is done. It is useful, and beautiful. When old Pósøvi takes a robe from his loom, it can be worn. It is finished. But this grinding and stirring and mending and sweeping, they are never finished."

"As the men plant, and hunt, and chip tools," Pamosi said gently. "Their way is no easier." She smoothed Talasi's hair away from her face. "Are you making canals there?" she asked. Talasi nodded. "That work, if it is to hold, must be done again and again, or the walls break, the water floods and the first work is useless."

Women's voices drifted on the air. Pamosi stood up and held her hand out to Talasi.

"Come," she said. "We will go back. The others do not need to hear what we say." They settled the full jugs into their carrying slings and started up the steps. Three women from East-Rising House descended. They smiled and waved and went on their way.

As the trail wound between low juniper, Pamosi slowed her steps.

"I have prayed a long time with those words, 'inside your woman's work.'

My prayers, my thoughts, even the seeing stone showed me nothing." She smiled. "Sometimes when we chase too hard after something, it slips away . . . and waits." She walked a while without talking. Talasi wanted to stop her. She settled the jug more squarely on her back and watched carefully where she put her feet. She made herself feel the jug's weight; the sun beating down on her smooth hair; the small rocks under her step. Pamosi pointed out some new plants, the bright green of early growth.

"There," she said, "that yellow blossom. That is mallow. It thickens the watery bowels of summer sickness. And that, with the pointed leaves, that is *suuvi*. It can be brewed and drunk to dull pains in the chest. Do you remember last winter, how old Nøødnø could not stop coughing, how pale and thin he grew? And, how Toho came and brought him back from going over with *suuvi* tea." Talasi nodded. Just that morning, she had seen old Nøødnø on the roof of his house, his arms outstretched in gratitude for the new day. Pamosi handed her a leaf.

"That one," she said, "how do you use it? What are the steps?" Talasi crumbled the fragrant leaf between her fingers and sniffed its scent.

"I ask the plant's permission to pick it," she said. "It is *sivahpi* and its uses are many. I steep the leaves and ask for blessing and give it to one who suffers from bone-shaking and fever."

Pamosi smiled. "I wish the Grinding Path were as clear as this one."

The plaza at East-Rising House was full of mothers and grandmothers and children, the little ones like bright butterflies, as wild, as welcome. Rupi's baby sister, Paayu, stumbled from woman to woman. She wore nothing but a tiny string of *tsorposi* around her fat neck. The women picked her up and nuzzled her and sent her on her tottering way. Somehow, with all the grinding and mending and cooking, no child fell in the fire, no child stepped out over the edge of the great rock. It was not always so. Last Going Home, a tiny boy had been carried, screaming, to Toho's dark house. His little legs and belly had been black as charred corn. Toho had eased his pain and no more. He had slept through his going over and been buried in the side of a narrow *tuukwi*, a braided willow deer at his side, a string of black beads around his wrist.

Ladle after ladle, Pamosi filled the big *wikoro*. She moved carefully. Even the smallest spill could make the difference between simple thirst and suffering. Talasi added hers. The *wikoro* brimmed full.

"It will be gone so quickly," Pamosi said. "There was so little snow. The springs run slower than last year. I wonder when the men will see this. They do not carry water. They do not see the small changes we women know."

"Can we tell them?" Talasi asked. She thought of Toho, of Kihsi, how they listened carefully, how Kihsi sometimes stepped aside and she led the way.

"They will not listen," Pamosi said. "Perhaps they cannot. Those bone dice rattle loud; sometimes I think that sound will drown out everything, the warnings, the guidance, our songs and prayers."

She took a bundle from the top of a wooden chest.

"Come with me," she said. "We will have to go to the plaza soon, but I have something to show you alone." They walked out into the small canyon half-hidden behind East-Rising House. The people did not go there often. There were places there, rocks, a tiny seep where ferns grow, old paintings on the cliff face, that held great power. The elders warned against what dwelled there. It was said they buried sacred objects in those places to draw strength, to draw that dangerous power, and to give it, Pamosi led her niece straight to a huge black boulder. It was rock from Two-Color Mountain, rough and ugly. The sun poured over them, burning out the scent of Talasi's clean hair and the perfume of the gray-green sage around them.

"Close your eyes," Pamosi said, "and hold your hands open in your lap."

Talasi squeezed her eyes shut. Bursts of light exploded against the red mist behind her lids. She held her breath.

"Breathe," Pamosi laughed. "That is the first lesson." Talasi giggled. "Here is the second, or is it the fourth, or the twentieth? It does not matter." She cupped her hand under Talasi's. "When your path hid from me, I put it from my mind. It was time to hunt as Toho does, to sit still and let the hunted find me.

"One day, as I prepared the clay for my work, as I ground the lumps of earth and sifted the dust through the basket made by your mother, and mixed the clean clay with water, It began to stalk me. You know how that is, nothing seen, nothing heard, nothing touched or smelled or tasted, but, nonetheless, the presence."

"Yes," Talasi whispered. She wanted to open her eyes. She felt the stalker there. It was small. It was solid. It moved at the level of the heart, without legs, without wings, soaring, as little hawks ride unseen air trails.

"I took some clay," Pamosi said, "only a little, and I let the stalker move into my hands. I coiled the clay and smoothed it. The little pot seemed to flow up through my fingers, a perfect globe, like a gourd, like the full moon. That night, while the pot dried, I dreamed and, in the morning, as I built up my fire, I let my brush trace the dream.

"I could scarcely wait for the firing to be done. I think I knew, in that long time, how you feel, how your quick heart beats. I felt as nervous as I had the days your uncle came to my courting window. I raked away the coals from the firing. I could scarcely look in the center, where the little pot lay. It was whole, finished, perfect as it could be. When, at last, it lay in my hands, I held it out to Father Sky and Mother Earth for their blessing."

Talasi felt a tear squeeze from between her lids. How blessed her aunt was, to have the hands, the dreams, the patience for the bowl-maker's work. Only women seemed to have that gift. She did not, nor any other, not for grinding, not for cooking, not for the sweet words that Rupi spoke, the shy glances she so easily gave. All she seemed to have was her restless mind, her strong body, her endless questions and a gift for waiting. That she could do. She could wait. She bowed her head and took in the silence.

Pamosi watched the tears dry on her niece's face. She waited till she saw Talasi's breathing slow and she could feel the child's pulse steady against her palm. She bent, took up the bowl and set it in Talasi's hands.

Talasi felt the pot settle into her palms. It was small and cool and perfect. It was just the right size. She ran her finger around the rim. It was a bowl, made for drinking. She could taste the water and how it would pick up the mineral scent of the clay.

"May I open my eyes?" she asked.

"Do you know the gift?" Pamosi asked. There was silence. Talasi opened her eyes.

"I do," she said. She held it up before her eyes. It was the deep red of winter sunset, of East-Rising House, of the cliff walls at dusk. A thin black line, sharp as Soyal shadows, trailed up and over the rim, winding down into the pot, circling from left to right, spiralling down to the bottom, then curving up around itself, till it met itself and joined, no beginning, no end. Talasi tapped the rim with her fingernail. It rang. She looked up and saw Pamosi smile.

"This will take a long time to unravel," Talasi said. "I will drink from it and thank you with each sip. I will spoon my burned soup in into it, till I burn the soup no more."

Twelve

THE PHONE SHRILLED. Liz grabbed for it. The morning sun was blue-white, the cabin icy. She tucked the phone under her chin and burrowed into the quilts.

"Liz," Deena said stiffly.

"I'm here."

"Can you get over here as fast as you can?" Deena said.

"Fifteen minutes," Liz said and hung up. There was cold coffee on the stove. She dumped it in a glass, added cream and brown sugar and gulped it down. The phone rang again. No one spoke.

"Hello," she said, "hello." There was nothing, not even the breathing of the man at the end, two or twenty or two thousand miles away.

"Damn you," she hissed. The connection clicked shut. "And if you're Nick, double damn you."

She pulled on her boots and finished off the coffee. The caffeine jolted in. She poured some cat food in a dish and went out to start the car.

The engine caught and roared. She set the brake and went in to close up the house. The phone rang. She walked away, locked the door and climbed into the warm car.

"Are you hungry?" Deena said. "We're having banana pancakes." She smiled down at Deej who was pouring a quart of syrup on her anything-but-short stack.

"She'll explode," Liz said.

"If that's the worst that happens," Deena said, "I'll be ecstatic."

"What's ecstatic, Mommy?" Deej asked. She took her napkin, dabbed at the syrup running off her plate, laid the sticky napkin in her lap, leaned her elbows on her knees and came up covered with syrup. Deena wiped her clean.

"Ecstatic is very, very happy," Deena said.

"Pancakes make me ecstatic," Deej said cheerfully.

"Good," Deena said. "Liz and I are going to sit in the living-room. You finish up, wash your hands and you can come play while we talk."

"I don't mean to be ungrateful," Liz said, "for these lovely pancakes, but it is seven o'clock in the morning and your call didn't sound like a casual brunch invitation."

"*He's* been cruising by the house every half hour since midnight." Deena said. She pointed to the front window. "Go ahead, you can see through that crack. He's about due."

Liz watched. A station wagon moved slowly down the street. The man inside pointed a camera at Liz's car.

"You think he stopped taking his lithium?" Liz said. "This is one sick hombre."

"It's not funny," Deena said. "He thinks I have a boyfriend. He told Deej that."

"Do you have a boyfriend?" Deej asked from the kitchen.

"No," Deena said. "You know that. I don't have a boyfriend. I don't want a boyfriend. You're my friend and Liz and Cody and Gorgeous. That's all the friends I have."

"Daddy says you have a boyfriend," Deej said. "And he says you're fat." She giggled.

"Ever try pesticide on pancakes?" Liz said. "Or a little codeine cough syrup? Works wonders."

Deena laughed. "Shut up," she said good-naturedly. "How'd your kids survive?"

"Bad genes," Liz said. "They did it to spite me."

"What do you call those things revolutionaries throw down in the road?" Deena said. "Like James Bond?"

"Caltraps," Liz said. "They're like big jacks."

"I got jacks," Deej said. "That's my daddy's name and he gave me some. I don't have no toys here."

"You lie," Deena said. She grabbed Liz's hand. "Come on," she said, "you show Liz, Deej. You show her all your stuff." She started to cry. "That's a damn lie, Deej, you've got crayons and dolls and a record player all your own and *fourteen* teddy bears."

Deej stared up at Deena, and tears welled up in her eyes. She wrapped her arms around Deena's legs.

"I'm sorry, Mommy," she sobbed. "I don't hate you. Daddy does."

Deena picked her up and sat at the kitchen table. She picked at the pancakes. "Oh shoot," she said, "I know you don't hate me. You make me ecstatic, that's what you do."

Deej jumped down. She came back with a fat box of crayons and a stack of newsprint. Liz set her up on the kitchen stool and washed her hands.

"You might call the cops," she said.

"On what grounds?" Deena asked. She lit a cigarette and glared at Deej. "Don't you say a word," she said, "or I'll turn you into a toad-frog." Deej giggled.

"My mommy always says that," she said. "But, she never does it. I wish she would. My daddy says she's a witch, right, Mommy? You could do it, huh?"

"I could," Deena said. "Your daddy better watch out or I'll turn *him* into a Republican."

"Is that very bad?" Deej said.

"It's pretty serious," Deena said.

Somebody pounded on the front door. Deej flew to the window, peaked out and ran back.

"It's Daddy," she whispered.

"I can't stand this," Deena said. She set the chain-lock and cracked open the door.

"Who's that woman?" Jack said. Liz stepped behind Deena.

"Who is she?" he said.

"I'm the social worker," Liz said. Deena stepped back square on her toe.

"This time of day?" Jack snarled.

"We like to observe the family setting at its most natural," Liz said. "It gives us a chance to see the communication between parent and child, to assess the interpersonal dynamics, to evaluate the cognitive parenting skills, to determine what socio-psychological factors might be coming into play."

"Oh," he said. "You from the court?"

"I'm not at liberty to reveal that information," Liz said. "Confidentiality, you know."

"Okay," he said. There was a short silence. "Can I see Deej?" he asked.

"Why?" Deena said.

"I just want to hug her," he said. "That's all."

"Okay," Deena said. Deej ran to the door.

"Daddy," she cried, "Mommy says she's going to turn you into a Republican."

"I already am one," he said. "And Mommy's not funny."

He hugged Deej, set her back in the house and closed the door.

"That wasn't so bad," Liz said.

"You don't understand," Deena said. "It's part of his routine."

"How so?"

Deena glanced down at Deej, who watched their faces as though she watched Big Bird and Santa Claus. "Later," Deena said. She grinned. "Tomorrow night at nine, the Concho; there's a great band."

"Excellent clarification," Liz said, "good communication skills, strong positive imaging, sound treatment plan!"

She went to sleep early that night; it was the easiest way past the loneliness. Hot milk and molasses, a good fire, the wind tapping at the rattly windows, the Phoenix newspaper lulled her brain and bones. She had hiked half the day in a little side canyon in the Verde Valley, found a tiny purple oyster shell on a ledge in the cliffs. It was a perfect mystery to dwell on . . .

. . . "Cousin, wake up! It is nearly First Dawn! Wake up!"

Talasi forced her eyes open. Rupi bent over her, prodding with her foot. She was dressed in her best summer robe and her eyes glittered.

"Cousin, will you make the Sun drag you from your sleep? He has enough to do! It is time! They go home today! Hurry! Come and see! The *salavi* are in the plaza!"

Talasi struggled to her feet. "Stop shouting," she said.

"I am *not* shouting! I am whispering!"

"How did you get in? Don't surprise me like this. I was dreaming and now it is gone."

"You and your dreams," Rupi hissed. "You live in your dreams. Come out with me. It is much better than dreams."

Talasi dragged the yucca brush through her hair and pulled on her robe.

"Where are your beads?" Rupi asked. They were nowhere in sight. Talasi hated the great fuss made dressing for the ceremonies, the young women endlessly playing with each others' hair, with ornaments and paint. With each necklace, each smear of face-paint, she felt more and more hidden from the Spirit. If Spirit knew her prayers before she spoke them, then Spirit had seen her naked and dirty and wicked . . . and blessed her still. With a fierce glance at Rupi, she started for the ladder.

"Put on your necklace," Rupi snapped. "You are growing more and more careless, girl. Someone . . . one of the boys . . . might see you. You are so messy. Do you wish to be *maana* forever, one of the never-married ones?" She pulled the beads from Talasi's sleeping robes.

Talasi flushed. Without a word, she let her friend drape the chunky blue beads around her throat and tuck the wild strands of hair back from her face. Beads and smooth hair made no difference.

"That is better!" Rupi said. "Now, come!"

They paused at the roof-edge to offer their morning prayers. "Look," Rupi cried and spun them both toward the *kiisonve*, the round plaza that lay between the southern mesa and the houses of the village; in that familiar, yet mysterious place, the *salavi* stood black against the sand, their shadows pale gray. *Pahos* fluttered at their base, the dawn breeze barely stirring the cloudy tufts of eagle down. An unwavering line of cornmeal had been drawn from the central shrine to the East. The rooftops filled slowly with the people of the village. They raised their arms in grateful prayer.

At the far end of the *kiisonve,* a young eagle bit at the tethers holding him to a scratched wooden platform.

I have been taught, Talasi thought, that his part is brave and joyous in my people's ceremonies, but when I see him fight the tethers, when he soars away, only to be yanked back to that perch, my heart hurts. Surely, he is meant for more than sacrifice, surely he is more holy in his flight than as breath feathers to bless some bride's robe. She put the thoughts from her head. More and more, as she drank from the pathway bowl and bent over her grinding and sang over the thickening corn stew, stirring and stirring, questions filled her mind and heart. Rupi glanced at her friend, saw the sadness in her eyes.

"Too much thinking makes you solemn," she said. "Stop now. See the smoke from cooking fires over the rooftops, smell the feasts. This is a happy time. Smile for me."

Talasi shook herself and forced a smile to her lips.

"You are right," she said and turned her eyes from the young eagle.

Smoke curled up from the rooftops, carrying the rich smell of stewing deer and antelope. Women appeared, beckoning their families to the morning meal. Each had labored for days, grinding, mixing the fine cornmeal with water and ashes, spreading the thin batter over the baking stones, peeling off wafer-thin sheets of *piki* bread and rolling them into flaky tubes. They had cut the meat of rabbits and small birds into chunks and made thick soups. Pots of *qa'ɸvala* had simmered for hours, the children stirring and stirring, their faces flushed, their arms aching. Fat, stuffed prairie dogs were seasoned with *tuitsma,* picked in late summer and dried in the sun. There were bowls of dried berries, smoked meat and roasted red and green chilies. Sweet *pikami* had baked a full day in the village's huge underground oven.

Despite the slow-running springs, it had been a good harvest and the hunts had been plentiful. For days, the women had hurried back and forth to each others' houses, carrying woven plaques filled with cornmeal or *piki* or sweet corn dumplings. No one went hungry, even those for whom the bone dice sounded stronger than their songs.

Talasi and Rupi climbed down the ladder into Choovio's house. The air was sweet with the smell of celebration. They bowed their thanks and settled near the hearth long enough to cram corn dumplings in their mouths. Choovio laughed.

"You must unwrap them first," she said. In the heart of her laughter was sadness. It seemed to happen more and more, that ache and joy in the same breath. She would not watch a greedy, bright-eyed grandbaby gobble down her food. Talasi would never feel the joy she felt watching the girls consume a morning's work in so little time. They giggled, wiped their mouths, bowed thanks and were gone, racing up the ladder, robes gathered around their slender legs. Choovio followed them to the roof. She offered her prayer for balance and for the healing of her daughter's sturdy body.

She watched them. At the edge of the roof they stopped and fell silent. As the sun's first rays touched the village, all was hushed. Then came the clear scream of the young eagle . . .

. . . By early afternoon, a good sharp sun had burned off the morning's clouds. Steam rose up from the dirt road. Liz stopped for food on the way to see Hatt. She remembered the "guests" at Lakeview, back East, and bought crackers and salsa and cheese and one ripe pear. The parking lot at the home was jammed.

Liz found Hatt perched on the edge of the neatly made bed, a stack of letters and papers beside her. She smiled up at Liz.

"I bet you're surprised to see me here," she said. Liz set her groceries on the nearest chair and leaned up against the dresser.

"I thought I'd take a chance," she said. "What's the story?"

"Rose called my son. He's out of town on business and my daughter-in-law is a cotton-headed nit. She had no idea what had happened. She sent those." She pointed to a stiff clump of chrysanthemums. "I'm sure he'll call tomorrow when he gets back. I decided to put this little episode to work and answer some long overdue letters. I'm glad you're here. I don't like to answer letters here any better than I did at home."

"I thought you might like some relief from the Tenderhome cuisine," Liz said. "I brought a picnic." She handed Hatt the pear.

"What a treat!" she said. She held the fruit in her hands, turning it slowly around. "Real food," she sighed. "Have you got a knife?"

"Why don't I ask the kitchen?" Liz said. "They'll give you stuff. Your insurance is probably paying ten times the cost of a five-star hotel."

"No!" Hatt said. "They seem to have the idea that I have high blood pressure. It's nonsense but they are very firm about my well-being. I'm afraid they'll confiscate this stuff."

Liz unclasped her camp-knife and handed it to Hatt.

"Get some paper towels, would you?" Hatt grinned. "This is going to get messy." Expertly, she halved the pear. The juice ran through her fingers. "Heaven!" she said. "Every Christmas John's people would send us a box of apples and pears. We ate them plain. I made pie. We gave a few to the families that were our regulars. They hardly knew what to make of them. They'd only seen them in cans."

Liz set out the food. She'd brought tea bags from home and a bar of chocolate.

"This is wonderful," Hatt said. "I'm dying for a decent cup of tea. I won't tell you what they give us here. I'm sure the nurse will give you a little jug of hot water. I don't think they can ruin that. They have some magic techniques here. They can turn perfectly good bread into leather."

When Liz came back with the hot water, Hatt had set out cut-work napkins. They were pale yellow linen, ivory lilies embroidered in the corners.

"What are those?" Liz asked.

"The Navajo girls at the school did them," Hatt said. "Nobody does work like that anymore. One of the teachers was an old German woman and she taught them the craft."

"What are those flowers?"

Hatt laughed. "They're the blossoms of the Sacred Datura. It's a common plant out here, quite beautiful. The vine and leaves are deep green and the blossoms are like great creamy lilies." She paused. "The Medicine People use them to induce visions. In the early '60s, we were forever hauling hippies from Kayenta to the emergency clinic for help. They'd read about datura and gobble it down without the proper training or instruction and start tripping their little brains out."

They sipped their tea. She'd set out little bowls, dark-brown, curved perfectly to fit the hand. Jasmine flowers floated in the tea. It tasted of Spring.

"Those bowls are Navajo, too," Hatt said. "Most people don't realize the Navajo have a pottery style all their own. We whites tend to lump all the Southwestern Indians together. It's a great mistake."

"They're wonderful," Liz said. "I've got my car outside. We could go for a drive. It's cold, but the sun's brilliant. We could sit out of the wind, maybe drive south, get some ice cream or something."

"I would love to do just that, but to tell the truth, I keep hoping that my daughter-in-law coaxed her two brain cells into action and got word to Roger. I would hate to miss his call." She patted Liz's hand. "Where *have* you come from?" she said.

"It's my pleasure," Liz said.

"Is it?" Hatt said. "Pleasure? Not charity?"

"The opposite."

"How so?" Hatt narrowed her eyes. Liz could see her, half a century ago, studying a silver belt buckle, studying no less the seller.

"The first time I saw you, you were fighting for your life," Liz said. "I admire that in a woman." Hatt laughed. "They gave you an evil medication and you fought it. Did they tell you about it?"

"Rose hinted at something, but I didn't ask. I lost over a month of my life and, I don't really want to know about it. Life's too short and precious to have to be reminded of the dreadful parts." She turned away. When she looked back, she was grinning.

"Did I do any damage?" she asked.

"The ping-pong table is still in the shop," Liz said. "A symbolic victory!"

"Yes," Hatt said. "My sister was in and out of mental hospitals for years. I never thought I'd end up within range of one of those things." She straightened up the remains of their picnic. "So I was an unconscious warrior, is that it?"

"There's more," Liz said. "I'm terrified of getting old. I need to know some old women who I respect."

"We're not going to have to worry about pointless tact," Hatt laughed, "I can see that. I *am* old, eighty-three years. We'll see if you respect me. I'll tell you something else. You might want to start looking closer at the old women you see. They survived. They're out and about. How do you suppose they did that? Women were still wearing hobble skirts when I started out." She studied Liz's face. "All that stands between you and me, Elizabeth, is forty years. That's all."

"After Rose told me a little about you," Liz said, "I went to the library and poked around. I want to know what it was really like back in the '30s, the '40s, out here. I wish that forty years didn't lie between us. I wish I'd been here when it wasn't shiny and clean and safe." She leaned forward. "I ask you, please, to tell me stories. I'll remember them. I'll keep them alive and pass them on."

"Well," Hatt said with a wry smile, "I *do* love to tell stories. You have to promise me one thing. If I pick up some anthropology journal and read about this 'amazingly articulate, still coherent ninety-year-old pioneer woman, etc., etc.' I'll put a curse on you. And, mark this, I know how to do it."

"No," Liz laughed. "Sworn, promised, vowed. What happened?"

"Some earnest soul trekked himself and his battery-operated tape recorder and ten steno pads all the way up to Kayenta," Hatt said. "He never told me clearly what he was doing. You know how those people talk. A year later, a friend sent me the article. I was ready to cast bones on him." She pulled a leather photo album out of the top dresser drawer.

"Ah," she said, "they haven't yet got this. I've already lost my best nightgown. I'm shocked they missed the cups and napkins."

"Here it is," she said. "*Latham's*, better known as Klethla Trading Post." Liz bent over her shoulder. The photo was faded sepia. A trick of camera angle made the building seem to float on the pale sand. She could see a boulder-choked wash, half an ancient Ford sticking up out of its bed. Junipers straggled along the wash rim.

Three scruffy ponies, blankets and bundles lashed to their rumps, were tied to the hitching rail. Under a flat, cloudless sky, a young Navajo woman in dark velvet covered with silver buttons turned her face from the camera. Two spotted dogs, the history of a thousand matings in their tiny bodies and huge ears, crouched at her feet.

Liz opened her wallet. "My place," she said. She set the photo in Hatt's lap. The house looked very big and gray. Patches of snow lay over the dark grass. The sky was quilted with clouds.

"You owned that yourself?" Hatt asked.

"I did, bought it myself, paid for it myself."

Hatt touched her wrist. "Do you miss it?"

"No," Liz said. "Too many memories. Do you miss the post?"

"Yes," Hatt grinned. "Too many memories." She turned a page.

"And there he is," she smiled grimly. "The dear old boy, my husband John." He was built low to the ground. His broad face was masked by dark glasses and the shadow of a wide-brimmed black hat. He wore levis made for a much bigger man, and his shirt was open to its second button.

"He always looked like he was standing in a hole," Hatt laughed. "And he hated tight clothes!" He was tugging on the ends of his long, silvery mustache and grinning at the camera. Somebody had draped a pile of Navajo blankets around his shoulders. A flicker feather soared from the brim of his hat.

"He loved to clown," Hatt said. "The Indians loved him because he could give and take a joke. The Navajo men were always playing tricks on him and he'd pay them right back. He knew how to drive a fair bargain, too. He was one of the few traders around who didn't jack up his prices on government check day and he refused to use trading slugs. I'll give him that."

"Trading slugs?"

"Like company scrip," Hatt said. "Some of the early traders, the ones who have roads named for them now, would pay the Indians for goods with slugs that could only be used at their post. Not John. He paid good hard cash. He had his principles."

"No husband," Liz said. "One true love who wouldn't let people take his picture. Thought the camera sucked his spirit. I think he'd seen too many cowboy movies."

Hatt nodded. "They never grow up, do they?" she said vaguely.

"You mean it was never different?" Liz smiled.

"In that," Hatt said, "nothing changes. That's the first law. In my day, all we did different was keep them from knowing we knew." She turned the page. Someone had hand-tinted the full-page photo. The girl wore a pale yellow bow in her russet hair. The boy was decked out in a blue cowboy outfit. He held a coiled lariat in his hand and his cornsilk hair was a mess.

"That photo says it all," Hatt said. Her jaw was set in a fierce elegant line. "Jeannie and Roger, the little miss and the buckaroo. She couldn't wait to get away from here, to get East, to leave the dust and snakes and heat behind. You should see her house now; it's all in ivory! All Roger ever wanted to do was be out beyond the beyond, on his pony, with nothing but a canteen and a sack of dry meat." She snorted. "Apparently, those days are over."

"What's 'beyond the beyond'?"

"John used to say it was where you could stop believing that civilization existed."

"I wonder if it's gone." Liz said.

"I know," Hatt said. "I'd be back in one of those canyons at Tsegi, no sound, nobody but me and my pony. Those old cliffs and caves have a silence beyond silence. The Navajo don't like to go there. They think they are places of death and, for them, that is the Great Silence." She ran her hand over her blanket. "I would be out there, maybe at full moon, being a crazy old coot, and look up in all that silence and light and see a jet trail across the night-sky and wish I had an anti-aircraft gun." She paused. "Still, I'd be a liar if I said I didn't welcome electricity when it came to the res, power lines and all! Let me see some pictures of those babies of yours."

"My babies," Liz said and fanned out the photos, Steve, with his lop-sided grin, his big jaw and soft eyes; Jen, her sculpted taffy-blonde hair, her three earrings in her right ear; Keith, in white t-shirt and sportcoat two sizes too big, laughing, making a movie of her taking a picture of him making a movie of her; Tina, crouching, smiling like a great-eyed, cocoa Buddha.

"Well," Hatt snorted, "I don't know about those earrings and that baggy coat, but they look bright enough. I like those faces."

Liz laughed. "I never thought I'd have battles with *my* kids about how they dressed, but Jen and I went a few rounds. I think I was just jealous."

"I wish Jeannie and I *had* fought," Hatt said. "I would have loved her to show some spark. She was in such a hurry to grow up, to get safely tucked away in a nice marriage. We could have used some fights. All we had were 'nice' silences." She tapped the photo. "I was so happy when she was born. It was darn lonely out there on the post. Some of the Navajo ladies and I could talk, but their ways and mine were so different. I figured Jeannie and I would be friends, but it never worked out." She flipped the page.

"That is Kwaayo," she said. "That was. He has been gone for ten years."

A small man held up his hand as though to block the camera. But he was laughing and the photographer had caught him full-face. He wore faded jeans and jacket, and he wore them well. His thick black hair was cut in bangs. A heavy silver earring shone in his left ear.

"His name means Gray Hawk in our language," Hatt said. "He was a Hopi farmer and trader, the hardest worker I've ever known. He'd bring us cornmeal and his sisters' pots and, sometimes, a hand-carved Kachina doll to trade. They carved 'em from cottonwood roots; still do now, the real ones." She glanced around the room. "I miss mine." She looked back down at the photo.

"He told wonderful stories. They have a word, *tuwutsmoki;* it means to be a bag of stories. He was that, *tuwutsmoki.* He taught me a little Hopi, just enough that we could joke together. We had been laughing at some foolishness that day. That's the only way he let me take the photo. He was off his guard. I had to promise him I'd never let it out of my hands." She gently traced his dark hair. "They're like your friend," she said, "they believe the camera does something dreadful to spirit." She turned the page to other, slightly blurred, photographs. "I should burn these," she said. "Let them go. They are of a very old dance, the Rabbitskin. I think it's no longer done. So many of them are gone."

"Them?" Liz asked.

"The dances, the people," Hatt smiled. "My friends."

The dancers wore rabbit robes that enfolded them in pale shadows. Clouds of feathers drifted in their dark hair. Blurred, sunlit mesas rose behind them. Two ancient women, in one-shouldered dresses and black shawls, knelt with shallow baskets of corn in front of the dancers. The chimneys of the pueblo were stacked bowls, broken made useful. The print was cracked and faded, a vision of a dream seen through mist.

"I stopped taking pictures of ceremonies after that series," Hatt said. "I don't quite know why. Maybe it was Kwaayo. Maybe it was the way these photographs looked, even when I knew I had set everything correctly before I shot. John laughed at me. He said I was as spooky as an Indian." She flipped the page.

"You'd have loved this one," she said. "He was a rip. He told everybody he was Comanche, even grew those pigtails to prove it, but whenever he'd had a few, pure Boston would creep into his accent. He called himself Sand Wolf. He was a roving trader and gambler. He'd won that wildcat kitten he's got in his arms."

Sand Wolf leered at the photograher. You could tell he was trying to suck in his big gut. A skinny pigtail hung along each side of his slab-jawed face. He wore a fur hat and filthy leather chaps and four strings of turquoise over a squash-blossom necklace.

"He'd trade stuff right off his body," Hatt said. "He'd even try to trade his body. He thought he was quite the ladies' man." She laughed. "One afternoon, he came out back into the summer kitchen. It wasn't anything more than one of those brush ramadas, but it did the trick. There were juniper boughs for a roof. You can't imagine how good it smelled after the monsoons swept in, wet desert and juniper." She closed her eyes.

"I was cooking some chilis and mutton for supper. He just rumbled in and grabbed me around the waist. I had onions frying on the back burner, so I grabbed that pan and whanged him over the head. I let out a holler and by the time John walked in, Sand Wolf was cussing a streak and wiping onions out of his eyes." She smiled down at the picture. "John loved to tell that story. He always said that the best part was that Sand Wolf was such a pig that you couldn't tell where his hair began and the onions left off."

"Were you afraid often?"

"Not as much as you might think. John was around a lot. Kwaayo stayed with us, off and on, helping out, teaching us about Hopi crafts, getting some of the old stories told. I wore a gun and knew how to use it. As it came to pass, I only used it once and that was to blow the head off a rattler that got too close to Jeannie's baby basket." She turned the page and laughed.

"Well, there I am," she said. "What you see is what you got. I must have been all of twenty-five. That's Roger hanging on my leg and Jeannie on my hip. I used to worry I wouldn't remember how normal people walk."

Young Hatt was laughing, showing a mouthful of strong white teeth. Her eyes were crinkled from laughter and sun. She wore a calf-length khaki skirt, pale velvet blouse and heavy silver necklace. The bright-eyed baby reached for the silver crescent that hung between her breasts. Hatt had hair so blonde it was white. She'd pulled it back in a bun and that was perfect; her good bones, her eyes and smile were open to the camera.

"What a joyful shot," Liz said. "You look like you've got it all."

"I thought I did. John had given me that necklace for my birthday. That's a moon for plenty. We thought we were going to have ten more children. I'd just found out I was pregnant again." She paused. "I lost that baby. Kwaayo tried to help. He brought me some teas from his grandma, but it was too late. I never got pregnant again. I had a bad time for a while, but, looking back, it seems a blessing. So many of the wives—of the traders, the railroad men, the ranchers—would just breed and breed till they were old women at forty."

"I almost did that. They had to talk sense into me when I was twenty-five," Liz said. "For a woman with no talent for motherhood, I sure had the equipment."

"I've wondered about myself," Hatt said. "What kind of mother I was. My life was so different from *my* mother's." She sighed. "And in those days, children were supposed to be a kind of wealth, hands for the fields, the herds, the work and, somehow, something more."

"More?"

"A way to pass things on, important things." They sat in silence. Hatt closed the album.

"There are more," she said. "But, I'm still getting tired easily. I don't think the dead air in this place helps. I'd like to get a little shut-eye before supper."

"I have to meet a friend in a few minutes," Liz said. "Your timing is perfect. I hope when we meet again, it's in Kayenta. I keep thinking about that fry bread."

"So do I," Hatt said wryly.

"If, by some chance, you're still here Tuesday, can I bring you anything? I'll call first."

"I wish fry bread travelled," Hatt said. "Cold you can use it for retreads. There *is* something I'd like. I got used to having a glass of brandy each evening. I'd sit out back of the hogan, watching the sun go down and sipping my brandy. I never got tired of it. Brandy and the warm colors of sunset just seem to melt together." She hesitated. "Remy-Martin's my brand. Is that impossible? I'll pay you when you bring it. They've locked up my money. Did I tell you that?"

"Of course," Liz said. "Of course Remy-Martin and of course they locked up your money. They wouldn't want you running amok in the Gift Shoppe."

"No," Hatt mused, "all those lovely bleach-bottle piggy banks and crocheted toilet paper covers."

Thirteen

REGGAE THUMPED THROUGH THE CONCHO'S CRACKED BRICK WALLS. The place was one of the originals, back when Cowboy Row was a place only cowboys wanted to visit. Slade, the new owner, was a tall nervous gentleman, from the Bronx by way of Lake Havasu City. He'd bought the Concho off the wife of its hallucinating former owner, cleaned out a truckload of empties and three stinking mattresses from the big back room and made a dance floor. Then, in a gesture of faith, he'd ripped off the boards covering the front windows and set in bullet-proof glass. His faith was not stupidity. He was still tense about the change. A couple of displaced cowboys had threatened his disputed manhood—he always wore dark glasses but you could see his eyes shifting behind them.

The windows had gradually darkened under the accretion of tobacco smoke, so nothing seemed that different. You could still get a beer or two on a bad morning and believe it was already night. The college cowboys and armchair Sundance Kids loved the place. They could order up a Dos Eq and pretend they were real sons of the Old West. They were all in there, bouncing to the Old West beat of Peter Tosh when Liz peered in the front window.

She saw Deena through the smoky glass, a cool island of blonde dignity in a murk of lonesome eyes, cruising desperation, drunk cowboys 'n' Indians and sullen mountain men. Liz pushed open the heavy door. The bouncer took her two bucks and stamped her wrist. She looked down. No grace note. A blue rearing stallion glowed on her skin. Deena sat quietly, sipping a beer with that careful inattention of a pretty woman in a bar. Liz tapped her shoulder.

"You all alone, honey?" she asked. Deena bowed her head.

"Have mercy on me," she said. "You're the fourth person to ask me that in the last fifteen minutes." She took her coat off the barstool next to her. "I am *so* glad to see you." She poked Liz and rolled her eyes toward the end of the bar. A man glared at them, a buckaroo in a spotless white Stetson and gorgeous business suit.

"Ralph Lauren?" Liz murmured.

"Not with that hair," Deena said. "I cannot abide hair spray on men!" He raised his glass to them and laughed.

"Hew ha," Liz said.

"He asked me if I was alone," Deena said. "I told him I was waiting for a friend. He asked me if he might be the friend. I said No. He called me Honey and allowed as to how I reminded him of his ex-wife. Who he'd left. Who wanted him back. Who he was squat through with. I ignored him. He sat down. He told me that he was not just some ordinary jerk. I said I could see that. He is a mining engineer. He has a master's in Engineering. He asked me if I knew the noise an armadillo makes when you run over it. At that point, the bartender told him to move on."

"You let him go?" Liz asked.

"Give me a break."

"Before you found out?"

"Before I found out what?"

"The noise!"

"No," Deena said. "I knew you'd want to know what with being new out here and all. That was his last shot. 'Between a crunch and a splat,' he said. He said that was the noise his heart made when I broke it."

"I'm glad I'm here," Liz said.

"I'm going to be celibate for the rest of my life," Deena said. "I swear it."

"I believe I will have that drink," Liz said. The bartender refilled Deena's beer and brought Liz a double gin and soda. She rubbed the lime around the edge of the glass and took a deep whiff.

"Lime and juniper," she said. "They were made for each other."

"That's how I feel about me and M&Ms," Deena said. "Born to be." She pulled a mini-bag out of her purse and dumped them on her cocktail napkin.

"No!" Liz said.

"Out here, greenhorn," Deena said, "it's real bad manners to comment on another man's drinking habits."

"Sorry, hombre," Liz said.

"You'll learn. How's Hatt?"

"She's great. She showed me pictures from her past . . . you'd love them . . . the trading post, her friends, her kids, herself. She was so warm. I can't get over how open it is out here."

"I think it's left over from the early days," Deena said. "I bet all those pioneer women had to make friends fast and enjoy the company while it lasted."

"Good idea," a voice said over Liz's shoulder. "Life's short." Liz looked at Deena.

"Those ventriloquism-by-mail lessons are working," she said. "Except you sound like a guy and you sound drunk."

Deena glanced down at her nails. "It's nothing," she said. "Did I ever tell you the one about the armadillo?"

Liz looked up into the long mirror behind the bar. One of the more-or-less mountain men stood behind her, wire rim glasses, beard, flannel shirt, graying ponytail. He was grinning blissfully.

"You're built for dancing," he said.

"Who?"

"You, Curly," he said.

"I hate reggae," she said.

"I do too. I just thought you might want to get to know me. My name's Ian MacLeod and I hate mining engineers."

"That's one thing we have in common," Liz said. "Now, what with good manners and the other ninety-nine things we don't, I think we better break each other's heart right now."

"George Hayduke is my hero," he grinned.

"Okay, that's two things going for you and, if you leave, we'll have three."

"I'm bored with preliminaries," he said.

"That's three and I'm out of here." She picked up her wallet. "Coffee?" she said to Deena. Deena sat tight.

"You know," she said, "you could just ignore him."

"Please!" Liz said.

The man lurched forward and tugged off his truck-hat.

"Listen," he said. "I'm no yuppie. You can count on that." Liz side-stepped his big body and stared him square in the eye.

"No shit!" she said. He grinned.

"A lady with spirit," he said. She headed towards the door.

Outside, Deena tapped her shoulder. "You okay?" she asked.

The evening eastbound train wailed in the distance. "Nice touch, that whistle," Liz said. "Yeah, I'm okay. Maybe not. I *liked* that. I liked that a drunk stranger talked to me. You don't know what it's like to be my age. I'm scared to death. I'm scared nobody will ever hold me again. Sometimes I get so lonesome I'd go with anything that had working male parts."

"I've got the answer," Deena said. "Come on. There's a great diner on . . . where else? . . . the edge of town." Liz stared at the late night traffic. "Come on," Deena said. "Coffee! Home fries! Home-made apple pie!" She grabbed Liz's scarf and tugged her around the corner.

Liz started to laugh. "Wait," she said. Deena stopped. "My kids," Liz said. "When I'd get like that, they'd hold a pity party for me. They'd stand around in a circle and sing 'Pooooooooor Mo-om.'"

"You should *not* have told me that," Deena said. "That was a big mistake."

The Queen Diner and Motel ("Get a Royal Knight's Sleep") blazed up out of the darkness. They parked, walked into the bright dining-room and took a booth on the highway side, the green watery glow of the big "Queen" neon sign flickering on their faces. The blonde waitress brought coffee in thick cups. She was smoking as she took their order; she narrowed her perfectly painted eyes against the smoke and called them "girls."

"Girls, what'll it be?"

Liz wanted to curl up in her voice, it was that warm, that welcoming.

"The usual," Deena said, "twice." She grinned at Liz. "Trust me."

She lit a cigarette. "Smokes, bless 'em. They calm me down, they pick me up." She sipped her coffee. "What was that all about back there? That tizzy in the bar?"

"It was all about a tizzy."

"What if I hadn't been there?"

"It would have been about trouble," Liz said. "I would have danced with him. He would have walked me to my car. He would have made a pass. I would have grabbed a significant body part. After that, your guess is as good as mine." She laughed. "I am a closet slut, sweetie."

"Oooh nice," Deena said. "You name it, you're gonna claim it, so shut your mouth."

"Well, what *do* you call women who sleep with men in order to feel pretty, to feel valuable, to feel like they really do exist?"

"Messed-up," Deena said. The waitress set their plates down on the table.

"Pie later?" she said.

"Check," Deena said.

"My kind of women," the waitress said. Liz stared out the window.

"I know," she said. "I just have big trouble with men, certain kinds of men, that's all."

"Well, who doesn't," Deena asked.

"Not like this," Liz said. "I lost count when I was thirty. I tried to stop after Nick left, but I always hope that it'll be different and it never is. Part of it is I love sex so much it's like praying, it's like belonging. It was always like that with Nick. There was a power, a mindlessness, I don't know."

Deena touched her hand. "I envy you," she said. "You've lived. You can't help that they're messed-up. You can't do a thing about that."

"Except stay away," Liz said. "The older I get, the easier it gets. But I've sure been dragged kicking and screaming into this time alone."

"I love it!" Deena said fiercely. "This time alone, I won't think about doing whatever you have to do to get something started. Shoot, I'm hardly home to myself. I don't know that I'd even know what that feels like. I went straight from Dad and more-or-less Mom to Jack. I want to be my own home for a while." She laughed. "I sound like one of those awful how-you-can-be-perfect new women's magazines. I hate 'em!"

"You can do everything they suggest. You just need twenty-eight hours a day and a full-time houseboy."

"I'd end up taking care of *him*." Deena laughed.

"I know. I'm still taking care of Nick's ghost. I see something beautiful, I think of him; I hear something funny, I think of him; I want to send him the light, the canyon walls."

"Listen," Deena said flatly, "as much as I wish it wasn't, Jack's ghost is with me every day. He was It!, in the sweetest way; now, he's It, in the nastiest. One minute I was lying on my beach towel, watching him ride the big ones in; the next, he's flipping the bird to my friend's car."

"The American Dream," Liz said. "We could write one of those magazines. We could get rich. We've lived through enough. Plus we're hooked on everything the average American woman, whoever she is, is."

"Take notes," Deena said. "I'm going to tell you the story of the marriage that couldn't be saved."

The waitress rounded the corner with two slabs of blueberry pie dripping with ice cream. "I took a shot," she said. "It's what I have for breakfast. You don't like it this way, I'll pay. It's been a boring night."

"I'd like to move a cot in here," Liz said.

"I'm sure the manager would love it. It'd take the pressure off the rest of us." She refilled their cups. "I'm at the counter if you need me."

Deena smeared the ice cream over her pie. "I am about to be very happy in the midst of telling a very unhappy story," she said. "He was my hero. Life at home was ridiculous. My mom drank, my dad roamed. Jack was big man on the beach and in my heart. He worked at it. He defended me. His family took me in. I was thrilled to be his girl, his *fiancée*, his wife.

"After a while, he seemed to think that I was his *thing*. We'd go to parties and he'd get mad every time I talked to someone, male or female. And the minute I started to have fun, he'd want to go home. If I was late back from the store or my part-time job, which he'd finally allowed me to take because he'd gotten us so far in debt, he'd sulk the rest of the evening. He wanted me to take on his beliefs, his atheism, his political party. I'd walk by the magazine rack and see *Ms* and wonder if I was living on the same planet. That was one year ago, Liz, one year ago."

"What happened?"

"It was Deej. That's what snapped me out of there. He had control of the checkbook, the car, my vote, my soul, but when it came to Deej, I couldn't let it happen. Mealtimes were nightmares. He had all these ideas about child-rearing. 'Spoiled' is a big one with him. He'd nag her and nag her, and her just a baby. Finally one night, he sat with her till midnight, demanding that she clean her plate. The food was cold and dried out and she wouldn't touch it. She just sat there, with her jaw set and tears running down her cheeks. She didn't make a sound. When I tried to get to her, he'd punch me. I had bruises all up and down my arms.

"Finally, he jammed the spoon into her mouth and cut her lip and I went crazy. I truly saw red—the air went red. I grabbed her and the car keys that, by some miracle, weren't in *his* pocket and I took off." She glared down at her plate.

"And it's no-way over," she continued. "It's just started. He's going after Deej big-time, I can tell. He's got the money and he's got the lawyer. His folks are rich."

"You're not alone," Liz said. "I watched my friend Lainie go through the same mess. I'm an expert in standing by."

"Thanks," Deena said. "Some days, all I want to do is crawl up in my dad's lap and have him tell me everything is going to be okay. He's great; he calls, he sends ten bucks every now and then. He'd hire a hit-man if I asked him."

"Where's your more-or-less mom in all of this?"

"She's really out there. Really out there. Earth-to-mom, you know? She nagged my dad till he left, then she took on California wine as her mid-life hobby. Her falling apart like that was weird. She'd always run the family, kept the checkbook . . .

"The craziest part is what *I* did night after night when he'd come home late, she'd be loaded, us kids down in the television room. She'd start in on him and I'd run into the bathroom and lock the door. I didn't want the other kids to see me because I'd be down on my knees praying to God. I promised Him that if He'd stop the fighting, I'd dedicate my life to getting married and making it work!

"So, *He* blew it and here *I* am, sitting in the Queen at two in the morning, smoking cigarettes, which my daughter hates, while she's asleep at her father's and he's drinking beer and watching a videotape of Kramer vs. Kramer and wishing I was dead."

Deena blew her nose on the napkin. "Twelve years of marriage," she said. "Do you believe that? *Twelve years!*"

"I think God, to whom I give little credit, owes you one," Liz said.

"I'm ready," Deena said. "He can make it in the form of full custody." She picked up the check. "You ready? I feel better, by the way."

"Pie will do that," Liz said. "I could curl up on this seat till morning."

Driving back to Deena's car, they were both quiet. The heater hummed and it seemed a fine place to be, in a warm car, with a friend and silence, rolling down a black highway into a town free of memories.

Home, Liz made a fire, and that, too, was fine, to feel tired and peaceful, to see the light dancing like Northern Lights on the dark ceiling . . .

. . . "They are coming," Rupi whispered. The eagle screamed. From the western *tuukwi* came an answering cry. Through the dusty wash, their feet sending up golden clouds in the morning light, around the black cinder cone, they came: first the Powamu Chief, unmasked, wearing a tall eagle plume and bright embroidered kilt; then the Kachina Father and his helper, in plain cloth, their Spirit faces stern and serene; then, pair after pair of Hemis Kachinas and the female Kachina Manas. Though Talasi had seen them for many summers, since before she could remember, they always made her breathless. They were Spirit and they were People, carrying mystery in their proud bodies. Hemis—far-away, their beauty stronger because they came from far-away and they would always leave.

Talasi took Rupi's hand. There was too much joy in her for one person.

"They are so beautiful," she said.

"Yes," Rupi sighed. Then, she giggled. "Especially that small one on the end, the one with the brown squirrel on his kilt. See how he moves. He is so young and so small, but he is full of strength." Talasi laughed. Whatever Rupi looked at, man or kachina, she always saw the same thing: a husband.

They were not husbands who came slowly into the plaza, nor sons, nor fathers; they were Hemis Kachinas, black, white brotherhood signs painted on their breasts. Feathery spruce hung from their belts and through their rain-blue armbands. In their left hands they carried spruce and a white *paho*, in their right a blue rattle. A string of copper bells chimed on their left ankles; deer-hoof and turtle rattles rasped on their right leg.

No human feeling crossed their stern faces. Power trembled in the feathers and wild grain that rose from their tiered wooden headdresses, painted with rainbows and white butterflies.

I have seen those every summer day of my life, Talasi thought, the little butterflies. By daylight they can be scarcely seen, by night they are like little spirits. I have seen everything the Hemis Kachina wears.

The Kachina Manas came into view. They were Spirit maidens, in black *manas*, red-and-white blankets and white deerskin leggings. White *pahos* shimmered on their heads. Each carried a gourd, a notched stick and a long deerbone. Male and female alike, they moved through the sacred patterns of the dance, tracing the migration paths, singing the story of the People. The old Kachina Father shouted encouragement in his thin voice. The sun moved higher and higher in the summer sky, the earth trembled under their dancing. The songs and bells and drums and rattles swelled together four times, four sacred times, till it seemed to Talasi that Father Sun Himself moved to the Kachina's praise.

As swiftly as the Kachinas had entered, they were gone. It was silent.

Mothers and grandmothers hurried back to their hearths. The children straggled back to their houses. Talasi felt snared, woven into the earth by the sacred music.

"Wake up," Rupi said. "Come to my mother's house for food. We can play dolls."

Dolls! Talasi thought. I don't want to play with dolls. I want to dance. I want to be one of the Kachina Manas, not play with a bit of root carved to look like them. She took Rupi's hand. They ran past the tethered eagle. Rupi sidestepped his scarred perch. Talasi stopped and studied his great, golden eyes.

We are not so different, she thought. I would free you if I could . . .

. . . Something scratched at the door. Liz stumbled out of bed. Sugar was curled on her desk, her tiny belly beginning to swell with kittens.

"Better you than me," Liz muttered. She opened the door. Bob strolled in, sauntering straight to the bed and curled up on her pillow. Liz settled back in with him and fell asleep to his bass purr . . .

. . . In mid-afternoon the dancers returned. With them came two brides who had married since the last Going Home. Rupi could hardly stand still.

"Someday," she whispered, "we will be there. We will kneel on the antelope skins. We will receive the Sacred Pollen blessing. We will be so beautiful." The brides were wonderful in their wedding robes, cloud-white breath feathers and woven fertility pods seeming to float from the hems. Their faces were solemn, their cheeks bright with paint and pride.

"Who will you choose?" Rupi giggled. "Will you choose that messy boy, that Shadow boy?"

"Hush," Talasi snapped, "we will be seen whispering and they will not give us gifts."

Rupi smiled at her. She poked Talasi in the ribs. "You are so serious," she said. "Everybody knows about you and that boy. No one cares."

Talasi smiled. "He is nothing to me," she said, "no more than a shadow." Ahqawu's grandmother turned around and stared at them. Talasi stepped on Rupi's foot. They both began to giggle, hands over their mouths, eyes fixed helplessly on each other, the laughter shaking their bodies.

"Stop," Talasi whispered.

"I can't."

The grandmother started to back towards them.

"Think of something sad," Rupi gasped.

"I can't," Talasi answered.

"Good," Rupi said, "I will." She made such a downcast face that it set Talasi off again. The grandmother moved in between them.

"Soyok Wuhti watches," she said. Both girls fell silent. The grandmother walked slowly back to her place. Soyok Wuhti, Ogre Woman visited every Bean Dance time. She had frightened little Sikya so deeply he had fallen ill and nearly died. Rupi shuddered. Talasi took her hand. They looked toward the gift-pile, toward the bows and arrows and plaques and dolls. Soyok Wuhti was far-away; the gifts were part, as she was, of the cycle of the seasons, the Great Spiral of the lessons.

The Kachinas began to move into the crowd carrying the gifts. There were the sweetest first corn and trays of red and white and yellow *piki*. There were woven plaques, made from yucca, split fine, dyed with sunflower seeds, red berries, smoke, even with the seasons' change, for the yucca spines were white in summer and yellow by the time of the Women's Dances. Set carefully at the edge of the gift-pile were the dolls: Hemis Kachina; Sowi'ing Kachina, with its antelope horns and tail; Mongwu Kachina, with its big staring eyes; Tsuku, the little clowns; Hahai-i Wuhti, Kachina Mother, with her many names and faces. There was Red-Tail Hawk and Toho and Eagle and Deer. They were toys and more. To see their flat wooden bodies and bright paint was to remember who Deer was and why Eagle was kin and how Toho hunted and killed, never with waste, always with respect.

The Kachinas walked slowly from child to child. There was no pattern to their path. A child could not guess whether she would be next or last. Rupi and Talasi stood tall and silent. They were beyond giggles, no longer tiny children to point or gasp or bounce on their bare heels. The smaller Kachina circled the plaza. His stern eyes looked straight ahead. He passed the girls, then turned and came back to stop in front of Rupi. His partner joined him, an old Kachina, his chest and legs wiry with years and hunger and work. They moved forward. The younger held out a plaque to Rupi; the other, to Talasi, a black doll.

She looked down and stiffly bowed her thanks. The old Kachina pressed the doll firmly in her hands. She did not want it. She wanted corn or *piki*. Nothing would have pleased her more. Her fingers closed around the flat body. She felt its power. She knew its shape, its dark colors. It was female. On one side Her hair was neatly coiled in the maiden's whorl; on the other it hung loose and uncombed. She was He'wuhti, Warrior Woman, hair half-done as it had been the day She rushed out to join the men fighting off a surprise attack. She led a guardian warrior band during the Pachavu Ceremony. *She* was so powerful that sometimes other Kachinas stood guard as shield against Her presence. Talasi pressed the doll to her heart. She raised her head and looked the old Kachina full in the face. There was only dark behind the narrow eye slits of his mask. He nodded, turned and was gone.

"Talasi," Rupi whispered. "Look." She held up her gift, a woven plaque, yellow and brown and sand. In its center, stood a little squirrel . . .

. . . Sugar leaped onto the bed and curled herself in the arc of Bob's body. He grumbled once and was silent. Liz absently stroked them, Bob's short, rough fur, Sugar like a warm cloud . . .

. . . Indigo shadows stretched across the plaza. Everyone, mothers, grandmothers, children, gamblers and weavers and babies and young lovers and the woman who made the best *piki* and the girl who made the worst, filed out onto the rooftops and crowded the alleys. The Kachinas filled the plaza, the Hemis Kachinas standing, their rattles and bells and voices silent. The Kachina Manas knelt. Setting the notched stick on the hollow gourd, each began to draw the deer bone over the stick. As the stick vibrated, the gourd sent out a great, dull buzzing. The Hemis Kachinas began to move, bells, turtle shell rattles, their heavy steps on the plaza floor, weaving in and around the great, dull buzz of the gourds.

Talasi pressed her hands into the wall behind her. She felt her heartbeat slip into the music's rhythm. She closed her eyes. The rough wall under her fingertips, the dirt beneath her feet were the only tethers for her spirit. She held to them. The music became a cloudy path. She could not sense beyond the next long curve. The air shuddered, the earth, as though a great being breathed, deeply, steadily, in perfect ease.

"Open your eyes," Rupi whispered. "You will miss them. They are going home."

The Kachina Father's farewell rang out. The Kachina leader shook his rattle, in answer, in good-bye. The People moved forward in a bright wave to receive from the Kachinas the twigs of spruce that would bless the fields. In silence, they stepped back. In silence, the scarlet curve of sun dropped below the black *tuukwi*. In silence, black themselves against the brilliant wash of light, the Kachinas filed out of the plaza.

No one followed. The light cooled. The shrill of crickets rose up and faded away. The women watched, their faces both weary and peaceful. A sweet evening wind came up; the dark bulk of the *tuukwi* closed round the tiny figures of the Kachinas and they disappeared . . .

Fourteen

THERE WERE NO WINDOWS IN THE LIBRARY OF QUMOVI TUUWA. It could have been ten miles or ten centuries distant from the main visitor center. Except for the mad buzz of the fluorescent light, there was no sound, and if you turned off the light and sat in the soft greenish glow from the outside corridor, it was a little like being underwater. There was the silence, the shifting light, the sort of dead, filtered air you might breathe through a mask.

Liz bent over old archeology reports that Paul was culling for juniper references. She copied names and numbers till her fingers ached, and filed away the neat cards. The light hurt her eyes. She switched it off and sat in the half-dark. Driving in, the night's dreams had lapped at the edges of her thoughts. The scream of a red-tailed hawk had frightened her, the sun had felt more welcome than usual, the shadows cooler, more poignant. Here, in the gloom, she could barely see the shelves filled with Pueblo II pots and ragged baskets and dusty mysteries.

A rattle, its head a gourd, its hair split raven feathers, grinned down at her. Two hawks' primaries hung from a twisted fiber cord tied four times around the handle. She climbed up and took the rattle down.

Its carved head fit perfectly in her palm. She tapped it against her hand, and closed her eyes. The rattle did not rattle; it gave sea-waves on sand, sleet on windowpanes, a diamondback's warning, a mother's hush to calm a frightened child, and a far older sound, a sound of making and unmaking, as though lava poured into icy water, steam exploding, rising, condensing, falling back as rain and rising again. A rhythm began to form. She remembered the Arabian music she had once danced to, the drone of old Irish dirges, the pulse of African planting songs. Behind her closed eyes, against that green light, she saw people dancing and corn tassels and flat figures with great eyes, their mouths unmoving and silent. She saw something golden struggling in light and shadow. Human or other . . . she could not tell.

The dream-door opened. White light flooded in.

"Liz!" Paul's voice came from everywhere. She forced her eyes open. He was standing next to her, and she could see every thread in the cloth of his uniform and smell the dust in its creases. She knew what small canyon was floored with that dust. She stared up at Paul. His skin seemed terrible, without color, without warmth.

"Don't drop it," he said. She clutched the handle of the rattle and sat down. The room wavered, the walls drifted and came into shape. Paul's face was gray.

"I'm sorry," she said. In the saying, she knew it wasn't true. She was angry. She wanted to go back, to the green light, the people dancing, the music, and to those flat, dark, silent figures.

"No," he said. "I'm sorry, I jumped the gun. I'm so touchy about the things in this room. They're fragile, irreplaceable, and we're losing so much." She nodded. "That one, in particular. We haven't even wanted to carbon date it, but it's easily eight hundred years old." He laughed. "You can't tell what you could shake up with something like that. Those raven feathers. That face."

"The warning may have come too late," Liz said.

"How so?"

"I've been having these dreams. I don't remember them clearly. Just bits and pieces. I sort of drifted off just now." She handed the rattle to Paul. He shook it once.

"You ever go up to Hopi?" he asked.

"Just once," Liz said. "I made a fool of myself. I haven't wanted to go back."

"What happened?"

"It was classic. I'd gone up to the mesas straight from Mesa Verde, with a heart full of good will and a head full of mysticism. I was with a friend. We were standing at the edge of the plaza in one of the old villages. There was a fierce wind. I had grit in my hair and my ears and my teeth. I remember a pop can blowing off a roof and clattering at my feet."

"Then the wind died," Paul said gently.

"Yes. I looked down at the pop can. I can see it right now. It was a Dr. Pepper, crushed on one side. There was total silence. The plaza had filled with people and the silence seemed strange to me. I thought I heard a baby cry, a drawn-out wail, but I couldn't see any babies within range. The cry came again, from above. I looked up. There was nothing, no bird, no speck in the sky that might have been a bird. It was a hawk's cry, I was sure of that. And then the silence deepened."

Paul touched the back of her hand. "And the dancers came into the plaza and the only thing you could hear was the sound of their leg rattles."

"Yes, that's exactly how it was. I could hear those rattles and the faintest chime of bells, then, suddenly, there were drums and wind and singing."

"And you forgot where you were?" he grinned.

"Yep, I plunked myself right down on some stone steps, oblivious to the looks I was getting. Davie told me about it afterwards. He said, 'Never mind, luv, you Yanks are always like that.'"

They worked on one of the small mesitas till dusk, repairing ORV gouges, Paul cussing steadily. Liz drove home toward the Peaks, their snow crimson and rose. The night was warm. She took her supper out to the pines and ate, watching the moon sail above the black branches, in air as silvery as moonlight. Bob and Sugar and a nameless ginger tom played mountain lion in the meadow, lifting their paws delicately out of the patches of snow that shone against the dark earth. Sugar leaped and twisted in mid-air, her tail a frosty plume. Bob waited, crouched behind a fallen limb, conservation of energy his creed. His green eyes glittered. His tail barely twitched. The ginger tom perched on a stump, his ragged ears pressed flat to his head. Liz tossed a pine cone. Bob erupted from his hiding place. Sugar tumbled over herself in terror, snow flying, glittering. The ginger tom yowled once and was gone.

She'd built the fire too high for the time of year. Propping the door open and settling in the rocking chair, she rested her feet on the desk, and began to read an old journal she'd found in the library. It was as though the writer sat with her, a pot of tea between them, their shoes off, the woman telling of following her stern husband across five states to settle in an isolated trading post near Canyon de Chelly.

Her husband had been a dark man, a silent, driven, hardworking man of granite. She had adored him. Through drought and flash flood, rabid coyote and rattlesnakes, illness and healing ceremonies, feasts and hunger, she had kept her journal, faithful to it and to the man who, she wrote, she would follow into death.

Liz closed the door and damped the fire. The bed looked cold. She remembered Paul's touch on her wrist, that light, companion's touch. Nick had never touched her that way. She didn't think he was capable of casual touch. She ran her hands over her body and cupped her breasts, warm and full under the flannel gown. She hated touching herself. It was a mockery. She thought of the thousand times she had told some grieving woman that she must learn to love herself, to please herself, to heal the hollow left by the lover. The best she could do was to rub the ache out of her shoulders.

"I would have gone anywhere with *you*," she whispered. He was so far, to the northeast, somewhere between the Sacred Mountains and where dawn would melt in. She faced that way and felt an old pull, as though her heart leaped toward him, then, tethered, fell back. "But without you," she said, "I've come here. And there's peace here. And dreams."

She settled into the quilts. They were warm from the fire, the pillow cool beneath her cheek. She remembered his touch, how the blood leapt, how she could not relax once his skin brushed hers. And for the first time, she saw clearly how little affection there had been, and she knew she was lonely for just that . . .

. . . "Aunt," Talasi said, "this is the hard path." She rocked over the grinding stone, her back burning, sweat stinging her eyes, the trough emptying, filling, emptying, filling. She did not pause. "I cannot sing with this work as the other maidens do. And yet, this is part of the path. I know that. I study the bowl, dawn after dawn, evening after evening. Curve by curve, the path becomes more clear." She smiled ruefully. "Three years and I know a small finger's length of it."

"You have not complained until now."

"No. Today Kihsi asked me to go with him to old Toho. He was afraid. I could not go. My mother had this work for me and there is a rabbit to clean for supper and, later, I will go to the spring with the other maidens. Last night, my mother and my aunt and old Tuvumsi went to the spring before sundown and did not come back till just before First Dawn." She scattered more cracked corn in the grinding trough.

"I saw this as a girl. This work is never-ending. We gather and cook and carry water and grind and wash and throw away and always there is more, more mouths to feed, more scraps to carry away. For the other maidens, there is hope. They can grind and dream of husbands, of babies. All *I* have is the work, and, for the cold times, the dark. I am away from the sun. I am away from the tracks and stones and changing light, the things that are my teachers. I am away from my life."

Pamosi crouched next to her. "I cannot give you comfort," she said. "Your woman's path is a mystery. I know this work must seem without meaning, save for what you learn of plants and healing. I pray you will be permitted to use that knowledge. I do not know why Spirit has chosen this harsh way for you. You are old beyond your twelve winters and this path is older."

Talasi pushed harder into the work. She was at the third stage of grinding, when the meal becomes fine as the red dust that blows off Two-Color Mountain. Pamosi pinched a bit between thumb and forefinger.

"This hard path," she said, "you walk it well." She touched Talasi's shoulder for a second.

"Thank you, Aunt," Talasi said. "For your words and for your touch." She bowed. Pamosi returned the bow and climbed up the ladder through the roof-hole. Her steps faded. The room was silent.

Talasi turned away from the grinding stone. She buried her face in her aching hands and, through tears, saw Kihsi by the grinding window, his face thinned out into manhood. He was fourteen winters, moving deeper into the men's world. He had long ago stopped hiding from her in boasting and mocking words. Again and again, they had slipped away, as gifted at being unseen as the cottontail, who, unmoving, might be rock or shadow. They had wandered the small canyons, studying the prairie dog and its underground cities; gathering plants for Pamosi's teas and paints; finding the broken bowls of the Old Ones and the sunken earth where their buried dwellings lay.

"Toho has called for me," Kihsi had said. "I am to go today. I am afraid. You know he is of both Snake Clan and Society. I do not know if my mother has promised me to them . . . in exchange . . ." He did not finish his words. They looked into each others' eyes. Tsohtsona's gambling and games with men had continued. She still walked with pride, her bold beauty unfaded. It was common, bitter gossip that someone's husband had been seen near her grinding window and someone's son had walked with her beyond the village. She wore many strings of turquoise. More hung from the walls of her house. She had no woman friend.

Talasi had waited for Kihsi to speak. He looked away, then, with his frightened eyes fixed on hers, he had asked her to go with him.

"You know this elder," he said. "I think he is kind, but he is called Toho for good reason. I have heard he can pounce on a person's mind, he can play with their spirit."

Talasi watched him. She knew what it cost for him to ask for help. Men did not do that. It was qahopi.

"No," she said, "I cannot go. I have work to do. I must do it."

Kihsi had touched her cheek gently with his rough fingers.

"You will be with me," he had said.

She turned back to the grinding. As she rocked over the stone, she thought of the grace and strength of his body; she was with the pulse of his heart, the breath that moved him over the long trail to Toho's place. These thoughts became a rhythm, then a story, then a song. She pushed into the work . . . she sang . . . the corn seemed to melt into meal and she knew another length of path was clear, no bigger than a corn kernel, deep and endless as a song . . .

Fifteen

ROSE STOOD IN HER MOTHER'S KITCHEN. The kids were gone. She had waked them twice, hunted down their lost sneakers, fed them and walked them to the schoolbus. Her mother was dipping day-old pastry in her coffee and talking. Talking, and talking.

"I do not know where he gets the money," she droned. "He does not send me what he should. I have to drive by Johnny's, that wicked place, and see him stagger out with some slut, some Tasavu whore. Your cousin, Connie, sees him and she thinks it is funny. She thinks it is okay to be in the streets, to be drinking with men, with strangers, pahaanas, Mexicans, black men, who knows? He was such a fine, young man. So strong. So hardworking." She sighed. Rose knew her feet could get her out of there. All she had to do was walk to the door. Class was at ten. She had an hour to sit somewhere in peace and quiet. But she stepped right in, and as usual, it was quicksand.

"Yes, Mother," she said patiently, "he does these things and as long as you let him come here and sleep off his drunks and eat the food I pay for, and cry on your shoulder about what a terrible man he is and how it is the *pahaana's* fault, and, how if only you would take him back, he would never, ever do it again, he will continue. He will . . ." Rose stopped. Her own stale words seemed to fill the room. She saw herself, her mother, trapped, sitting and standing at this battered formica table for months, for years, for centuries. For centuries they had done this. For more centuries, they would go on, complaining and advising, whining and comforting, an abyss far wider than the ugly tabletop separating them. She patted her mother's shoulder.

"I need to go," she said. "I will be late for class." Her mother's dark eyes snapped into focus.

"Class is not till ten," she said.

"I have to stop at the library," Rose said. Her mother sighed.

"Well, if you must. I will make stew for supper tonight, some fry bread. You like that."

Rose nodded. It was an old and familiar offer of peace.

"That would be good," she said.

"Are you going to wear those pants?" her mother asked. "They are too tight. You must watch your weight. We Indian women need to be careful, you know that. We need to make a good impression."

Rose pressed her palms onto the edge of the table, the small pain clearing her thoughts. She could step back into quicksand, into a spiral of criticism and defense, defense and criticism. She would skip class and spend the rest of the day eating and hating herself.

"I will wear my long sweater," she said. "At work, I have my lab coat. I must go."

Her mother poured another cup of coffee and sighed bitterly.

"I only mean to help," she said.

"I know. I will be home right after work, if I can. If not, I will call." She bent and kissed the part in her mother's hair. There was not a strand of gray. She might have been a young woman, a child.

"I mean no harm," her mother said and folded her worn hands in her lap.

Rose gathered her purse and coat, walked calmly to the front door and stepped out into full sunlight, icy blue sky, woodsmoke heavy and sweet in the air. She carefully closed the door behind her and started to laugh.

"Ah, Great Mystery," she said, "thank you for helping me escape that kitchen. Thank you, whoever You are, whatever You are, for this day. Whatever it brings." She climbed into her car, started the engine and turned on the radio. Somebody was singing something about loving somebody. She clicked it off and pulled out of the muddy drive, singing, singing a silly old song she had learned in Girl Scouts ten centuries ago.

"The eentsy-beentsy spider climbed up the water spout . . ."

The day rolled along. She got an A for a research paper; there were parking places whenever she needed them; she treated herself to lunch and watched, without pain, all the beautiful boys. If she could walk out of that kitchen, she could walk out of anything. Beautiful boys were for the looking; she didn't have to stay any longer than a sweet fantasy. Beautiful boys were just another kind of quicksand. She sipped her coffee, licked the whipped cream off her lips and watched the honeys saunter by.

The Camaro was in the Tenderhome parking lot. Liz had slapped a sticker on the back bumper: "Life's too short to dance with ugly men." Rose grinned. She had a door to reopen with Liz. Good to have a joke for the unlocking. She found Liz waiting by the nursing station, looking worried.

"Let me change," Rose said. "I'll be right back."

Liz sat on the edge of the low bookcase. The blinds were open. She could watch the sun drop behind the fat hills that rose beyond the parking lot. An aide wiped off the tables. She remembered how their surface felt, the film of something, soap, grease; she imagined eating at them and shivered. Rose tapped her on the shoulder.

"How are you?" she said. "It's been a while." She blushed. "I had terminal pre-menstrual syndrome the last time we talked."

"I nearly died from it a few times, myself," Liz laughed. "Or my family nearly did, I'm not sure. How's today?"

"Ovulating," Rose grinned. "If my aunt heard me, she'd swat my butt."

"Ooohh, women's things!" Liz said.

"Powerful!" Rose said. "*Now* is when I feel like I can do anything!"

"That's the trouble," Liz said. "Those hormones start firing-up and I get dumb."

Rose laughed. "I like that bumper sticker."

"That was vengeance. I saw a sticker on some jerk's truck that said, 'Save the whales; spear a fat chick.' Voluptuous as I am, it irritated me."

"Plus, it makes no sense."

"Mine does."

Rose looked up at the clock. "I've got to get to work. Why don't you stop by after you visit Hatt?"

"I'd love to. I've got a couple questions before I go in there, though."

"Shoot."

"What's happening with the family?"

"For the last two weeks I've tried to get the son to come in. He sets a time and then something always comes up. He is *so-o-o* pleasant, Ms. Willard this and Ms. Willard that."

"When you tell her? How does she take it?"

"She breaks my heart," Rose said. "She thanks me and asks me to set up another time. The social worker keeps saying Hatt's in denial. I don't know what good it does to stick those labels on." She shook her head.

"Did you forget?" Liz said. "There are stages in grief, you know. Denial, anger, sadness and acceptance. So much neater that way. No despair. No rage. No pride. And nobody has to face responsibility, except the one who grieves."

"Expertly said," Rose grinned.

Liz laughed. "I've been in denial for five years. I'm going for the record."

"Where's relief?" Rose asked.

"Ovulation," Liz said. "Hatt doesn't have that option anymore. What's she doing with her time?"

"Joining in a little, but she told me she doesn't want to get too close to anyone, because when she goes home it will hurt too much to say good-bye. She reads, writes letters, looks at old photos. We talk when I get the time. She told me about her friend, about the photos. I couldn't believe those dance pictures. So beautiful!"

"What are her options?"

"I don't know. I talked with my head nurse and she says there isn't anything *to* do. The kids took the matter to court, the doc testified, the judge decided, the money comes in and she's signed, sealed and delivered." She paused. "I guess I'll do the anger part. I'm getting better and better at it." She stood up and walked to the archway. "Liz?" she said, "Do these pants look too tight?"

"They look great," Liz said. "Why?"

"My mother tells me that we Indian women have to make good impressions."

"No, no, no," Liz said. "It's middle-aged women who have to do that, Not Let Themselves Go."

"I think," Rose said gravely, "that the future is not going to be pretty, because in ten years I will be a middle-aged Indian woman. It sounds hopeless to me, so I think I'll go right now and finish off the peanut butter cups that are sitting in the staff lounge."

"Medicine," Liz said. "Good medicine."

Hatt's door was closed. She hated curious strangers. She hated sympathetic eyes.

"They look in and give me these sickly smiles," she had said. "I wish I had my shotgun."

Liz knocked.

"Come in," Hatt called. She sat writing at her small desk. Liz perched on the windowsill and opened her bag.

"What have you smuggled in today?" Hatt asked. She waved at Liz's hoop earrings. "You look like a lady pirate!"

"Demon rum," Liz laughed. She held up the bottle. Sunlight caught in the heart of the brandy. "Look at that," she said, "spirits." Hatt took the teabowls from the dresser and set them on the desk. The brandy **was** sunlight going down, golden, a soft, hot shock to the throat.

"To the future," Hatt said. "To uncertainty."

"Meaning?" Liz said. "I'm careful what I drink to."

"There's something going on," Hatt said. "Roger keeps agreeing to come in and not showing. He's never there when I call and wifey is sugar-sweet. 'Bless you, Mother,' she says and hangs up." She slugged down the brandy. "I'm going to have more than one. Tell me. What's going on!"

"What's your guess?"

"Rugs and bowls and a hundred thousand dollars worth of Indian silver."

"Good guess."

Hatt held up her teabowl for a refill. "What can I do?" she asked. Liz poured for both of them.

"You got a lawyer?"

"Of course," Hatt snapped, "but I suspect he's in cahoots with my kids. I put a call in to him. He hasn't returned it." She looked around the room. "I'd like to scream, but then they'd sedate me."

"There're other lawyers. We'll find one."

"We?"

"Who else? Tell me some things. I need to understand more."

Hatt nodded. "I never thought it would come to this. I saw it happen to old people. I thought I had arranged my life, my independence. I worked very hard at that." She tilted up the last of her drink. "What do you want to know?"

"What happened to Roger? What happened to the buckaroo, the boy who loved freedom?"

Hatt poured herself another shot. "I'm going to need this," she said, "telling family secrets, digging up ghosts that won't stay dead." She moved into the rocker and hunched forward, her elbows on her knees, the brandy held in front of her face. She stared down into it as though she might see something there. "I'll never know what really happened. Roger was a part-man part-boy, part-critter. They called him 'Cat.' He lived hard, drinking, gambling, lots of willing women and he was honest and generous with everybody. He apprenticed to a Navajo medicineman for a while. He might have been married to a Navajo lady for a while. I'm not sure.

"Then, something happened. He had his fiftieth birthday and one day he showed up in my kitchen and told me he'd found Jesus and stopped drinking and he'd come to bring me a message of Love . . . Love, with a capital L. He found It. He was born again and he couldn't go to his grave knowing his mother was doomed to burn in hell. I tried to jolly him along, but I absent-mindedly poured myself a brandy and he stomped out."

"Jesus!" Liz said. They looked up at each other and started to giggle.

"'Fraid so," Hatt said, "if ever a perfectly nice man has been misunderstood, it's Jesus Christ. Well, Roger found himself a nice, yammering, born-again wife and parlayed his inheritance into a nice, safe, born-again business, joined one of those born-again businessmen's groups and stopped being 'sentimental' and 'Godless.' He and the wife pray for me every day." She shook her head. "I'm so glad John didn't live to see this. It would have broken his heart. Roger cannot stand that I live in Kayenta. He thinks it's just part of my heathen ways. Truth is, after all those years on the post, I hate these modern times. I know how to go to dinners and art shows and all that fol-de-rol, but I'm happier gossiping with my friends or poking around back of Tsegi or getting coffee at the cafe, blasphemous as that coffee is." She picked up the brandy bottle and took a slug. Liz stared down at her teabowl. She was getting weepy, she could feel it. Hatt leaned over and pinched her arm.

"Cut that out," she said. "I don't need people crying over me. They're already praying. I can hardly stand *that*."

"We've got to fight," Liz said fiercely. She stood up fast. Dizziness rippled up from her belly. "Oops," she said. "Believe I'll sit here a while."

"Good," Hatt said. "We'll fight. I promise. For now, don't leave. For now, just stay with me."

They sat quietly sipping brandy, watching the sunset burnish the low hills. Hatt's face was peaceful. Once, she roused and said "Someday, I'll tell you about the blanket on the bed. You'll love it." Then, she settled back and began to drift into sleep. Liz helped her to the bed and covered her. She waited till Hatt slept, then leaned down and kissed her cheek.

It wasn't till she tried to knock on the nursing station window and missed, that she realized she was thoroughly drunk.

Rose looked up. She saw Liz, swaying, her face bleached out by fluorescent light, blurred by something else. Liz leaned her head against the glass and grinned. Rose clenched her fists. She was hanging on her thumbs the way she always had, when her father had stood so, nights and mornings, bleak afternoons, his powerful arms limp at his sides, his old jacket stained with wine and vomit. She unfolded her fingers.

"I'm sorry," Liz mouthed.

Rose opened the door. "Come in here!" she said. "What happened?"

"I'm sorry," Liz said. "I smuggled some brandy in to Hatt. We had some."

"Some?" Rose said. She heard her mother's voice: Some? How much is some, you wicked man?! Rose poured them both coffee.

"Here," she said. "It won't sober you up, but you'll be a wide-awake drunk." Liz sipped the coffee.

"I am *so* sorry," she said.

"Oh, shut up," Rose said. "Just be quiet. Sit here, drink your coffee. You scared me, that's all."

Liz watched her work steadily through her stack of reports. Aides drifted in and out. Somebody set a plate of nachos on the desk. They were perfect, cheesey and blazing hot. Rich came in and slumped in a chair.

"Thank God for eleven to seven," he said. Liz smiled politely and kept her mouth closed. Rose handed her some papers to alphabetize. Rich was right. Night shift was the best. Somebody moonlighting could stretch out his long legs and close his eyes; somebody could raid the kitchen; somebody could sit near a friend, quietly recovering from carelessness, without making long-distance calls or writing letters she just might mail or taking someone home who was only a poor substitute for the silence at the end of the phone line. She thought about writing a country-western ballad and ate another nacho. Rose looked up.

"It's nearly eleven," she said. "You're still in no shape to drive. Let's get early breakfast. All you've had are those nachos and you were in there with Hatt for nearly seven hours."

"I'm okay," Liz said. "You don't need to do that."

"Listen," Rose snapped, "it's not out of kindness. I used to pick my dad up and bring him home. I've seen it. I'm not letting you out on the roads like that. You can come with me or you can sleep in one of the vacant rooms."

"No contest," Liz said.

"Good. Let's go."

Lena's was bright, it was Mexican, it was buzzing with late-night-, uh-uh, uh-huh, can't-go-home, don't-want-to energy. Most of the customers were sharp-faced and red-eyed, bearded men with grimy t-shirts and tattered black sneakers, women in sheer blouses and down vests. A Hopi family sat at the counter, quietly eating five-dollar specials. Rose nodded to them. She and Liz slid into a back booth.

"How're you doing?" she asked.

"Embarrassed," Liz said. Rose nodded. They ordered huevos rancheros, flour tortillas and coffee. Rose started to put fake sweetener in her coffee, shook her head and spooned in sugar.

"I'd rather get fat than brain damaged," she said cheerfully. "So, how was the lady?"

"Mad," Liz said, "She knows. She tried to call her lawyer. He hasn't called back."

"I figured she knew. I thank you for telling her."

"It's more like she told me. She said something about a hundred thousand dollars worth of Navajo silver."

"That sounds about right," Rose said. "What are you going to do?"

"I don't know. If she could get public sympathy, make herself a test case, but she's so private. I can't see her doing that."

Somebody dropped change in one of the little booth-side jukeboxes. Liz looked at Rose.

"I think this place makes me lonesome," she said.

"Every place makes me lonesome," Rose said.

The owner's black-eyed kid, his hair in skateboarder spikes, brought their food. He touched Liz's bracelet.

"Cool," he said. "So plain, you know?" He held up his arm. He had bangles and bright woven bands and studded leather half-way up to his elbow. "For good luck," he said. His mother was behind the cash register.

She glared at him. "I'm gonna need it," he said and scooted back.

"Well, this is about perfect," Liz said.

"Let's talk about Hatt." Rose said.

"There are other lawyers," Liz said. "There might even be one out there with principles."

Rose nodded. "I could talk to my brother. He's worked on that Big Mountain stuff. I'll ask him." She stopped.

"No!" she whispered. "Damn!"

"What's wrong?"

"Nothing," Rose said. She folded her napkin carefully in front of her. "Just my cousin, Connie. I shouldn't have come in here, I knew she comes here, but I wanted you to see the place, taste the food." She looked into Liz's eyes. "She will come to speak with us. When she is done, I would like to leave." Liz nodded.

"Hey . . . Baby." The voice was tender, only a little slurred. A long-haired woman smiled down at Liz, then at Rose.

"Hey, cousin," she said warmly, "what brings you here?" She slid in next to Liz, slapped her purse down on the table and shrugged out of a stone-washed denim jacket, a cloud of expensive perfume and sweet wine rising from her. She was painted beautifully, lilac eye-shadow, black eye-liner, a little apricot rouge on her broad cheeks, her lips outlined with coral. Her hands were wide and strong, silver and turquoise on every finger. When she reached across Liz for the menu, her blouse fell away from the tops of her full breasts. Rose stared down at her plate.

"Hey girl," Connie said, "where are your manners?"

"This is Liz," Rose said stiffly. "She visits at the home." Connie grabbed Liz's hand and squeezed it hard. "I'm Connie," she said. "Rose's cousin. I'm the bad girl in the family."

Two men at the counter had turned around and were watching every move she made. She crossed her legs, pulled her blouse away from her breasts and fanned herself with the menu. "Damn," she said, "it sure is hot in here." She smiled at the men. They turned back to their coffee.

"Jerks!" she laughed. "They're out of money, got nothing left. On Friday night! I saw 'em up at Johnny's, on their last beers. Couldn't even buy a lady a glass of wine. Now, they want a free look." She waved to the owner's kid. "Danny, get me some coffee." He blushed. "I love 'em young," she said. He brought her coffee.

"I did it how you like," he said. She pinched his cheek.

"*Muchacho*," she said. "You wait for me, you save it for me, you hear?" He ducked his head. "You want anything to eat?" he said. She roared with laughter. He bolted.

"Lizzie," she said. "How'd you get the little rabbit out on a Friday night? She's usually home, holed up with my aunt and the two cutest kids in town . . . next to mine, of course." She opened her purse. Rose turned her head. "Rose, Rose," Connie said. "How are those kids?" She pulled out two five dollar bills. "Hey, a little love-gift for those babies."

Rose let the money lie.

"C'mon, cousin," Connie said. "It's clean money. I got paid today. Take it. Besides, like the Tasavu say, you have to take a love-gift. It's bad luck if you don't and you've sure as shit had enough of that." She pushed the money closer.

"Rosie, cousin, take it!"

Rose picked up the bills, folded them carefully and put them in her coin purse. She looked hard at her cousin.

"For a love-gift, Connie," she said. "Only for that. I am sorry to be so cold, but you know it hurts my heart to see you like this."

Connie stubbed out her cigarette and reached across the table to take Rose's hand. Rose didn't pull away. Her hand lay limp in Connie's.

"Little rabbit," Connie said. "Remember when I used to call you little rabbit and you called me sparrow. Remember? Remember Gramma? For the sake of that, listen to me. It's Friday night. A friend bought me a couple drinks. I will have some coffee, something to eat and go home. The kids are with my mom, just like yours. How is that so different? How does that hurt your heart?"

Rose stood up and gathered her coat around her shoulders.

"I have told you," she said, "that I would be your true cousin when you no longer drink. You have seen my father. You know." Connie shook her head. "Thank you for the children's gifts," Rose said, "but I have to leave." She picked up her purse.

Liz started to ease out of the booth. Gently, Connie blocked her.

"Liz," she said, "please tell my cousin that there is more to life than work and school and mother. She was born, my cousin, then she became an old lady. She has never been a girl, she has never been a woman. From her mother's house to a no-good pretty husband. No fun, no laughter, no Friday nights."

"Shut up," Rose said softly. The Hopi family walked past them. "We will be news, now, cousin," she said. "They are already discussing us on Third Mesa."

"Excuse me," Liz murmured. Connie touched her sleeve.

"Tell her, sister, tell her," she said.

"Connie! Yo!" The voice was soft and strong.

She turned, grinned, jumped up and sailed toward the front door. Rose walked stiffly to the cashier. Liz dropped a tip on the table and stood up.

A tall, big-bellied Navajo leaned against the cigarette counter. She could *not* stare at him. He wore a black leather jacket and a black Stetson, brim circled with gold conchos. He was another one of those men born to wear jeans—long-legged, narrow-hipped—he wore them, proper ones, faded from sun and wind and work. The cashier glared at him. The Navajo dropped his dark glasses down on his nose and stared at the guy. Connie punched his arm. With a low howl, he swept her into his arms and out the door.

Rose's fingers trembled on her coat buttons.

"Dutch treat?" Liz asked. She kept her voice neutral. Her head ached.

"Sure," Rose said. She turned to the cashier. He wore a hairnet and a stained white shirt, and he stared at Rose.

"You got loud friends," he said.

Rose stared back. She opened her purse, pulled out her wallet, her money and never dropped her eyes. He looked away and punched the register keys.

"Sorry," he said. Rose nodded. She picked up her change.

"Let's go," she said. "The air is bad in here."

They stepped out into crystal cold. There were gossamer halos around the streetlights; The stars hung low enough to catch in their hair. Liz breathed deep. Rose stopped and turned to her. The flush had faded from her cheeks.

"Please," she said, "let's forget this happened."

"What, Rose?" Liz said, "I don't remember anything."

Sixteen

LIZ FELT A NEW AND SHIFTING PATTERN TO HER DAYS: time with Hatt, light and shadow in Qumovi Tuuwa, drinking coffee with Rose; hard meetings with Katz, the new lawyer, a fierce, skinny man who took on impossible cases and occasionally won one; long afternoons, warm and peaceful, next to the library fireplace; dancing with Deena to the White Boys Band; walking . . . in town, out of town, in the pines, in a late spring blizzard, always under the light-etched beauty of the Sacred Mountains. She felt as though she were coming home. Opal light flooded the meadow on those April evenings. The first pale flowers pushed up through the dark pine needles. Ravens and zoot-suited Steller's jays screamed from the trees.

By mid-May, the grass had turned to gilded silk. Hummingbirds quivered near the eaves; Liz put up a feeder and waited for them. They came, their wings iridescent, their throats claret and pulsing. The tiny birds, the grass, the trembling feathers and stalks seemed as fragile as blown glass, as luminous.

She opened her journal and wrote: *May 28, Started garden.* Paul had delivered firm instructions: last killing frost second week in June, grasshoppers, soil so acid you could trip on it. She dug a square out of the cinders south of the cabin and hauled soil and horse manure from the stables across the road. She started tomatoes and banana peppers and squash in little pots on the windowsills. It was only a little odd that the seed catalogue Paul had handed her came from her hometown. First frost, last frost, length of growing season; she could have been, except for the sun and the pines and the mountains, in her old backyard. Even the white evening moths were the same.

172

She sowed spinach and lettuce around the edges of the patch and set in marigolds—against bugs, for beauty; at sunset, they burned red-gold. Fuschia bells of penstemon sprang up at the meadow edges; locoweed, lush and magenta, sprawled along the fence-rows. Some afternoons, thunderheads swept in from the south, burst and were gone, leaving everything glittering.

She transplanted the tomatoes, peppers and squash and watched for the spinach and lettuce to sprout. Weeks passed. She wondered if the seed had died. It was an odd, dreamless time, the days the sweetest she'd lived in a long time, the hours passing almost by rote. There was little mail. The phone rang just enough. She was slowly running out of money and was glad she'd put the garden in. Each slow morning, each evening were jewels, holding light, letting go.

One early evening as the rose faded from the pinetops, she sprayed the garden. A last trick of light caught the first trace of new lettuce, the pale green of new spinach, set them shimmering in the black dirt, their track as liquid as a snail's. A raw tomato perfume etched the air and, when she carried the hose to the side of the cabin, she crushed wild mint under her feet. Sugar, her body stuffed with kittens, lurched beside her. Liz walked up the road to catch the last of the one-shot, lonesome light.

She leaned on the splintered fence that bordered the neighboring pasture. Three horses, still and dark as shadows, stood at the edge of the pines. The ivory moths fluttered over the thick grass, doing their disappearing act with the light. She looked up toward the mountains. The light on their flanks had faded; against the pale sky, they were no more than ink-strokes. On the highway, car lights were ghost lanterns. Someone had built a campfire near the distant farmhouse. The smoke drifted across the road.

Liz had run into the lawyer that afternoon.

"I was going to call you," he said. "It's over. There's nowhere left to go." Liz had stared at the silver bracelet on his left wrist, at the sun shining there.

"What now?" she asked.

"Legally," he said, "there's nowhere left to go. That's all I can tell you. I'm sorry."

"*Legally?*" she asked.

He had set his dark glasses firmly over his eyes and nodded. "Yes, call me if you get any interesting ideas," he said and loped away.

One of the horses whinnied. A small plane glinted in the last wash of sunset. She walked out toward the highway ghost-lights. She wondered where the cars were going, who they carried. She wished Hatt were in one of them, going anywhere, because as she had begun to fight, to hope that she might win back her freedom; the home had become unbearable.

"Rest home," she had snorted. "There's not one moment of silence."

Liz brought her a tiny tape player. She sat for hours listening to the operas she loved and to tapes of Indian dances that Liz had found in the library. The lawyer had brought more, Hopi, Zuni, Apache. He had given her a curved rock from the San Juan. He had told her his name was Robert Katz and made her laugh. It hadn't been enough.

Each day, she rose and moved carefully through the hours in that strange place, blessing the routine. She made her chores last as long as possible, sorting her photographs, burning some in the metal waste-basket, the window open, the smoke alarm fooled. She burned juniper there, and sage, and washed the smoke down over her body. She wrote letters in her precise hand and showed Liz how she had once signed her name, the spider's web of the old calligraphy.

"Those things mattered then," she said. "Don't let me forget. Don't let me be sentimental." At three, she lay down for a nap. At four, she made one phone call, to her daughter-in-law or Katz or Liz or to Sally Roan-horse in Kayenta. She waited for mail. They handed it out at supper, along with the food she barely touched. She would leave the letters, the notices unread by her plate. They were for the long evening.

"They think it gives us something to anticipate," she said. "But today, another of my letters came back, marked, 'Moved: forwarding expired.' She was an old, old friend, a teacher in southern Colorado, up by Wolf Creek pass." She had closed her eyes. "I'm getting like a child," she said, "waiting for that mail like it was Christmas."

One day, she had returned to her room to find that someone had stolen the little sweet-grass basket that hung from her mirror. Then some chocolates disappeared and her blue sweater didn't come back from the laundry. She filed complaints. Regrets were expressed on the director's letterhead, money to cover the losses paid into her account. She called Sally Roanhorse and told her to send nothing more; love-gifts were stolen. Sally listened quietly.

"When so many go there to be left to die," she said softly, "it is an evil place. You must leave." They had cried together, all those long, light-struck desert miles apart.

A car raced past Liz, throwing up clouds of dust and cinders. She stepped back into the pines, into the dry needles and sturdy lupine. The moon was a paring of light. It was the Water-Holding Moon, Hatt said. She had taught Liz the moon's names and the signs on the gray blanket: Changing Woman, the early One, and her two sons, Born for Water and Monster Slayer. They kept the balance, those two, restored *hozhoni*, when the forces of evil tried to do their dizzying work.

Liz walked back in the darkness and moon-shadow of the trees. The earth, the pine needles smelled raw and wild. She knew that celery-green shoots were pushing through the mold, that black beetles tunneled just beneath the surface. To think of Hatt, sealed away, while this dark perfume rose from the earth, this living earth, was dreadful.

She closed the cabin door, opened the windows wide and blessed the summer nights. They were cool, breezy, often shattered by monsoons, lightning a dazzle in the skylights, the rain solace on the roof. She undressed, stretched out on the bed and thought of Hatt, lying half-awake, hearing all those televisions in all those dark rooms. Liz shivered. It was death-in-life.

She could feel the gentle pull of the moon. The Water-Holding Moon. She remembered black water holding stars, meteors, the moon cupping light. She remembered Nick's black hair, silvered, his pale skin, the sweat shining on both of them. It had been forever since then, forever since it had been good. The other men had been no more than summer air, a touch, a comfort, only that. Her touch was honest, only that; it kept her faithful to the memory. That death-in-life.

She slipped her hand between her thighs. "Give me back my body," she whispered. "Give it back . . ."

. . . Blue moonlight washed over the spring. Wrapped in heavy robes, Talasi and Rupi watched the slow trickle of water into a tall pot. Rupi shook off her robe and stumbled to the water.

"Is it full yet?" Talasi whispered.

Rupi turned. She was naked. Her body was round, her breasts already womanly. She splashed water towards Talasi.

"No," she hissed. "You are always in such a hurry. It won't be full before First Dawn. Go back to sleep. I am turning it. The seep has moved." She tugged the pot into place, then ran back to the warmth of the robes.

"I don't want to sleep," Talasi murmured. "All day, I *am* asleep. Grinding, stirring, making *piki,* over and over again, it puts me to sleep."

"Stop complaining," Rupi said. "Think of something happy."

"Night, no walls, no voices, nothing but the small sound of animals, the smell of earth, stars, all shapes of the moon. Were it not for the Raiding Ones, I would leave you for a while and think of happy things."

Rupi huddled deeper in her shawl. She poked Talasi's side.

"You are always giving speeches," she said. "You are always complaining. *This* is what we do. Grinding and making *piki* are what we do. Even the young men do not go out alone at night." She shivered. "How are you going to find a husband if you do not change these ways of yours?" Talasi shrugged away from her.

"You know nothing," Talasi said. Her throat tightened. Tears filled her eyes; through them she gazed up at the moon's cool disc. It blurred and shimmered and doubled. She nearly forgot her pain. How did her tears change the moon? It was always and never-changing. She thought of Pamosi's seeing stone. Tears were the same. She blinked them back.

"You know nothing," she repeated bitterly. "I do not dance. I stand with the married women and the old ones and the children, watching, only watching. Have you been so blind, cousin, not to see?"

Rupi sat up straight and threw her robes over Talasi's shoulders. She pulled her close into that warm cocoon.

"No," she said, "I have not been so blind. Nor have the others. We saw and asked questions and were told to say nothing. We did not mean to hurt you." She reached for Talasi's hand. It lay limp in hers.

"There is so much hurt," Talasi said. "So much anger. So much that is *qahopi*. When I was little I knew only the words of my sorrow. But, now I am fourteen winters old. For the last three dances, I have watched all of you with sunflower dust on your bodies, with the red paint on your legs, with your faces so full of promise and I have wanted to walk away. To go to the night, to the silence and not return." Rupi pulled her close.

"No," Rupi said, "you must not think those things."

"Not Going Over," Talasi cried, "but to live alone, to go away from always having to see babies and mothers and Kihsi." She stared out at the pale desert. "I would go there. I know how to live. Kihsi has taught me hunting."

"Do not be foolish," Rupi said. "He cannot teach you how to lie under a Raider's body, or feel their blade cut your throat."

Talasi curled into Rupi's warmth, trembling.

"I will never marry. I will never carry my husband's love in my belly. I will never hold my babies in my arms," she said. "We will not do the Corn Blessing. No name will come." She pulled herself away and crouched on the cold sand. Rupi said nothing. She placed her hand flat against Talasi's spine.

"I have asked Spider Grandmother and Taiwa and Masau'u Himself why I was given this path and there is no answer," Talasi said.

"If you knew why," Rupi asked, "would the pain be less?" She rubbed Talasi's shoulders. She could feel the pain in them, the strength. It was the strength of the grinding. It was a woman's strength. She waited, her strong hands moving steadily, working out the pain.

"If I knew why," Talasi said, "I could see more clearly the next turn in my path. All I see is mist. All I see is pointless grinding, nothing but the busy work of an empty woman. It might be better to be Tsohtsona, to burn with her fires. This coldness is like dying."

Rupi rubbed her back in ever-widening circles, pressing into each bone of her cousin's spine. Talasi grew warmer under her hands. Her cries grew softer. At last, she was still. Rupi wrapped her in her own shawl, warm from her body and pulled her into her lap. Unthinking, she rocked Talasi gently, drying her wet face with the ends of the shawl. She did not sleep.

First Dawn flickered along the horizon. Talasi woke and stepped to the spring. Water brimmed in silver sheets from the *wikoro*. She caught it in her hands and scattered drops to the light.

"Thank you," she whispered. "For this day. For my friend."

"Those are my prayers, too," Rupi said. Talasi turned. Rupi lay full length on her belly, watching her.

"Are you sorry you have told your secret?" she asked.

"I am glad to no longer be alone with it," Talasi said. The light crept up, trembling, deepening, thin stripes of purple cloud along the horizon as though the world was held in the curve of a huge shell.

"That boy," Rupi said, "does he know? Every day, he passes your grinding window. He never looks, he does not stop, but all his errands take him that way."

Talasi unwrapped their bundle of *somiviki* and dried meat. Rupi crouched next to her and poured water in their bowls.

"Rupi," Talasi said, "that boy and I have not spoken in two winters. He was called to the house of Toho one morning and came to ask me to go with him. I could not. The next afternoon, as we guarded the corn, he started to walk towards me, as always, then turned and ran to the far end of the field." She paused and bowed her head. Her shining hair, freed from the maiden's coils, hid her face.

"What is it?" Rupi asked. "There is more?" Talasi nodded. She shook back her hair. Rupi saw how beautiful she was, her cheeks red in her broad face, the light glinting off her hair, her eyes gleaming; she thought of He'wuhti, her hair hanging loose, her wide shoulders, her power.

"That boy knows," Talasi said. "We do not have to speak. He is with me and I, with him," Rupi unwrapped a *somiviki*.

"I know how that might be," she said. "I have dreamed of that since I was small, but, as yet, there is only Sakuna's teasing." She laughed. "It suits me."

She looked into Talasi's eyes. "What do you wish of me? The others know you are my heart-sister. They ask me about you. They guess things. I have said nothing because I knew nothing."

"Tell them the truth," Talasi said. "Better, send them to me."

"I am glad to do that," Rupi said. "There are too many twice-told stories with our people." Talasi smiled. They ate in silence, the sun warm on their hair. It seemed to her that they *were* blood sisters, and had been, for a long, long time, kits in the same litter, wolf-pups tagging after the same mother, young hawks, trying their wings, in terror and joy, on the same trails in the air. Rupi pulled her close.

"I ask you," she said, "and swear to it, if you will be my first-born daughter's Spirit Mother? My husband will know that we have made that vow. He will agree to it, or he will not be my husband."

"I swear it, sister," Talasi said.

"And I," Rupi said. She giggled. "And Sakuna, too."

Seventeen

MONSOON THUNDER BY-PASSES THE EARS. It goes straight for the belly, the spinal column, the bones themselves. "Monsoons," the gas station guy said, "are like eight-hundred-pound gorillas; they go anywhere they want." He told Liz to stay in the car and ride it out. Cars have tires. People don't. She thought about asking him for date. He seemed both metaphorical and wise.

She wondered if he might have an idea about how to tell Hatt Latham that which was untellable. But he scuttled out in his yellow slicker, gave her change and that was that. She pulled out onto Santa Fe and was abruptly visited by the last dream. The streaming windshield became a cliff-face. There could have been vines growing there, a seep, spilling in glinting sheets of water. She heard the echo of a woman's sobs and remembered a Viet Nam vet who had told her about driving from Page to Flagstaff, the screams of a Vietnamese woman wailing in his ears. She wondered mildly if she was finally going crazy.

And drifted into the left lane. A horn blared. She came alert as a guy in a Dodge pick-up roared past and threw her the finger. She returned the compliment and feeling like a hundred-and-fifty-pound gorilla, hit the gas. She cruised past him and repeated the compliment. He beeped. She swung in front of him, mouthed "Up yours," into the rear-view mirror and saw him come up fast. She suddenly remembered that they shot people on Southwestern highways.

The Dodge swerved into the slow lane and cruised next to her for a while. Traffic began to pile up behind them. The Dodge cut in front of her. She swung back into the slow lane and he stayed parallel. He beeped and leaned across the passenger seat, grinning, driving with one hand, pulled back in front of her and leaned out the driver's window. He swept off his hat.

"Curly," he yelled. "I forgive ya!"

Liz swung off onto the feeder road. She realized her palms were wet. The dream was gone, her vision clear. She drove up to the light, turned left and pulled into the Safeway parking lot. Black clouds scudded north. She could see lightning splitting the black air above the Peaks. She rolled down the window. Rain misted her face. The Dodge pulled into the space ahead and stopped.

She rolled up the window and locked both doors. As he ambled toward the car, she sighed. It was all there, the levis, the legs, the beginning of a gut, the skunk-stripe beard and cheerful smile. With ironic gallantry, she could tell, he carried his hat in his hands. His stride was something. Her belly went hot. He set his big hands on the roof of the car and leaned in towards the closed window.

"Curly," he said. Liz turned her head. She hoped the lightning would strike. She didn't think he'd be wearing sneakers and those good-old-boy leather boots were perfect conductors. He'd fry. She sighed. It was going to be a different kind of lightning. It had, in fact, already struck. She thought about trying something new, started the car and turned off the engine, wondering how it was that the same old, same old always felt so new.

"Good," he said. "Now, this rain's stopping. The sun's going to come out and, in about fifteen minutes, the inside of that car's going to be about a hundred degrees. How about you open the window? Give yourself a little fresh air?"

She rolled the window down an inch.

"Well, hel-*lo!*" he said. "Like I said back there at the bar, my name's Macleod and I'd like to get to know you."

By the time she pulled into the Tenderhome parking lot, she was hopelessly high. They were going to meet for dinner, maybe a little dancing, a little ride out Lake Mary Road for the moon. Maybe. She was already through four or five maybes and lying back to take a look at him.

"It's the sweetest drug," she said to herself, "I hate to ruin it by getting to know him."

Hatt's door was open. Her purse lay on the bed and she was pacing back and forth in front of the window.

"Get me out of here," she said."We can go anywhere. Just get me out!"

They swung down the hairpin curves into Oak Creek Canyon. The gray, broken cliffs, the pine and aspen, the yellow stars of cinquefoil, the slender bells of penstemon, the salmon-red rocks in the distance were straight out of a photographer's dream. The bumper-to-bumper traffic wasn't.

"It used to take us three days to drive to town," Hatt said calmly. "There wasn't even a road. You always carried two-by-fours and a shovel with you. You knew you'd get stuck three times and blow out two tires . . . at least."

They stopped for water at the little spring. Hatt drank from her hands and smoothed the rest over her face.

"I'd trade everything to be back there, back then," she said. "Stuck. Digging sand that won't stay dug, under that white sun, frying, wondering if they'd find my mummy years later." She sat on the mossy boulder near the spring. "I'm so afraid I'll never see Kayenta again. I've lost faith and retaken it so many times since January, but last night I dreamed of John and Kwaayo and a Yei-bei-chi ceremony I once watched. At the end, a coyote came up to me and put its warm muzzle in my hand." She held her wrists in the water and shivered.

"I can't seem to get cool these days," she said. They climbed back in the car and headed toward Sedona.

"Ice cream?" Liz said.

"I would love that." She took a yellowed, lace-trimmed handkerchief from her purse and dried her face. "One of the girls learned to do this at the old Indian day school," she said. "I told you that before, didn't I?"

"Once," Liz said. "The napkins."

"Liz," Hatt said. "Tell me. What did Katz say?"

Liz signalled, hoping the tourists might learn something from the gesture, and pulled off under a stand of cottonwood. Golden light filtered down through the leaves. They could hear the wet rill of the creek. A dragonfly swooped in and hovered, its wings an iridescent blur of green and turquoise.

"He said we've done everything that can legally be done," Liz said. Hatt stared out the window, the handkerchief stretched tight between her fingers.

"We can keep fighting," Liz said. "There are ways. A class-action suit. The Gray Panthers. You've got rights, you must have. And if you don't, it's time you did." Hatt said nothing. Liz grabbed one end of the hankie and tugged it.

"Hatt, come on, we can fight." Hatt didn't move. The hankie trembled between them.

"Hatt, you stubborn old woman. Think. They haven't broken you, not with the dead food, not with the dead air, not even with that medicine, that poison."

"Corpse-powder," Hatt said quietly. "That's what it was. Sally says they are Skinwalkers in uniforms, those doctors. She says I should run away."

"I'll help you," Liz said. "We'll do it." She wanted to yank the handkerchief out of Hatt's grip. She was the stronger. It would be easy. Hatt held steady.

"You could sell some of the rugs, some of those old pots. They are worth tens of thousands of dollars. You can win," Liz said.

"You don't understand," Hatt said. "I can't sell those things. They were either love-gifts or they were given by those who had no right to give. Those must go back; we stole them. They will never belong to us."

"Then we'll raise money, a defense fund, benefits. I know how to do those things."

Hatt's hand trembled and she held steady. "There is more, Liz. You were right. I am a stubborn old woman. Old. Eighty-three, nearly eighty-four. Right now, in this car, in this bright sun, I'm fine. But in shadow time, dawn, dusk, night, I drift. I can feel it. I lie in my bed and I am not sure where I am." She tugged at the hankie. "We could fight. There are a few pieces I could sell that would bring in money. We might even win. This time, I might return to Kayenta. And, the day will come when I *will* fall, I *will* forget to close the damper on the stove. Then . . ."

"No," Liz said.

"Yes," Hatt said fiercely. "Liz, child, there was an old Navajo couple who lived up near the post. The old woman was from those people who hid away when the government rounded up the Diné and death-marched them to Bosque Redondo. This old woman, she was a real long-hair, a fine weaver, a strong shepherd, a tough, beautiful soul. She got sick. A terrible illness. They had a ceremony. It did no good." Hatt tugged on the handkerchief and smiled.

"You might as well let go," she said. "I'll tell you something about the Navajo so this story makes sense. They are terrified of death. They do not believe in an afterlife. Their souls go wandering. If someone dies in a hogan, the death-fear is so terrible that they abandon the hogan and everything in it. They just ride away. No other Navajo will ever go near that hogan again.

"This old woman knew her death was near and she knew her husband could not afford to build a new hogan nor outfit it, so, one evening, she just hobbled off into the desert. She was a skillful woman. She wiped out her tracks. She was never found. Sometime later, the old man found himself a new, young wife and they lived for years in the old woman's hogan."

Liz glared at her. Hatt pulled the handkerchief away and wiped her face.

"That's not right," Liz said.

"That was how it was," Hatt said. She took Liz's hand in hers. "Let's get some ice cream," she said. "There's time to talk."

Liz pulled back out onto the road. Hatt took a deep breath.

"Can't you just smell summer?" she asked. Liz said nothing.

"Where are your manners?" Hatt said. "An old lady just asked you a question." She tapped the back of Liz's hand.

"Of course I can smell summer," Liz said. "The question is, why do you want to shut yourself off from this?"

"But I'm not," Hatt said. "I'm enjoying every second of it. Why, aren't you?"

They brought Rose a pint of double chocolate, chocolate-chip ice cream. She checked Hatt in.

"I'm surprised you came back" she said.

"Where would I go?" Hatt said. "You two are conspirators."

"Innocent," Rose said.

"Come talk with us," Hatt said. "I have some requests."

Rose glanced at Liz. "I'm fine," Hatt said. "Especially my eyesight. Don't treat me like a child."

"I'll get my ice cream and meet you in the solarium," Rose said.

The big room was empty and silent. They could see the moon through the windows.

"The Water-Holding Moon," Liz said. "I never learned that . . . how to hold back."

Hatt smiled. "Then what do you have for yourself?" she asked. "Those women who went to huts during their periods, they weren't outcasts. They were going to store up. To be with-holding."

"The moon just makes my loony," Liz grinned. "My period makes it worse."

"I wonder," Hatt said. "Are we loony or are we just moonrun?" She patted Liz's hand. "You see, it's evening and I am drifting. What I really remember is cramps and headaches and washing out those damn rags!"

Rose sat down. "I read that chocolate is the answer," she said cheerfully.

"For periods?" Liz asked.

"For anything," Rose said. "Women know that. It's innate."

"I need more than chocolate," Hatt said. "I think you've acquired a permanent guest."

"Are you sure?" Rose said.

"I think so," Hatt said. "I dreamed so. And, much as I'd hate for Roger to know I said this, 'For every season, there is a time . . .' This season, I will stay here."

Rose was quiet.

"I still don't understand," Liz said.

"You don't have to," Hatt said. "All I ask is that you listen and consider whether you can help with some things I'd like to do, to have done." Liz nodded. Hatt stroked her hair.

"For instance, I've wanted to do that for the longest time. You have beautiful hair."

"It's fake," Liz laughed. "It's a perm."

"No," Hatt said, "it's how you want it. That's not fake. How I want the rest of my life to go, is with honesty. And, forgiveness. I know I am dying. That's a gift, to know that. I want to die clean. There are old grievances to lay to rest, old misdeeds to mend. I won't die as a fool. Or a victim."

"Isn't giving into this place being a victim?" Liz said.

"Not if I can use these last days," Hatt said. "But I can only use them with your help."

"You have that," Liz said.

"And mine," Rose said quietly.

"My daughter-in-law," Hatt said, "let slip that she and Roger had emptied the hogan. For 'your peace of mind, Mother,' she said. My things are safe in their garage. They've even put in a security system. So no one can steal them. I get to take them with me when I am better and can go home."

"How thoughtful," Rose said.

"I certainly have slept better since I heard all this," Hatt said. "What she doesn't know is that I did a little detective work a few years ago and discovered that she's from one of those fine old families up in southern Utah who have been looting Indian graves and selling the pieces to rich New Yorkers and Angelenos for years."

"You wouldn't believe what they have tucked safely away in their garage," Hatt said. "I have the inventory up here," she tapped her head. "I need to get it on paper and locked up somewhere. There are Pueblo I and II pots, a Whirling Logs rug, some very old Second Mesa plaques. There's even a Hopi wedding robe and marriage case."

"How did you get that?" Rose asked. Her face was stern.

"Since the story is only half mine, I can't tell it," Hatt said. "I promise you, no blasphemy was intended."

"Let's hope none occurred."

"That's why I want these things returned," Hatt said. "Failing that, peace of mind lies in knowing they will never be sold, that they will never fit into somebody's color scheme."

Rose and Liz looked at each other. "I like a challenge," Liz said.

"Me, too," Rose answered. "There's also the question of balance."

"*Hozhoni*," Hatt said.

"*Su'antsaki*," Rose said. "Doing right."

"Vengeance," Liz said. "Don't get mad, get even. For your peace of mind, Mother!"

"I wish Roger had met you," Hatt said.

"I *am*," Liz said, "frequently, beyond the beyond."

"So, Rose," Hatt said, "I ask you to find ways, they must be discrete, to give these things back to the tribes. Kwaayo, Shining Woman, the others, they are all gone over. These things must be returned. It will be difficult.

They are very beautiful. There is a turquoise-and-coral plaque, a lion-skin quiver. For so many years, they were a part of my life."

"They will stay with you," Rose said. "In your heart." Hatt nodded.

"As stories do, memories. I have some of those to pass on. Once I'm gone, make sure others hear. I would have told my daughter, but she wanted nothing to do with them." She paused.

"To see her, that is my last request. There is something only she can give me. I may die without it, but I must try to reach her. Her children call. They write, but, for forty years, she has given only silence. You could tell her, Rose, that I'm dying."

"I can do that," Rose said. "I will gladly use my professional judgement. Tonight, according to the "Diagnostic Manual," you might be exhibiting signs of depression, early Alzheimer's complex, organic brain syndrome. The salad bar of the brain, take your choice."

"Which one doesn't call for medicine?"

"Early Alzheimer's."

"Fine."

"Could you develop a little irritability?" Rose said.

"Delighted," Hatt snorted.

"Your other request," Rose said, "to return those things. That will be more difficult. I was not raised in my peoples' ways. I have only bits and pieces. But I can begin to ask questions."

"And you, Liz?" Hatt asked. Her voice was tired. She played with Liz's hair.

"I like a little project now and then," Liz said. The air-conditioner suddenly blasted on. Hatt shut it off and opened the windows. Rose and pine-scented air drifted over them. Liz remembered waiting, one perfumed summer night, crouched in the back of somebody's van, watching, waiting, while in a low concrete building, Michael shredded Draft Registration papers. He had come back to her, his face peaceful, his hands covered with paper cuts.

"They're useless now," he'd said. "A couple thousand. I pissed on the scraps."

Liz built a fire in the barbeque. Rose had said to burn juniper or sage. She had both, juniper from a lone tree on the black sand and sage from three places: a meadow near the South Kaibab uranium mine site; a mesa, steep, with gray-red veined walls sloping down to the Green River; and an eerie, sunless grotto north of Las Vegas. Thin blue smoke curled up through the black branches. The juniper flared and was gone. The sage sent up its scent, bitter as her prayers. It had been a long, faithless time since she had come willingly into the presence of smoke and prayer.

Bathed in dazzling light from a stained glass Station of the Cross, she had once knelt in front of the Virgin Mary's pale statue, begging Her, the

Woman with downcast eyes and meek mouth, to stop her mother's pain. She had watched the statue for a sign. The eyes stayed blind, the hands outstretched. Candlelight flickered off the gilt edges of the robe, and no more. There had been the stink of burning wax.

"Smoke carries our prayers," Rose had said as they parted. "They told me that much."

"To what?" Liz whispered to the smoke. She thought of her mother in the bad old days, of Hatt, waiting for sleep. "Better to walk out into the desert and brush out your tracks," she whispered. She thought of that kneeling child, of the guttering candles, the cold painted plaster, and she wished she could scoop that girl up and carry her out onto the black sand, sit with her under the sheltering juniper and count the visible stars . . .

. . . Talasi sang in her mother's house. The way through the grinding had emerged. She bent over the corn, her arms strong and rounded, her body easy with the work. One who watched would have seen a woman, young and yet, unripe. There was a steady sadness in her dark eyes. When visions hovered, she forced herself to see *through* the sadness, as though it were a kind of seeing stone, a stone that taught how sadness can shift the shape of what one sees.

She threw a last handful of corn in the trough and dropped the grinding stone on it, breaking the kernels into smaller chunks. This first grinding was most difficult. It jarred the arms. Her fingers ached. She swept the cracked corn into a shallow bowl and carried it to the roof. Coals smoked in a raised firebed. She placed an old bowl on the fire and poured in the corn, stirring as fast and hard as she could, steadily, without pause.

Below, the plaza was quiet except for a few men gathered in the north curve, crouched over the game. She missed her aunt's house. The gamblers had not come to East-Rising. The night before, her father had come from the game with gossip of drought to the South and whole villages of southern clanspeople heading towards Place of Water.

"They have heard," he said, "of our black sand, how it holds water, how the corn grows long and full. The *kikmongwi* talk of how we must help these people. Some of us think there is not enough." Choovio had not missed a stitch in her mending.

"And yet," she had said quietly, "there is enough for trade, enough for the game."

Nuuva had turned his face. "The others," he said, "they are caught by it. I am not. We have enough to eat."

Talasi straightened and stretched out her aching back. She stared up into the sky. There was only sun, no cloud, no sign of vapor, only the white-hot sun, so bright that she could not see the fire in the coals. The parching corn gave off its rich smell. She bent again, stirring, singing one of the maidens' songs.

Kihsi stood quiet on the path below. He watched her move, heard her sing, heard how she changed the words of the grinding song. He folded his arms across his chest, as though he could protect himself. When she stood and stretched her arms to the sun, his body ached. He wanted to touch her, to use his big hands to move the pain from her back, as he had once moved boulders in fields that seemed from another lifetime.

He could not guess how womanhood might be, what mysteries she had learned, what secrets she now carried, but manhood had sometimes been nothing but pain. They said there was joy in the force that moved in him, insistent, constant; they said it was the joy of new life. He did not think that new life should spring from such longing, such loneliness. Night after night, he lay on his sleeping mat, restless, seeing Talasi's wise face, her sleek, strong shoulders. He wanted to talk to her, to hear her, to touch her smooth skin, to hold her. And there was more.

He had heard his mother and father in the night, he had guessed at the sighs and small sounds. He had heard the other young men talk. He guessed at what was said about his mother and why his father had left. He wondered why so much was made of it, of the mating and, why, since all felt the longing, some were scorned. He had heard his friends talk of Rupi's round shape, of Sawya's sweet behind as she swayed up the trail from the spring, of the pleasure that a man might find between a woman's thighs. Before they were taught, the young men knew these things. They knew what lay beyond the courting window. No one had ever said a word about Talasi. He would have killed them if they had.

He wanted to speak to her. Her song was in his bones. *Qahopi* as it was, he sang it with her, in silence, his lips not moving. Once, quiet on the trail of a lizard, they had turned suddenly toward each other. She had nodded and he had known. In their separate hearts, they had been singing the same song, a song for the lizard, a song of taloned feet and green-yellow scales and the taste of ants. He wanted to call out to her, to say aloud what was singing in his heart. But, as always, he heard Toho. He heard the words that were a wall between him and Talasi, as thick and gray as the broken stonework of the Old Ones.

"We are in danger," Toho had said. "A time of thirst and hunger moves toward us. It is time for the Ladder Dance." Kihsi had held himself still. He had heard of Saqtiva. It was deadly. It held the power that sings on that border between life and death.

"You are asked to dance," Toho had said. "If you accept, you will dance in your sixteenth spring. You will give four years to your preparation, to become skilled, and more.

"If you accept, you must put all women, even your mother, from your life. You must live alone. We have a room. You are to touch no woman, neither in friendship nor in lust. You will speak with no woman, walk with no woman. During the rabbit chase, you will stay away from any girl." He paused and studied Kihsi's face. "Not even one wise as Talasi. You have heard of this dance.

It is in all the wild stories that boys tell. You know the dangers, you know the work. I cannot tell you why or how you were chosen. I can only say that this is vital to the children and the children's children of this place."

"What must I do?" Kihsi had asked. He remembered that his voice had trembled and Toho had smiled. "I ask you," he had said, "to take water and *piki,* only that, and go out beyond the farthest cornfield, into the red wash near the big cottonwood. You will find a rock-and-brush shelter. Inside, there will be a mat, a robe and a pouch containing certain roots. Do not sleep the first night, though you may rest on the mat. On the next day, chew two of the roots. You will be still . . . dream, maybe . . . and walk for some days . . . I do not know how many. At the end of that time, rest and drink and eat . . . slowly. During that night's sleep, you will come upon the answer to your peoples' request . . . yes . . . or no, only that . . . yes or no."

Kihsi never knew how long he walked, or where. It seemed a long, solitary dream. Later, he remembered clouds like smoke and smoke like clouds; where the fire came from he could not guess. Once, he stepped off the mesa-edge onto air solid as rock. There had been the shining leaves of the cottonwood and its twisted branches, as though snakes bore leaves, all arching over him as he lay on warm sand, the hot gush of his first ejaculation pouring out over his belly. And then, He had appeared, God of Life and Death, with His tender, ugly face, His gentle eye, His burning eye. He had said nothing, only waited, and Kihsi had whispered, "Yes."

Talasi heard the clatter of pebbles, as though someone walked below. She peered over the roof-edge. The path was empty. She eased the pot off the coals and waited for the parched corn to cool.

Eighteen

LIZ AND PAUL STOOD AT THE WESTERN BOUNDARY of Qumovi Tuuwa, looking out over the shimmer of near-ripe oats. The noon sun bleached out everything, and turned the brain to lava. Paul glared at the oats.

"Damn 'em," he muttered. "They gotta go. They fall off the feed-trucks up on the highway, blow over here and take off like plague. Plant breeders' voodoo makes 'em zombies, you can't kill 'em, they drive out the native plants. This patch used to be loaded with beeweed and four o'clock."

"But they're pretty," Liz said. "Like white gold."

"So's Lake Powell," Paul snapped, "and jet-trails and those redwood *Architectural Digest* mansions down in the red rocks. Pretty!"

"Oops, my dear," Liz said. "Pre-menstrual? Or whatever it is you fellows go through?"

"Sorry," Paul answered. "You know. It's not personal. We're being eaten alive by budget cuts. If it weren't for a couple research grants I had to sit at my desk and dig up . . . when I should be out collecting plant samples, monitoring water, keeping Phoenix heathen off the ruins . . . I'd be doing squat."

"Anything else?"

"You leaving. Because you have to earn a living. Not being able to offer you money. All of that."

Liz shaded her eyes and peered up under the shadow of Paul's hat. His eyes were miserable.

"Paul," she said, "I'll be out. As long as you and Claire keep feeding me, I'll appear."

"I know," he said. "I'm just fed up, that's all. I could leave. I've put in some applications, but you know how this place is. Some days, I think It wants me here. Others, when Roy is off into the backcountry with some lithe archeology student, I don't care what It wants. He's about as useful as tits on a stallion." He threw his hat into the shimmering heart of the oats.

"Hew ha," Liz said.

Paul glared at her, at the oats, at the molten sun and the spot where his cap had disappeared.

"And I don't have my hat," he said "I'm gonna fry what's left of my brain."

"Did I ever tell you," Liz said, "about the pity parties my kids used to hold?"

"You did," he said.

"So," she said, "how do we do this?" She picked up a plastic garbage bag.

"Pick 'em," he grinned. "Right where my hat fell in."

"Fell in?" she said.

"Right."

She crouched in the middle of the oats. Bend, decapitate and toss, bend, decapitate and stow. Her knees started to ache. She moved to the oats' border and bent from the waist, using both hands to pull and stow. As the hour wore on, she started to feel good, strong and sweaty and good. She straightened and stretched up toward the burning sky. She could smell her sweat and the faint animal scent of her hair. The oatheads were full and rough—they chafed her hands.

She thought of the women who had worked here centuries ago, the women of her dreams. They were here, around her. A light breeze dried the sweat on her forehead. She wondered if they had hauled water here for the corn, if here the boy had stepped back into the shade of the juniper, if here the girl had followed. She guessed that if she parted the oat stalks, she would find in the hot sand broken pieces of water jugs, rough and gray, the coils still visible, the finger marks unblurred.

Paul moved near her.

"How's Hatt?" he asked

"It's not good," Liz said. "Katz says there's nothing legal left to do. She could sell her stuff, but Roger's had her declared incompetent, because she talked about *chindi* and had the hogan protected by a medicinewoman. He said she seemed to be 'unable to differentiate between reality and superstition.' So she can't get her hands on her stuff. Katz thinks it would only buy her time. Roger's very powerful, and he's rich enough that he'll just appeal and appeal till she runs out of money and strength. At that point, of course, it would only be reasonable that she be put back in the home . . . for her own good. That's Roger's favorite phrase, . . . 'for her own good.'"

"Must be land involved somewhere," Paul grunted. "You know how the city's growing. Deeeeee-velopment! It's the God of God-loving businessmen." He yanked up a clump of oats. "What're you going to do?"

Liz straightened and watched the monsoon clouds charge in from the south, their shadows weaving across the pale and black basalt, sucking the light from the earth.

"Do what she wants," she said. "Roger apparently ripped off her hogan and has the stuff secured in his garage."

"For her own good," Paul said.

"She wants the stuff returned."

"Who to?"

"Indians. Maybe you can help. She said there are Pueblo I and II pots, a mountain lion quiver, jewelry."

"Wait" Paul said. "Roger's taken *those* things? It's illegal for anybody to have those pots if they came off public land."

"Hey, Ranger Rick," Liz grinned. "Maybe you could put on your uniform and your gun and pay Roger a visit. Don't be surprised if he's ten steps ahead of you." She tied the garbage bag shut and turned to toss it in the back of the truck.

"Paul?" she said.

"What?"

"You and Claire, you go to church?"

"We do."

"I've got one question."

"Shoot."

"Where is Jesus H. Christ now that we need him?"

"Does this have something to do with money-lenders and temples?"

"It does."

"Maybe we're Him. Maybe it's our job."

Liz waved toward the Sacred Mountains. She held her arm straight and turned in a slow circle, from the clean line of the mountains to the burnt sienna western cliffs to the shimmering northern horizon and the squat eastern mesas that watched over it all. "This is the temple," she said. "All of it."

"Heat's getting to you," Paul said. "I've been uneasy about you right from the start." He swung his oats up into the truck. "Come on," he said, "we'll get you back in the air-conditioning and feed you some of our swell Black Sands coffee."

"You mean the stuff that tastes like it's made with black sand."

"Check," he said. Liz climbed up into the passenger seat.

"Whoa," she said. "My back hurts. I think I'll skip the coffee. I'm going home and lie flat and drink heavily."

"Yes, Doctor!" Paul said. "Make that two prescriptions and hold the ice." They pulled onto the park road.

"Paul?"

"Yeh."

"Why didn't we just cut the damn things, then rake up anything that was left?"

"Liz," he said, "I've been asking myself the same question."

Gin works some miracles. There is the scent, there is the dance of ice and crystal, and light seen through them. There is the time somewhere between the first drink and the third, when one thinks with infinite grace and clarity, as though one was cool as ice, bright as crystal. It is better to be alone while the miracles work. They require only the complicity of the gin. They require the pure freedom of solitude. They do not kill pain.

Liz had forgotten the first rule about being drunk and in pain. The pain doesn't go away and, somewhere between the third double and oblivion, you realize that you are going to wake, in pain, *with* a hangover. Oblivion moved in. Behind her lids, she saw the rogue oats glittering in the wind. She thought she would go there. She would lie down in them, press her back against the warm sand. She would stay there till the pain was gone . . .

. . . They climbed the steep trail to the black mesa. Along its edge, shadowed against the pale evening sky, like creatures half-human, half-hawk, flute players, drummer and the old, old singers stood quietly. Just below them, a death's step to the desert floor, the ladders had been set in a narrow ledge. Rupi squeezed Talasi's hand.

"I am so afraid Sakuna is one of the dancers," she said."He has been so shy with me. You know what that might mean."

"And I am afraid for Kihsi," Talasi whispered. They moved through the crowd to the cliff-edge. Talasi did not say that she had dreamed of Kihsi, dreamed him, half-eagle, half-man, soaring out from the cliff-face, sunset blazing on his wing tips and his golden head. She no longer dreamed in riddles. Each dream was clear, many were dreadful; none held comfort.

Rupi closed her eyes.

"I will wait like this," she said. "I am too afraid to look. When they appear, tell me." Talasi stepped near the edge and looked down. A Hu Kachina moved towards her, its sharp teeth glinting in the fading light, its great eyes bulging with rage. It switched at her with its yucca whips.

There were to be no women near the ceremony. She knew that. She stepped back and studied the ledge below. Two poles, swaying gently and topped with a crossbar, were set deep in the eastern end. A twin pair stood to the west. The eastern poles were stripped nearly bare, a few limbs left to serve as rungs. The western poles were completely smooth. Long buckskin thongs had been tied to their crossbars and wound evenly down the length of each pole. Two dancers stood near the eastern poles, two near the others. The young men were naked, painted white as for death, their faces grave and tranced under the ghostly powder. Hawk and eagle feathers trembled in their shining hair. "Stripped," Talasi thought, "they are stripped, the trees, the men . . . they have nothing to protect them."

Sakuna was not there. Talasi shuddered and closed her eyes. Unbidden, the vision had come. Though his back was turned, she saw Kishsi's gaunt face, his eyes, black as fire rock, burning.

"Open your eyes, Rupi," she said firmly. "Sakuna is not among them, but Kihsi is."

Rupi looked down and gasped. Behind them, a matron said to her daughter, "These maidens, it is as though *they* were standing on the ledge . . . "

Talasi straightened her shoulders. She touched Rupi's hand. "Sister, please be strong and let me hold your hand. No one must know my feelings."

. . . Liz turned, as though to look away from the dream. Pain blossomed across her back like a terrible colorless flower. She thought of fish in underground pools, the white of them, the clammy translucence. The pain was gelatinous. It burned like fox-fire. Cold. She thought that if she raised her arm and held it to the light, she would see through it, but she could not move.

Her heart sledge-hammered against the arc of her ribs. The place where the fishes' eyes were not kept coming to her, the blind lump of flesh or scale. She wanted to throw up, but she couldn't move her head. She forced her eyes to look out the south window. If she let her sight rest on the black trunk of the nearest pine, she could keep the sickness away.

SOUTH

For a woman of Alsace, name unknown
in our history books,
who resisted, who stood fast.

Nineteen

LIZ LURCHED AWAKE, FISTS CLENCHED, HEART BANGING, gasping as though she had been running. She moved to sit up, to push up into full wakefulness. Gray light bleached the skylight, the stars gone. Her sheets were drenched, dreams no longer a riddle, comfort in none. The pain waited. She knew that. She shifted and it sprang, white-hot, nauseating.

The phone was beyond reach. She was terribly thirsty. The gray light softened, became rose. Bob climbed in through the cat window and gave her a cool look. Liz took a deep breath pulled herself up, and cautiously wedged the pillows behind her back. Bob ate, belched and jumped up on the bed. She started to move her legs to the side of the bed. The pain pounced, breathtaking. She was too scared to cry. She stayed still. Sugar pawed frantically at the door, her babies were in a box by the bed.

Liz forced herself to breathe, got her legs positioned and swung her feet to the floor. The room spun. She bent her head till the whirling stopped. Through each move, she kept thinking how ridiculous it was. She expected that something would suddenly give and she would wake up, go to the kitchen, put the kettle to boil, let Sugar in and settle down to watch the kittens nurse.

Clutching the bookcase, she dragged herself upright. If it was a dream, she might as well keep moving and see what the effort would bring. Her first step was all right, the second easier. Setting her bare feet carefully on the rough floor, she hobbled across the room and leaned against the desk, a huge old roll-top. She thought about curling up in it and knew she was not dreaming, the pain would not relent.

"When you're terrified," Eva would say, "do something ordinary." She dialled Deena's number and started to cry.

"Who is this?" Deena said. "Mom? What's wrong?"

"It's me. Liz. I hurt my back. I'm okay, I mean, I'm not dead. I can't move, that's all."

"What do you mean you can't move?" Deena said. "That's serious. Can you wiggle your toes?" Liz giggled.

"Liz?"

"Just a minute." She tried to calm herself, to gather breath around the panic, but she couldn't. Tears poured down her face. For an instant, she seemed to lose language; there were no words, only the giggles and tears bubbling out of her, drenching her inside and out.

"Liz. Answer me." Deena sounded mad.

"I'm sorry," she said. "It's not fatal."

"It's okay," Deena said. Liz heard her light a cigarette and wished she had one. "You just sounded like my mom for a minute. I get these midnight calls from her."

"It's more like six."

"Close enough. What happened?"

"I worked with Paul yesterday, pulling up oats. I must have hurt my back. It's not like I'm paralyzed. It's the pain. The crying just keeps happening. I don't know. I'm going to do it again." She felt the giggles pressing against her throat.

"Go ahead," Deena said. "Deej is asleep. I'll just sit here. Then, we'll figure out what to do."

"Thanks," Liz whispered. The tears jammed, the laughter like labor. She took a breath. The tears broke loose. This was it, the dam gone, her body helpless, the pain too sharp to be blurred by daydreams, the daydreams washed out, washed away, Nick gone, cut loose from her shoreline, from her dreams. She'd come two thousand miles to let the dam silt over and it hadn't been good enough. There had to be this, the powerlessness, the dam blown up. She took a breath. The air moved easily into her body; it tasted sweet. She let herself down into the old library chair Nick had given her, that she had hauled all that long way. It was perfect, straight-backed and hard.

"Feel better?" Deena said.

"Yes," Liz said. "Essential, that's how it felt."

"I couldn't tell if you were crying or coming," Deena said.

"Don't. It only hurts when I laugh."

"What now?"

"The emergency room, I think," Liz said. "And, don't let them give me any tranquilizers."

"Forget that," Deena said. "They'll charge you as much as a regular doctor and you could wait for hours. I'll drop Deej off at day-care, get somebody to cover at work and be there in forty-five minutes, okay?"

"Oh, lady," Liz said. "I'm so glad you're there. I'll just sit here and cry some more."

"You do that," Deena said. "I'm on my way."

Liz leaned back gingerly in the chair. She was terribly cold. One of Nick's shirts lay across the back of the chair, and she hooked it around and pulled it over her shoulders. Each move was a small victory. She thought of Hatt's neighbors, the women with the walkers, with their treasures tied up in handkerchiefs swinging from the hand-grip; the old rancher, struggling to bring his spoon to his mouth; the skeleton in the wheelchair, how she nodded and smiled and wove patterns in the air when the aide, against the rules, switched the television to MTV.

The door shook. Sugar finally butted it open and peeved into the cabin, complaining all the way. Sunlight and sweet piney air poured in. Bob opened his eyes and watched Liz for a minute, yawned, tucked his great head on his paws and slept. Liz leaned slowly forward and rested her head on her arms. She felt the sun touch her face . . .

. . . The harsh, haunting notes of Saqtiva floated out from the mesa top, the flute and drum weaving through the old men's voices, the crowd swaying to the music. All went silent. Talasi pressed close to Rupi.

The two eastern dancers began to climb their poles, reached the crossbars, slowly raised themselves and stood upright. Only their years of discipline and the People's prayers balanced them; nothing lay between them and the sand below.

The dancers lifted their heads, as deer might, or wolves. The watchers on the cliff heard nothing. The dancers flung themselves out, atlatl and arrow, thrower and thrown. They passed in mid-air, grabbed the opposite crossbar and swung out over the precipice. In that instant, Kihsi and his partner leaped to the top of the western poles, clutched the leather thongs and swung out into space, soaring in a great arc as the thong unwound, spiralling, out away from the solid rock, out on the evening air, burnished by the last rays of sunset, Kihsi's dark head golden, his body an arrow, shining. With every breath, Talasi sent him her strength, her love. It seemed forever that he soared there, hovering on the warm air, hovering on his Peoples' prayers.

The eastern dancers dropped to the ledge and raised their arms in gratitude. Kihsi and his partner drifted in, touched earth, drew breath, and leaped up, arms flung wide in joy. A triumphant cry rose from the old men. The flutes soared. The drum pounded through the earth, its rhythm solid as the stone, firm as the people planted on that ancient sand. Talasi watched through her tears as Kihsi walked to the hand-holds pecked in the *tuukwi*, and began to climb . . .

. . . Deena touched Liz's shoulder.

"Don't move," she said. She traced down her spine. "You're stiff," she said. "Where does it hurt?"

"Lower. There." Deena's hands seemed to gather up the pain.

"Don't try to get up," she said. "I'll be right back." She returned with a grocery bag in each arm. "Here's the paper and o.j. and a green chili omelet. I'll start the coffee. You feed yourself. We'll talk after we've both got some caffeine in us."

"I love it," Liz said, "Love it, love it, love it." Grinning, tears streaming down her face, she said cheerfully, "I'm a mess, just a mess."

"That's fine," Deena said and helped her sit up. "As long as you can cry and eat at the same time." She hugged Liz gently and set a tray in her lap. Liz sipped the orange juice and watched Deena. She ground coffee, put the water to boil, found cups and cream as though she were home. She leaned over the breakfast bar. "How you doing?"

Liz smiled and shrugged. "Weirdest crying I've ever done. Painless. It's like the tears have a life of their own." She dug into the omelet. It was stuffed with jack cheese and chilis and topped with guacamole. She cried through every forkful, till she started to laugh.

"Be careful," Deena said. "You're in no shape for that whatever maneuver!" Liz closed her eyes. She heard Deena humming to herself.

"Get ready," she said. "Here it comes." She poured water over the grounds and the dark perfume of fresh coffee filled the air. "That's it," Deena cried. "That's the reason to live!" She pulled up the rocker and handed Liz a mug of coffee laced with honey and heavy cream."

"I'm yours," Liz said. "I'll do whatever you tell me. I'll do anything, I'll even *babysit!* . . ."

"The tape's on," Deena said.

Liz laughed. "So this is what it's like."

"I'm supposed to say 'What?', right?"

"Being taken care of," Liz said. "Being a grown woman and being taken care of."

"Oh, yeah, that," Deena said. "That happened to me, once, when my sister came to visit and I had the flu. Yeah. Women get one shot at it a lifetime. Shut up and enjoy it."

"It's so simple. Really."

"It's a pleasure. Really."

"You'll get your turn. I promise. You'll get two shots at it in this lifetime and you don't even have to be sick."

"Dirty magazines," Deena said. "The kind with enthusiastic, dumb young men . . . and all the cocoa I can drink, with all the whipped cream for me."

"You're consistent."

"I am. Keep it simple!" She refilled their cups. "We better figure out where to go from here. I bet you sprained it. I called Lou Alonzo.

He's my doc. He'll treat you like you're not quite bright, but he knows his medicine."

The nurse wheeled Liz into the waiting room and waited by the chair. Liz's face was gray, her eyes bottomless, gray-green wells of nothing good.

"I don't believe I let them do it," she said.

"Do what?" Deena asked.

"Give me a shot. I told him I can't take drugs. He asked me how I knew. I told him I get depressed; it's in the genes. He said, 'Your jeans look fine to me.' The nurse came in and said it was a muscle relaxant and I let her give it to me. It's a tranquilizer. I can feel it. Listen to how funny I'm talking." She giggled and started to cry.

"You're getting yourself upset," the nurse said. "That will only make things worse." She turned to Deena. "She needs to stay flat for at least four weeks. And she needs to take these pills. They're anti-inflammatory, and they help the pain."

"Don't talk about me as though I'm not here," Liz blurted. "My God, that's how it was for Hatt. That's how it will be." She looked up at the nurse. "I'm here. I'm alert. It's my body!"

"I'm sorry," the nurse said. "I *am* sorry. When I had my last kid, they did the same thing to me. Do you want to ask me anything?"

"Tell us what I have," she said.

"You sprained your back. Then you kept moving. It's as though you carried a bowling ball with a sprained hand."

"I think I resent the part about the bowling ball," Liz grinned.

The nurse laughed. "That shot must be working," she said. "That one shot won't hurt you. You'd have to take pills for a few days. You're right about the pills. Forgive Alonzo. He doesn't believe in the mind except as a tool for logic."

"Thank you!" Liz said. "You're the best tool he's got."

"I suspect that's true," the nurse said.

"I do feel splendid," Liz said. "I think I can walk." She started to move and stopped. "Well, I could if I could get my arms to work."

"Can we talk about you in the third person now?" Deena said.

There was no answer. Liz fought to open her eyes, to agree with Deena, to let her know how very grateful she felt, but it seemed that she was turning into something wonderfully soft, something luminous and powerful. There was no pain. There never had been any. They floated her to the car, and then, there were light-years and light-years of the most gorgeous trees she'd ever seen, pine cathedrals, light pouring through them.

She gave a trial thought to Nick. Nick who? The pills were a logical and delightful idea. The cabin appeared. Deena parked and walked up to the door, tall and golden, clearly a goddess, a woman of Light. She re-appeared, tossed some bags in the back seat, and smiled at Liz.

"You are messed-*up!*" she said.

"Mmmmm," Liz said. Deena tousled her curls, saw the easy rise and fall of her breathing and, gently, shifted into reverse . . .

It was a long, hot trail that led to the western villages, to House of Eagles, Nest House, Water-Holding House and Fire Rock House. There were few juniper and, at mid-day, the *tuukwi* gave no shade. Talasi had been walking since First Dawn, up the dry washes, past the black hills, along the *tuukwi* top where wild flowers swayed over the cinders, purple and yellow and bright red. The moon-colored bells of sacred Datura lay along the trail, forbidden to her. Only the men used their luminous blossoms for sight.

She was thirsty. Before she drank, she scattered a few drops of water to the earth and turned in a slow circle, studying the horizon, the bushes, the shallow wash hazy with heat, all those shadowed beautiful places that might hold more than beauty; there was always danger in what could not be seen, for a woman . . . alone . . . so far from any village. Not many summers ago, not far from home two women had been raped. "Everywhere," the gossips had whispered. "Beheaded," they said. "Heads gone, never to be found." It was Kunya who had stumbled on their bloody bodies. For many moons, he had stayed away from the bone-dice, and when he had come to throw again, his hand trembled and he lost.

"*Powaqa,*" he had whispered. There was talk of a healing time for him, for the husbands and children of the two women. Talasi did not know what had happened. She was grateful to have been spared that work.

This work, the walk alone, the vigilence, her heart pounding in her breast, the blessed silence: she took it to her with joy. She drank slowly. One drank often and in small swallows. Travellers had been found, people from the mountains, dead from dry sickness, their flesh withered, water in their closed canteens.

A sparrow hawk swung low over the desert, hunting the small creatures frightened into motion by Talasi's steps. She thought of the dead women. She could not imagine rape. She had heard the sounds from her parents' mat. Sleeping at friends' houses from the time she was a little one, she had heard their mothers and fathers and peeked at them from under her sleeping robe. It was a strange dance, sometimes gentle and pretty, a man's hand trailing over a woman's unbound hair; sometimes sad, when a woman reached for a man, and he turned away; sometimes fierce and disturbing, lovers entwined, gasping, crying to each other, their bodies almost violent, their eyes closed, whether in passion or pain, she could not have told. Then, the dance seemed a battle.

But for a man to force a woman who did not want him, did not know him, that was unthinkable. Perhaps Kunya was right. Perhaps only the *powaqa*, the cold, two-hearted ones could do such a thing. She shivered and took another slow look around. All was still and peaceful, only heat-ripples and the gray-green leaves of the *sivahpi* moving. She tied the half-empty jug in her carrying sling and stepped out onto the trail.

Though she was a little afraid, she was happy. One was *always* a little afraid. Since the Old Ones, there had been raiders; forever, there had been danger. Masau'u had welcomed them to the harsh world, and one used one's fear to see the beauty. It was a harsh beauty, not for the careless. Had the trail been less-used, she would not have been allowed to go alone. She was happy for her solitude. It was the rarest gift, a gift few women received . . . or sought.

She thought of Kihsi. He had more than survived Saqtiva. His flight, his dance had been so sure and joyous that the elders saw rich harvests ahead for the villages. Many evenings, she looked up from her grinding to see his eyes just outside the window-slit. They were no longer children, permitted to meet outside that narrow space. She did not speak. She could only grind and sing. What she had to tell him could not be said in the maidens' songs. There was no song for it, no word. She waited patiently. He returned again and again. He was in her path, this man, his dark spirit woven in with hers. They had only to wait.

The sun walked with her. The juniper were few, one or two gnarled piñon rose from the shimmering grass. She saw a family of antelope, feeding quietly, too far away to be frightened into flight, close enough that she could see their black horns, the perfect heart of their white rumps against their pale brown coats. Two calves butted at their mothers' bellies. Tiny gray lizards scuttled across her path. She remembered the Spotted One and the ancient wall and Kihsi, his smile, his black, black eyes searching hers.

By the time she reached the northward turning, her shadow was long and thin. She had never taken this path, the faint trail to Toho's house, his kiva. He lived alone. His wife had died and he had taken no other. His one-room house was built from rough, black firerock, on a small *tuukwi* just north of Nest House and it's mother house, Kwaahuki; that great dwelling looked out over the valley where the eagles flew, where she and Kihsi had watched. He had taught her to see, to use her power to slow their flight in her mind's eye, so she could tell one from another: tattered old grandfather; sleek, nervy bucks; proud females, soaring above their nests, a king snake or lizard hanging from their beaks.

At the turning, she stopped, drank water and scattered the last drops to Mother Earth. She bowed to Father Sun and cast cornmeal to both, to Earth and Sun, in thanks for her safe journey, for childhood, for Pamosi's teaching. She gave thanks for the sweet and bitter-scented days learning medicines, for the dawns with the seeing stone, for the mysteries and recipes, the charms and teas, the lessons Pamosi had barely to speak, so strong was her teaching, so deep Talasi's hunger to learn.

She had not wanted to leave. It was good work there. Within. The grinding had become skill and comfort and path to Sight. But she had been summoned to Toho. It had never happened before. One sleepless night, Masau'u had returned, and the message had been clear. Talasi had dreamed the path, Pamosi, the story that would satisfy the gossips. Talasi was to care for him in his aging. No one knew how old he was—no one remembered his birth.

Masau'u brought more than a summons. He guided her into dreams, into a vision of a frail Toho, hesitant, yet burning, it seemed, with words. She had stood behind him, holding his trembling body, before them a great circle of elders. She had felt the words come through her, flowing from her breast into Toho's flesh, the words, her words stuttering from his lips.

"Beware," he had whispered, "there will be famine. Chaos. There will be dying babies and men mad with hunger. Many hungers. I come to tell you of winds tearing the soil from Mother Earth, of trees ripped from Her hillsides, their heart-roots withering in a new Sun's breath . . ." The words had become visible. They had twisted in on themselves and become a tongue, guttural and thick, a tongue not the People's. As the sounds poured, like poison snakes into the dark Kiva, the elders, one by one, closed their eyes and turned away, till all sat in a blind circle, each one alone.

She shivered. The shadows were moving in, blue and cold, and she was very tired. She settled the carrying sling firmly on her shoulders and took the path to Toho's house.

Twenty

DEENA LOOKED DOWN AT LIZ. She was huddled on the couch like a child, crying in her sleep. Deena brushed the damp curls away from her face and thought of Deej, of nightmares, of terrors beyond a mother's touch. Liz opened her eyes and stared at Deena's face.

"Good," she said and went back to sleep. Deena sponged her forehead, her wrists, her throat with cool lemon water. Deej wandered out of the bedroom, clutching her stuffed rabbit to her chest.

"Can I have some?" she said. Deena smoothed the water over her round arms.

"Is Liz very sick?" Deej asked.

"I don't think so," Deena said. Deej set the rabbit near Liz's arms. "She can borrow him," she said. "But she has to give him back."

"She'll be glad," Deena said. "She loves rabbits. She has them all over her house, big ones, little ones, funny ones, grumpy ones."

"Will she let me play with them?" Deej said.

"You bet." Deena leaned back against the couch and pulled Deej into her arms. "She's got kitties, baby ones. When she's better, we'll go have a picnic and you can meet them all." Deej stroked the stuffed rabbit with her bare foot.

"If Daddy says it's okay," she said . . .

. . . The trail wound between pairs of *tuukwi*, a narrow path, worn deep, curving in and out of sun and shadow, opening to a stretch of high desert, dotted with firerock, sprinkled with wildflowers and rabbit-brush. Talasi leaned against a boulder and looked up at the squat *tuukwi* ahead.

In the fading light, Toho's house could have been no more than a pile of fire-rock, thrown by Two-Color Mountain. Ladder poles thrust from a rock pile at the base of the *tuukwi* marked his kiva. There was no smoke, no light, no children or dogs, no cooking smells drifting out on the evening air. She had been told the trail; there were surprises there, dangers. No one ignorant of the trail's story could reach the top.

She let the boulder's warmth ease her aching body. She was hungry, but that was nothing new. As the droughts had held, all the people walked and worked and sat with hunger. She had fasted for three days and on the fourth, made the journey without food. She felt dizzy. The sunset blurred, and the last fiery arc dropped below the far mesas, a wave of brilliant green flaring and gone. The breeze sprang up, rattling the dry leaves of the *salavi*. She felt the pathstone cool in her palm.

"What?" She whispered.

The air shimmered to her heart-side. Light flickered across the path. She bowed her head.

"As You wish," she whispered. She wanted to settle the carrying sling on her back and run, so she pressed her palms against the rough boulder, the pathstone holding her steady. The light stopped, drew in on itself, burning brighter and brighter till she could not look. When she raised her eyes, she saw the woman, a woman who raised *her* eyes to Talasi, eyes that shifted color in the changing light, green to gray to blue, their centers shot with sunset gold. Talasi had heard that the *toho's* cousin, the short-tail cat, had eyes that color, but this woman was as human as she. *Pahaana* . . . and human. Talasi wondered why she had returned, and how.

The woman raised her heart hand. Around her wrist, she wore a circlet of shining metal and one of blue beads, *tsorposi*. Talasi touched her own beads and took heart. She studied the woman; she was very tall, her arms round and strong, as though she had known the grinding. Her fingers were long and thin, her bare feet delicate. Around her full face, not so different from the People's faces, her hair curled like hawk down. It seemed to catch fire in the setting sun. No one, not woman nor man from any direction, had hair like that. The woman looked frightened and tired.

Talasi held up her heart hand and the woman spoke, a harsh sound that made no sense. Others had come to Black Sand from far away, speaking strange tongues. Sometimes they stayed through a winter, talking only with their hands. This woman's hands did not speak. They trembled in the fading light. High above, the half-moon became brighter.

Talasi pointed to her bracelet. The woman nodded.

"*Wuhti*," Talasi said, "*Um waynuma? Um hin maatsiwa? Nu' Talasi yan maatsiwa.*"

The woman shook her head. She did not understand. Talasi stepped towards her. She pointed to her heart.

"Talasi," she said. "Talasi." She pointed to home "*Hoopoki. Hoopoki.*"

"*Hoopoki*," the woman smiled and pointed east. "Talasi," she said. She touched her heart. "Elizabeth," she said. Talasi could not repeat it. She shook her head and smiled.

The woman touched her heart again.

"Margaret," she said. *Ma'φqa'at* . . . perhaps . . . bones of the hand. Talasi's heart began to pound. The pathstone glimmered. She held up her heart hand and began to walk toward the woman. The woman slowly raised *her* hand and waited. Talasi beckoned to her and, step for step, eye to eye, they closed the distance and pressed their palms together. The woman closed her eyes. Talasi gasped; her head filled with a chaos of words and sounds and pictures, the pictures familiar, the buildings that pierced the clouds, huge terrible metal birds, a sky that burned and was not consumed, ashes covering the earth, babies cradling babies, old ones alone. She snatched away her hand. The woman opened her great eyes. She stepped towards Talasi.

"*Paas,*" she said. "Slowly." The light had gone cold. The shadows were gone. Only thin moonlight caught in the woman's hair. "*Paas,*" she said again.

"*Paas,*" Talasi said and stepped forward . . .

. . . "Liz! Liz!" Deena shook her. "Wake up! You've got to wake up. You're breathing funny." Liz opened her eyes. She smiled.

"No," she said. "Not yet." . . .

. . . Talasi watched the woman breathe and breathed with her. Again, they stepped forward and touched, only fingertip to fingertip. For a moment, there was skin on skin, the warmth of it, as delicate as milkweed down. In perfect Hopilavayi, Talasi heard the woman's words.

"I am Elizabeth Margaret," she said, "and you are Talasi. I have been dreaming of you."

"And I, of you," Talasi thought and smiled to see the woman nod . . .

. . . Elizabeth! Wake up! I'm going to pour water on you if you don't." Liz turned her face away. Her breath was slow and shallow. Deena checked her pulse. It seemed thready. She slapped her. "*Paas,*" Liz said.

"No paz," Deena snarled. "You're gonna wake up, girl!" . . .

. . . the woman's eyes locked with Talasi's. Her fingertip drifted back, as smoke fades, as water seeks the sun. She said something in her harsh tongue.

"*Wuhti,*" Talasi called. "*Pahaana. Tuumoki wuhti.* Dream Woman. Come back." There was no answer. She stood alone on the path to Toho's house . . .

. . . "Oh God," Liz said. "I'm dead. I know I am." Deena shook her. She grabbed Deena's hand.

"I'm not dead," she said. She tried to sit up. "I wish I was. Something died in my mouth. I can taste it."

"You're fine," Deena said. "But I wasn't sure for a minute."

Liz closed her eyes. "I think I'll just rest my eyes for a minute here," she said. "If I slip away, just let me go. I have the worst hangover I've ever had. It would be an act of mercy." Her eyes snapped open.

"I met her," she said. "I met Talasi."

"You said 'Paz'," Deena said.

"No," Liz said. "I said something else. I knew what it meant. We talked through our hands." She closed her eyes. "I told the doctor not to give me that stuff. I've gone over the edge. Can I have some water before they take me away? I smell lemons. I'm hallucinating."

"You're fine," Deena said. "Drink this." She held the glass to Liz's lips. "If you could just approach life with a little more imagination," she said, "you'd be fine." She smoothed lotion on Liz's arms. "That's the lemon. That's all it is." Go to sleep, rest . . . "

"How can I stay here?" Liz asked wildly. "Camped in your living-room? You won't have one minute of privacy."

Deena sighed. "I didn't think of that. You're right. With my social life . . . all the men . . . the intimate little dinner parties . . . the wine tastings . . ." She tucked the sheet under Liz's chin. "Why don't you shut up and *go to sleep*. It's nearly morning." She kisssed Liz's forehead and turned out the light.

The streetlamps threw shadow-branches on the walls. Liz could hear the faint clang of trains in the freightyard. The house was silent. She knew she was finally unmoored from home's shoreline. The big man wasn't swimming out for the rescue. She wanted his arms around her, holding in the terror, holding out the pain.

"Hey," Deena whispered from the bedroom. "Are you thinking about Nick?"

"Of course."

"I know. I do that, too. Whenever I'm sick or scared, I remember this boy I never even dated."

"It's a habit."

"Well, cut it out. See if you can think of the last time he took care of you . . . if ever."

"Thanks," Liz said. "I needed that." She was abruptly grateful Nick was far away. He'd run from sickness. Hers. His. Sick or hungover, he'd retreated to his cabin. She had always imagined him there, high on good dope, curled into the coolest, darkest shadow of the bed, going half-dead, as a wounded cat might. She did that, burrowing into her dark and trying to find the path there, the path that led back . . .

. . . Talasi searched the empty wash behind her, the *tuukwi*, the shadows and pale patches of moonlight. The woman was gone.

"As You wish," she whispered again. Her palm was empty. She traced the curve of the *tsorposi* bracelet, its stones luminous, its touch cool and familiar. It was her father's gift. He had traded two bags of salt for it, precious salt, brought up from the heart of the great *tupqa* to the west. A night-bird hummed past her head and swooped down over the floor of the wash. She looked up. Above, one star blazed, then another, and another. Below them, Toho's house squatted like a great cat.

She crossed the last stretch of sand to the boulder that marked the trail's beginning. Its shadow broke away and moved toward her. She smiled and bowed.

"Welcome, my niece," he said. He was smaller, thinner, more hunched than she remembered.

"I am happy to be here, uncle," she said.

"I have sent my helper, Owasi, to tell your family that I will need you here till winter."

She bowed.

"Follow me," he said, "This path is difficult." Sure-footed but slow, he led her across a long line of rocks. As they stepped onto a sandy trail to begin the climb, light glimmered to her left. There was no woman shining there, no Spirit-shifting. It was only moonlight on the ragged curve of a snake pecked in the dark rock, and higher, twined around a boulder, another, and slithering down from the *tuukwi* edge, another. Toho and his shadow wavered in and out of sight, weaving between boulders and cliff-face, as graceful as the snake, as mysterious as their clan. Of all the kivas, the least was known about those men who called the snake Brother, even *tsuu'a* with its terrible poison, Brother.

Toho appeared at her side.

"You are strong," he said, "and you pay attention."

"Thank you, Uncle," she said, and bowed. He waited in silence at her side.

"I have been told that you will be my teacher," she said. "I have come here to listen, to know if that is true."

Toho smiled. "I see that you are tired," he said. "I think food and sleep might be welcome." He eased the carrying sling from her shoulders. For an instant, she felt herself drift, as though her robe, the cornmeal she had brought as gift, had held her to the earth. She steadied herself on the boulder.

"That is ordinary magic," Toho said. "You have felt it before. It is in the body, not Spirit."

"You know my thoughts," Talasi said.

"No," he replied. "I too pay attention. This will be easier than you might guess. They say I am called Toho because I pounce. That is true, but I am called Toho for many reasons, as you are called Talasi because you are graceful and stubborn and a worker for Life. I can be quick. I can be fierce. I can be silent and I can scream. And I can be slow as the stalking lion and kind as a mother cat." He turned. "For now," he said over his shoulder, "I have fresh *pik'ami* and a warm house. Come and eat."

Talasi sighed. Her belly was a knot. She could endure it. She knew, as did all the People, how to do that: to wait, to be hungry. The hunger *to know* was starvation; to feed it was to ease the emptiness of her womb.

"I have heard you are impatient," Toho said. "That was not a sigh of relief." He slowed his pace and reached for her hand.

"Know this, child," he said quietly, "you began long ago."

Twenty-one

LIZ WOKE. THE HOUSE WAS NEARLY DARK. Deena sat in the tiny kitchen, reading, the radio murmuring, a small lamp glowing on the table.

"Yes," she said quietly, "you lost a day."

Liz stretched and caught herself. The pain pinched in her back, along the tops of her thighs.

"It was probably better lost," she said. Deena picked up a tray and brought it to the couch.

"Welcome," she said. "Can you eat?"

"Always," Liz said. She started to push up, went gray and flopped back. "Whoa," she said. "Whoa." Deena set the tray on the coffee table and took Liz's hand.

"Your pulse is jumping," she said.

"I'm scared," Liz said.

"I can help."

"Do it."

She helped Liz sit up, plumped the pillows behind her and set the tray in her lap.

"You've made my fantasies real," Liz said. The tray was beautiful, old, chipped enamel, cabbage roses and one iridescent bug-eyed butterfly; it held an iris in a pint milk carton and a sandwich garnished with tomato roses and sprigs of mint. Under the plate lay a magazine, from the cover, a young man with impossibly beautiful shoulders smiled vaguely.

Deena set a goblet near the sandwich. "Fresh-squeezed," she said. "Cheers."

"I don't believe this," Liz said. She sipped the juice. "Grapefruit," she said. "How did you know?" She grabbed for the napkin. "Oh no," she said, "here I go again." The tears rolled down her cheeks.

"Not again," Deena said. "This is the last time I do anything for you."

"You wait," Liz said. "You just wait." She blew her nose. "I used to be like you. I'm scared I'll never get it back."

"Get what back?"

"Wanting to do stuff like this. I used to. Really. I used to give great everything. I can't anymore."

"What happened?"

"Well, I figured I was this dark, sturdy, not particularly beautiful package of brains who ought to be grateful if some sucker saw the beauty inside."

"You got part of it wrong."

"What part?"

"Dark . . . it happens to big blondes, too! Plus, we're only half of the equation. The other half are the women who are gorgeous and keep hoping some sucker'll see past that to what's inside."

"So, as though I need to tell you, I became The Giver. At first, they loved it. Nick said once, "Great food, great sex, great talk." That summed it up. I was very, very careful. I studied them. I listened. Men don't like demands. They don't like too much deep talk. I worked hard to be 'different from other women.' That's what they always said. 'You're different from other women. I can talk to you.' You know what that means?"

"Uh uh."

"It means 'you're not pretty. I'm not threatened by you. I will shortly lose interest.'"

"I'm taking notes."

"So they'd hang out and wear the embroidered shirts and come in late or not show up at all and, finally, just have to be honest with me because I was such a good woman, about the other woman, the real love, the one they'd found while they were coming home late. And, they'd be on their way. I was everybody's 'in-between' mama, she who is on the way to the real thing."

"I detect a touch of bitterness here," Deena said.

"No, not me."

"That's why I like *these* magazines," Deena said. "These guys will never turn on you." She patted the pretty boy's butt.

"I thought Nick was different. He was honest enough to warn me. 'Don't fuss over me,' he said. 'Don't keep my brand of beer around and send me cards . . . I'll walk all over you.' So, of course, thrilled as I was to have this beautiful young man in my company, I did, and he did. Of course, I never heard him complain while he ate all the beautiful meals and drank the great wines."

"Was he really beautiful?"

"Who knows? I thought he was. You want to hear the most pitiful part?"

"Sure."

"Even though I hated him smoking cigarettes, I kept a spare pack of his brand in my dresser. He never knew about them. I didn't throw them out till the day I packed to come out here."

"I let Jack hit me," Deena said flatly. "More than once."

"I see."

"I was an idiot."

"No. It's something else. It's not stupidity. Nick hit me and I hit him."

"It's over, right?" Deena said. "It's over."

"That part."

"It's *all* over for Jack and me, every speck, the hitting, the thinking we'd get back to the beach-bunny days, whatever dreams we thought we had." She nudged the plate toward Liz. "I can live with it. You eat. Mocha Fudge ice cream for dessert." She kissed Liz's forehead and went back to the kitchen.

Liz ate slowly, a perfect *BLT* on whole-grain bread. She heard the dishes rattle in the sink, the rush of water, Deena's faint song, her hushed footsteps in the hall.

"See you in the morning," she whispered.

"Sweet dreams," Liz answered. She closed her eyes. Elmo, Deena's magnificent long-haired tabby, nosed her hand with his wet nose. "Later," she whispered. Deej giggled in her sleep. Liz let the tray slide to the floor. A motorcycle, a big one, screamed around the corner and up Mars Hill . . . not Nick and his damn bike, but she half-expected to hear eastern doves, the steady rumble of the bigger city, Keith's notes floating up the stairs.

"Oh no you don't," she whispered to herself. "That's gone." Gorgeous settled in against her hip. She wondered if Deena had left food and water for Bob and Sugar, and knew she had. She started to drift and heard the sigh of silk. A shadow loomed above her; it spoke English.

"Here," Deena said, "Mocha Fudge" . . .

. . . Talasi lay awake. Toho had built a fire.

"These cool Pamuya nights hurt my bones, " he had said. "And this is for my guest." He cast a powder on the flames. Sweet smoke billowed up. In the fire's heart flashed sunset and green after-glow. He watched her closely, she had felt that. Even as the last pinch of powder exploded in a shower of sparks, she had not flinched.

Rolled in his robe, Toho watched her face in the firelight. Her eyes were closed, but he knew that she was awake. Earlier, he had watched her move through the cluttered room. He had seen that she was not fooled by the apparent carelessness. She asked permission, touched a few things, picked them up and set them back where she had found them. He had seen the treasures of the room through her eyes: the baskets of the Old Ones, painted with scorpions and three-headed lizards and horned men; the shadowed niches holding turquoise birds and gleaming shell bowls; the wounded owl, its great eye burning like an ember; and, hanging from a beam, the atlatl quiver, made from the lion's tufted tail. She had set it swinging and watched its shadow on the wall.

"How was she taken?" she had asked.

"She came to someone," he said. "Long ago. The atlatl, the darts have not been used since before my time." She had reached up to touch a cluster of hawk feathers that hung from a plaited cord.

"And these?"

"I do not know," he said.

"This cord," she said. "Its four colors are not of the directions."

"No," he said. "It came from an old house, half-buried on the side of Two-Color Mountain."

"They did not use dyes," she said. "White, brown, this light green, this sand; they are the colors of the plants themselves. Our sacred cords are dyed. Yet, the work is so carefully done, as though this were for a ceremony." She watched his face.

"I have no answer," he said. "Perhaps as you work here it will tell you its story." She nodded. He had smiled to himself. He had known her calm was well-crafted. When he handed her supper, he was happy to find that her hands were damp with sweat. It was good that she was a little afraid; that was the beginning of wisdom. It was good that her face did not show fear; that was the sign of courage. He had watched her grace as she cleared away the dishes. She moved well, without hesitation or waste.

She had set their dirty bowls by the hearth. "The ants are not yet returned. I will clean these with our morning dishes," she said. "I am tired." Perhaps most important, she was not driven by habit. He had nodded and handed her the sleeping mat and pointed to a pile of blankets. He had watched while she chose one beautifully woven from cotton, in the manner of the people of Salapa. His second teacher had given it to him long ago. She examined it carefully, running her fingers over the weave.

"There is heart in this work," she said and they went to their sleeping places.

Talasi listened for Toho's breathing. She heard the slight shift in rhythm that meant he slept, and she opened her eyes. She wondered if she would ever sleep again. Her teeth chattered. She pressed her hand over her lips. Firelight played over the hawks' feathers, the swaying golden tail; the baskets, their figures dancing with the flames. In the shadowed niches she saw the glint of turquoise and shell, as one saw moonlight or stars.

She thought of the *pahaana* and wondered if she had been Toho's creation. "Bones of the Hand." It was a most unusual name. She turned on her side, fidgeted, stretched and rolled back. The fire died out. Star Beings moved across the roof-hole: lizard's head, atlatl point, snake's tail and scorpion's sting. As always in summer, she missed Hotomqam and the seven shining sisters of Tsovawtaqam.

Just as she felt sleepy, there was the faint shift in the black sky that signalled night's end. First Dawn melted in. Without a word, Toho rose stiffly from his mat and climbed to the roof. Talasi waited for his return. As the light warmed from gray to yellow, she cleared away the ashes and laid the morning fire. Toho returned, moving slowly, his face tight with pain. She offered a cup of water. He smiled.

"Go," he directed. "Say your prayers. Say one for me, for *us*, that Taiwa will light our work . . ."

. . . Waking and dreaming blurred, the days slipping by in a haze of pain and medicine, the evenings a comfort. The house was cool and quiet, its thick walls holding out the June heat, the street noise. Only the train whistle, the motorcycles came wailing through. Liz felt insulated and peaceful, lost from time. Deena brought her library books and ginger-ale and, when the pain had lessened and she could sit up, a pile of clothes and buttons. "Earn your keep," she said. It was part of the gift of that month that they lived together cheerfully and that Deena could so thoroughly read her mind. Books and work were anchors; unmoored by her faithless body, she was grateful for both. Books had always been shoreline and sea. She remembered a long childhood fever, how you could float on it in the company of stories, The Green Fairy Book—and Red and Gold and Blue—a rainbow of old tales, as though a child lay, on a raft, drifting from shore to foreign shore. In Deena's empty house, ginger-ale going flat on the coffee table, she went back to those stories . . . and forward.

She read till her eyes burned: *The Once and Future King, The Magic Journey, Grendel* and *Surfacing*. She thought of the years she had feared being dreamy and helpless . . . and her helplessness, her dreamy hours seemed the sanest she'd ever been. Without Deena, without the stories she might have been lost. Without shelter and friendship and craft she might have drowned in isolation and nostalgia; those were the deep, stale waters.

Deej brought her a candy bar.

"You can keep the rabbit till you go home," she said, "but you can eat the candy bar." She watched Liz unwrap it. "My back hurts a little bit," she said.

"About this much?" Liz measured a chunk of the bar with her thumbnail.

"That much," Deej said. She was a serious child.

"She's a Watcher," Liz said. "I was one too."

"Me too," Deena said. "I wish she wasn't. Sometimes, I wish she'd just lie down on the floor and scream and turn blue. Even when she's crying, a little part of her stands back."

Deej fetched in her books and sat on the floor, her back straight against the couch, while Liz read. She had a special treasure, a bug-eyed, long-lashed pink unicorn. Deej carried it everywhere, its gargoyle head peeking from her pocket, her tiny purse, her backpack. She braided its flowing mane and glued beads to its back.

"Me and Kya," she said. "We go places." She wouldn't tell them where.

On Wednesday and every other Friday, she and Kya went out to her father's car.

"I hate this," Deena said. "Every time. I'm scared he'll kidnap her and I hate the returns. Every visit with him is Christmas: restaurants, shopping, new clothes, new toys, on and on, ice cream and candy and everything she wants. I can't do that. I won't. You've seen her. 'It's no fun here, Mommy. You take Daddy's money. Daddy buys me *that*.' He's killing us."

"No. She's alive. He can't start beating you and finish with her. There's that."

Deena shook her head. "I'm telling you. The day is coming . . . . If I didn't know other women who were going through the same thing, I'd just give up. It's like some soap opera." She stomped into the kitchen. "Sherry takes tranquilizers all the time. Did you know that?" she yelled. "She passed out a few nights ago. Came to, in front of the television, with a pint of ice cream melted in her lap." She laughed. "Why am I laughing? It's not funny, not really." She leaned against the door-jamb and looked down at Liz. She wore an olive-green t-shirt. A Mother's Day present, it had a cheerful heart-eyed bear on it.

"Change that shirt," Liz said, "and come in and talk to me."

"Not now," Deena said, "I'm gonna wallow for a while. Sometimes the wisest thing a friend can do is let her best bud wallow."

A few days later, Paul came by with home-made beer, a bag of Claire's green-corn tamales and a rueful story.

"It's not funny," he said. "Stop laughing. You're supposed to have a black belt in sympathy, right?"

"Empathy," she said, "with empathy, you get to snicker. Go ahead. Really. I'm listening, honest."

"Okay," he said. "This is very serious. The reputation of Qumovi Tuuwa is at stake. He gets this glazed, predatory smile every time he sees certain tourists."

"Scholars. Anasazi addicts?"

"No."

"Bodacious ta-ta's?"

"Yes."

"I thought so. There's a clinical term for it."

"What's that?"

"Testosterone poisoning. It's fatal."

"Poor guy! I'm so glad you can clarify this for me. I failed the mental health crises part of my training. Here's progression of symptoms: He spots her; she spots him. I think it's pheromones. He drops everything and insists on escorting her on a personal tour of one of the more remote ruins. Okay I'm not denying that they both come back with that look of job satisfaction so crucial to the well-being of ranger and visitor, but when he gets like that, he can't think, and when he can't think, he can't read and when he can't read, he can't figure out grant requirements and when he can't write grants, we don't get any money." He sighed. "Testosterone poisoning?"

"A classic case," Liz said.

They split a bottle of the gamy beer.

"Reminds me of Wales," Liz said. "My ex-professor took me there on your taxpayer money. We went to this little pub where the ale looked like horse piss, right down to bits of straw floating in it. I drank it straight down, right in front of the three old guys at the bar. You could hear the sigh of relief when we left. I've never known if it was because I was a woman, or because Lazar was wearing one of those lord-of-the-manor khaki jackets with flaps all over it."

"You've got a real soft spot in your heart for him, don't you?"

"He was an unforgettable kind of guy," Liz said cheerfully. "He had the same problem with research assistants and secretaries that Yates has with tourists. Fortunately, he's there and I'm here. That's the only cure for innocent female victims of testosterone poisoning: isolation."

"Liz," Paul said.

"Paul."

"We're not all the same," he said.

"Yeah, but the good ones are taken. Okay?"

"Change the topic?"

"Fine."

"Tell me about Wales."

"Not so different from here. The northern part is mountains and semi-charming towns and hordes of tourists. The south is trashed. The people are warm and gloomy and the restaurants fully as awful as ours. The Welsh seem to feel the same way about the English that the Indians seem to feel about us."

"Every which-a-way," Paul said.

"Yeah, and they've got mountain streams, we've got high desert. And we've all got mutton!"

"I've wanted to go there since I was a little kid," Paul said.

"You like these old places, don't you?" Liz asked.

"I do. Sometimes I stand out there near Juniper Spring at dawn and I can feel those old guys around me, just that: no vision, no voices, just a feeling."

"Would you have been drinking much of this fine beer the night before?"

"Could be," he grinned. "Wales . . . could you feel them there, the old ones?"

"We went one afternoon," Liz said, "to a little spit of land on the northwest coast, near Anglesey. According to the old stories, Anglesey was one of the strongholds of the Druids. On this point, its western wall green with seaweed, was a beehive cell, big enough for one monk. It had been built in 900 A.D. I stood on that ground and I was home in a way I've never felt before, on rock that was there long before the monk, long before my people."

"We can't do that here," Paul said. "Not like that. They can."

"They?"

"The Indians, here. The Welsh, there. We're aliens. We always will be. Aliens everywhere."

"I'm glad *you're* out *there*," Liz said. "They need you."

"They sure hold onto me," he said. "I try for other jobs, other places, and when I get rejected, I'm always glad." He smiled. "There's two of me now. There's a new ranger. She's Hopi and she breathes fire. She's quiet and polite and she—ever so respectfully—keeps letting us know what's what, where things belong." He grinned. "Get it?"

"Hatt's things," Liz said. "She's a link."

"I think she'll be perfect. She'll do it exactly as it needs to be done. You'll meet her soon. Don't let her scare you. She can be very cool."

"So can I."

"Right," Paul said. "Poker face, that's you." He tipped up the last of the beer. "Keep the bottle," he said. "It's desert glass. Nice for posies." It caught light and held it, lavender, a bottle filled with evening.

"What's her name?" Liz asked.

"Ms. Tewa," he said. "In a way, it means fighter. She'll tell you some-day. Especially if you don't ask."

"Sounds like most of my lovers."

"Liz."

"Paul."

He tapped her gently on the head with the bottle. "Find some posies, will you?" he said. "Those days are over. Celebrate!"

"I do," she said. "More and more. Every day."

"I see it," he said.

"Thanks. And tell Claire that the next time we eat, I'm doing the cooking. This has gone far enough."

"Just get better," he said. "Claire loves it. She loves what she does, and so do I."

"You're very lucky."

"I am," he said. "That luck includes friends. Be clear about that."

Deena pulled in the driveway a little after dark. Liz held up the bag of tamales.

"Claire strikes again," she said. "And there's beer in the refrigerator. It tastes just like horse piss. I didn't have the heart to tell Paul."

"If it's cold, I'll drink it," Deena said. "The air-conditioner went down." She grabbed the tamales. "I'll warm these lil' darlin's up."

The tamales were pure genius. Claire had done something magical with the sauce. It was hot and gentle and spicy, warming the throat and lingering on the tongue like good lust.

"I love that woman," Deena said. She iced some coffee and brought it to the low table.

"I think I can walk outside," Liz said. "Let's sit on the stoop and watch the traffic go by."

"Whew. I don't know if I can handle the excitement."

The sun dropped behind Mars Hill. Green twilight lingered. Deena's peach trees were ebony.

"Those peaches look like jade," Liz said.

Deena looked at her.

"Solitude makes me poetic. Enjoy it!" Liz smiled.

The western clouds flared rose-gold.

"I love this place," Liz said.

"Me, too. I'm going dancing tonight. In how many other towns can a lady go dancing alone?"

"Moab," Liz said, "if they allow dancing."

"I don't think Mormons are quite like Baptists," Deena said. "I do believe they allow the pleasures of the flesh. It's just caffeine that's out." She stood. "Hurry up and heal that back. I'll miss you." She kissed the top of Liz's head and walked away down the quiet street. Elmo crept through the flowers, stalking something invisible and dreadful. Liz missed the cats. She wondered about Sugar's kittens, the garden, whether Bob was eating enough. She hoped they had survived. The phone rang. She hobbled in and caught it on the sixth ring.

"Stranger," Rose said. "Where have you been? I called your cabin for days and all I got was that electronic creep on your phone machine. Even he finally died. I drove out there and this number was pinned to the door."

"I hurt my back. I'm at Deena's. I should have called, but this is the first day I've been up. I ain't faithful, honey, but I'm true."

Rose snorted. "I'm sorry. It's awful here. She's having a rough time. I think your visits kept her connected. When are you coming back?"

"I have to stay put for another week or so. Can you bring her here?"

"I don't know if she'll come. She's hardly in the present. She's somewhere else; back on the post, I think. It's awful."

"My favorite aunt went that way. She'd been a classical pianist and the funniest woman alive. She ended up tied in a chair, muttering switchboard extensions from a job she'd had when she was thirty."

"That's how it is," Rose said. "She's trading, arguing, afraid of something, but the worst part is when she comes out of it. She realizes she's made a mess. It's awful, the shame."

"Try to bring her here. Please."

"Staff isn't supposed to take out patients. There's some rule about insurance and favoritism. But I'll see if I can get one of my cousins to come with us, like a volunteer." She sighed. "What a crazy place."

"I'll be there as soon as I can," Liz said. "I'll write her tomorrow. I've got to settle back into the cabin, find a job. It should be ten days, maybe less."

"I'd like to visit," Rose said. "Is that okay?"

"Of course," Liz said. "Any day, any time." She paused. "Are you all right? You know you didn't need to ask me that."

"I'll tell you when we're face-to-face," Rose said. "My life's . . . I'll tell you next time we talk. Gotta run."

Elmo knocked over Deena's glass and lapped up the creamy coffee.

"A wired cat." Liz said to him. "I tell you, Elmo, these are some crazy days."

Twenty-two

"THIS PLACE REMINDS ME OF MY AUNT'S," Rose said. "We'd have mats and sleeping bags and old mattresses spread all over. We had a ball. We'd steal chips and stuff, see who could stay up the longest, spy on the grown-ups. When they came in to see what was going on, we'd be all huddled up, just like puppies in a pile." She took a little cloth-wrapped bundle from her pocket.

"For you," she said. She looked around. "Yeah," she said, "this place is about the size of my Aunt Leora's. You couldn't turn around in the kitchen without bumping somebody in the living-room. She used to make enough food for twenty people in that kitchen. Every weekend. She was magic!"

She wrapped Liz's fingers around the bundle. "For healing," she said. "Aunt Leora taught me a little. Not that she knew. I used to hang around and spy. Please open it."

Liz spread the leaves on the table. They were still supple. Their scent filled the room.

"Willow herb," Rose said, "and juniper and groundsel and sage, and rosemary just because it smells so good. You can make tea with them. You can make smoke. You can sleep with them under your pillow."

Liz picked up the rosemary and the sage. "They're beautiful together," she said. The sage was soft as a kitten's ear. She crushed a few leaves in her fingers and rubbed the oil into her wrists. "Rosemary makes a wonderful rinse for dark hair."

"Did one of your aunts teach you that?"

"No. It says it on the Nature's Pathway All-Natural Herbs and Natural

Plants and Flowers Rosemary Shampoo bottle. Plus, there's this model on television swinging enough hair for three women around on her head. I have been studying these things the last few weeks. You can read for only so long."

"The ways of your people are like the ways of my people," Rose said dramatically. She picked up Deej's doll. "This She-Ra, who my daughter also follows, you know of her?"

"Of her," Liz said, "and He-Man, her sacred consort and the great fuzzy bird and the One Who Eats Cookies. It is powerful teaching, not all of it good."

"Perhaps one of my people will write a book someday about all of this," Rose said. "And make much money and fame off your peoples' legends."

"It is time," Liz said. "Perhaps this person of your people will call the book *Revlon Woman* or *Tales of Visa*."

"*Antsa,*" Rose said. "That means 'very well, let's get on with this story.'"

"How's Hatt and how're you?"

"She's slipping in and out. I got permission for my cousin and me to take her out, but when I told her about visiting you, she said she would rather stay put." Rose paused. "I'm not sure she knew who you were, but she covered it well. I think she's afraid of letting anyone see her confusion. It must be awful. Knowing. Better to have a stroke and get it over with. Forgive me."

"I've thought that a lot," Liz said. "I'd guess she thinks it. Has she said anything more about her belongings?"

"She talked about a bracelet some Hopi man had given her. Kwaayo. That's what she called him. She looked sad when she said his name. He was a trader. I think he was a friend to her and her husband. There's a picture of him in her album."

"That's odd," Rose said. "We don't like pictures."

"I know. I knew a man like that. I burned the only picture I had of him." She laughed. "He was in bed, wrestling with my dog."

"The ways of your people are strange," Rose said.

"*Antsa.* I think we're going to have to get her stuff as soon as possible. What can you do about her?"

"Hey!" Rose said. "I am extended-care facility personnel. No problem. We just use Standard Operating Procedure. This is an ancient ceremony in which the old one is allowed to deteriorate until she needs medical care, shipped off to the hospital, rehabilitated at great expense and shipped back, so she can fall apart again. Many of the old ones have gone through this two or three times till they died. This gives many people jobs. It keeps much silver flowing into the hands of the Rich Ones."

"And how are *you?*" Liz said.

"Like that," Rose said. "Nasty. Fed-up." She sat on the floor and leaned against the couch.

"My husband wants to come back. He's getting out of this thirty-day treatment program he's been in for a year. He says 'things are different, baby.' My mother tells me to take him back, 'for the sake of the family.' She is very busy cleaning up after my dad's money messes, 'for the sake of the family.' Hatt is dying. Worse. Her body is fine and her soul is dying. My daughter really has a She-Ra next to her Hé-é-e Kachina. She asked me yesterday where we come from and I had to go to the library to get some *pahaana*'s book on us. Sorry." She blushed. "And I'm so lonesome I can't see straight."

Monsoon air drifted over them, wet, perfumed with Deena's flowers. Rose breathed deep.

"I love that," she said. "Aunt Leora says we Hopi are born with joy for rain, that our hearts lift when we smell rains coming."

"Aunt *Leora?*"

"I know. They took her away to school when she was little. Her mother hid her, but the government found her. They named her Leora. Her real name is Osuwa. It means sprig. I don't *have* a real name, but my kids do. I got a dictionary at school. I'll tell you, but you mustn't use them. It's a double secret I suppose."

"I promise," Liz said.

"My boy's name is Saami. It means fresh corn. That's very sacred to us. My girl's is Soona. It means the heart of something, the seed."

"Those are wonderful names," Liz said. "We used to give children names like that, back in the full-tilt hippie days. I thought about it for my kids, but didn't do it." She smiled. "I guess I knew times would change. In my heart, I wanted to name them Wolf and Jay and Orphé. Can you imagine a corporate lawyer named Wolf Morrigan?"

"I think," Rose said, "that a secret name is a source of power. I don't think it goes on a nameplate. Those are good names, Wolf and Jay. What is Orphé?"

"French for Orpheus, an ancient musician, a singer. I would listen to Keith's guitar and think of him. The name is doubly powerful because a French artist, Jean Cocteau, made a film about Orphé. Keith loves Cocteau, and he loves movies."

"You see," Rose said. "You *pahaana* have your stories. You have your Spirits." She paused. "Before I am much older," she said, "I want my stories, my Spirit. I want to know my real name."

"And I," Liz said. "There are two of us, dis-spirited, un-named."

"No," Rose said. "There are tens of thousands. I think of Connie. My mother. Hatt. I will not let that happen to my children. Soona will not be told that because she is a girl who was raised in town, she is only half-Hopi."

"There was a girl who was told that?"

"Yes."

"It sounds Catholic," Liz said, "1940s Catholic. The nuns did the work, the priests did the mysteries. There was nowhere for a nosy little girl to go, except to Mary, and she just stood there."

"But she was a mother," Rose said. "She couldn't have just stood there!" She laughed. "I put some things together, from Aunt Leora's whispers, from these books. We have Mothers in our Way. Grandmothers, too. Spider Grandmother. Mother Earth. Kachina Mother. Crow Mother. That much I got!"

"I did get hawks," Liz said. "They came to me back East and they come to me here, so it's not so empty."

"Be careful who you say that to," Rose said. "Not everyone out here accepts those things. People could be afraid of you, especially Indian people." She paused. "Me, too. They come to me, hawks. They have talked to me and helped me. Once, I was visited by a friend who had died. He came to me in a dream while I was driving. He woke me and saved my life."

Liz nodded. "A friend woke me, a year before he died. Michael looked like a red-tail. The day after he died, a little sparrow-hawk flew into the fence he'd built. We buried them together. Under a pine tree, so he could go into the earth and feed it, become it."

"You see," Rose said. "You know what to do. He knew. We call the red-tail *kyeele*, because her name is a little like her hunting cry. To be greeted by one of them is the best thing that ever happened to me." She crushed a sprig of juniper between her fingers and held it under Liz's nose. Her eyes were wet. "Look at me," she said. "I am so emotional. My cousins tease me. They say I'm like a white lady." She poked Liz gently and stood up. "Can we find some coffee here? Would Deena mind if I made some?"

"She'd be delighted. She's been doing all the nursing lately."

Rose clicked on the coffee-maker. "She had it all set up."

"She's a wonder woman. She's a Hé-é-e. All working woman are," Liz said.

"You're a feminist, aren't you?" Rose asked. "I'm not joking. I want to know."

"I am," Liz said. "That's a real name. That's a Spirit."

"My Aunt Osuwa says that feminists are nothing new. She says she's been doing it for years. She says, 'Some of these Hopi mens . . . what choice do the ladies have?' The other ladies in the village say she has a big mouth." She laughed. "She does."

She brought them both coffee. "You know, it's hard up there these days. I'm not the only one with one foot in Hopi and one in *Pahaana*-land. My mom, she lectures me about my butt being too big and her feelings are destroyed if I don't eat her fry bread and *nok qui vi* and dumplings. My cousin Connie, she dances the women's dances, she can tell the old stories from dusk to dawn . . . and she takes money from men, for booze . . . for that damned cocaine. My other cousin's little boy . . . " She stopped. "He got messed-with," she whispered, "by that dirty old teacher, that *powaqa* man." She shivered.

"I read about that. I'm sorry." Liz waited.

"I shouldn't have said that," Rose said. "There were fifty or more of them, all little boys. It makes me want to throw up." She set her coffee on the table. "There's more. People are killing themselves. Young people. Some of the drunks have sold sacred objects to *pahaanas*." She rubbed some sage on her throat. "And here I sit with you, because I can't talk to my cousins, because the only one that *will* talk to me is Connie and I'm not speaking to her."

"You can't talk to your cousins?"

"Not really. I don't grind corn. I don't make *piki*. I don't go to all the dances and I won't let my husband come home. I have white friends. I am *qahopi*. They are nice to my face and they gossip behind my back. 'That town-girl, that pahaana-lover.' It hurts my heart. My cousin, Bernice; she'll stand there, in her AC/DC t-shirt and act so sweet and the whole time, she's getting information to take back to the others."

"We do it, too," Liz said. "Make no mistake. We kill each other with gossip. Maybe we're doing it now."

"No," Rose said. "We are lightening our hearts." She sipped her coffee. "Somehow, I think it helps. Someday, when I know more, when I am stronger, I will talk to my cousins this way. I can start with Connie."

Deena poked her head in the front door.

"Lose your key?" Liz said. "Remember, you live here?"

"Are you decent?" Deena whispered. "You've got company."

"Company? Almost everybody I know in Arizona is here."

"It's Macleod," Deena hissed. "He's in the driveway."

"Wonderful," Liz said. "Give me a break."

"He followed me. He's all apologies. What'll I tell him? He's unusually persistent."

"Tell him to come in," Liz said. "I'll deal with it."

Deena stepped in. Behind her, hat in hand, grinning, stood Macleod. Rose glanced up. Something closed her smooth face. It was barely perceptible, a tightening, a caution. Liz saw that, saw Deena head for the coffee, saw Macleod's big hands crushing his hat and felt a lurch of heat in her gut.

"Macleod," she said. He stepped to the foot of the couch.

"Don't blame your friend," he said. "I made her an offer she couldn't refuse."

"You might have called to see if it was visiting hours," Liz said. "That's not your style, is it?" He shook his head.

Rose briskly gathered up her purse.

"Liz," she said, "I must leave. I'm late."

"Rose," Liz said, "this is Macleod. Mac, this is Rose Willard." Rose nodded. Liz felt she had been caught out at something, had seen the lurch of heat, the dumb hunger that lay behind it. She looked up into Rose's eyes. They were flat.

"Thank you for the visit," she said. "For the herbs. I'll use them. I think I'm going to need them."

"You better," Rose said. Her eyes softened. "I will come again, if you like. Just call me."

"Any time," Liz said. "Any time is a good time."

Rose bent and kissed her on the forehead. She stepped back and gave her a searching look.

"I'm all right," Liz said

"This is no hawk," Rose said.

"Really. I'm all right. I know that."

"Hey," Deena said. "This coffee is great. Come back, Rose. Any time." Rose left. Macleod stood by the piano, looking like a man who had stepped out for a beer and found himself on another planet.

"Pretty intense lady," he said cheerfully.

"Ladies," Liz said.

"Right," he said. She watched him look around the little room for a place to sit. She thought of a Sun Bear she had once seen in a zoo. Bulky and graceful, it had circled its tiny cage. She wondered why she was thinking in metaphors.

"Grab a pillow," she said. She could hear Deena taking a shower.

Macleod hunkered down near her. He smelled good, a little sweaty, clean, the waft of a recent beer on his breath.

"Haven't sat on a floor since I was a pigtailed hippie," he said. "Did the whole shot, lived in a school bus, had a dog with a bandana, grew my own, the whole enchilada."

It was time to talk code: I am. You are? Do we speak the same language? She wanted to press their palms together and get it all over with. She looked across at this big hands. There was a softness in them that surprised her. Macleod caught the look.

"No ring," he said. "I'm a committed bachelor."

"I'm not," Liz said.

"What?"

"A bachelor. I've been married four times, at least . . . two of them legal. Been seriously in love once and never got over it. Nice track record, but it's mine."

"Well," he said slowly, "truth is, I'd be glad to know a lady with some miles on her. There's a lot of 'girls' in this town."

"Get this straight," Liz said. "You just insulted me. And them. I was just as smart when I was eighteen."

"Whoa," he said. "You *are* intense." He grinned.

You better love it now, Liz thought, 'cause you'll hate it later. "Consider yourself warned," she said.

Deena sidled into the room.

"Well," she said. "I have to pick up Deej and it's Friday night, so she and I usually do a little shopping and get a bite to eat and maybe see a movie, so, I'll just . . . "

"Do your Diane Keaton imitation?"

"Leave you two alone." She stepped behind Macleod and gave Liz the raised eyebrow.

"That will be fine," Liz said.

"You can take my driver's license," Macleod said. "I can see you ladies run a tight ship here." "She'll be safe."

"That's okay," Deena said. "I memorized your license plate number and my boyfriend's a cop. No problem." She strolled out through the door and the house was, suddenly, small and quiet. Macleod cleared his throat.

"You ladies really take care of each other," he said. "I feel like a fox in a hen-house."

"Nicely put," Liz said. "So. Who are you and why are you here?"

"I'm a sub-contractor, framing, wiring, wallboard, finishing. I've got a degree in education, unused. I can't stand to be indoors for more than a couple of hours at a time. I was in Viet Nam and it made me a man. Nasty time, but I grew up there. I live an hour south of town, and I've wanted to get in the sack with you ever since I first saw you."

"I *am* a terrific dancer," she said.

"I bet."

She glared at him. Under the blanket, she was hanging onto her thumbs.

"Have you ever loved anybody?" she asked. They both looked stunned. She bet her eyes were all pupil. "*And* been loved?"

"Yes," he said carefully, "I think I have. It was a long time ago."

They were silent. Liz was sharply aware of everything: the threadbare touch of the cotton blanket, a kid yelling down the block, the scent of sage, her pulse beating in her throat. She twisted Nick's bracelet on her wrist, the silver cool against her skin, slipped it off and tucked it behind the couch cushion.

"Look," he said. "I'm an ordinary guy. We're not kids. Let's just make love. I'll take precautions. I'm a big boy." He closed his eyes and reached out to touch her face. "I want you," he said. "I'll show you. I've been thinking about it for weeks."

"My back," Liz said.

"I'll be real good," he said and bent to kiss her eyes.

"I bet," Liz said. She grabbed his gray-brown curls and pulled him to her lips.

Later, after all the easy hunger of her and the good heat of him; after he had eased her off the couch onto the hard floor and his lips and tongue had travelled everywhere, she said, "You were!"

"I was what?" he murmured. He was like a great, sleepy animal, curled on his side, quite beautiful in his nakedness and satisfaction.

"Real good," she laughed.

"Baby," he said, "you were the best."

Twenty-three

THEY DIDN'T GO WISELY, THEY DIDN'T GO SLOW. They ignored all the "Building a Healthy Relationship" books. They agreed never to say the "R-word." Macleod was there, above her, beneath her, beside her every chance he got. They didn't communicate. They didn't negotiate. They barely talked. It was basic.

"I can't get enough of this," he growled. In his absence, she thought of his big body, his adolescent zeal and middle-aged skill and she used him even then, making love to herself whenever the house was quiet.

"You're my woman," he said and she began to believe him. She thought she had abandoned the idea of mating. He was not Nick. There was no fire, no flight, no dark wit and incandescence. But when they were pressed belly to belly and the blood ran warm and peaceful in her veins, she let herself think of mating, of wolves, of wild geese. She let herself think that some humans might behave as well as animals, might be together for the long run, the daily round.

"They were wrong," he laughed, "you *can* do it on the first date and not screw up."

"You're such a wordsmith, Macleod," she said, "but we haven't had our first date." On his next visit, he brought a rented VCR and *High Plains Drifter* and good pizza and bad red wine; they had their first date and broke the rules again.

A week later, Deena and Deej drove to Santa Cruz for the weekend and he stayed the night. Liz's back was better and they rediscovered all the marvelous places and possibilities for making love, as though it were all new, as though a fine amnesia had seized them both. They told each other all the old lies. They were convinced the rules were made to be broken.

Long after midnight, while he snored beside her, Liz lay watching the street shadows on the ceiling. She'd tucked Nick's bracelet in a pocket of her overnight bag. She was getting used to her wrist being bare. She touched Macleod's shoulder. It was meaty and muscled. For an instant, she searched for the bones under the flesh. He turned towards her. Half-asleep, he kissed her breast. She gathered his head close to her and buried her face in his hair. He smelled of both of them, of her pleasure, of theirs. Gently, she moved away from him and turned on her side.

She woke a few hours later to his body on hers, and the emptiness that came from sleep with no dreams. They made love a long time.

"Sunrise service," he said. "This is my kind of religion."

"Promise me something," she whispered. She felt him tense.

"Maybe."

"Promise me you won't suddenly wonder why I like it so much, how I got so good. That's all," she said.

"What's that about?" he said. His face was flushed and tight.

"Other men. Liking it. Then, for some reason, getting frightened. Thinking I'm over-sexed or something. I've never really understood."

"That's not me," he said. "I *love* your attitude. You're a real liberated lady."

She knew the power of "don't," how it's a charm that makes the person to whom it's said want to do precisely that which has been prohibited. She knew that and she was still surprised when, kissing Macleod good-bye, she heard him say, "Mama, you can't get enough, can you?" She said nothing. She watched him stride to his truck. She could smell their lovemaking sweet in her skin.

The rules were made to be kept. That was the first rule. She stretched out on the couch and closed her eyes. Don't. Do. Dreams had no rules and for that she was grateful . . .

. . . Beyond Hotomqam's dazzling helmet, the Seven Sisters were back, circling in their slow, shining dance, spinning towards the cold time, the time of renewal. Talasi watched them from the windy *tuukwi* rim. She looked out across the desert to Nalakihu and Eagle House. Smoke curled from the rooftops. She saw people moving in the chill twilight. She felt far from them and eager to be close. It was time for her to go back, to the grinding, to the stirring and mending, to the fire in her mother's house. Toho had said that she learned quickly. He praised Pamosi.

"There is heart in your work," he said. "A woman's heart."

Talasi pulled her shawl tight. She thought of the lessons, how simple some of them had been, as simple as weaving, and, for a woman, as forbidden. Sometimes, she had been giddy with new knowledge; she would find herself out of breath and take herself to the grinding till she was calm. There had been the namings, the legends behind the names, the necessity behind the legends. There had been survival within the mysteries and mystery in the survival. Each day was in the work, of the work, the work itself. So much heart, so much body; it was as though her very blood and bones had studied.

There were no secrets. The knowledge only waited to emerge. All had the knowledge. The emergence was the miracle. Silence was the *sipapu*. Knowledge was rock, was light, was cloud, was grinding, stirring, weaving, waking and sleeping, was what passed from Spirit, daily, through the teacher to the student, from the student to the teacher . . . even to the last lesson and farewell.

Toho's shadow fell beside hers, thin and long in the last light. She would leave soon, to stay with a cousin at Nest House, and, then, at dawn, to leave for home.

"I have brought your belongings," Toho said. "There is food and water for your journey back and a gift for Nest House." He smiled. "There are some other things . . . things you have earned . . . and a gift for you."

She turned to him. He was moved by her beauty. She had not changed physically. Her face was still full and smooth, her eyes bright as polished stone. Her hair was straight and thick and shining, but behind skin and bones, a beauty burned, and a power that time would not touch. With his wonderful Sight, he watched her age as she stood there. He saw the old woman she would become. Wuhti Sonwayo, woman of beauty. Wuhti Øgala, woman of power. She blushed and bent to the parcel at her feet. He saw the girl she still carried in her.

"Do not open it now," he said. "It is good to walk with unknown gifts. They lighten the way."

She settled the bundles in her carrying sling and pressed her cheek to his. They had never before embraced. He breathed in her scent, warm skin and juniper smoke and clean hair and something female and ripening. He thought of his youth, his manhood, the many women, how each had had her own fragrance. He sighed.

"Thank you, Uncle," Talasi said. He bowed. She set out down the winding trail, away from his shadow, his small dark house, the glow of his fire and his teaching. She passed between the great boulders, past the three snakes, silvery in the dusk, away from the little kiva and out onto the path that led through the wash, past the turning in the trail where the *pahaana* had appeared, out onto the wide path that led home . . .

. . . Liz rose carefully from the couch. The pain was completely gone. "Dr. Feelgood!" Macleod had crowed the night before.

Elmo poked his huge head up above the windowsill and cried. Liz let him in and stood in the doorway, looking out across the straggly lawn to where Deena's garden struggled and faltered.

"Not one of my strengths," Deena had said. "Any plant that makes it under my care ought to be patented."

Elmo gently pawed her ankle. She fed him and settled in at the kitchen table with coffee and the Sunday paper. She opened to the want ads. It was time to go back; not just to work, to the cabin, to her garden and cats, but to admitting that there *was* a future and she *was* forty-five, alive and well in the dubious Eighties.

She thought of her garden . . . gone. It would be the first autumn in eight years that she wouldn't eat her own tomatoes, dry her own rosemary, drench her own sweetcorn in butter. Monsoons had blasted the town every day since she had been at Deena's. They had hammered the earth with rain and hail. Nothing could have survived rain like this rain; the sky opened and the world went away.

Those fierce rains made her think of home, the old home; the long, sunless days, the gentle rains that went on and on, leaving the world a soft and brilliant green. Summer evenings, she had walked to Nick's little house in the heart of the city, under emerald trees, through drenched grass, past glittering shrubs and dandelions, everything luminous, everything smelling of damp and dirt and mushrooms. It was a liquid season. Here, the rains came and left the mountains in an hour. Nick and those green evenings were gone somewhere; and, locked away, the lean question mark of him, the answer.

Macleod already worried about her caring more than he. She guessed it had become habit with him, to either adore or be adored, to pursue what he couldn't have, to say "You're my woman," and mean "I'm not your man." For a while, she had tried a little experiment, the bed the laboratory, her words the variables. She'd watched him retreat from affection and reach out for silence.

But his body was reliable, his enthusiasm irresistible, so she smiled and came and came and smiled and waited for him to push her away. She was guarded. Even with Nick's bracelet tucked away, she could feel a circle of something around her. She met him with her body, not with her soul. And always, she stood back. She was closer to Elmo, the cat. It was no big deal . . . maybe.

It *was* a big deal that she had nearly run out of money and that she had no idea where she'd find work. She read through the want ads. There was nothing. Not by her standards, which began to develop rapidly as she read the ads. No Administrative Assisting, no "People-kind-of-Gal-Fridaying," whatever that was, nothing that required wardrobe and hairdo, nothing requiring her part in the conspiracy that the boss was a very, very big man. Nothing that would bury her alive, in dead air, under fluorescent lights, from eight to thank-God-it's-five.

"I'm an aging hippie princess," she said to Elmo. "I don't know computers, don't want to. I'm not young and adorable. I'm about to be flat broke." There was nothing to do but go for a walk.

By the time Deena, forlornly post-Deej, drove up, Liz was walking toward the house.

"Look," she said. "I did it. I'm ambulatory."

"You should be," Deena said. "All that physical therapy; you've probably got the hip muscles of a thirteen-year-old gymnast."

"Come on," Liz said. "Don't be glum. Look at that sky, look at those thunderheads, look at this gorgeous asphalt. I'm free!"

"You're stir-crazy," Deena said, "and I'm depressed. Let's go for a drive and find something decadent to eat. I need it."

They headed out for Liz's cabin. The sun was hidden below black thunderheads, its light up-thrust and golden, so that the road and the pines, even the ripped-up earth of the new monster shopping mall burned red-orange under that dense sky. It was her first time out of town since the accident, with that dippy quality of the beginning of a vacation, when you find yourself noting with amazement that they have fences here! And cows! And guys on bikes!

The cabin still stood. The garden was gone. It had gracefully given in to silver dandelions and purple beeweed and some un-named pale yellow, nodding blossoms. There were three restless kittens tucked under the dresser and a fierce mama. Liz grabbed some clothes, pulled a month's mail from the box and they headed back out.

"Anything special?" Deena asked.

"Just the kids. I'm so stubborn. Nick never writes, never wrote even when we were lovers, and I always hope there'll be something from him."

"Could he write?" Deena asked.

"What do you mean?"

"Most men I know have a congenital inability to write, remember holidays and walk into florist shops, unless they are trying to get in your pants."

"No, he couldn't."

"Well, then, there's only one thing to do," Deena said firmly.

"It's got something to do with chocolate, right?"

"Right! You've got to drown your disappointment. It's my job as your best buddy to help. A woman shouldn't have to drink mocha alone. We're going to the café."

"What if I'd gotten something wonderful?" Liz asked.

"Then," Deena said, "we'd celebrate!"

The roads were a dusky dream, all gilded grass and wine-red light; the café the inside of a kaleidoscope, mirrors and glare and voices, the Talking Heads blasting. Deena parked Liz at the window and went for their coffees. Liz looked around. She could have been watching a foreign film . . . in a foreign country, just off the train, just touching down, released from a blessed cocoon of books and silence and cool gray light. She watched the people talking, heard the buzz, wondered if she knew the language in this new land.

A slight redhead sat near the old Victorian coffee roaster. She wore black running shorts and a magenta tank top. She was reading. Liz could imagine her in taffeta, back straight, hair piled on her head in a french knot. The woman's eyes were moss agate, huge, lined top and bottom in black. A tattooed dragon curved round her wrist. She had hung crystals and feathers from her ears. The music ended and, in the silence, she turned to Liz.

"Are you all right?" she said. "I haven't seen you around for a while."

"I hurt my back," Liz said. "I'm better. Thanks."

"Have you done anything for it?"

"I stayed flat for a month. This is my first day out."

"Wow," the woman said. "This must seem like that bar in Star Wars!"

"Close."

The speakers crackled, U2 wailing over the noise. Liz mimed being deaf. The redhead laughed and went back to her book. Deena set two cups on the table and a fat wedge of chocolate fudge cake. She nodded at the counter.

"They're looking for a baker," she said. "Five bucks an hour and all you can eat. An old hippie baker ought to be able to handle it. I took an application. It asks for your name, your address, your Social Security number and your sign."

"I'm on the cusp between burned-out and heartbroken and I don't want to cook for people," Liz said.

"What *are* you going to do?" Deena said. The music suddenly cut out.

"Not cook," Liz said. "All I've ever done is feed people. Lazar and his charming quasi-hippie faculty dinners. 'You must try this. Liz is a genius with vegetables and tofu. Oh, you've never had tofu? blah, blah . . .' and Nick's bachelor buddies, drinking my Dos Equis and wolfing down East Coast enchiladas. No thanks!" Deena stared at her. "I'm whining," Liz said.

"It's not a pretty sight," Deena said. "Look, you'd be cooking for *money*, not for love. You'd have flexible hours, physical work, wear what you want, be your own boss, make lousy pay. It's perfect for you."

"Plus," the green-eyed woman said, "I'd be your boss. I'm the regular baker." She pointed to the disappearing fudge cake. "I'll teach you to make that."

"Take the job!" Deena said.

"I'm Liz. My friend and I are interested."

"I'm Artemis. Friends call me Artie." She grinned. "Yeh, mom was a hippie, still is. I have a sister named Twilight and a brother named Tree. We call him Slick. He insists on it."

"I like Artemis," Liz said. "I nearly named my kids Wolf, Jay and Orphé."

"Poor Orphé," Artemis said. "All those awful women tearing him to shreds. I suspect it was the other way around." She stood up. "Can I sit with you a minute? Give you a discrete sales pitch? I've seen you eat here. You know what's good. Let's talk a little." She nodded at the counter. "I invented everything in there. Even Grandma's Scones. I'm Grandma."

"They're the best thing in the case," Liz said. "The sesame seeds are perfect. And the currants. You soak them in something, right?"

"Sherry," she said. "Good cream sherry. See, you're a natural." She looked into Liz's eyes. "Besides, I think you could learn a lot here. We could work together. You've got good eyes." Liz leaned back in her chair.

"Whoa," she said. "I've never done commercial baking, just some commune cooking, a couple festivals. You know, five thousand whole-wheat, oatmeal, chocolate chippers." She laughed. Artemis smiled. Something, some trick of the heart, caught her. She saw herself then, draped in a rainbow poncho, smiling, only a little stoned. She'd been standing behind a sawhorse table, dishing out beans and salad to a line of people, most of them young, most of them in tie-dyes and jeans, some of them in red headbands. In the background, she heard the voice of one of the musicians. "I am Roland Kirk," he said. "I have a message." Michael had been at her side. He had gone silent, as had everyone.

"Children," Roland Kirk had said, "you got Mr. Nixon on his knees. If you let him up, children, I'll curse you forever. I can do it, children. Make no mistake. I am a *Black* Black man and I carry rats and razors in my pockets!"

Most of the kids had laughed, but the tall boy in front of her had become pale. He had looked down at her with his red-rimmed eyes and he had said, "It's true. He knows we'll give up." He had turned and stomped off into the crowd. Ten years later, she had watched him climb the steps to her door. She had not seen him in all that time, but she knew the anger in his body, the gold star in his left ear, the sullen set of his jaw. 'He could be the death of me,' she had thought and waited.

"I'm Nick Oliver," he had said. "I sat in on one of your classes. I might like to talk with you."

Deena touched her hand.

"Hey you," she said. "You in there?" Artie knelt in front of her.

"It's not your back, is it?" she asked. She set her palm against Liz's brow.

"No," Liz said. "I wish it were. I have a little problem with ghosts."

"I can help," Artie said. "With your back. I do massage. Let's make an appointment. You can fill out that application at the same time."

Deena helped her move. They carried in groceries and jugs of water from a little spring in Oak Creek Canyon. Sugar twined around their ankles. The kittens' eyes were open and deep blue. Bob sulked somewhere; they could hear him grumbling. Spider webs laced across the skylights. Deena started to sweep them away.

"Leave 'em," Liz said. "The light comes in."

Deena unpacked the groceries. "I'll miss you," she said. She waved a huge chocolate bar in the air. "A house-warming gift, a bribe. I'm scared, you know."

"Of what?"

"Macleod taking over. You disappearing. It's happened to me before with womenfriends. A new romance. Priorities. Etcetera."

"Not a chance," Liz said. "I learned that lesson long ago."

"Good." She opened the bar and handed Liz a chunk. "A toast," she said. "To reliable things."

After she left, Liz opened the windows and set the kettle on to boil. The cabin seemed spacious and lonely, familiar and a little dreamlike, as though she'd returned from a long trip, a slow one, on foot, part of it alone, part of it with Deena. She made coffee and sat on the stoop, drinking it, watching the sunset glow off the mountains.

Macleod called as she was getting ready for bed. He was glad she was home. They'd have all that privacy. Soon. Maybe outdoors, in the long grass. Under the stars. He'd gotten himself so worked up thinking about her that he'd had to take a lunch, har har, break. But it wasn't as good. She was the best. Could he tell her how she tasted? And the weekend? The long grass? The stars?

After they'd set a date and hung up, she stretched out on her bed. She could hear the kittens thumping and whimpering. Sugar was absolutely pompous with motherhood; she'd relegated Bob to outdoors, with a scar across his black nose. The moon silvered the walls. The air was soft on Liz's skin and she realized she felt completely happy. It made her nervous . . .

. . . The journey to Toho's had seemed so long. Homeward, the same trail flowed under Talasi's feet. She wanted that long walk past black hills, under clear cold sky, with time and silence to let the memories settle in. She saw the days with Toho as precious beads, some perfect spheres, some rough as firerock, some stars and moon and lightning; others earthen, clay and sand, as plain and essential as dirt; some shaped by dream and skill, others fresh-taken from the Mother. She told herself a story of a necklace, three crystals for Hotomqam, then chunks of firerock, of clay; then seven purple crystals, the Sisters, and more firerock, black, dense, the winter sky.

Though she walked slowly, it did no good. Place of Water appeared on the horizon, lifting above the rock and sand, gray in the Hawk's Moon sun.

A man emerged and began to climb toward her. In that late afternoon, trick light, he seemed tall as two men and quick as a cloud's shadow. She stopped. He waved to her. She secured her carrying sling and moved steadily toward him. There was no one else in sight. She felt it took forever for them to close the distance.

They faced each other and bowed.

"Cousin," she said.

"Not cousin," he said. "Welcome." He wore a robe of spotted-cat fur, framing his face in black and silver. She wanted to feel both, skin and softness, under her fingers. Beyond his shoulder, the people of the village were no more than ants. There would be no one to see. She reached out her hands, palm up, the pathstone shining clear as moon on water. Kihsi bent and pressed his cheek to the stone, then took her hands and pulled her to him, burying his face in her hair.

"You smell of that dark house," he said. "Of those smokes and plants and powders. I will never forget them."

She said nothing. She held him to her. And then, it was as though *he* had cradled *her,* at birth, and held the child who cried with a skinned knee, and comforted her that night at the spring and stood, as Toho, on that mesa top, the kinship, the knowledge in his arms.

Twenty-four

AN OPAL DAWN WASHED UP FROM THE HORIZON; Liz remembered an early dream, Talasi's world cupped in a great shell. She was almost too sleepy to drive, hazy as the mist rising off the pines.

She made it to the cafe, parked and knocked at the back door. There was no answer. She waited. A man staggered out of one of the packing cartons stacked along the trashed banks of the riverbed; he took a leisurely piss onto the dry earth and wandered off toward the Jesus Loves You Rescue Mission, where, unlike some of the more respectable charities, they put the coffee on promptly at six. Liz knocked again. She heard footsteps, a bolt slid back and Artemis waved her in.

"Welcome," she said. "You can hang your jacket here. There's an apron in the metal can. Wash your hands and stand back. I came in late, so I'm on automatic, not too rare for me. Watch, learn where things are, watch my hands and don't try too hard. It's just like learning to dance. Maybe later you can try a few things on your own." She took a deep breath and flopped a huge ball of dough out onto the big baker's table that filled the middle of the room.

By late afternoon, Liz had met the twins, Beryl and Shel, and their sister Viv. They were not identical, the twins, although they were both dressed in baggy black camp-shirts and white pedal-pushers. Shel had hennaed hair and purple eyes. Beryl wore gold-rimmed glasses and peach ankle-socks. Her hair was a brown rooster's comb. "We're twenty-one," Beryl said. "We grew up in London and we just got to these bloody States." Viv was small and quiet and blonde. She showed Liz how to fill out a time card. She was twenty-two and she had the oldest eyes Liz had ever seen.

She slid a tape into the stereo. It was Kate Bush, singing "Wuthering Heights."

"She's wicked good," Viv said. "That's my favorite song. That's how it is when it gets like that. You're standing outside and he's in there, all dark and terrible and beautiful. And you think you'll die from cold."

"Your eyes don't lie," Liz said.

"That's what people tell me," Viv said, and ambled off to fix some customer a Fresh Fruit Frappe.

Jeri, the Deadhead, a compact, red-cheeked woman with splendid breasts, blew in at three to start prep for the next day. "Red Rocks," she said, "'82, it rained in all the right places," and popped the Dead tape in. Liz thought wistfully of Luther Allison, of Aretha, and realized she'd have to take a stand. Jeri had wound her ginger hair with strands of cotton, black and red and purple. She wore a Bob Marley t-shirt and refused to shave her legs.

"Call me Jer," she said. "Watch. Ask questions. Don't be scared to make mistakes. Artie makes 'em all the time. She's such a genius, though, she turns 'em into miracles." She tucked her semi-dreads up into a hairnet and scrubbed down the table.

"Go ahead," she smiled, "try something. We could use cookies. Do it. It's the only way to learn."

The Poet slammed in past her, late for the afternoon shift. "Yo, Jer," she said. "Phil's gonna kill me. I screwed up again." She tossed an apron over her black jumpsuit and charged out to the counter. Little wood parrots swung violently from her ears. Liz dropped a pound of butter into the big waist-high mixer and started the beater.

"This is a time-warp," she said. "I've been suspicious of this town right from the beginning. It's all fake. This is really San Francisco, 1963."

Jer spooned whipped cream into a plastic tub. "Sure," she said, "until you try to change anything. Then you know we're on redneck Republican turf for sure." She showed Liz the baking sheets and the ice-cream scoop. "Makes perfect-size cookies. It's the closest thing we've got to a production line. By the way, don't mind The Poet. She sees things in extremes. Phil never killed anybody. It once took him five months to fire some woman who was dipping into the till."

Liz added slivered almonds and currants to the cookie dough, folded in chocolate chips and scooped the babies out. She stood by the window of the big convection oven, watching them. She was drenched in sweat, sticky with honey and flour, bone-tired and inordinately content. It occurred to her that she just might be able to do this work. Nobody had asked her age. Nobody had bright ideas for a flattering hair style. Nobody had told her to hurry. Nobody had wanted anything from her but the flour scoop, a clean whisk and two pans of killer cookies.

Three hours later, she wasn't so sure. She wrestled the giant mixer bowls into the sink, in scalding water, scrubbed their gluey insides for twenty minutes in scolding water, and wrestled them back in their slings. She'd been in the tiny kitchen for twelve hours. Artie had gone home at noon. The counter folks were closing up and she was more tired than she had been since her kids were babies. The Poet had put on a Sex Pistols tape and was dancing between the tables, scattering napkins, twitching salts and peppers and vases of dried flowers back in place.

"Have you got a key?" she yelled to Liz. "Hey, try that Laurie Anderson tape. You'll love her."

"Okay," Liz yelled back. "All set. Laurie Anderson. Will do." She heard the front door slam. She turned off the tape and listened to the ringing in her ears. Then, as evening cooled the light outside the front windows, blessed silence drifted in. She heard a train go by. She gave the baking counter a final swipe, tucked the chocolate chips back into their battered paisley canister and carried her coffee to the front room.

Her arms ached; her back was more than a little stiff. She was mildly alarmed. The old romance of doing simple work, using her hands and body, had seemed so clear back when she'd done that other work, cutting through that fog of human pain; watching her clients go back to that which had driven them to her. She had longed for work that created and was done. You could make a bowl, a house, a tray of cookies. She felt disenchanted, flabby and thoroughly middle-aged. The Deadhead, The Poet, Artemis and the three sisters; they seemed fearless and indestructible. Their energy was infinite. They glittered. They were the Pleiades minus one.

She sipped her coffee. She nearly wanted a cigarette. The room grew dark, the old gilt lettering on the coffee roaster shimmering in the streetlight. As tired as she was, she realized she felt an easy satisfaction. The case was empty; she'd earned a day's wages. Fairly. Harmlessly. No one was in more or less pain because of her. She'd never been certain about her presence as healer. Women had grown stronger, men had found their tears, couples had separated with more grace than bitterness; some had let their wounds heal, had accepted the scars, had stretched and moved on. But in it all, she had always been afraid.

There had been mistakes, some of them innocent; some of them the result of her own pain, her own hungers and emptiness. Her arrogance. There had been Nick. She had betrayed him.

She thought of Talasi, of her teachers, of herbs and smoke and prayer. She thought of apprenticeship, the kind that might lead to the healer's knowledge that she knew nothing, that all she had were dreams and will and surrender. It was easier to grind. It was easier to set cookies on a bright red tray.

In that instant, she saw how Talasi touched her. She knew why she did not speak of her, why she had told so little of the dreams. They were deep within, barely framed in words. Talasi was *her* pathstone, secret, silent, glowing cool and clear in her mind's eye. In thought or not, surfaced or buried, Talasi was her guide. She lit the way and she allowed the traveller to stumble. Liz cleared the table, locked the back door and walked out to the empty parking lot. A man stood in the phone booth, his face, his gestures eerie in the flicker of the street-light. He yearned toward the receiver. She heard him laugh. Her belly tightened. She wondered why Macleod called so little. She decided to visit Hatt.

Tenderhome was shut down for the night. Rose, bent over her paper-work, a circle of light shining blue off her long hair. Liz tapped on the window.

"Look at you," Rose said. "You jumped right in. You've got frosting in your hair."

"I am an old woman," Liz said. "I am one hundred and nine thousand years old. You have never seen so much pure, random energy in one place. I am shattered."

"You'll get tough," Rose said. "Aunt Leora says that the only reason women's work is women's work is because only women are strong enough to do it. In her day, the women picked the corn, hauled it, shelled it, dried it, ground it three times over . . . before they could even start to bake."

"Hey," Liz laughed. "When the going gets tough, the tough start whining . . . Well, it wasn't the baking, it was the cleaning." She held out a bag of cookies. "I liberated these."

"Come right in!" Rose said. "I've got coffee." She opened the door. "I'm glad you stopped by. I want to prepare you for Hatt. I've seen her every day, so it's not a shock for me."

"How bad is it?"

"She's pretty confused. Sometimes I'm sorry she's my friend. It would be easier if she was just a case."

Liz looked down at her hands. "After all the years at the place back East, I never got used to it. The consulting shrinks would tell us that the people were in less pain than we were, that they didn't know, that it's natural for old people to detach. I never bought it.

"There was one woman. She was fifty-five. She'd worked all her life, mostly in bars, waitressing, hostessing, bartending. She had an inoperable brain tumor, one of those spidery ones that they can't touch. She wouldn't go into the day-room without her make-up and wig. She wore high heels till the day she convulsed and they took her fancy shoes away. A week later, I was sitting in her room while she dozed. She came to. In this tiny tired voice, she said, 'Liz, if you ever get one of these things, just drive into the lake.' She grabbed my hand. 'It's so boring. Pain. They don't tell you that.'"

"Hatt's not in pain," Rose said. "Not physical, anyhow. She's just not here most of the time. Who would blame her? And, when she is, she's a little ashamed."

"Would you go in with me?" Liz asked. "That way, if she doesn't remember, you can introduce us."

"Sure. Let's take the cookies." Rose paused at the door. "When I was small, my grandma got like this. She'd be sitting at the kitchen table. We'd go to greet her and she'd shoo us away. She was scared we'd step on the chickens. She hadn't kept chickens for twenty years. Connie used to pretend to feed them.

"After my grandpa died, she'd ask for him. My aunt would patiently explain what had happened and Grandma would just shake her head. 'These mens,' she'd say, 'they're always running round.' She'd pick up whatever she was working on, shake her head and tell us kids to watch out. Between the men and the chickens, she had her hands full."

Hatt was awake. She wore a chenille robe. In the peach light, her cheeks seem flushed. As she drew closer, Liz saw that the flush was rouge. Someone had painted her fingernails plum and tucked a silk daisy into her hair.

"Your friend Liz is here," Rose said softly.

"I'm all set," Hatt said cheerfully. "The girl was here earlier." She looked hard at Liz. "Oh, forgive me," she said. "You're not the girl." She narrowed her eyes. "Do I know you? I do, don't I? Was it long ago we met? At home? At one of Mother's parties?"

"It was long ago," Liz said. "I'm Liz Morrigan. I'd like to visit for a while." Rose slipped away. Hatt gestured to a chair.

"I'd be delighted," she said. "I don't get many visitors out here." She looked around the room. "My family seems to have disappeared. Usually, they'd be buzzing around like flies. John's probably taken them off to help him. He's fixing that back fence that Mrs. Chee's big ram knocked down. We like to have them help out on chores. Too many children these days have easy lives. It spoils them."

"It's true," Liz said. "Have you been here long?"

"Years," Hatt said. "Though sometimes when I see Roger saddle up all by himself, or Jeannie fussing over her sewing, it seems as though it were only yesterday that they were babies. Time is strange out here. Clocks don't matter. We go by the light, by the seasons, by the lambs being born, the shearing."

"I've been having dreams like that," Liz said. "Time doesn't count."

"It's the light," Hatt said. "It touches you. I have the oddest dreams. Nightmares, very nearly." She shivered.

Liz opened her bag. "I brought some cookies. Home-made. I thought we could have tea. Get reacquainted."

"I'd love that," Hatt said. "I'll put the kettle on . . ." Her voice faded as she looked around the room. Her eyes rested on Liz.

"Never mind," Liz said. "I can get the water." Hatt nodded. By the time Liz returned, she had measured tea into an earth-brown teapot and set out cups and spoons. Liz hadn't seen the pot before. It was red-rock brown, its shape a perfect curve. Along the bulge of its belly lay sprigs of violets, bound with gilt ribbon in the style rich young ladies once learned at school.

"I have some lemon here," Hatt said. "I hope that will do. The Navajo drink it with evaporated milk. I can't get used to that."

"Lemon is fine," Liz said. She touched the pot. "How beautiful."

"I painted it," Hatt smiled. "A Hopi friend brought it to me, unfired, from his mother. She had dug and ground and shaped the clay. He packed it back up to the mesa, so she could fire it. I wasn't sure it would work, but it did. He told me she thought the glazes were magic. 'Spirit-paint,' she called them. She thought I had dreamed the flowers. They don't have violets up there."

"It's a treasure," Liz said. "And the cups?"

"They are bone china," Hatt smiled. "My mother's mother's. She gave them to me just before John and I came out here. She didn't think they would survive. I don't think she thought I'd survive. We did." She nodded. "We assuredly did." She smiled at Liz. "I'm so glad you've come. Tell me about yourself. Tell me about those dreams."

Liz flopped on her bed, too tired to undress, to tired to do anything but pull the sheet up to her chin. The tea buzzed in her brain. The cabin seemed a little strange, impersonal. She felt as though she'd come off fourteen hours of straight driving. Sugar carried her kittens, one by one, to the foot of the bed; Liz wiggled her toes to make space. "Dreams are prayers," Hatt had said. "That's what my neighbors say." Moonlight poured over the meadow and through the skylight. The kittens nursed and purred. Liz thought of Macleod, all the silence between them. He seemed no more than a story, much less than a dream.

Twenty-five

"YOUR AUNT SENT ME TO BRING YOU TO THE VILLAGE," Kihsi said. "There have been many people from the South resting here, many strangers. She was afraid for you."

Talasi stepped away from him. "I am not going to my mother's house?"

"No."

"Is there trouble in her house?"

"There is trouble in the village. The bone-dice roll everywhere. They have touched our mothers' houses." His face closed with anger. Talasi laughed.

"You talk like Toho," she said. She dropped her voice. "'The bone-dice roll everywhere. They have touched our mothers' houses.' How? How have they touched our mothers' houses? Tell me, friend. I have not changed. I am not some priestess."

He cupped her face in his hands. "Look at you," he said. "You have changed. We have not talked with each other for years and that is all I've dreamed of, to look at you, to talk with you, to touch." He dropped his hands.

"I know," she said. "We must not be seen. We are no longer children." She stepped away. "There will be time. You do not have to come to the courting window to know that. We can talk on our way back, if you remember how to talk to a friend." She picked up the carrying sling and settled it on her shoulders.

"My mother. What about my mother?" she asked.

. . . "Liz . . . Liz, let me in!" She heard Macleod. He pounded on the door. "I've got a problem, Liz," he whispered. "Hurry up!" She burrowed back into the pillows. She wanted to go back, to follow the lovers down that cold trail. The door shook.

She stumbled to the door, slipped the bolt and was hauled into his big arms. In seconds, he was naked. "I couldn't wait," he said.

"How do you do that?" she murmured sleepily. "Get undressed with no hands."

"Ranger training," he said and carried her to the bed. He slid in beside her and butted her hip. She went limp, faked a snore. Just ten minutes more sleep. That would answer the question.

"Wait," she whispered.

"No wait," he grinned. His fingers found her, slipped in and she went blissful and stupid. She pulled him on top of her. As he pushed inside, he buried his face in her hair.

"Oh lady," he said, "I swear we've been lovers a hundred years." She rose up to meet him, slipped her hand between their bellies and felt a quick rush of affection. Before she had time to be scared of it, she started to come.

The alarm jolted her awake.

"Oh piss off and die," she muttered. Macleod opened one bloodshot eye.

"Not you," she said. "You just rest up. I'll see you tomorrow."

"Now?" he said.

"Tomorrow. I've got to pay my rent." He turned on his back and eyed her. The sheet slid off his body. He was a pretty thing. She had to admit that.

"You sure?" he grinned.

"I'm sure," she said and dropped her night-gown over her head.

"No," he moaned. "That makes it worse. Flesh under silk. You can't leave me like this."

"I guess," she said, "you'll just have to . . . har har . . . take matters into your own hands."

"I have," he said sadly. "It's just getting worse."

She bent and ran her tongue over his neck. "We've got time," she said. "Years, if need be." She watched him flinch.

"Hey," he said, "no long-range plans. Okay?"

"Is tomorrow short-range enough? I'll be off about noon, but I want to see Hatt for an hour, so two o'clock would be good."

"Book me," he said. "We could meet here, distract ourselves for a while, hike up to Lockett Meadow. You'll love it. Come back, distract ourselves some more, go to a movie . . ."

"Distract ourselves," Liz said. "Do you like fried chicken?"

"Am I a semi-redneck? Eat some fried chicken, distract ourselves some more."

"Sounds distracting," she said and moved out of range. He whimpered. "Tell you what," she said. "I'll put some coffee on, get myself dressed and bring us both a cup. You keep right on doing what you're doing and I'll enjoy the show." He stared at her.

"I have never met a lady with an attitude like yours," he said. "Has anybody ever told you, you think like a man?"

"A few," Liz said. "And they were wrong."

She watched Artie shape poppy-seed dough into soup buns.

"I don't know," she said. "I'll give it a try." Artie tossed her a lump of dough.

"Watch," she said. She folded it in her smooth young hands. Liz looked down at her own hands. They seemed to be doing the same move. She thought of her fingers gliding over Macleod, tracing the thick muscles of his chest. The dough was warm and resilient as his flesh. It could be that simple, as simple as bread and friendship. She sighed. Bread and sex, you couldn't get more tricky; wrong temperature, weak hands, impatience . . .

"I got it," she said and set the bun on the tray. The next one went quicker, the third without thought. Her mind drifted to Talasi and Kihsi, to Macleod, to their flesh. As she had moved over him, she had wondered if they were at the beginning of something special and guessed they weren't. She had thought of the lovers on the trail, of Talasi's fingers on Kihsi's face. Those two were fire; she and Macleod were smoke. So much for simple things. She set the tray of buns on the warming rack and scraped up the remaining dough. She had known the fire, and it sure enough had burned. She wondered if she could settle for the smoke.

"Hey," Artie said. "You're quiet."

"I'm having deep thoughts," Liz said. She smiled. Artie looked wonderful. Though she'd been there since before dawn, she was bright-eyed. She wore three onyx studs in her right ear, a long silver plume in her left. She'd tied a black cotton shirt over a fuschia tank top and gray harem pants.

"I love the way you dress," Liz said.

"I mostly dress for cheering-up. For celebration. Another morning alive, another night got through. You know. If it's a gray day, this gets me through."

"A gray day?"

"Oh yeah," she said. "No big deal. I have 'em. Things get out of hand, so . . ." She pointed to the plume. "I love feathers. Whatever," She scraped down the table. "You want to try something new?"

"Sure. It's all new. I did cookies yesterday after you left."

"She certainly did," Viv said. She hung her jacket on the rack and tucked her backpack under the desk. "I'm going to sue her. I ate three. They're a sure cure for Heathcliffitis."

Artie handed Liz an old notebook, its cover scrawled with marker, a peacock going up in smoke, the smoke condensing into flame, the flame blossoming, the flowers the tail of another peacock.

"Speed?" Liz said.

"Brain," Artemis said. "A blessing and a curse. Feel free. We need a coffee-cake. The cardamom-pear's a sweetheart."

"I know," Liz said. "It got me here."

She was happy that night to sleep alone. Nights next to Macleod were nights without dreams. She built a fire in the pit at the edge of the meadow. She could make fire alone, *and* smoke. Rose's words came to her, Talasi's. The prayers of the heart, how they were heard, how they could not be hidden. The juniper burned to coals, the nightwind died. She cast sage on the fire. As the smoke rose, she thought of the incense at High Mass, the sweet weight of it in the lungs. She thought of the scent that clung to Eva's hair when she returned from *sesshin*, from those breaths and hours and days of meditation. "The stink of wall-gazing," she had called it. She wondered if Eva sat right then, incense smoke curling, her back straight, mindless and mindful, two thousand miles away. Liz watched the smoke trail up through the trees. The sky was pale turquoise, the clouds apricot, the shadows held a woman's shape. Sitting.

"For Eva," she whispered. "For her work. For dreams. For Hatt." She paused. There was no use not speaking the last. It was in her heart. Always. "For Nick," she said clearly. "For his return." There was no answer. No raven screamed. The moon stayed steady, the stars in their sockets. But, as though Eva sat near her, thin and strong as shadow, she heard her voice.

"Be careful with your prayers, Liz. You must live with the answers. . . ."

. . . "How is Uncle?" Pamosi asked. "Is he still pained by the cold? Does he sleep? How is the owl?" She set *piki* and *someviki* in front of Talasi and sat beside her. Talasi bowed her thanks. She was grateful for the *piki's* lightness, her throat tight; she had been shaken by Kihsi's words.

"Your mother has put your father and his belongings out of her house," he had said. "He visits my mother. She gives him gifts. They are feared. There is talk of Powaqa because they both win so often at the game."

Talasi unwrapped a *someviki* and nibbled at the edge. "The owl is gone," she said, "though Toho fusses every day because he misses it. It kept his house free from mice, but there was more. You could see it. They would look at each other with their old eyes. Once, as I came in with water, I caught him talking to it. Its wing mended, and we carried it up to where the small pines are thick. It rode on his shoulder without a tether. When he set it free, it did not fly away. We had to leave. Then, without a cry, it flew into the tops of the trees and disappeared. We could hear the beat of its wings long after we could no longer see it."

"Bag of Stories," Pamosi said. "You tell it well. I hear *him* in the story."

Talasi flushed. "He is a hard teacher. Once, he set the bones of a hare in front of me and told me to tell a story that would bring the bones to life."

Pamosi smiled. "And?" she said.

"The owl ate the hare," Talasi said. She smiled. "And took the story with him. Now, he will never go hungry." Her smile faded. She looked down at her hands.

"Toho is in great pain," she said. "He asked me to tell you that his bones hurt more in this cold than the last. He asks you to visit and bring your medicine."

"I will go," Pamosi said. Talasi saw how tired her eyes were, how there were lines on her smooth skin, how gray streaked her hair. "Now that you are here, I can leave. My husband will be in the kiva for the rest of the moon." She paused. "What of you and Kihsi?"

"First," Talasi said. "What of the village? What of my mother and the man who was my father?" Pamosi smiled at her niece. This was no childish messenger, no lost girl who sat at her table. She waited. In the silence, Talasi would find room to speak.

"Toho saw something, something unknown and dangerous. We were unable to make out the direction. Every gate was clouded, all trails thick with mist," Talasi said. "All villages were in peril."

Pamosi frowned. "There are no directions to see. The evil does not come from outside. It comes from within, within your mother's house, Tsohtsona's house, Høwi's rooftop, the plaza, the ball-court . . . perhaps, even in some of the kivas."

"The bone-dice," Talasi said.

"The people; the games, the hunt, whether boy child is born or girl, whose corn ripens first, how many visitors come. It is a fever. Men and women burn with it, even some of the elders. I see the children playing at it. You have seen Kunya, how his eyes shine, his terrible smile. There are many like that. They are fired with greed, with the longing to own things, more things than they can possibly use."

"My mother?"

"She is not free to welcome you. Though she has banished Nuuva from her house, she is snared in her anger, in her longing for him. It is no chance that we women weave bird nets from our own hair. Would that we could remember that!"

A pebble clattered through the roof-hole. Kihsi peered in.

"Welcome," Pamosi said. Talasi glanced at her aunt. "Time is too short to wait for the rabbit hunt," Pamosi said. "I will stay a while, then you two may leave. You know the gossip, you know how to stay clear of it," Pamosi said. "Do nothing to bring attention to my house."

. . . Drowsy, Liz stirred soup; she watched the chopped herbs swirl on the surface, a spiral of basil and cress and chives. She could have stood there for the rest of the day, barely moving. The dream drifted in her blood, yearning, ominous. She set the ladle on the counter. Beryl said something. Liz turned.

"Earth to Liz," Beryl said. "You in there?" She poked her gently in the ribs. "I asked you to do the chalkboard . . . would you?"

"Sure. I'm sorry. I didn't sleep well." She started for the dining-room. Beryl caught her apron-tie.

"What's wrong?" she asked. "Man troubles?" It was their favorite theme.

"No. Yes. More like no-man troubles . . . or wrong man troubles. I don't know." Liz grinned.

"My mum just told my dad to get lost," Beryl said. "It's the fourth time. Fourth dad, that is. Your generation is sweet but strange."

"True," Liz laughed. Beryl kissed her on the cheek. "Does your daughter talk about you, do you think?" she asked.

"I'd bet on it," Liz said. "And her kid will do the same. Your mum's probably answering the very same question this very same moment, somewhere."

"Coo, it's a funny old world, in't it?" Beryl said and ambled out to the counter. Liz chalked in the day's specials. Veggie Lasagna. Vichy-more-or-less-soise. Chive-Cheese Buns. Broccoli Quiche. The rolls were hers, the soup, the lasagne. She felt comfortable. She smiled at a customer. The regulars were becoming familiar, the professor who spread his papers on the biggest table, drank one espresso in three hours, and never tipped; the hippie mechanic with purple bandana and gray hair, who flirted sadly with Shel and never tipped; Les Girls Marvelous, who arrived in shrieking bevies, stuffed cream cheese brownies into their perfect bodies, and tipped like maniacs.

The place was crowded. The sky had drizzled sulkily since morning. Through the big steamed-up window the Peaks were doubly blurred, veiled in pewter clouds. Liz finished her clean-up, grateful to settle the last bowl in its rack and pull off her apron.

By the time she stepped out the back door, the sky had cleared. The little cottonwood on the riverbed's bank was silvery-green, the air clean and cool. She took a deep breath, rolled down the car windows and drove out of the parking lot.

Rose met her at the entrance.

"She is still in bed. She does not want to get up," she said.

"Do you blame her?" Liz said. Rose shook her head. "Can you stay a while? It's spooky around here today."

"I can't," Liz said. "Macleod and I are supposed to hike up to Lockett."

"Okay," Rose said. "No big deal." She shrugged.

"Nice non-verbal communication," Liz said. "More workshops?"

"Hopis have feelings," Rose said.

"No!"

"It's not that you won't stay," Rose said. "It's why you won't stay. I don't trust that man. I haven't liked him from the first time we met."

"Why?"

"I'm not sure. He's so big. You seemed so little next to him. He could hurt you."

"Well, yes," Liz said. "He probably will."

"Why do you see him then."

"I'm a junkie. He's good dope." Rose turned away.

"How can you be so disrespectful to yourself?" she asked.

"I have feelings, just like Hopis," Liz said. "One of the feelings is loneliness. He soothes it a little." She stood in front of Rose. "Is that disrespectful? He gets laid. I get to feel pretty for an hour. It's not an unusual bargain."

"You're not pretty," Rose said. "You're beautiful and if you won't see it, all the men in the world won't make a bit of difference. I'm not pretty either. Hardly anybody is, just those ladies in the magazines and they're all fourteen years old. What difference *does* it make?" She laughed. "Aunt Leora was worried about me and my cousins, that we wouldn't be pretty, that no boy would want us. She thought we were much too thin for any good Hopi man to ever desire. Connie curled her hair once and my aunt wouldn't let her out of the house for a month."

She pulled Liz into the solarium. "I wanted you to stay because Manny is coming back in three weeks. I don't know what to do and I can't talk to anybody else. Manny thinks I'm pretty. He thinks I'm so pretty that I shouldn't go out by myself, that I should be home from work in exactly the times it takes to drive from here to there, that I should only dress up when we're together. What's worse is I miss him! The kids and I have learned to live without him. I feel guilty. I don't care. He thinks everything will be the same as it was. It can't be."

"Hopis have feelings," Liz said. "What are yours?"

"Fear, anger. I'm going to give it a chance. I'm not sure why. Maybe I owe the marriage. I don't know. Maybe I'm just a thinner version of my mother. I hope not." Rose smiled. "Do you want to know why I said that about Hopis having feelings?"

"No," Liz said. "That's why I keep bringing it up."

"Because people think Indians are stone-faced. Because I was taught to be polite. Because politeness gets misunderstood. Because I'm sick of being misunderstood. With everything that's going on these days, up on the mesas, down here, we can't afford to be misunderstood any longer. That's why."

"Thank you," Liz said.

"Thank *you*," Rose said. "Ever polite, we Hopis. Go see Hatt. Then go get your exercise!"

"That's exactly what it is," Liz said.

Hatt was a stone woman under the soft blanket. Liz remembered a dim cathedral in Bath; soft puddles of ruby and emerald light had fallen across the marble tomb of a Lady, the Lady dead since the thirteenth century, her statue serene on the tomb's lid. She was dappled in that colored light, bejewelled, her eyes closed, her mouth set in a firm, sweet line. The light in Hatt's room was peach. Her face was not serene, nor sweet. The air outside the window was dry and golden, not wet and green.

As Liz watched, the stone face softened. Hatt smiled. She stroked one hand with the other. Her hands were as pure and gnarled as juniper roots. She had become totally a thing of the desert, her skin parchment, her bones jutting white under it. The nurses had loosed her hair for sleep, and it spread across the pillow in a luxury of silver. Liz slowed her breath. She wished she could muffle her heartbeat. It would be violence to wake Hatt, to rouse her away from that smile, that blind caress.

"Where is he?" Hatt whispered. Liz waited. Hatt curled on her side. "He said he would be here. Where is he?" She plucked at the pillowcase.

Liz set her hand over Hatt's. The veins pulsed against her palm. Hatt shook her off, reached down and tugged at the sheet.

"I am so cold," she said. "I am wet. He said he would come. He promised. The child is coming. I am wet. The bed is wet. I want my robe. I must change these sheets." She tried to sit up and fell back.

"I'll get your robe," Liz said. "We'll make the bed fresh."

"Find him," Hatt whispered. "Bring him. Tell him where I am. He will come to me. He's out riding. That's all. Take my pony. The spotted gray. Find him."

"She opened her eyes and clutched Liz's hand.

"Elizabeth," she said. "What have I done?" She closed her eyes. "Make it stop," she said. "Please. Let me wake up." She burrowed into the pillows.

Liz pulled the sheet over her. She saw the rise and fall of her breath. For an instant, she felt the pillows under her hand, thought of death, the sweet smile of the stone Lady. Hatt sighed. Her eyes roved under their lids.

"I'll stay," Liz said. "I'll stay for a while."

Twenty-six

LIZ WAS LATE. Macleod would be too, according to the message on the phone machine: "Something came up. Three." She heated the morning's coffee and moved the rocker out to the edge of the meadow. She thought of Hatt waiting, Roger out riding, Macleod somewhere, of mothers and sons, women and lovers; what she knew, what she guessed, what she feared. Mothers loving blindly, sons who would not free themselves from hope and blame, hope that each new woman would be the perfect one, the one who held on and let go, knowing magically when to be there and when to go away, the wo-mother who would not take offense at the message, "Something came up," and when something came up, would adore it. And, when no woman could be the perfect woman, the son moving to the new woman and, again, to blame, to new woman, to blame, to new woman, to blame. Never to himself.

The women blaming themselves: not pretty enough, not smart enough, not loving enough, not young enough, thin enough, accepting enough, not Mother enough, or too much. She remembered the first night with Nick, how his kiss, his hands on her had been nothing till he had pressed his face against her breasts and held her to him, silent and sexless, and she had smoothed down his rough hair and known him for kin. Without that, without the recognition, what was there? Without the ancient forbidden links, mother-child, father-child, sister-sister, sister-brother, brother-brother, without the hope that we can find with the lover what was lost with the family, what was the point? The sun angled across her lap. A breeze came up and caught the pale grass. She heard a raven screaming and willed herself ignorant of everything but light and wind and warning cry.

She stepped under the shower, felt the hot water working on her aching shoulders. The shower house was one of the treasures of the place. It stood at the center of the half-circle of cabins, a big room with an endless water supply. She could stretch without tangling in the shower curtain and, when she had finished, could walk, wrapped in a thick robe, under clouds or sun or stars or snow. Snow was the sweetest, its flakes falling on her warm skin, stinging, melting there, gone to rain. She had never felt so clean.

She was rubbing rosemary shampoo into her hair when Macleod whacked the door. For an instant, she kept still, holding to the last few seconds alone.

They hiked up through pine and slender aspen into the Inner Basin, Liz moving fast and joyous, from shadow to shadow, from purple larkspur to fire-red paintbrush. She was breathless, half from altitude, half from beauty, and alone when she stepped out into the full sunlight of the meadow. Mountains rose up in three directions, blue-black thunder-clouds above their peaks. Meadows of brilliant wildflowers stretched as far as she could see. Macleod caught up.

"You know," he said, "I used to do that kind of macho hiking myself. You still got that East Coast hustle in your muscle, honey."

'Bullshit,' Liz thought. She waited. Let him fill the silence.

"Seriously," he said. "You'll enjoy it more if you go slower."

"You're right," she said. The little woman. She was still willing to play. If he'd just shut up and use his mouth for what it was good for. Those were the stakes. They were high. She'd never, not even with Nick, had so much fun having fun.

"Now, look at that," he directed. She did and all of it, the contempt, the subterfuge, all of it dropped away as they came full into the meadow. The tall grass shimmered. Thunder echoed back and forth against the Peaks. In the grass, as though stars had fallen and floated there, were blossoms of blue and bitter-sweet and twenty shades of purple. Tiny ivory lilies sprawled along the trail. Macleod swatted her butt.

"Do I know how to treat a lady?" he crowed. "Another goddamn day in paradise!"

"You know," she said, "sometimes I actually like you."

"Huh?" he said. "Where did that come from?"

"I mean, you keep things from getting sentimental."

"Hey," he said, "keep it light. That's the American way." They walked slowly up a trail that wound through the meadow, curving up toward the high peaks, past ancient twisted snags and black boulders. At a turn, blocked from trail-view by a big pine, she pulled him to her and kissed his salt skin. She almost loved him then. She felt as though she could survive anything, his thickness, his unspoken, unconscious contempt, as long as he brought her to places of rock and pure light and air. She pushed him against the tree.

"Close your eyes," she said.

"You're crazy," he said and grinned. She unzipped his jeans. "But you're my kind of crazy," he said. When she looked up, his eyes were closed, his face tender. He held her head gently in his big hands and began to guide her.

"Oh no," she whispered. "Let me do the work." He shivered. With a last deliberate slow trail of her lips, she stood up.

"Hey," he said. "Didn't anyone ever tell you to finish what you start?"

"I will," she said. "Trust me."

She had set candles around the dark cabin. In their glow, she stood at the stove, frying chicken. She felt positively female and ordinary. The oven was warm against her belly. Macleod's beer, her gin and a Caesar salad were cold in the refrigerator. He stood behind her, kissing her neck.

"I love your chef's outfit," he said, tugging at her nightgown straps with his teeth. "Hurry up, Pierre. You owe me."

She set the lid on the frying pan and moved into his arms, her mouth open against his, her teeth nibbling gently on his lips, her lace-covered breasts sliding against his naked chest. He ran his thumbs over her nipples.

"You drive me crazy," he said.

"You would have loved me in high school."

"I would have lusted you," he said.

"Oops," she said, "the L-word. Sorry."

"Just want to keep it on the up and up," he said.

"Mmmm, yes," she said. "My boyfriend liked to keep it on the up and up, and up, and up. We played with each other for hours."

"Was it fair?" Macleod said.

"What do you think?" she asked, touching him beautifully. "Now, what do you think?"

They barely made it to the bed. Later, as he moved deep inside her, she felt a great softening within her, spreading up, moving, transforming to tears, catching in her throat, welling in her eyes. She held Macleod to her.

"Ah, love," she murmured. "Ah, love." She felt him oblivious and was grateful. Some wisdom cautioned. 'Be careful,' it said, 'this is what he, unknowing, works for. This is what he fears.' She stopped moving and pushed gently at his shoulders.

"Whoa," she said softly. "No joke. The dinner's burning." He looked up, hazed with sex. "Come back," he whispered. "Please come back." She stood over him. She knew she had been only partly right. This was what *she* worked for. "Come back." It could be personal. That was possible. Perhaps their bodies were wiser than their minds. Perhaps something ancient would win out.

She filled their plates with chicken and salad and home-baked bread and carried them back. She felt beautiful, the food an offering, her aging body, with its full drooping breasts and soft belly, a second offering of passion and skill and response.

He took his plate and looked over at her.

"This is wonderful," he said in his tranced voice. "Are you some kind of . . . I don't know . . . sorceress, temptress . . . sent to tempt me . . . to . . ?" He looked down at himself, at the chicken leg he clutched in his hand, at her, who had stunned them both, by starting to cry.

"Hey," he said, "it's okay."

"No," she said. "You don't know. Nobody ever said anything like that . . . like they saw the ways I'm beautiful. Lazar never said 'I love you.' Nick slapped me, told me to get out . . . then he said it. Never anything friendly like that. Never anything normal."

Macleod sat up straight. "Hang on," he said. "I didn't say 'I love you.'"

"Oh, I know that," she snapped. The tears stopped as abruptly as they had started.

"Wait a minute," he said. "Don't get mad. You're too sensitive. Oh shit," he fumbled, "don't assume anything, either way. I like you. I love the sex. I can talk to you. You're a great lady, but I just don't have those stars in my eyes." He stared at her. "Liz, don't let me hurt you. I'm afraid I'm going to hurt you."

Liz smiled. She took her plate from the shelf above the bed and began cutting at the baked potato. Her mouth was dry, but she was damn well going to eat something. She looked straight into Macleod's scared eyes.

"Two out of three," she said. "Not bad."

"What's that supposed to mean?"

"I have this rule, which I am probably going to break. I will leave immediately if a man says any of the following things to me: a) Don't be too nice to me.; b) I've never been able to talk to any woman the way I can to you.; c) I'm afraid I'm going to hurt you.

He looked down at his hands. "Yeah," he said. They sat in an odd, almost friendly silence for a few minutes.

"But," Liz said, "you are the best practitioner of the horizontal bop I've ever met." She laughed.

"Likewise," he said.

"Maybe our bodies are smarter than our minds."

"Don't know. I've got my doubts that I can get close to any woman."

"I've got the same doubts." She left it ambiguous. "It does seem a sacrilege to walk away from this gift we've got."

"Once a Catholic," he laughed, "always. I'm scared you want more than I do. Shit, it's either that way or the other." He looked down at himself. "Besides, we're having one of those Eighties talks and, look at me,

I'm hard as iron." Liz set down her plate and moved toward him. They stopped the Eighties talk and started moving old. It was, for the moment, so easy. It was almost friendship.

When he left, he stopped at the foot of the stoop. He looked dazed. His voice was edgy. She stood just inside the door and smiled.

"It's okay," she said. Her heart pounded. Her hands were numb, her throat tight around the questions that must not be asked: When will we see each other again? Is this good-bye? How do you feel?

"I'll call," he said, almost sullenly. "I'll be in touch." He walked away. She saw the caged bear again, pacing up the path, grumpy, helpless, a little dangerous. She wanted to run after him . . . she wanted to run home.

She made herself turn around and walk into the kitchen. Fear burned in her, that fear that marks the beginning of the end. It had become tedious that the beginning of the end occurred so close to the beginning of the beginning. She wrapped the left-over chicken, grateful she had not given him any to take home. She brought in water for the dishes and heated it, wiped down the counter, finished off the salad and crumbled bread at the edge of the meadow for the jays. This was the way home.

Washing dishes, looking out through the fogged window to the gray light and black pine, she came back to herself a little more. A jay fluttered down and pecked at the bread. The plates and cups and silver gleamed in the rack, the warm water was soothing on her hands. She could smell Macleod on her body. She decided to take another shower, to wash her hair with rosemary, her body with sage. She changed the sheets and poked up the pillows.

The phone rang. She gathered up her shampoo, soap and sage water and left the cabin. Something a nameless poet had once said came back to her. He had landed on her doorstep on the way to New York; he'd been hitchhiking from L.A. and it had taken ten days. They had been talking about drugs. She had offered him a joint and been surprised when he turned it down.

"I'm going to feel so high when I step out of your shower," he had said, "I won't need anything but a good night's crash." She guessed, and it was true, that returning from the hot water and soap and her own hands on her body, she would find only changes in the dark, the faint shifts in light and shadow, the sheltering stars and her scent, returned and welcome . . .

. . . Pamosi's step faded away. In the dark room, Kihsi watched fire-shadows play across Talasi's face. She seemed old, her eyes deep as a grandmother's. She smiled. He took her in his arms and pressed his face against her hair. She reached up and stroked his.

"We have both washed our hair," he said. "As though it were our marriage. I crushed the yucca, prepared the water and rinsed away the suds myself. There was no mother, no grandmother."

"Pamosi helped me," Talasi said. She sighed and moved away from him. "We must leave here and we must bless ourselves. I could grind the wedding corn for a lifetime, carry the wedding case, wear the robe, kneel in front of our families and be no more your wife than I have been since that day we met the lizard." They cleared away her supper and swept the hearth clean. She gathered her bowl and sleeping robe.

"I know a place," she said. "Few go there. You will see why."

Pamosi watched from the rooftop. All she saw were shadows, shadows that slipped along the base of the *tuukwi* in silence, as though the moon drove them, shadows that flowed together, then disappeared.

"This place is beautiful," Kihsi said. "Why do people fear it?" She pointed up. On the cliff, far above their heads, wonderfully painted figures caught the moonlight, that cold silver glittering on their twisted bodies, their starved eyeless faces, their horns and claws and gaping mouths. Kihsi turned his head away.

"I see," he said. "I see." He turned to her. She led him to a shallow pool at the base of a low mesa. There was a seep in the cliff-face, a frail cottonwood, its last leaves rattling in the wind. There were tracks, delicate and broken. Where the water puddled, where it trickled in broad sheets against the rock face, where it glittered on the ferns clustered at the pool's edge: all shone like shell. Talasi bowed her head.

"Undo my hair," she said. He loosed one knot, then another, and the maiden whorls uncoiled and tumbled. He brushed a strand away from her face.

"And you," she said. They knelt at the edge of the pool and washed their hair; and, turning, shivering and clumsy, they braided the ends of their wet hair. They knelt a long time in the moonlight, the silence, the trickle of the seep, their hearts' rhythm their wedding song. When they moved apart, Talasi spread the sleeping mat on the black sand.

"Hurry," she said. "I am freezing." Kihsi hesitated. "I have waited for you," he whispered. "I do not bring skill." He saw her smile.

"Skill is cold," she said. "And I am freezing." She lay on her back watching him move toward her, so dark, his wet hair gleaming in the moonlight. She closed her eyes and felt his breath on her throat. Behind her closed lids, she saw the cool light of the moon, then, as he moved over her, no light, and, as his body joined hers, colors and light beyond dreaming . . .

. . . Liz jolted awake.

"Oh no," she said. She felt for Nick's bracelet, to turn it, to let the cool metal slip between her fingers, a prayer wheel, a charm for sleep. Her wrist was naked, her heart doubly so. Before she could trick herself back to sleep, Macleod's face drifted in, his terrified eyes, his mouth set in that "Take no prisoners" line.

She tried to find a cool spot in the bed, threw off the sheets and let dawn air wash over her. The skylight was silver-gray with clouds. She could hear thunder in the distance. Abruptly, at some unheard, unseen signal, it became the kitten hour. They leaped into action, as loud as a herd of tiny elephants. Something crashed in the kitchen. Liz gave up.

As she poured water into the kettle, she thought of Hatt, the sweet sleep, the terror, the swirl of silver hair on the pillow, as though Jean Harlow slept there, or Marilyn or some other goddess. They were all gone to end-point, beyond hope and gratuitous pain. There need be, at end-point, no more offering of yourself. You didn't need to watch men your own age goofy over some shining child, or study your date and realize his middle-aged self was both dangerous and dull with passivity, with hidden rage. The white kitten sank its needle teeth into her ankle.

"Thanks, pal," she said. "I needed that." She scooped him up and buried her face in his sweet fur.

That afternoon, she sat at Hatt's side and heard her cry out for lost love. Not for her husband, not for her son or daughter or kin, but, for some dear lost ghost.

"Please," she begged. "Bring him here. I only want to see him. There will be no violation, only that we can see each other."

Rose watched from the doorway.

"Who is he?" she said. "Who? What violation? That is a strange word."

"I don't know," Liz said.

"Please," Hatt whispered. "You are cruel." She opened her eyes and stared at Liz. "*You* know. YOU KNOW!" She sat up and threw the blanket to the floor. Her eyes were blue fire, her rage burning perfectly, pure flame, clean. She pointed at Liz. "You know," she whispered. Liz stepped closer and picked up the blanket. Hatt's face crumpled. You could see the eight-year-old girl she once had been. She gazed up at Liz.

"What's happening?" she cried. "Where am I? Who are you?" She glanced at Rose and huddled back into the pillows. "Keep her away from me," she whispered. "I have suffered enough. He is gone from me. That's enough." She glared at Rose. "Isn't that enough? You and your two-hearts. Your *powaqa* curses. You won. Isn't that enough?"

Rose went ashen. She covered her mouth with her hands. Hatt let loose a high-pitched cry.

Rose shuddered. "I do not talk with two-hearts," she said. "Never!" She turned to leave and stopped.

"Forgive me," she said. "She is delirious. She has mistaken me for someone else." Hatt turned her face away and closed her eyes. Liz touched Rose's shoulder.

"What did she say? I must know." Pamosi's warning, black birds, wheeling, circling in, relentless, dropping out of the eastern sky with a great whisper of wings.

"Outside," Rose said. Liz draped the blanket over Hatt's motionless body. She slept, or not. It didn't matter. The waking was as terrible as the dreams.

"I want to sit near sunlight," Rose said. They pulled two chairs near the solarium window.

"A two-heart is an evil being," Rose said. "I will not say witch, because I know your people have witches who are good. A two-heart is dreadful, intelligent, clever . . . strange that they are called two-hearts; they should be called 'no-hearts.' They are absolutely ruthless. They keep the balance."

"How?"

"The world needs both," Rose said. "Hopi and *qahopi*. Only when the balance is off is there real trouble."

"And Hatt?" Liz asked. Rose shook her head and touched Liz's hand.

"This is ghost-time," Rose said. "I hate it. I wonder if we will all go through it?" She stood up. "I must go back to work. Let's have supper some night, Thursday?"

"I'd love it," Liz said.

She sat a long while with Hatt, watching her dreaming face. The turquoise ring was gone from her hand, slipped off, slipped away. More loss. Another curse. Around midnight, she pulled the blanket over Hatt's shoulder and left.

Her own bed felt cool and safe, ringed by books and moonlight and juniper, doubly ringed by pine, held in a great hand of dark earth, watched over by cloud-veiled stars . . .

. . . First Dawn lay like blue ice along the horizon. Talasi pulled the robe over Kihsi's shoulder and her back, pressed against his warm body and saw he was watching her.

"I am still freezing," she said.

"No," he laughed. "Freezing is all the mornings of my life till this one." He moved over her. She thought of the rabbit, the hawk, of that dance.

"*Inǫǫma*," he whispered against her skin. "Wife."

Only for now, she thought, and as though he had heard her, he said, "Forever." He sighed against her and pressed his wet face against her shoulder. She held him carefully. Above them, the wonderful, terrible paintings leaped into Second Light.

"Not forever," she whispered. "Hold me and listen." Kihsi traced the line of her naked shoulder with his lips.

"What is it?" he said sleepily. "What is so important?"

"Not forever," she said. Silent, he gathered her closer in his arms and she told him their truth . . .

Twenty-seven

BY MID-WEEK, LIZ HAD STARTED WAITING. She was good at it, experienced, as most women are; she was bad at it, thoroughly. She had waited for Lazar, for Nick, even for men who didn't matter, for a letter, a touch, a gift, a surprise, gratitude, honesty, for the pain to stop, for the love to resume. But, most often, if you were a woman and the waiting had begun, so that you put away your life . . . to concentrate more fully on the waiting . . . you, a woman, simply waited for the phone to ring.

By Friday, she was bored. That was the great curse of the waiting: it leached the light from a good life. Early evening, she lay on her bed, sulking, wiped out from work, grouchy. She had dragged the waiting with her twenty-two hundred miles, to a new place, a new man, a new ghost-time. The ghosts were interchangeable, touch for touch, lie for lie, dream for dream. The waiting stayed the same, the jammed beat of it, the static, the gutburn. She could get up, go out, give in, call Macleod; that would stop the waiting for the duration of his welcome, his tease, his laugh. Then not only would she resume waiting, she would wait in the cold company of no pride at all.

So she made herself warm milk and cinnamon, played Kate Bush and Aretha, half-read a book on pre-Columbian astronomy, brain dancing between stars and stones and the knot in her belly. The phone rang. She made herself wait three rings. The man's voice was cranky and only remotely familiar.

"Listen," he said. "I've got a proposal. I can't discuss it on the phone. Can you meet me at El Primo?"

"Who is this?" she snapped.

"Katz," the voice said patiently, "Mrs. Latham's lawyer. Look, I don't want to say anything over this phone. It's probably tapped. Will you meet me?"

"When?" Liz said.

"Now," he said. "I've got a crazy weekend. This is the only time I've got free."

"I'll be there," Liz said. "Wear a rose or something so I'll know it's you."

"You'll know," he said. "By the terminal bags under my eyes." He hung up. No thank you, no good-bye. She found a clean shirt and pulled it on, and, as so often with the way of waiting, no sooner did she reach the door, then Macleod called. He was warm, he was sexy. He had ideas. They would this, they would that, more scenery, more food, more more. She was grinning as she left the house. She felt beautiful. She felt like a junkie.

Katz was morosely stirring his coffee and sneaking glances at the long-haired young waitress. His khaki pants were too short; his feet, in heavy boots, looked as though they belonged to a much bigger man.

"Jeez, you've got big feet," Liz said.

"You bet," he leered sadly. "So what?" He smiled at the waitress. "What does she care?" The girl patted him on the head. She had terrible teeth and a sweet smile.

"I care," she said, "but so does J.W. and he would tear you limb from limb."

"I love you," Katz said, "truly and deeply."

"Wait," Liz said. "I know who you are. You're every man I ever met. You're looking for Guinevere? Right?"

"No fair," he said. "No fair to expose a man to the cruel light of a bad Mexican restaurant in a sad little mountain town, in front of this hippie angel who may someday leave J.W."

"Fair," Liz said, "fair?" She sat down. "If life was fair, we wouldn't be here." Angel brought her coffee.

"Right," he said. "And we wouldn't have to leave. Let's go. There's too many ears. We'll take my truck, I don't think it's been bugged . . . yet."

"May I drink this?" Liz said. He was getting on her nerves, with his tense ferret face and that opacity she'd seen in men who didn't really see women unless they were angels. Every time the front door opened, he jerked around. She wouldn't have been surprised to see him slide off the stool and go loping after some oblivious prey, his eyes bulging, jaw clenched around an imaginary cigar, the ghost of Groucho, *still* stalking. He smiled at her.

"Sure," he said. "But hurry up. I'll buy." He dropped a dollar on the counter.

"Ooooh, big spender," Angel said. "I like that in a guy."

They headed out the lake road in his spotlessly clean truck. Liz bet herself that the interior of the camper was without flaw, all the forks in the right place, a full set of condiments, clean underwear in case of luck or emergency. She guessed she'd never find out.

"What's up?" she asked. She glanced at the little lake and still didn't much like it. Manmade lakes were always out of synch; you could imagine the earth cringing at their shorelines, the animals wondering what the hell was going on. There were little pieces of styrofoam in her coffee. Her back ached. The Macleod high was gone.

Katz looked at her. "We've got to get her stuff," he said.

'Agreed," Liz said. "How?"

"Any way we can."

"Who's we?"

"You, me, maybe that Hopi nurse. I've got a copy of that book by that guy in Tucson . . . *Ecosurgery,* or something. If we get maybe four other bodies with brains attached, we can do it."

"This is so sudden," Liz said.

"She haunts me," he said. He turned the key, stuck a tape in the player and turned to her. She remembered how much she had liked his eyes. They were winter blue and he had ginger eyelashes and no secrets she couldn't see. "I've been to see her a couple times." Katz said. "Before she spaced out, she told me she wanted the stuff back. Then, the Feds busted that nice, Mormon, county commissioner with those looted Anasazi pots . . . they were right in plain sight in his office . . . that arrogance!" He paused. "She said something about a Hopi bracelet and she cried."

Liz fished the styrofoam out of her coffee and flipped it toward the window.

"Hey," Katz said. "This truck is new."

"Swell," she said. "A compulsive Robin Hood."

"Well," Katz said thoughtfully, "actually, I'm an untreated manic-depressive, Deadhead, hopeless Romantic, Jewish-American Prince lawyer river-rat. And, as far as I can tell, you're a burnt-out middle-aged chronically dissatisfied Hippie American Princess with too many miles behind and who knows what ahead, okay?"

"Nice," Liz said.

"So," Katz said, "swell, nice, are we a team?"

"Hey," she said, "what you said used to be true. But I'm doing okay here. I work, I can actually sleep, I like morning, I get laid a little. I don't want to go to jail. I deeply do not want to go to jail."

"I believe you," he said. "But do you want to let her die, let Roger sell that stuff to pigs?" He stopped. "Listen, you've got no reason to trust me, but you've got to trust this. What we've been granted out here is very precious. It's a privilege. You know that."

"Oh piss off," she said. She wanted to punch him. She considered the long walk home. "I could just tell you to take me back and leave me alone. I don't work with men. I don't like men. I sleep with 'em, that's all. I've got a delicate balance here. I like it."

Katz stared out the window. She looked at his profile. She thought of Michael, the big nose, the hawk brow. Michael would have loved this project. Katz turned up the music. It wasn't the Dead; she was grateful for that.

"You ever hear of Monique Wittig?" he said.

"I'm feeling very stubborn," she said.

"That's okay," he said. "My ex-wife was a killer Feminist. She had this quote by Wittig over the bed. It said, among other things, 'There was a time when you were not a slave . . . you may have lost all recollection of it, remember . . . make an effort to remember, or, failing that invent.' I memorized it."

"Go on."

"If I end up like Hatt," he said, "I want to remember I wasn't a slave. I don't want to have to invent. I want a real memory."

" 'You walked alone, full of laughter . . .' " Liz said. "I know Wittig. It's over my desk. You win."

"So," he said. "We need vehicles; surveillance on the security system and the Latham daily routines; some other zealots, a safe place to store stuff, a way to give it back."

"Maybe a plan?"

"I think the plan will invent itself." Katz fiddled with the feathers that hung from the rear-view mirror.

"I've got a friend," she said, "who has a friend . . . "

"That's exactly who we need."

She was trembling by the time she crawled into bed. Katz was like five cups of bad coffee. It had taken them an hour to stop talking. The bones of the plan had emerged. From the size of the skeleton, it wasn't a very big beast. She hoped they could bring it alive.

"Help," she whispered to Sugar, who was grooming Lurch, her large, blue-eyed boy. "I'm in over my head. I'm going to be shot or hung or put in jail for the rest of my natural life." Lurch closed his eyes. She could hear him purring from ten feet away. She thought about packing the car, driving back East, home, buying an apron and supplies for a million ginger cookies. She thought of holding Tina in her lap and wishing for more grandchildren and shopping for a nice dress for any weddings left to come. She thought about driving past the road that led to Nick's cabin. She thought about the failure of sun, of memory. She thought about slaves remembered, masters brought down and forgotten, and, as she turned on her side in that last move toward sleep, she thought, I'll have to ask Katz. A river-rat. What that means . . .

. . . Talasi rolled up their mat and brushed away its mark in the sand. Kihsi watched her. The women of Black Sand were graceful, but she moved in such beauty that he wished a terrible thing, that they might die there, together, that his last sight would be of her. He turned away and began to tie up their bundles.

"What will we do?" he asked. "I do not care if we have no children. There are many children, and too little food. Our house, our food could be shared."

"The elders will not allow that" she said. "I have my work. It is not the work of a wife." She touched his shoulder. His body, known, was more mystery than before. She had never guessed that a woman and man could feel such joy.

"You *are* my mate," she said. "I am yours. Nothing can change that." He nodded.

"In another time . . ." he said.

She smiled. "If we live well, there will be another time. Now, in this chaos, we must stay in balance. I don't know how." He took her face in his hands.

"This is balance," he said.

"Remember," Talasi said, "the two who ran away? Both from Antelope Clan?" He held her close.

"That was long ago," he said. "In another time." He pressed his face against her hair. "I will follow you," he said. "In these times, even in this cold, there are strangers. I will watch to make sure you go home in safety."

She held him tight. "You are my home," she said. "There is no safety."

EAST

For you: reader, dreamer, weaver, lover,
who stands fast,
who surrenders,
who might find, in remembering,
in invention,

your real name.

Twenty-eight

FULL MOON AT SUMMER SOLSTICE, clear sky, not so much as a thread of cloud; they could go up to a mountain meadow, Macleod proposed . . . sleep out under the stars. She'd love it. Liz didn't tell him how the light worked on her, how the full moon shone into the wild corners of her skull, how the longest day of the year was celebration, and good-bye, how she longed to sleep under that bright sky alone, how she couldn't, how no woman could, safely, while strangers moved in the world.

"Sure," she said. "I'd love to."

She stumbled through work, burned a pan of corn bread, a dozen pitas and a batch of molasses cookies before she discovered that Artie had set the oven twenty-five degrees too high. She started over. The ovens were usually off by noon; by two, the kitchen was Death Valley. Shel burst into tears. The Poet blew up an egg in the microwave. Liz slammed the sticky bowls in the sink, pinched her finger and stopped dead.

"I'll be back later," she said to no one in particular and stomped out. The seat belt burned her fingers. The monsoons were taking a break, the locals said. Must be the Hopis hadn't danced right, they said. Meant a mean, early winter, strangest weather they'd see in years, hotter 'n a jack-doe in heat, they said. Liz draped her apron over the seat and took off.

There was more than the weather wrong. Macleod had resumed. As it were. She wondered if he rationed time: one careful call a week; one tender sentence; a slew of instructions on how she could read maps better, close the truck door, lighten up, take it easy, take it slow. Her dreams were richer than her days. She ran Macleod's body as Katz ran rivers. She'd learned what river-rat meant. She wondered if she'd ever again run a heart, a mind. They called it running, taking a tiny craft through great

264

water; it was not running, it was being taken. She wondered if she would ever again let herself be taken.

She drove to Tenderhome; there were no questions there. She could sit with Hatt, bear witness, hold that hand, like a handful of bones, its pulse beating under her fingers. She could drink bad coffee with Rose, gossip, feel her heart lurch every time Rich stretched out his long, lean legs. He'd grown a mustache and he was always a little nuts from amphetamine. He eavesdropped. He gave advice.

"You're wasting your time," he'd said. "Macleod. We're all the same. Losers. Lovable losers." In the right light, in the right nostalgia, she could pretend he was Nick, watch him tilt his chair back and hang on the edge of disaster.

Hatt's curtains were open; she lay in the glare. The room smelled of urine and old food, of ghosts and disinfectant. "Die," Liz whispered. "Get out of here." She closed the curtains and brought a basin of water to the bedside. She sponged Hatt's face, trickled water over the pulse in her wrists. Hatt licked her lips. Liz poured a glass of water; it was warm. She took ice from the snack kitchen and touched it to Hatt's lips. She sucked at it and pressed her fingers over Liz's.

"We're going to get your things," Liz said. Hatt circled Liz's wrist with her fingers. "I know," Liz said. "Katz told me. We'll find it if it's there."

"She's hanging on," Liz said.

"I know." Rose said. "For what? That daughter won't come in. She's so polite. Busy summer. Getting the kids ready for college. She's sure I understand."

"I'm sure you do."

"Hey," Rose said, "they gave me a gold star in the last Family Communication workshop."

"No!"

"You better believe it. A little gold star just like the kind we used to get in school. Rich stuck it on my forehead. He wants to start a union, but only when he's ripped."

"I want to start something," Liz said.

"Trouble?"

"Maybe." She closed the nursing station door. "I talked with Katz. We're hunting a plan."

"Stay still," Rose said. "That's what my uncle taught the boys. You stay still and sing. The animal comes to you."

"Believe me," Liz said. "If I sang, the animal would kill itself, right there!"

"Does this plan which we are waiting for include me?" Rose asked.

"If you wish."

"I wish."

"We're having a little picnic Fourth of July," Liz said.

"I'll bring a surprise." Rose said. She set her purse on the desk. "Here's another surprise. You won't believe it." She took out a paper and unfolded it in front of Liz. It was a six-month lease on a one-bedroom apartment. There was one signature. It was Rose's. She traced it with her fingernail.

"I'm taking the children," she said. "We're going to live by ourselves. When I told Manny, he cried. It was terrible, this man who prides himself on being the baddest of the bad." She smoothed the creases in the paper.

"You should frame it," Liz said quietly. She dug down in her purse. "This isn't a gold star," she said. "It's an antique." She held a purple button in her palm.

"Uppity Women Unite," Rose read. "I sure don't feel uppity." She pinned the button to her collar. "He is so beautiful to me and so ugly." She sighed. "My mother thinks I'm crazy. 'He didn't run around with women,' she said."

"Well, then . . . "

"I know. He didn't cheat, didn't hit me, didn't steal my money. But, even when he was there, he wasn't. I went alone a lot. I went inside alone. You know?"

She folded the lease and balanced it on her palm.

"What did you find?" Liz asked.

"What I found inside me, way inside me, was not Manny's hold on me. I found my hold on him, on fixing him, on making everything the opposite of my mother and father. Once I knew that, the rest was possible." She took Liz's hand.

"You can do the same thing" she said fiercely. "With Macleod. With Nick's ghost. Be alone. Go inside." She laughed. "That is *qahopi*, that aloneness. I learned it from *your* people. How solitude is a dear friend."

"And if there's nothing inside?" Liz asked.

"Then pray," Rose said. "Find a tree and talk to it. Talk to the light . . . it's always here." She blushed.

"Will you be my primary when they bring me in?" Liz laughed.

"Listen," Rose said. "If that is crazy, then all wise people are crazy. You gave me this button. I want to give you something." She touched Liz's forehead. "Remember *E.T.*?" she asked. "Take this with you. It's from my grandma, through me. *Your* prayers are in you. As are your answers. Shut up and listen for them." She took her finger away from Liz's skin and kissed the spot. "There," she said. "Now, it's yours."

Macleod rolled away. He flung his arm back and took her hand. "Gotta catch my breath," he said. Liz tugged the quilt over their bodies.

"It's the altitude," she said. She pressed her hands into the grass outside the sleeping bag. There were flowers there, penstemon and lupine and tiny daisies. They were frosted in moonlight, tiny bells of ice, fireworks seen in December. She turned on her back. The stars were invisible, lost in the moon's radiance. She thought of Rose's gift, of talking to light, to the moon, the perfect looniness of it.

She moved closer to Macleod. He curved his body against hers.

"Are you okay?" he whispered.

"Ecstatic," she said. She imagined the moonlight on the tears that chilled her skin, how they would be a silver thread. Thunder purred in the south. Macleod began to snore. She wondered if deer watched, if they grazed oblivious, moonlight dappled on their pale hide. She wondered what perched on the black limbs at the meadow's edge, what wing caught light, what bright, unblinking eye.

"Moon," she whispered, "I think it's *all* medicine, this, prayers, touch, listening. Please. Let me feel peace next to this man. Let me feel peace away from Nick. Let me feel peace in my own company."

She listened. There was only the perfect silence of the unseen stars' circling dance, and Macleod, like a great bear, uffling in his sleep . . .

. . . Talasi knelt in front of Toho's gift.

"Look," she said. "Even the wrappings are gifts, this four-colored cord, this cloth."

"He wastes nothing," Pamosi said. She watched Talasi unwrap the bundle.

There was the black and white bowl Talasi had used at meals; some unstrung beads, black and purple and clear; a pair of new sandals. She remembered the firelight on his face as he bent over the reeds, stripping them, wetting them, plaiting them into shape. One corner of the wrapping shawl was knotted around a leather pouch. Pamosi glanced at it and stepped back.

"That is for you alone," she said. "Join me in the morning. We must travel to Place of Water. Three babies have Gone Over there." She climbed the ladder. Talasi shivered. She felt alone, not just in the firelit room, but as a pebble is alone, a star, a footprint on a solitary path. She tried to imagine Kihsi and could not. She called up Toho, and he would not stay. She turned to the leather pouch.

It was made from a white dog's skin, legs and head drawn up and webbed with colored cords, their knots stuck through with eagle feathers, hung with *tsorposi*, woodstone and striped shells, knots encircling other knots, the cords as many colors as earth and sky. She studied the web; to work quickly would be useless. That had been her hardest lesson.

She began. Blue-gray knotted with red, white woven with black, sand and sage and cedar-green braided. She saw that it was a path and followed it. Slow. A touch, a breath, the work tucked away in memory, for she saw that she was to re-tie the bundle as he had tied it, that in the pattern lay power. He had taught her that, how opening and closing must be the same, how the knots and turns and choices made between, shaped the power, held the charm. The fire died. In the roof-hole, above the bone-cold room, the woman warm with work, Hotomqam hovered and descended.

Yellow and firerock gray and jay-feather blue, the color of the seasons, a pattern of protection, for what lay within, and without. She undid the final knot and set the gray and scarlet cords aside. The skin lay in that unwoven web of color, cradled, as though Spider Grandmother had labored there, unweaving and weaving, making and unmaking, as is her great work. Talasi unfolded the head-flap, the back legs, the sides and found a polished stone box. It was nightstone, black, veined with white and purple, glittering with crystal.

She bowed, scooped water from the *wikoro* and scattered drops over everything. As she bent over the gifts, she could smell Kihsi in her flesh and Toho's smoke in the unwrapped bundle.

"Thank you," she said and opened the box. It held the tools: dried *pale'na* blossoms, packets of herbs, an ancient twig deer no bigger than her thumbnail, a gleaming shell as big as her palm. She sniffed the shell. It smelled of the Great Water.

There were ground minerals, each in its own bag, black and copper-red and yellow-green. What she needed was there, yet without the old man's teaching, each blossom, each stone, each shell would have been nothing but a trinket. Talasi set everything carefully on the skin, then tilted the box into her palm. The last gift slid out. She had not known it was missing.

It rested in her hand, cool and bright as ever. It lay where Masau'u had placed it, but this time it was hers to bring out at will. She held it to the dawn light. At first the stone was clear; then clouded, pierced with colors, shot through with moonbows and lightning and the shimmer of First Dawn. She watched and wished and he was there, black against the light, the old one, his arm raised in farewell . . . in greeting . . .

. . . Liz woke alone. Amethyst light moved up through the pinetops. The grass was wet, the lupine rhinestoned with dew. Macleod ambled out of the trees. Naked and grinning.

"Another goddamn day in paradise," he howled. "We're not doing too bad," he said, "are we?" He crawled in beside her and grabbed her close.

"I missed the moon," he said. "but, I'm sure not gonna miss the dawn." She thought about the mysterious nature of gifts and, turning to hold him, took them in, his body, the dawn and pleasure, flooding like the light.

Turning back, they saw the ghostly gift of deer in the dark trees. They were both quiet and that too seemed a gift. He dropped her off at work. The kitchen was peaceful, only the thin sweet notes of a Navajo flute sounding from the stereo. At one, when the rush slowed, Deena stuck her head in the back door.

"Where have you been?" she snapped. "I've called for a week. That damn machine isn't working." She scooped chocolate chips from the jar and dropped them in her mouth. "I'm a mess," she said.

Liz untied her apron and tossed it on the bakers' table.

"Let's grab something and go outside." They placed their orders and found a seat at one of the outside tables. "I turned it off," Liz said. "I was having a fit every time I came home and there was no call from Macleod."

Beryl shouldered her way out the screen door and brought Deena's soup.

"You'll like it," Liz said. "It's hot borscht, no beets, just cabbage and dill and sour cream. It has the Katz Seal of Approval."

Beryl waited at Deena's shoulder.

"Yes?" Liz said.

"Aren't you going to introduce me to your friend?" Beryl said. "It's only manners, mate."

"Beryl," Liz said. "Deena. Vice-versa. You've heard about each other."

"Not . . . " Beryl said.

"Yes," Deena said. Beryl plucked an olive out of Deena's salad.

"It's not true," Beryl said. "Not a word of it."

"I never thought so," Deena said.

Beryl curtsied and wandered down the line of outdoor tables, stacking dishes, scooping up tips. A lanky boy set his bicycle against the lightpole. She jumped on and rode it around the block.

"Was I ever so blithe?" Liz said.

"Last week," Deena said. "I remember. *I* was never so blithe," Deena said. "I was born old." She held out a piece of paper. "Check this out."

Jack wanted custody. Deena could have Deej in the summer. She got every other holiday and the right, woman's libber that she was, to pay child support.

"The shit," Liz said.

"Indeed," Deena said. "That's mild. He had this couriered to my office. The staff just loved it. 'How Deena's World Turns.' They're probably still chewing it over." She stood up.

"Where are you going?"

"After a brownie, what else?" She stomped in and stomped out, the brownie trembling on the plate.

"The trouble is," she said, "I'm worn out. I'm ready to let him have her. That way she isn't being torn apart. Every time I stand up for myself he goes after her. 'Who's Mommy seeing?' 'Why doesn't Mommy buy you more toys; she's taking all my money.' 'Whose car was in the drive?' It's so ugly. I read those damn women's magazines and they always make it sound like there's a way out, a way to be decent."

"You cannot give her up," Liz found herself saying. She slammed her hand on the table. She and Deena both looked at it.

"I don't need that," Deena said. "I don't need to be yelled at."

"I don't care. You can't give in to him. It's child abuse, as plain as if you hit her yourself." Deena's face went pale.

"I don't need this," she said and gathered up her purse.

"Right," Liz said. "Do you want me to tell you to give up? After what you told me? After what I saw in my old work?"

"I'll tell you what I *don't* want," Deena said. "I don't want you saying things that make me feel guilty." She stood up, threaded her way between the tables and disappeared into the parking lot.

Liz picked up her coffee and ambled casually past all the curious faces. Deena leaned against the wall, studying her sneakers. She looked up, her blue eyes flat.

"What?" she said.

"I was out of line," Liz said.

"You were. If I want a lecture I'll pay for one. Life is not therapy."

"So, Assertive One, what can I do?"

"You can drive," Deena said. "And you can listen."

Beryl stuck her head out the door. Liz pointed to the car and waved good-bye. "That's two days in a row," Beryl yelled. "I'll clean up." Liz blew her a kiss.

She drove north, past the dusty grove where dusty people gathered for Sunday flea markets, the truck stop called "Mom's" where the biscuits were so bad you knew the old saying was true: "Never gamble with a man named Doc, never eat at a place called 'Mom's' . . ." All that hot, gritty way, Deena said nothing.

They curved up the highway to the cinder cones, to the place where the black and pale sand braided together.

"Let's go to that overlook," Deena said. "I haven't been there in years."

Liz pulled in. They sat on the picnic table. Below them, the desert flowed away, a sea of sand and shadow. Beyond lay the violet mystery of rock and light that one could never reach. Between them lay easy silence. Deena wiped her eyes and smiled.

"This is so good," she said. "I forget how it is to be out here."

"I love it," Liz said. "And I love our friendship."

"You know?" Deena said. "That's what I remember when I remember to go to these places. The simple stuff . . . 'I love our friendship,' 'Deej is worth a fight', 'Letting go and taking back are things we never learned.'" She stretched out her bare legs. "I don't even want a cigarette. I don't even want him dead. I'm just glad to be here, that's all."

"There's big medicine here," Liz said. "That's what Paul told me. I've got one more simple sentence."

"Shoot."

"Whatever you decide, I'll be there."

"Well, then there now," Deena said. "What's the big deal?" The sun beat into them. Liz tried a little prayer. "Burn the pain out of us," she said to the sand, to the heat-waves rippling in the sage, to the twisted skeletons of piñon.

"Amen," Deena said. She poked Liz. "I wonder about something. I wonder: do men go through this?"

"I'm not the person to ask," Liz said. "I cannot give an unbiased answer." She stared up at the black hills. "I am one bitter bitch."

"I'm getting there," Deena said.

"Know this, too," Liz said. "That's no deep psychological demon you're fighting there. Jack is a real monster. If you fight him, he goes after Deej. If you lay back and he starts feeling safe, he'll need a new victim, one that's close at hand."

"I can stand that," Deena said. "It's when the doubt starts, the guilt, then I get nuts. That's when I need help."

"I'll listen," Liz said. "I'll drag you to places like this and listen. Do the same for me."

"Vowed," Deena said.

"You know?" Liz said. "You could talk to Katz. He's on the flip side, a kid he loves and sees six months out of the year. You could call him."

"He's crazy busy."

"He loves it. He loves being Saint Katz of the High Desert. Trust me."

"We'll see."

They heard a truck crunch in over the gravel. Liz turned. The truck stopped inches from the Camaro's bumper and a ranger got out, a ranger with a gun and dark glasses, a ranger with the meanest mouth she'd ever seen.

"Your right front tire is on a patch of beeweed," the ranger said. "Did you read the signs?"

Liz stood up.

"I'm sorry," she said. The ranger nodded.

"I'm Annie Tewa," she grinned. "Paul told me about you. I hear you've got a plan."

They caravanned to Paul and Claire's. Around a table filled with eggrolls and cold spicy noodles and ginger fruit salad, they talked. Claire watched them.

"You've got to do it," she said. "Where I come from, they have stolen so much—sacred carvings, scrolls, even the bones of our ancestors."

"Keep feeding us," Liz said, "and we'll get *your* things back."

Claire patted her hand. "That's okay. It's bad enough when Paul's off fighting forest fires. Thailand is another planet."

They cleared the table and piled into Paul's van. He'd found some new petroglyphs. They hiked through prickly pear and rabbitbrush to a trail that curved between two mesitas; sunset turned everything soft pink, the sky a lens of rose.

"I can't stand to think of leaving here," Paul said. Annie nodded. "Then don't," she said.

"Come on," he said. "You know the story. 'Trim the fat,' they just told me. Where? How?"

The light deepened to garnet; in it, the shadows were black, Annie's eyes unreadable.

"What if the park closed?" she asked. "I think of that. Some of the old people want that."

"Then who'd protect it?" Paul asked. "Who'd keep the ORV's off the sage, the Phoenicians off the ruins?"

"Maybe those who live here," she said.

Liz stopped. "I'll catch up with you," she said.

Ahead lay a little mesa. Deena and Claire were a few hundred feet behind her. A jackrabbit crouched at the side of the trail, its slate eyes luminous; a jet seamed the sky, its trail pink, then gold, then gone; and the horizon flared yellow-green. Darkness melted up from the east—there was just enough time. Paul had said that just after sunset, the little snake carvings were silver.

"Thank you," Liz whispered. She looked down. A pebble shone in the black sand, like a tiny moon. She picked it up and saw, next to it, a half-buried scrap of pottery, bone-white, laced with a delicate web of work. She turned it over in her hand, put it back, the pebble beside it, and started up the trail. The mesitas had held the sun's heat; she could have been swimming in tropical water, through currents of night-wind. Ahead and behind, the voices of her friends echoed in the bright air. She touched the bracelets on her wrist, Nick's silver circle, the string of turquoise beads.

Twenty-nine

"WE DON'T USE SPICE," ROSE SAID. She turned the chunks of mutton in the iron stewpot. "Way back, we didn't use meat that much either. We didn't have sheep till the Spaniards came." She sprinkled salt over the browning meat. "So, we just used *paatsami*, that's the parched corn, and ashes from saltbush and maybe even a little salt, if there was any to spare. Salt was really precious. The men got it from somewhere in the Grand Canyon."

She poured in the hominy, added water, covered the pot and turned down the heat. "That's all there is to *nok qui vi*," she said. "Except the waiting. It takes a long time to taste right. My cousin lets it cook overnight. She makes the best *nok qui vi* on Second Mesa."

Liz poured them both coffee and they sat on the stoop in the early afternoon sun. Thunderheads were moving in from the south; the air was thick with the promise of rain. The scent of *nok qui vi* drifted past them. Rose leaned back against the woodpile and closed her eyes.

"Sometimes this place reminds me of my aunt's," she said. "She did not have running water. She burned wood for heat. That smell, that mutton and corn, the rain coming, it really takes me back."

A raven screamed. They looked up. It flew in from the southeast, black against the thunderheads.

"That too," Rose said quietly. "Up there, some of the people believe that ravens can be *powaqa*."

"I wonder about them, *powaqa*," Liz said. "My people called a lot of uppity women witches and killed them."

"No. Ours are different, both women *and* men. They came with us when we emerged. They buy wisdom, they sell themselves for power." She watched the raven.

"Can you imagine what he knows?" she said. "How to ride the wind, how to fly away . . ."

Liz leaned forward out of the shadows, into the sun.

"When I think of Hatt," she said, "I understand how people make those bargains. If we had more power . . ." The raven cocked his head and defecated on her car.

"So much for talking to birds," Rose said. "We'll have to rely on something else."

"On us," Liz said.

"Who's us?"

"You, me, Paul, Annie Tewa."

"And Richard, the one that makes you nervous."

"How can he help?"

"He wants to. He's strong. He's nuts. He's one of the most private men I've ever met. He'll cover for me." She smiled. "And he wants nothing back. Nothing. He just wants to get even."

"I can't think of a better reason to do this work," Liz said.

"This Annie, what's she like?" Rose asked.

"Tough, soft-spoken, Hopi-Tewa, raised in BIA schools. She told me she spoke only Hopi when they came to get her. They hit her, those BIA teachers, when she spoke it. Somehow she didn't lose her mother-tongue . . . or her anger."

"She's lucky," Rose said. "I would trade my soft girlhood for all of it."

"She wants to meet you."

"So she can feel superior?" Rose said. "I told you before. Some of those traditional Hopi are so cold to someone like me. That is wrong." She looked down at her hands. "I may not have danced in the Women's Ceremonies, but I believe the way is compassion."

"Then don't judge her," Liz said. "She's harsh, but I've only seen her with white people. Do you blame her?"

"I don't know. Some days I want to be harsh with everyone, Hopi, *pahaana*, young, old, woman, man. Some days, all I want is solitude. Some days, I think we humans are Spider Grandmother's greatest mistake.

"That Roger finally came in. He didn't even go in to see her. He said the same thing his sister said. 'I know you understand, God bless you.' I wanted to knock him down and shoot him up with drugs and lock him in the broom closet and listen to him scream till the drugs worked."

"Well," Liz wondered, "how about breaking into a suburban garage, hauling out dusty rugs and boxes. Waiting. Never quite knowing where the things went, maybe visiting somebody at Hopi or on the res someday and seeing an old pot on the fridge and knowing. Maybe."

"That's the story of my life," Rose said. She grinned. "I've got the perfect place for short-term storage. Rich has a surfer wagon with painted windows. Connie's got an old truck up on Second Mesa. It runs. We can throw some mud over the license plates or get some hot ones. She's good at stuff like that."

"Connie?"

"Connie," Rose said, and blushed. "And Yazzie. He's a master thief. He knew Roger in the old days. He says he lost a brother to the Jesus Way. He says he works for Hozhoni, for balance. He says he saw a movie about Robin Hood when he was a kid. He wants to be as good as Robin Hood. So we've been talking, me and Connie. Turns out we're the main gossip topic . . . both of us." She laughed. "Turns out I knew more than I thought I did. She's been re-teaching me."

"There's more," Liz said.

"Meaning?"

"Meaning Annie Tewa, she knows about you." Liz paused. "Meaning I've been dreaming about a Hopi woman," Liz said. "She was a child when the dreams started. They're more than dreams. I've known that for a while."

"What are you saying?" Rose said.

"I'm not sure. It's like having a second life, one where I don't have to do anything. I'm just a watcher."

"What do you watch?" Rose asked. "What does it have to do with me?"

"I am watching a woman surrender to a difficult life," Liz said. "Not be defeated by it, but move through it. I know where she is; I can guess at when. Last week, Paul took us out to see some new rock art he'd found. Across from House of Eagles. I saw three snakes carved in the mesa, I saw where the sun set—it was the place of my dreams."

Her voice sounded odd to her, like that '60's rock 'n' roll that had once faded in and out of the desert night.

"Black Sands," Rose said. "When?"

"As they were leaving, maybe a little before."

"Parrot Clan was there, Aunt Osuwa says.

"Yes. The woman is Parrot Clan. Her name is Talasi . . ."

"That means pollen."

. . . She knelt over the grinding stone, pushing into the corn as though it were her worry, as though she could grind her fear to dust. She ground for Powamu, for the late winter ceremonies of renewal. It had been a harsh time. The people needed to remember that Spring moved in Mother Earth, that the pale beans sent out shoots in the dark, as the people gathered underground, awaiting the visit of Crow Mother and her terrible helpers; and the children of those who had been children took in the teaching and moved on . . . to the next season, the next cycle, the Powamu when they sat with *their* children, remembering, looking forward, knowing the beans sent out their green, living shoots, knowing dark became light . . . and light became dark . . . in perfect balance.

Talasi smiled. She remembered turning from the sight of Kihsi's naked body. She no longer turned away. The sight of him, the touch, she gathered them in, storing up for the long, hungry time ahead. He was eighteen winters. Already, some of the gossips called him *qataaqa,* Not-man. He would be challenged, soon, to take a wife. The people needed more people, for work, for family, for the future. The elders saw—in his hard work, his songs, his skill at hunting, at weaving, at preparing *pahos*—that he was a good man. He would be asked to pass on his goodness to his children, to his grandchildren.

Talasi's wrists ached. Her thoughts moved with the rhythm of the grinding, forward, back, forward, back. There were few baskets of corn in the caches. Droughts left too little water for storage, too little for the corn and beans and squash. The women travelled further and further to gather greens and berries. The rabbits brought back from the hunt were as small and withered as the village dogs. Rupi carried a child, her belly enormous, her legs scarcely thick enough to carry her, much less the child.

Pamosi had seen that the birth would be hard. The child was big, and was not turning as it should. She gathered herbs to slow the labor, had Rupi moved to her sister's house at East-Rising. All that could be done had been done. In the long evenings, Talasi sat with Rupi. Her friend's face was thin; it was becoming too quickly the face of a grandmother. Her eyes were feverish, her words desperate.

"My baby must live," she said. "I have lost too many. I see Sakuna look at the younger maidens." Talasi had set her hand on the baby's shape; it was turned sideways. Rupi had felt water leak from her; then, for days, nothing.

As she rocked over the grinding, Talasi saw her friend's bright eyes, the lop-sided bulge of her belly, how her skin was dry and yellow. Rupi did not eat. All she wanted was water. Her sister had carried a jug from Nest House, all that long way. If Talasi thought of that, of the work that lay ahead, of Pamosi's visions, of what the women knew, what the men would not hear, she could keep Kihsi from her mind. She kept his marriage from her mind.

Her hair swung forward and she smelled the smoke in it. There was too little water to waste on bathing. She remembered the winter pool, the shock of it, their hands fumbling together, the icy single braid of their wet hair and his skin warm beneath her hands. She could not grind the memory away . . .

. . . The phone rang. Liz uncoiled from the sheets and pulled herself up. It was barely dawn. The air was icy. Clear gray light poured in through the east window.

"I'm in a phone booth on the edge of town," Macleod said cheerfully. "I woke up with the birds . . . and a hangover and hard-on."

"Forget the first and second," Liz said. "I'll take the third."

By the time he walked through the door, she had showered and started coffee. He kicked her big patchwork pillows into a heap and hauled her down. Without a word, he pulled her robe apart, unzipped his jeans and nailed her delightfully to the floor. Afterwards, she looked up and saw his hat still jammed squarely on his head.

"Class!" she said.

"Hey, Macleod's my name, good lovin's my game." She was liking him again. She rolled out from under him, pulled on her robe and went to the stove.

"Chemicals!" she said.

"A good woman," he said. "You know what's important: morning exercise, stimulants and the wit and wisdom of George Hayduke."

She carried coffee and bagels to the pillows and snuggled up against him.

"In that tradition," she said, "I've got a promise to keep. I'd like you to help."

His face went tight.

"Huh?" he said warily. She recovered from liking him.

"I've got a job for us, stealth, excitement, vengeance, good works. We honor the spirits of the dead, the living and those not yet born. Hayduke lives!" She grinned and cuddled closer. He stretched and moved away.

"Sorry, dear," he said. "Nothing personal. Hangovers need space."

She sat up. If that was what he needed, she'd give it. She'd learned, if nothing else, the consequences of not giving men 'space.'

"You know how I am," he laughed. "Mr. Sensitive as long as it's up."

She sipped her coffee. She could smell their juices on her body; she wondered if they dulled the brain. It occurred to her that he did manage to say what other men kept silent.

"Macleod," she said, "do you remember Hatt?"

"That Hopi girl?"

"That's Rose, that Hopi *woman.*"

"Scuse *me,* Gloria," he said.

"Hatt is the woman in the nursing home, the trading post woman?"

"Oh yeah," he said vaguely. "How is she?"

"She's lousy," Liz said. He got up, ambled into the kitchen, re-filled his cup and ambled back.

"How about mine?" Liz asked.

"Oops," he said. He brought the pot over and filled her cup.

"Macleod," she said again. She could hear the whine. She thought about stopping, but her mouth had other ideas. "Do you ever listen to me?"

"Sure," he said, "especially when you talk dirty." He took her breast in his hand. "Damn," he said, watching himself as though it was one of the greatest miracles, "you make me seventeen again. Look at that."

"Stop," she said.

He glanced at her and dropped his hand.

"Sure," he said. "Be that way."

"Wait a minute," she said. "If all we ever do is screw, we're not going to want to do even that after a while."

"Even that?" he said, sliding down and starting to bury his face in her body.

"No!" she said. She pried him away. She couldn't believe she'd done it. She couldn't ever remember saying no. You didn't say no to that which made you pretty.

"Hey," he said, his big face flushed and surly. "I told you. I've got a hangover. Keep it simple. You want more than I do. You and I, we hike, we make each other feel good, I take you out to some of the best damn scenery you've ever seen. What more do you want?"

"I want you to listen to me," she said. Am I still saying this to some man? a cool, clear part of her asked. "I want you to open up. I want to relax with you, know you. I want us to do this plan together. I want us to do something real."

They stared at each other. She pulled her robe together.

"Lizzie," he said.

"Don't ever call me that," she snapped. She remembered Nick's eyes, his voice. "Lizzie," he'd said, "who's going to call you Lizzie?"

"Look," Macleod said, "you're a fine person. That's the highest compliment I can pay anybody. I respect you even when I don't agree with you. We *do* talk. You know we do. I've said more to you than I have to a woman in years. The thing is . . ." He paused. "The thing is I do want to be with someone someday. And even if I don't know what I'm looking for in a woman, I *do* know what I don't want. And you're it. You're too high-strung, too sensitive. When you're upset, it's like a black cloud. It fills up the room. You clam up and I feel guilty and I get pissed-off and I don't want to feel that way."

"No," she said. "Who would?" He took her hand. Swell, she thought, now he's personal.

"Mac," she said, "when I'm quiet I'm just trying to figure out how I feel. Or I'm just off someplace else. That's all."

"Can't you just lighten up?" he said. "You're too damn heavy for me." He seemed to shrink down into his big body.

"That too," Liz said.

"What too?" he snapped.

"No big deal in the body department. Macleod, if I were twenty-five and skinny and blonde, the stars in your eyes would look like Times Square. You'd love anything I did. Sulking, demands, games. I'd be a big challenge. You'd trip over yourself trying to figure out how to win me." She slammed her coffee cup on the floor. He flinched. She grabbed his face and made him look at her.

"Am I right, sweetheart?"

"In a way," he said. "I *am* looking for someone special. But that stuff about looks, that's not fair. You're in great shape for a woman your age."

Liz dropped her hands. She looked at him, his thinning hair, the gray in his beard, the softness in his shoulders and arms, his gut, and she grinned.

"Gee, Mac," she said, "you too. For a middle-aged guy, you do all right."

"Yeah," he said. His face brightened. He pulled her to him.

"Listen," he said. "You're a great gal. I can be honest with you. I couldn't talk like this with just anybody. Most of the women in my life have been girls. I like you. I really do. But, I just don't have those stars in my eyes and I can't make 'em happen."

Liz took a deep breath and kept her mouth closed. This was the point where she always vowed to help the man light the stars. Macleod's eyes were going to have to stay dim.

"The funny thing," he rambled on, "is that I *hate* that feeling. Those stars. I get jealous and crazy and have to know where she is every minute. I feel empty when she's not around."

"I know the feeling," Liz said. "You get the stars, you get the Black Hole."

He turned and held her close. "Oh God," he said, "I knew I was going to hurt you. I knew this would happen. I've been right where you are. Don't feel that way about me."

She looked up into his broad, bewildered face and she saw, clearly who his pain was for.

"Hold on," she said softly. "You better get this through your head. I am not in love with you. I am not going to self-destruct from not seeing you." As she said the words, she realized they were breaking-up. "Macleod, really, I'm fine. I know how that other is. When Nick left, the only things I hung onto were my heartbeat and my breath. This isn't like that."

He kept looking at her with grave compassion. He'd gotten a little hard again.

"I'll miss *this*," she said, touching him. "I truly will." He looked down at her hand, then up and saw her sadness.

"Oh no," he said. "Don't cry. You'll make me cry!" He turned away.

Well, Liz thought, let's get this over. She wiped her eyes on her sleeve and took him into her arms. He was crying. That didn't stop him from being ready to roll. After he'd calmed down and moved into her, whispering "You're my woman . . . you're my woman," into her flesh, she took a deep breath and sat up.

"Macleod," she said, "this has got to be the last time. I fool myself because the sex is so good, then I want more."

"Of course you want more," he said benignly. "You deserve more. You're one hell of a fine woman. I wish there were more like you." He patted her back. She wanted to kill him.

"Do you feel *anything?*" she asked.

He smiled at her. There was admiration in his eyes. She thought she might have to pick up the coffee cup and hit him square between them. It would be justifiable homicide. Any jury of her peers, any twelve middle-age women, would agree.

"I gotta be honest with you," he said. "You deserve that. You're such a straight shooter. I feel relieved. Hey, we've had a great time, we're being adults about this. No hard feelings. You're great!" He pulled on his clothes. Liz tightened the belt around her robe. Her hands were numb.

She walked him out to the truck. He put his arm around her.

"You've taught me a lot," he said. "I'll never forget this." He kissed her cheek. She thought that if he said one more warm, appropriate thing, she would smash his windshield. He waved once before he pulled away. He was smiling.

They always walk away stronger, she thought. What's with me? I don't particularly like him. I sure didn't love him and I feel like somebody just yanked out about twenty feet of intestine. She kicked a rock. "What the hell," she said out loud, "he could have disagreed."

Thirty

"DEENA," SHE SAID. "THIS IS RIDICULOUS. I can't sleep. I can't sit still. I can't get off my butt. I can't read. I can't eat."

"Be grateful for that last one," Deena said. "It's the saving grace of misery. Hold on. I'm lighting a cigarette."

Liz shifted the phone to her other ear and sipped her coffee. She was drinking ten cups a day since she and Macleod had talked things over like adults. She made herself put whole milk and honey in it and told herself it was nutritious. She had managed to get herself to work. In fact, the sweet monotony of it had been soothing.

"Okay. I'm back," Deena said.

"This is ridiculous," Liz said and started crying.

"You said that, and I'm inclined to agree."

"Tough love? Right?"

"You knew who he was."

"That's what's ridiculous. I knew who he was. *I* told *him* I wanted to stop things and I feel like he rejected me. I feel like he was just moseying along, not really into it, not making much of an effort and he didn't even have to end it. I did it for him. I should run this ad somewhere: 'Passive Men. Enjoy a love affair without effort. Our dedicated staff does all the work, from start to finish.'"

"I'm almost enjoying this," Deena said. "I do think I'm going to be celibate forever."

"Great, I'll send my bill for your mental health. I can't believe I'm going through this. I don't even like him."

"Really?"

"Really. I do that. I'll be lovers with men I'd never have as friends.

That's why Nick was something special. I liked him. I even respected him."

"Liz," Deena said firmly. She was sweet reason. Liz could imagine her looking down at Deej. "What have you really lost?" She asked.

"The best sex I ever had in my life. The last man who will ever want me." She paused. She heard Deena snort.

"You *are* kind of drying up. I've noticed that. Just shut up about that, Liz. You'll play right into it if you keep this aging bullshit up!"

"I know! That's what I hate."

"So. What else?"

"The big one. The hope that he might eventually realize who I was and treasure me."

"That's great!" Deena laughed. "You want a man you don't treasure to treasure you. That's just great."

"I know," Liz said miserably. "I know. Right now, I can't help how I feel."

"I could come over and smack you around. Would that help?"

"Thanks. I'm doing a good job myself. I'm just glad you're there. I'm going for a walk. I think that's what I need."

"I'll be home after nine. If you want to spend the night here, Deej's bed is empty."

"I'll call," Liz said. "I love you."

"Likewise," Deena said. "I'm like you. I pick friends a hell of a lot better than I pick husbands."

Liz drove up to an old trail at the foot of the Peaks. It ran through fields of wildflowers and dry grass. A few jack pine and ponderosa gave the hawks and ravens a place to hang out. Meadowlarks trilled warnings so beautiful they were lures. She stepped out onto the cinders. A gray snake rippled across her path, leaving its trail of delicate waves.

She walked from late afternoon through early evening; sat on a boulder for a while contemplating life, love and a meatball sub for dinner; and walked out into a wash of apricot light from the setting sun. The Peaks were purple, the grasses caught last light. She headed east, tears running down her face, a hawk cruising behind her, silent and alert, hunting the little field-mouse meatballs scared up by her passage. She had never enjoyed misery more.

The light faded, the path became a dark curl in the shimmering meadow. By the light of a late summer moon high in the south, she picked a handful of penstemon. She stopped under a squat pine just before the trail head and faced the mountains.

"Thank you," she said. "That's the best I can do."

Sugar and Lurch were curled at the foot of the bed. The other kittens had gone to live with Katz. His cynicism and despair melted away as soon as he had a kitten in each hand. He'd named them Rose and Anne, for Roseanne Cash, who he loved from afar. Liz straightened up the cabin and put the two coffee mugs in the sink. She hadn't touched anything for three days. He'd left nothing behind. No shirts, no stale cigarettes, no vacuum that wouldn't fill on its own.

She put the penstemon in a glass of water and held them to the light. In the meadow, they had been cool violet; against the candlelight, they were tiny rose lanterns. She set them on the windowsill and slipped into bed. Her legs ached. She felt hollow and grateful, for the snake, the rosy light, for Deena. She pulled the phone into bed.

"Hey," she said, "I'm okay."

"Good," Deena said. "I had no doubts."

"Thank you."

"Sweet dreams." . . .

. . . Talasi knelt over the stone. She prayed for the rhythm to do its work, for the swaying bach and forth to clear her mind. No matter how she tried, she could not blot out the vision of Rupi, of her mouth stretched huge in a soundless scream. She could not blur the sight of the tiny, clay-colored body, perfect, female, the life-cord tight around its neck. She saw her own hands, shining with blood, useless. She saw Rupi slide down to the birthing mat and curl on her side, her arms crossed tight over her breasts. She saw the tiny wrapped bundle, saw it again and again.

A shadow darkened the courting window. She turned. What few boys had once come there were long married, were fathers, were Gone Over. Kihsi knelt.

"Why are you there?" she whispered. She wanted to throw meal at him, as the maidens did to rid themselves of an unwanted suitor. She did not want him there. They met in secret. She was frightened that he had appeared there, as though he were courting, as though he would say something not kept secret.

"They have told me what I must do," he said. "We have never had *this*. We have never had even one morning of time together without being frightened. This is a gift."

"But I *am* frightened," she said. She set down her stone and moved to the window. He took her hand. They had not seen each other for many dawns and he had sent no word. She had ached for him, but she had waited. Her dreams had told her nothing. She had not used seeing stone or fire or smoke. Those visions were not for lovers. Waiting was for lovers.

"Talasi," he said. His voice broke. He dropped his head to their linked hands. "Let them talk," he said. She set her hand on the back of his neck and pressed her face against his rough hair.

"You smell like Toho's smokes," she said. He nodded.

"What did he say?"

"You know," he said. "Will we meet?" he said wildly. "Will you see me?" She set her naked fingers on his lips. Without the pathstone, her palm felt unprotected. His mouth was warm. She was gathering him in, the touch of him, the sight, his scent.

"Say it to me," she said, "what he said you must do."

"Not here," he said. "Come with me tonight to our place. We have only tonight. I am to leave tomorrow."

Talasi knelt at the little pool. It was barely a damp smudge against the red sand. Young ferns struggled at its far curve, cool-shadowed by the cliff. She pressed her hand into the damp sand. Behind her, Kihsi unrolled their sleeping mat. They were both silent. She looked at her hand-print, saw in the dark hollows old memories: Crow Mother's black eyes; the blue ring of Qalavis's mouth, his black hands holding a child still; Ongchoma's stone, whose touch will make a child strong. She remembered Kihsi's eyes, his straight back; and then the red haze behind her closed lids.

She stood and let her robe slip from her body. He touched her shoulder. His fingers burned. And then she was surrendered to his body, his passion beating her back into the warm rock. The bones of his face ground into hers. She rolled away. He would not hurt her with his sorrow. She struck him once, became a blade, her nails searing across his cheekbone. They stared at each other.

"Did you think I was only sad?" she asked. "Did you think only a man felt anger?" He touched his face.

"What will we do?" he asked. He reached for her. He saw her. How he had loved her, would love her, how the betrayal was all he had to give. He marked her face with his blood as she moved up against him and he poured into her, as seed, as water, as life and fire and smoke.

"No," he whispered against her skin. "We can find a way."

"My husband," she said clearly. She moved up on the mat, cradling his head on her arm, and wiped the blood from his face. "There is no way," she said. He sighed and settled into her arms. She held the weight of him, took it into her heart. She would carry it to her Going-Over and beyond. She watched his face until she saw his eyes roving under the lids and she knew he slept. Even after she had folded her robe under his head for pillow and stood up, she felt him in her arms.

At the cliff-base, the water had puddled. There were tiny fish there, their pulsing hearts visible in their transparent bodies. She dipped her hands in the water; a spiral of blood swirled away. The fish scattered. She offered water to the four directions.

"Thank you," she whispered. By morning, she would be gone, the fish gone, too. And yet, with the next rain, *they* would again flicker through the water. She wound Kihsi's kilt around her and climbed up the faint trail to the signs. They were painted in the ancient way, in colors, in red and yellow and blue. They glowed against the dark cliff-face, as though the setting sun lit them from within. They were *lay'ta*, perhaps dangerous. They were neither deer nor migration sign nor corn nor cloud nor smoke.

She sank to a boulder and watched the fading light play over their strange forms: the headless beings, the twisted arc, the broken shield covered with beautiful animals, lizards and bats and hare. None of the pictures was whole or unaltered. A breeze blew down the *tupqa*. It smelled ordinary, of juniper and faint woodsmoke and the sweet wet of the spring. She looked up at the pictures and cleared her mind. The prayer leaped out.

"Let me see clearly." The pictures stayed a mystery. She murmured one of the lesser charms for clear vision. Nothing changed. She took the pathstone from her medicine pouch and willed her heart to slow.

Daylight was fading; there would be no moon. She had only a little time. She held the stone to her eye and saw the shield. The animals were as finely drawn as the designs on Pamosi's bowls. She knew she was barely breathing. She could have been at the grinding stone, letting the rhythm take her. Suddenly, the hare leaped from the shield, the lizards followed; the bat soared up into the dusk. The shield darkened and she saw, as though drawn in fire, tree stumps and fallen pine, deep gouges torn in the black hills, the bones of animals and people, scattered, broken. She saw *yaapuntsa* swirling over the land, towering up into cloudless skies, blotting out the fiery eye of Father Sun, who was no longer Father. He was Destroyer; he was pure rage.

The shield vanished. She lowered her arm. The pathstone lay cool in her palm. She wondered if she would ever move again. Behind her, the Sacred Mountains swallowed the last of the light. The cliff-face darkened, red to black; she saw how rock came from fire.

Kishi walked toward her. He waited till she stood and held out his arms.

"We are the same now," he said. "You no longer maiden, I, carrying your mark." She touched his cheek.

"Did I hurt you much?" she asked.

"Enough," he said. "There will be a scar."

"As everywhere," she said and told him what she had seen . . . the old, terrible vision . . . again . . .

. . . "Liz, it's Rose. I'm sorry to wake you. She's had a very bad night. She's terrified. Nothing works. Can you come?"

"I'm off today. I'll be there as soon as I can."

"Get some breakfast," Rose said. "I need to finish some things. My mom can get the kids off to school." She paused. "Liz, I've written that she not be sent to the hospital. If anybody asks you, just agree. Okay?"

"Of course," Liz said. "See you."

She set the phone back on the bookshelf and stumbled out into the kitchen. She found herself thinking of Mac, of his big warm body, those sweet dawns. Desire washed over her. That was how it always worked when you only wanted what wasn't there. She made herself think of how his eyes could go cold, how he flinched, how his face looked when he said, "lighten up." Fool's Grief, that's all it was.

She showered and put on a bright shirt. There was something about losing sex that made her want to fade away. After Nick, she had lived in jeans and beat-up flannel shirts for three years. She slipped his bracelet on her wrist and turquoise blossoms in her ears, turquoise for joy, silver for the moon and how it moved in her, pulled on her jacket and left.

The diner was crowded. She ordered and sat waiting, wishing she still smoked cigarettes. That was all she wanted, coffee, grapefruit juice, a cigarette. Last night's meatballs and Fool's Grief were playing field hockey in her stomach. Some sadist played Bob Seger. Tears stuck in her throat. The late-night, all-American truck-stop waitress appeared.

"Hey," she said, "it's you. Where's your girlfriend?" She filled Liz's cup. "Are you all right?" she said gently.

"The usual," Liz said.

"Hey, jerk 'em," the waitress whispered. "There's a million of 'em out there and I've met 'em all, and laid half of 'em. Forget them."

"Thanks," Liz said. "I'll come here the next time some pretty young thing catches my eye."

"Was he pretty?" the waitress grinned.

"Not quite."

"Young?"

"Not quite."

"Well, then," she said, "it must have been his thing." She sat across from Liz. "I'll get killed for this. You gotta learn a few facts. I can tell from your accent that you're from back East. With cowboys, you gotta remember two things: they all got one; when it ends, go for protein. It's that low blood sugar that'll get you every time."

"Sausage and eggs over easy," Liz said. The waitress patted her hand and scooted back toward the kitchen.

Rose met her at the edge of the parking lot. She tilted her face to the sun cresting the far trees.

"I'm so glad to be outside," she said. "Summertime, I can't stand the indoors." She looked at Liz.

"Are you okay?" she asked. "You look different."

"Macleod and I parted company. He allowed as to how he might hurt me. He's really glad he met me. I'm a real woman, one you can talk to, not just some airhead pretty face."

Rose smiled. "What a loss!" she said. "I'm sorry you feel bad, but he was nothing for you." She opened her purse. "I have something for you!" In her palm rested a tiny carved onyx animal, bound to its back a sliver of turquoise with tiny red eyes. A thin coral line ran along the side of the carrier animal.

"It's a Zuni hunting fetish," she said, and dropped it in Liz's hand. "You must find a bowl to be its house, and feed it cornmeal. The red line is its heartline. It is a bear carrying a badger, a bear for curiosity, badger for healing." She shaded her eyes. "I made up the part about the bear. Traditionally, the bear is for strength, but you already have that. Curiosity is more fun."

Liz held the bear up to the light. "You can tell," she said. "That is one curious bear." She dropped it into her shirt pocket. "I'll carry it right there," she said, "near my heart. I'll feed it."

"Use this," Rose said. She held out a plastic bag. "It's medicine. Connie brought it in to me. Manny's in the picture again. She figured I'd need it."

"What do I do with it?"

"Feed the bear. And when you first get up—dawn is best—offer some to the day. Ask to keep your heartline open. Say thank you." She grinned. "It's inner. You know what to do."

"I used to pick flowers," Liz said, "and put them in my mom's jelly glasses. I had a statue of Mary. I'd surround her with flowers: dandelions, violets, paintbrush. I'd light candles, burn this awful incense you could get at the dime store. Then I'd kneel there in my dad's blue bathrobe, which was the closest thing I could find to a nun's habit." She patted the fetish. "I've got just the house for them. It's Pennsylvania Dutch redware. My mom gave it to me. It's from where her people used to live."

"The ones with hex signs?" Rose asked.

"They *were* the ones," Liz said. "They're nearly gone. There's one market that's left, food, some cute sayings, designs."

"There might be more," Rose said, "if you hunted."

"There might be. I might get to it someday. I've thought about it. I'm scared there won't be anything there. Their Chaco Canyon is Pittsburgh."

"You mean yours."

"Mine."

A beautiful car swung into the parking lot and pulled up near them. It was dark red and shining. It even had a heartline, pinstriped from front to back with black flames. Rose shook her head.

"That's my man," she said. "Come on. Let's get the introductions over with. He's scared to death of you. He thinks you'll warp my mind."

"Wonderful," Liz said. "I feel so relaxed."

Manny rolled down the window. Liz knew he was studying them behind his dark glasses. What she saw of his face was infuriatingly beautiful.

"Take off your shades," Rose said. Manny dropped them to the end of his nose. "This is Liz," she said. She turned to Liz. Her voice went soft. "This is my husband, Manny."

"I'm pleased to meet my wife's friend," he said.

"I've seen you before," Liz said. "You were on that picket line at

Peabody about a month ago. You gave me a flier."

"We try harder," he grinned. "Rose tells me you've got a plan."

"We do."

"She wants me to watch the kids that night." He laughed. "You gonna get her to join that Women's Lib?"

"I think it's a little late for that," Liz said.

"Yeah," he said. "She doesn't need that button, you know."

"You gonna watch the kids?"

"Yeah."

"You wear the button," Liz said. He pushed his glasses back up. He was smiling. When he turned to unlock the passenger door, Liz saw that he had braided one strand of hair in a skinny pigtail. He set his thin hand on hers.

"She give you that medicine?"

"Yeah." She wasn't going to start lying now.

"It's cornmeal," he said. "My sister ground it. Rose's cousin brought it in. You be careful."

Liz traced the black flame. It curved up and disappeared into the door-crack.

"I am *very* careful," she said. "And I'm pleased to meet my friend's husband."

"It burns inside," he said. "Look." He leaned away and opened the door. The flame blossomed out onto the roof into huge white flowers. She backed away. *Datura*, moon flower, flower of Sight and madness.

"You be careful," she said. "They can kill you."

"In a way," he said, "they have. Rose can tell you." He started the car. Rose leaned across the seat. "Just sit with her," she said. "That's all you can do."

Hatt's voice wailed through the halls, crying out words and syllables and the strangled sounds you make in nightmares. The day-nurse walked by, pushing the medicine cart, lost in counting syringes. She nodded to Liz.

"You'd think the moon was full," she said.

Liz's hand slipped on the doorknob. She realized she was frightened. She wanted to turn and leave, outrun the nostalgia in her body, maybe settle herself in the passenger lounge of the west-bound express and drink till she hit the station in Santa Barbara, and stumble off and stagger west till she stood hungover and hip-high in the green salt water.

She opened the door. Hatt lay on her side, her sheets bunched under her scrawny buttocks. There was a puddle of urine on the mattress cover. Her nightgown had ridden up over her swollen belly. She clawed at the edges of the mattress. Her eyes were wide open and burning.

"I am so cold," she said clearly.

Liz grabbed a towel and mopped up. She folded in a dry bottom sheet and covered Hatt carefully with the Navajo blanket.

"I can't breathe," Hatt said. "The ceiling is closing in. The walls." Liz yanked open the curtains. Hatt turned toward the light. She circled her naked wrist with her fingers.

"I have lost your gift," she said. "They have stolen it. The *chindi*, the *powaqa*. They work together. As it was foreseen." Her voice rose and cracked. "Where are you? Are you out there? With them?" She threw off the blanket and smiled.

"I will go home soon. There has been a mistake. Your gift is in the stone box, where it has always been. Dear love. Don't be afraid." She lay still and closed her eyes. "I will sleep," she said. "I will see you." Liz covered her again. Hatt wove her fingers through the fringe.

"You must not cut your hair," she said. "I am cold. You can wrap me in it." She reached up into the air and drew the ghost to her breast. "You are here," she said. "My friend, my dear friend." She spoke, some other words, sibilant, more breath than language, and fell silent, her fingers stroking the blanket, her face as smooth as a girl's.

Liz watched over her. It comes to this, she thought, nothing, not marriage, not true love, not motherhood, not beauty, not even work can prevent this. This waking dream and nightmare. This room with no light and too little air. This love with ghosts. She pulled the blanket up over Hatt's shoulders. She could smell the wool, that strong animal scent, pungent and alive.

"Changing Woman," she whispered. "All I know is the name, the scrap of story. We never had time for you to teach me." She took Hatt's hand in hers.

"I'd like you to come back," she said. "I don't know you well enough to mourn you as you deserve." There was no answer, only the slow rise and fall of the blanket. Liz looked down at their hands, hers veined, hanging on, Hatt's refined to bone, ready to let go. She kissed Hatt's pulse.

"He didn't leave you," she said. "You did nothing wrong." She dropped to her knees and rested her head on the rough blanket. In the delicate light, they slept.

"I must marry before the harvest," Kihsi said. "They prayed over this. Toho said I would be allowed to court a girl from another village. There are two, one on a slope near Neuvatukaovi, another above Soowi Lake, far to the south. I leave tomorrow. I am to find a girl whose mother has gone over and I am to bring her here."

He took hold of Talasi's hair and gently pulled her to his side.

"They are wise," Talasi said. "I would push the kiva in on their wise heads.

They did not pray for me. To see you here, with wife, with children. How could they be so cruel?" She moved away from him. "I have given up everything. I have done as they wish. As They wish." She faced him. "You agreed?"

"Yes," he said. "As you do." He took her in his arms. "'In another time,' we said. This girl will be my bride. She will be the mother of our children, the village's children, but she will not be my wife. You are my wife." He held her face in his hands. She closed her eyes.

"No," he said. "We have this time. Do not shut it out." . . .

. . . the door opened, then closed. Liz came awake. Hatt slept on, snoring. They had left the breakfast tray on the nightstand. There was cold tea, some thin yellow juice and a divided plate holding three blobs of gray. Liz guessed at scrambled eggs and applesauce; she gave up on the third. Someone tapped on the door.

"Time for breakfast," a girl's voice said. Liz pulled the blanket over Hatt's feet, kissed her forehead, and left.

She drove straight to Katz's storefront office. He was hunched at his desk, glaring at a pile of papers, a half-eaten chocolate-chip cookie and a can of organic fruit pop. He didn't look up. She leaned against the file cabinet and studied the map of the Colorado River that covered the back wall.

"I have to find Benny Wilson," he said. "He lives near the wash marked by the big forked cottonwood, the one that made it through the last monsoon. He lives a few miles south of that tall mesa where old lady Begay . . . not old lady John Begay, but old lady William Begay . . . runs her goats. I have to reach him by Tuesday so he can be arraigned. If I don't, he could go to jail for a long, long time and the one thing the Wilson men hate more than jail is *belecana* lawyers who don't keep them out of it. What do you want?"

"Old lady John Latham is dying in the house of the dead. Let's go talk."

"Wait," he said. "The neighbor's dog barked all night. I've got to find a place to live in two weeks and I think I'm in love with a married woman. I can't handle this."

"Let's go," she said. "The only thing I hate more than old ladies being ripped-off is lawyers who won't help them. It's your plan. We're going to go drink coffee till we think of something." She patted his bony shoulder.

He tossed Benny Wilson's warrant in the in-basket. "Coffee gives me the shakes, and don't mother me. You know I hate it."

"You love it," Liz said. "Let's go."

Thirty-one

LABOR DAY CLEARED THE TOWN OF LOCALS and filled it with last-ditch tourists wandering in search of the Grand Canyon, bathrooms and hand-carved, genuine Kachina Dolls for under twenty-five dollars . . . "Do you have one with the snakes?"

Half the conspirators had fled to Liz's back meadow. She brought out a platter of smoky ribs, double-stuffed baked potatoes and thin-sliced purple onions. Rose piled sweet corn in a basket and Katz uncorked a bottle of champagne. They stood a minute in the strong sun.

"This is perfect," Liz said. Pine pollen blurred the blades of sun. A spider looped a web of light between the porch-edge and the woodpile. Rose emerged from the cabin with coffee and warm peach pie. Liz watched Katz roll up his sleeves and set the half-empty champagne deep in an ice-filled bailing bucket, and she wished she could stop time. She didn't miss Macleod, she didn't miss Nick; she missed no one and nothing.

They pulled their chairs to the shaky table and touched hands.

"Thank you," Rose said. Katz nodded. "Normally I'd add a few disclaimers," he said, "but I'd rather eat." He forked a slab of ribs and three ears of corn onto his plate. Rose glanced at Liz. "Where do you put it?" she asked. "I want your secret."

"Anxiety," he said, "and senseless yearning." Liz and Rose glared at him. "I wish that worked for me," Liz said.

"It's worth it," Rose said. She sprinkled salt on her corn. "Tell me this isn't worth it."

"We better earn our bliss," Katz said. "I'm not keeping any notes, but I know we don't have enough bodies for the plan. We don't even know how much stuff is in there."

"A lot," Rose said. "She told me some of the things. I haven't wanted to make lists, but I remember that there are fifteen to twenty old rugs, a couple huge water jugs—*wikoro*, we call them—old baskets, some Pueblo I and II pots and four or five cigar boxes of jewelry, the old kind, the good stuff. Those were all from the post. Then, she said there were things that had just been around the hogan, gifts, a sacred pipe, a quiver made from mountain lion hide, Kachina dolls. She figured Roger would have gotten rid of those and the Yei-bei-chei rug. Pagan idols, you know."

"We need to get as much as we can," Liz said. "I keep thinking about the security system."

"Talk about senseless yearning," Katz said.

"Joe wants to meet with us," Rose said. "He knows security systems, but he doesn't really know us. He would have come today, but his cousin's doing a Blessingway and needed him there. Connie went with him."

"A Blessingway?" Katz said.

"Yeah," Rose laughed, "he said it was either that or Vegas and he figures he's getting older, so . . . " She scraped the bones off her plate and took another potato. "I talked with Annie Tewa. She's going to meet with a medicinewoman she knows up there and see if they can arrange for the holy things to be purified. Those old guys have to pray over it for a while. She thinks they can get most of the stuff back where it belongs. I described one of the wood pieces to her and she cussed and cussed. She said it's an altar object and that it's been missing for years."

"So," Liz said, "let's look at our assets. We've got two trucks, Rich, us Paul and Annie for afterwards, Yazzie's expertise . . ."

Rose laughed. "He'd love that . . . expertise. His gambling buddies all talk like that. You'd think they were big government officials."

"We need a car for look-out," Katz said.

"I've got some fake i.d. left from the weird old days," Liz said. "I'll check out rent-a-wreck."

"Just don't get the yellow Cadillac," Katz said. "Everybody watches for it ever since some hookers rented it for the rodeo parade."

"Check," Liz said. "We know what not to do. We know the Lathams go to Palm Springs for the holidays. We know they don't use a house-sitter. We know they just lock up and trust to Jesus."

"And we know we're crazy," Katz said cheerfully.

"Check," Rose said.

Katz poured the last of the champagne in Liz's glass. She held it to the light.

"Here's to the Monkeywrench Gang," she said. "They didn't know anymore what they were doing than we do."

"Yo," Katz said. "Do you like that? The quintessential hipness of it? Yo!"

"I don't think hip is any longer hip," Liz said. "We are distinctly old-fashioned."

"This is Arizona," Katz said. "We *are* the cutting edge. We are *it!*"

"Oh lord," Rose said. "I think I'll have a piece of pie."

"Hey! You!" Deena climbed out of her car and strolled down the path. Liz could see Deej's little head in the front seat. She was bouncing up and down, Michael Jackson's banshee cry drifting from the car radio.

"I can't stay," Deena said. "We're going to Slide Rock. If I'm not back in three days, send a rescue team. It's going to be a madhouse, but the precious child wants to go." She grinned at Rose. "Hey, lady, how you doing?"

Rose held out the pie plate and raised her eyebrow. "Hmmm?" she said.

"Get thee behind me, woman," Deena laughed. "I barely got into these shorts."

Katz nodded happily. Deena wore faded cut-offs and a halter top. She'd gathered her blonde curls on top of her head.

"I'm Katz," he said. "Where have you been all my life?"

"Filing," Deena said, "and typing and buying groceries and cooking them and throwing out the garbage and cleaning the bathroom floor and answering questions like that."

"Oh," he said. He pushed his pie around on the plate. "Me, too."

"Sure," Deena said.

"Really," he said.

She smiled past him. "Well," she said, "I want in. Not the planning or anything like that. Just tell me the time, the place and my job and I'll be there. Then we all develop amnesia."

Rose nodded. "Don't be too hard on Katz," she said. "He suffers from senseless yearning. You know how that is." Katz bit his knuckle.

"I'm going to do it," he said. "I'm going to try again." He looked up at Deena. "Okay," he said, "I never cleaned the bathroom floor. You're right." She picked up his fork and took a bite of pie. "Better," she said. "Liz tells me you've got a kid somewhere." He nodded.

"Cody," he said. "He'll be here at Christmas."

"Okay," Deena said. "Liz has my number. You can call me. We may have something in common besides unilateral attraction." She ruffled Liz's hair. "Call me. Remember, three days, then send 'em out. I'll be ready."

"You want the guys from the hospital or the firemen?" Liz asked.

"Make it a Forest Service hot shot crew," Deena said. "That will do very nicely." She sauntered up the path.

"Does she ever just walk?" Katz said.

"The day we met," Liz said, "she was wearing hot pink Spandex.

She's relentless."

"Why me?" he moaned. "Why am I visited by unattainable angels?"

"I once asked myself the same question," Liz said. "I think it leaves more time for real life."

After they left, she sat with evening, the champagne turning to blue gloom in her blood, the sky above the black trees in glory, pink and orange and a last wash of copper that burned volcanic on the Peaks. She watched and felt lonesome and realized she was glad to be alone. The plan seemed a dream.

The light faded away. She took the pie plate into the chilly cabin and wrapped herself in the last of Nick's shirts. It was nearly gone, cuffs and collar threadbare, buttons missing, a three-corner tear in the left shoulder. It was no good for warmth, but the worn flannel was velvet against her cheek. When it went, all she would have left were the bracelet, the crystal glass and ghost she could barely call up. The real thing, the work, came without her calling . . .

... They did not sleep. In silence, they held each other through the short night. When first light warmed the horizon, Talasi whispered into his skin, "How can I thank the dawn?" Kihsi pressed his face to hers. She watched him walk into the shadows. She knew he would pray. She raised her face to the light.

"Thank you," she whispered. "Help me live through what lies ahead." She scattered cornmeal, looked up and saw Kihsi, walking away, his figure black against the dawn. She saw him clearly, as though he stood in front of her, and she saw the cornmeal like a powdering of stars against the black sand; she knew she would remember that clearly, and not the sight of the man, the shadow, against the gray morning.

Autumn moved in, aspen golden overnight, comfrey and mint withering in the cold. Nights were damp, mornings bleak, a cool white sun clearing the horizon just as Liz drove into work. She could feel the light shrink; it tugged at her. The love songs and chatter in the cafe kitchen grated. The plan seemed yet more dreamlike, absurd, fantastic, less real than the stories that came to her in sleep.

Macleod didn't call, he didn't write. She missed him and called herself an idiot for thinking that he would suddenly do that which he had never done. Her loneliness seemed odd till the morning, she pulled Nick's shirt out of the washer and held only a torn rag. She walked calmly out the back door, across the catwalk, over the dry riverbed, into the little bathroom at the back of the cafe and threw up. It did not seem at all extreme. She realized that Macleod had been a shield. Without his good touch, without his thick flesh, his generous mouth, Nick's absence rang cold against her. Crying about Macleod, she'd see Nick, frozen in time, always twenty-four, always in dark blue. She sensed she was losing him completely. Finally. Against her will, in the shadows of autumn, in the fading light, to the stubborn healing of time. Lying alone, night after night, she wandered in her dreams, bearing witness, watching . . .

. . . Talasi was grateful for the long summer chain of ceremonies. She blessed the hungry kachinas, the feasts and offerings and prayers. Work was all she had, grinding, stirring, grinding again, away from people, away from the sun, her head filled with simple songs of grinding, blocking thought, blocking memory, blocking the wicked pain. She could sing above her numb heart, which would not pray nor be grateful, which only nagged: "You are out of balance, you are bringing evil, you are *qahopi*."

She worked in the gray light. Pamosi brought her corn and carried away meal. The people had begun to use stored corn. What corn survived was withered and discolored; two patches of squash had died. Pamosi told these things to Talasi and was given back only silence . . . and cornmeal, ground fine, ground with hope, with the memory of Kihsi, ground to nothing, hope and shadow ground away.

Talasi did not know if he had left the village. She did not know if he was on the trail south to the girl who might wait there, or if he had gone out into a far canyon, to live alone in that *qahopi* solitude that could only lead to madness. She knew him in memory and that was unbearable. With him, she had come to womanhood; without him, she was woman no more, never to be girl again.

Only Pamosi came to the grinding room, only Rupi, of all the women, asked for Talasi.

"She eats only enough to stay alive," Pamosi said. "She grinds and sleeps and if I help her, washes herself. She says there's too little water. I have combed her hair and taken away her dirty clothes. I think she would not even dress if she were alone."

"I was that way after the last child," Rupi said. "She is ashamed. I will wait to visit." They looked up at East-Rising House, no more than a boulder in the setting sun, no light in the grinding room, no smoke rising.

"She is buried alive," Rupi said . . .

. . . Liz dragged herself up out of sleep, the dreams like drowning. She pulled her grandfather's robe over her nightgown and built a fire. The cabin seemed shrunken with cold. She wanted to crawl back under the quilts, but the dreams lay there, bleak. She thought of those dying fields, the cold firepit. She thought of a pot the color and shape of the moon buried in a concrete garage. She thought of that mine site in the Kaibab Forest, its sage and wildflowers bladed flat, nothing left but a heap of dying juniper, no track but that of coyote, the Navajo death-dog, his delicate prints leading from drill-hole to trailer to oil slick, as though he hunted and found only death.

She took her coffee to the woodstove and brought the ravaged dream to fire and morning light. Rupi's dead babies, the shrinking piles of corn, two patches of blackened squash plants, the dice, the ball-court, the marriage not for love, but survival: the village was dying and, somehow, the people were the disease, as was Talasi, given up, given in, grinding in silence, dying from rage. She could have been any of the women Liz had listened to. Those women, abandoned, had told their stories: He wanted someone younger . . . older . . . sexier . . . less demanding . . . dumber . . . smarter . . . other than, always other than. He needed space. He needed challenge. He needed . . . he didn't know . . . he simply didn't need her, that he knew.

She sprinkled sage on the woodstove. As the oils vaporized, she smelled summer, the sweet grasses of the Inner Basin, sage and flowers crushed under her naked body, under Macleod's weight. No elders held them apart. No law kept them separate. It seemed a waste. She wanted to call him. There were cards to send. There was her craft. She knew it thoroughly. She knew what would draw him back.

She fed juniper to the fire and went back to dreams . . .

. . . The Kachinas danced the Home Dance; the messenger eagles were sent on their way, the Spirits went home. Pamosi brought no more corn to the grinding room. She walked Talasi to the fields, to the plaza, to the squash patch and the wild berries. She watched her niece stand silent as the other women offered their prayers for the blue-black thunderclouds of late summer, the clouds that did not come. She scolded her.

"If you were small, I would hang you by your heels in the smoke," she said. "We need your prayers. You know winter was warm. The snow melted into the air. Now, when the Cloud-People gather, the rain does not reach the earth. They take back their blessing. We must pray. We must sing stronger to make up for those who hide in the safety of the plaza, away from the hunger, away from the sick children, away from the songs and prayers. They see only the dice. They hear only their rattle."

Talasi heard through fog. She did not care. It was *qahopi*, the fog that enfolded her. She saw it spread. She saw the children listlessly waving the crows away, their legs and arms little but bone, their bellies strangely fat. Though they were fed first, it did not matter. Many had gone over with summer sickness. Without water, without prayer, they could not fight the terrible draining of their bodies. till Pamosi took her home.

She was grateful for the dark; in it she could stop pretending to be alive. In the black time, she could lie, eyes open, watching the stars plod across the roof-hole. She dreaded the moon, the reminder, the mockery of its cycle. There, in the dark, she would feel something hovering near her heart side, something thin and black and shifting, whose flesh gave off a bitter smoke. Grinding, she had smelled it and turned to find no one, nothing there. It never came to her in full waking or in dreams. It was summoned only by the rocking of her body over the stone, or the slow wheeling of stars in the roof-hole.

Her dreams were few. She saw herself, ugly, bent over the grinding stone, or crouching by a seep, waiting for a mouthful of water to trickle into her bowl; guiding the precious water around the stunted corn. As dreams were waking; waking was a gray dream. Once she saw Kihsi, terribly thin, return from a hunt with empty hands. As though it were a story told by gossips, she watched his new bride greet him at the door of Tsohtsona's house.

That night, she ate nothing. The others gathered in the plaza to mend and talk and rest, their voices drifting in the purple light. She watched a while and saw, in horror, that she could *see* their words. Their stories, their gossip, their fear and hunger and cruelty took shape before her eyes, ugly and twisted as ogres, as powerful, as dangerous. Sight, too, became sound. The mountains were sometimes a ringing in her ears. The sunset screamed above her, its light dying away as sobs do.

In her quiet room, there was some peace. She closed her eyes and imagined small things, the grinding stones; the cold firepit; the *wikoro,* so close to empty that it rang when you touched it; the faded basket that held her robes; the niche that sheltered the dogskin bag. She wondered if she would open it again. When she thought of the pattern of the knots, she heard only silence . . .

. . . Liz made a vow. She took out an old workshirt, no one's but her own, and she stitched the vow into its faded blue. Each word was a flower, the starflowers of the Inner Basin, the lupine and asters that grew outside her door. She worked when she was lonely, she worked in peace; she worked when the urge to call Macleod, to send a charming card burned in her. She stitched at home, in the woodstove's warmth, and she stitched in the silence of Hatt's room. The stitches flowed, the flowers melted across the cloth—lavender and coral, magenta and cream, each a call not made, a card not sent. When the not-doing was hard, she made a flower the color of her reluctance, gray-green, charcoal, sand, drab and honest, useful, in honor of healing, in honor of that oldest vow.

Sitting with Hatt, it seemed she sat with an ancient spider—far from the world yet caught in it, webbed in the clear threads of the i.v. lines. She and Rose turned Hatt's body, heavy with half-dying; padded her chafed elbows and knees, cradled her ulcerated heels in thick cotton.

"I hope she cannot smell herself." Rose said. They burned juniper, scattered sage on the radiator top. On good days, they could persuade her to swallow a few spoons of applesauce; on bad, she moved restlessly in the high bed, throwing off the old blanket, tearing at the i.v.s, crying and mumbling and suddenly coming alert, her eyes sharp and haunted, her fingers clawing at Liz's hand.

Viv came, and Artemis. They sat with her in their bright clothes and wonderful perfumes. Artie massaged her gently, smoothing scented oil over her parchment skin. She set her hand over the smaller sores and they healed. Viv sang to her; they were old, old songs, Irish, English, Welsh and Scots, hymns to the Lady, rounds to the Mother, praise for our Sister, Moon. Deena came often, with coffee ice cream, with a ginger-striped kitten, with a bunch of violets she had found half-hidden in the florist's case.

"They have no smell," she said, but Hatt pressed them to her face and smiled.

One evening, as the four of them sat together in the dim room, Deena said, "It's strange. I look forward to coming here. When the day is over and it's quiet like this and she seems peaceful and we're just sitting here, it feels so familiar to me. It feels like the opposite of everything that breaks my heart."

"We sat with my grandma like this," Rose said. "But for her, there were no tubes. I often think that if Hatt could tell us, she would ask to have them gone."

"I don't know," Liz said. "She could die right now if she wanted to. She's hanging around."

"Perhaps," Rose said. "Perhaps she has that much faith in us."

They were silent, Hatt still, her breathing shallow and steady under the old blanket, under the sand and gray and black, under Changing Woman, under Monster Slayer and Born for Water, under those who could restore balance, those who would not die.

Thirty-two

MACLEOD'S CAMPER SAT SQUAT IN THE TWO-BY-FOUR PARKING LOT, windows steamed up, bumper stickers blotched with mud. Liz tapped the brake. The stickers were new: "He who dies with the most toys wins"; the other to do with anybody who didn't like his driving. She looked down at her sleeve, at the gray-green flower blossoming there, and drove on.

She had waked early, too restless to fall back asleep. The road was slick, the horizon pale yellow. She eased the Camaro around a patch of ice and turned onto the side street that held the cafe. Dawn lifted above the far cinder cones, shining opal. She stood a moment on the back stoop. She thought about sending Macleod a post-card saying, "Park elsewhere," pushed open the heavy door and went into the cafe kitchen.

Artemis was frosting plum danish. She was herself a symphony in plum and purple, hair bound up in a fuschia-strewn scarf, a tiny silver star painted on her cheek, skirt striped emerald, plum and silvery-gray.

"Samhain?" Liz said. "We've got a month to go."

"It's for you."

Liz hung her coat on the rack and tied an apron over her Fool's Grief shirt. Artemis touched a violet, left it frosted with flour.

"It's to honor what you're doing." Artie said.

"It's no big deal," Liz said. "In fact, it's a not-deal: not-calling, not-writing, not-dwelling on the good parts. I saw his camper today. I not-stopped. Now I'm here. Sometimes, it's that simple."

"And sometimes it's not. You know I drink too much. Not-drinking—sometimes that's impossible. Men are like that for you. You know that."

"Ouch" Liz said. "And thank you for the beauty about you, for your colors this morning. I miss those days when people bejewelled themselves. I saw Janis Joplin once. She was a solid woman, but on stage, with her glitter and bangles and crazy hair, she was a cloud, of snow, of moonlight." Liz dumped butter into the big mixer. "I had a picture of her in a silvery chemise, ankle bracelet, tattooes; legs all sprawled out, bottle of Southern Comfort, her hair like a drunk angel's. Nick thought she was me."

"She sang about love being a prison, right?"

"Yeah," Liz said. "That's what she sang about . . . you know that. Why ask?"

"Because I saw something about you. I want you to ask me about it." Artie began sliding danish onto the black laquer tray. Liz broke eggs into the bowl. It was her favorite part of the job, tap, crack, fire the egg into the bowl, tap, crack, fire, keep the yolks whole, watch the pile of neatly halved shells rise. It was precisely the kind of doing that made not-doing no big deal.

"Artie," Liz said, "you know how I feel about some of the stuff you believe. I'm dubious." She folded in flour and berries.

"You're scared."

"Mighty huntress," Liz said, "my friend Rose tells me the best way to hunt is to let the prey come to you."

"Yes, and here you are."

"So, here I am." Liz poured batter into the huge pans.

"There are no strings attached. You don't have to join anything, follow any rules. It's just a gift I have. Most times it's a pain-in-the-ass. It's just information, that's all. Use it. Don't use it. It's up to you."

Liz nodded stiffly. "Go ahead." She scattered sugar and cinnamon over the top of the cakes and shoved them in the oven. She washed out the mixer and set it back. Cookies were next, then soup buns, then pie. Artemis shoved her bracelets up on her arms and leaned into the bread dough.

"Well," she said, "you need to see Nick again. You will."

"Don't play with me," Liz snapped.

"No," Artie said. "I wouldn't." She moved to Liz's side and touched her shoulder, her fingers, gently tapping no more than the quick beat of a wing. "You can use Nick," she said. "You must. And maybe even Macleod."

Liz opened her eyes. Walls, light, Artie's face shimmered as though she looked through ice or an old, old window.

"I really can't fool around like this," she said. "I get lost. I have to stay with things I can touch, things that are solid."

"That's what this is." Artie fed her a wedge of plum. "There. Can you taste that?"

"It's sweet," Liz said.

"And Macleod," Artie said, "was he so sweet?"

"No," Liz said.

"And Nick? Really?"

"No." Liz saw his hand moving toward her face, his cold smile, his drunken mime one night when he had pretended to kiss her and vomit, kiss her and vomit. To let her know. Who was boss, who would come out on top. "No, no." The plum's skin was bitter. Her breath caught. "Oh my," she said, "I hate it." She felt the weight, the men, their dead, dead weight, when they were done, when they were gone.

"I can't breathe," she said. Artie led her to the back door and the harsh air.

"Breathe," she said. "Breathe." She held Liz in her arms. "You have stopped giving your power away. Now you must start taking it. If you don't, you will become a bitter and foolish old woman."

"Please stop," Liz said. She took a ragged breath and felt her tears let loose. "You've made your point."

Artie rubbed her back. She worked her strong fingers down every bone of Liz's spine, as though she circled each with a small silvery ring of light, of kinship, of strength.

"I'm done," she said. "Th-th-that's all folks!"

"I thought it kept me young," Liz said. "He'd be inside me, he'd be saying things, moving, his face so soft and I'd think 'I'm not old yet.'" She felt the icy rail under her hands, her tears freezing on her cheeks, her breath warm in her body.

"Someday," Artemis said, and her voice was kind, "someday no man will want you. Someday, no man will want me." She wrapped her young arms tighter around Liz. "Now, how will you live with that? How will I?"

In the dark perfume drifting from Artie's hair, Liz closed her eyes and saw Nick's face, heard him saying, his breath soft against her skin, "Nothing means nothing, Lizzie. All we've got is this second. Maybe the next one. That's all." And she knew he was wrong.

"The phone," Artie said. "We better get moving." . . .

. . . Summer withered into harvest. The people went to the ravaged fields, faithful to the ceremonies of gratitude. The ears of new corn were pinched and dry. Half-hearted, the people played in the fields, smearing black corn smut on each other, chasing the children, whose laughter was thin, whose small legs couldn't carry them far. Silence fell. The people looked at each other and saw on their thin faces the black smudges like a terrible illness. They wiped themselves clean and wandered back to their homes, thinking of that ancient celebration, wondering if they would sing it again.

Toho did not travel to the eastern villages for their ceremonies; he needed help on the rough trail and their was water enough for only one traveller. The lesser priests performed the blessings. The garments, the headgear and wands and rattles were faded, the *paho* carelessly prepared. Few people watched the dancers. There was too little corn for feasting, too little joy.

The traders' visits dwindled, and yet, the gamblers huddled in the plaza, no longer playing for *tsorposi* or bright feathers. They silently cast their dice for corn, the kernals that lay scant and luminous in their dark palms.

Just before the Women's Dances, at a time when no rain had ever fallen, there were days of violent storms. Bruise-dark clouds pounded the earth with huge hail-stones, sent winds that ripped branches from cottonwood and juniper. Lightning split the tallest pine. Floods tore new gullies in the cleared fields and though the skies emptied themselves, the springs ran slow.

Before Soyal, the weather cleared. Talasi saw cool light fall through the courtroom, out into the *tupqa* behind the village. The damp wash was scrawled ked away from her stone, the airless with tracks, of mice, of rabbit and the fat, clawless print of a spotted cat. She sat on a low rock-slab. A long time ago, it seemed, Kihsi had taught her how to read the tracks, the deep prints of times of plenty, the shallow marks of famine, the lightning zig-zag of prey and hunter, sometimes the torn earth of death . . . and feeding.

She broke away a sprig of juniper and sniffed it. That last night, there had been the scent of crushed juniper, of sage. She dropped the twig, stepped into the tracks, blurring them, wiping them out.

She woke that night to voices from the rooftop. Two shadows crept down the ladder, the first half-falling, dragging itself to a place near the cold firepit. The other knelt trembling at Talasi's side. It was Pamosi.

"I must use your room," she whispered. "I must make a fire. Tsohtsona has been hurt."

Talasi lay as though asleep. She remembered that once long ago she had known how to brew healing teas, that she had been able to touch a wound or bruise or broken bone and release the pain. She wondered when that had been, in a dream perhaps, a vision. She watched Pamosi build the fire. Even in that, she remembered, there was healing in certain woods, in powders, in the color of the flames. In the fire's shifting light, she saw Tsohtsona's old broken face, her bloody mouth, the eyelid half torn from her flesh, a trickle of blood shining black. Pamosi stripped off the ruined robe. There were deep gouges in Tsohtsona's shriveled breasts. She whimpered once as Pamosi eased the cloth from her body.

Talasi turned to the wall and closed her eyes. She drifted. It had become her greatest skill. She heard their voices, Tsohtsona's hoarse, blurred with something more than pain. She heard water trickling. She wondered if it was time for the Home Dance, if the rains had come. She smelled juniper smoke and herbs. The sound became sight and she saw willow-herb, steeping in a gray bowl; groundsel, pounded and spread gently on the places where the skin was not broken, where the pain lay deep. Their sharp scent pierced her fog. She pulled her blanket over her face and burrowed into the stale dark. Only the voices came through, only the strange and terrible story.

Some had gone to gamble, Tsohtsona the only woman. They had smoked something. The men had begun to shout and laugh and boast. She had been frightened but had not shown her fear. The smoke had helped. It had numbed her. It had been strong in her bones. She had begun to win and win, the dice seeming not to fall from her fingers, but straight from her luck. At her side, the piles of corn had seemed to live, so quickly had they grown. At first, the men had only played harder, boasting that they would win.

Then, Kunya had turned toward her. "You are *powaqa!*" he had hissed.

"His eyes were evil," she said quietly. There had been a white-hot pain across her brow, then nothing but sound, only the thud of fists on flesh.

"I was not surprised," she said. "I was ashamed. That I have gone with these men, I, who am about to be a grandmother. I go with these men, who do not work, who have cut the sacred trees, who watch our crops die and do nothing. What is most terrible is that I cannot leave these men. I cannot promise you I will not go back. Their game is a heavy hunger in me. I cannot breathe unless I play. Nothing else matters, not even the things I win . . . "

Talasi saw the child being born into a broken family. She saw the young wife. She felt her fear. Who would hold the child to Father Sun? Who would choose the Mother Corn? Who would give names? Who would hear *her* prayer: that she might die and not have to live through this. She stuffed her mouth with cloth. It did no good. Her breath moved stubbornly, cruelly, in her breast. She spit out the cloth, covered her ears with her hands and slept.

She woke to Pamosi's touch. First Dawn shimmered in the roof-hole. She wondered dully how there could be such beauty. Tsohtsona was gone. The fire was dead. Nothing remained from the night before except her anger.

"Dress yourself," Pamosi said. "Your warmest robe. I packed some food and water. You are going from this room." . . .

. . . Rose woke wrapped in Manny's arms, her heart pounding, her throat dry. She rubbed her arms and felt her hands like ice. The light in the east window was gray. It seemed the coldest she had ever seen. She pulled Manny closer.

"You okay?" he whispered into her hair.

"Just hold me," she said. "Bad dream." Talasi had come to *her*, to the one with so little teaching, the one who should know. The light warmed, became yellow, became pink and orange. Manny grunted and turned on his side. She pulled his ponytail away and kissed the back of his neck.

"Coffee," he murmured.

"I love you, too," she said. He reached around and patted her growing belly.

"None for you," he said. "Drink your milk." He rolled on his back and studied her face. "I love you, too," he said. "You be careful today."

"Bless me," she said. He nodded and closed his eyes.

By the time she saw Annie's red Maverick turn the corner and roll slowly down the street, she was washed and dressed, her hair tucked into the married woman's coil. She grabbed the grocery bag that held the gifts.

"Good-bye," she whispered to her sleeping family. "I'll see you tomorrow." She put the big coffee thermos and plastic bags of mountain plants in her purse and walked out to Annie's car. The ranger grinned. She held out a fresh danish.

"Trail food," she said. "Got 'em where your friend works. It's a two-hour drive." Rose pulled the coffee from her purse. It stuck. She looked down and saw that it's handle was caught on the little purple button. She looked at Annie.

"I've got to make a quick call," she said. "I'll be right back."

"We're travelling on Grandmother Time," Annie said. "The old lady dreamed you. She said you'd be late."

Liz set the phone on the hook.

"It was Rose," she said. "She dreamed Talasi."

"Good," Artie said. "It was too much for you alone. I'm glad you've got company." . . .

. . . Talasi pulled the dusty robe over her head and watched while Pamosi folded the shoulder and caught it with a bone pin. It did not surprise her that her aunt draped *tsorposi* around her neck, nor that she tied the unfinished strand of white and black and purple stones around her heartwrist. She had lost the circle of *tsorposi* somewhere in the clutter of her room. Pamosi stroked paint on her face. She was not grateful. She did not want the protection. She knew she was dying and she did not care that it was the death most cursed: the death of not-living, of giving up.

"We should wash your hair," Pamosi said, "but there is too little water." She lifted her basket into its sling and handed Talasi hers.

"I know you are weak," she said harshly, "but you will have to carry this." Pamosi seemed as tall as the traders from the north. Her hair was not bound. She had smeared corn pollen on her face. Her dark eyes were huge and flat, her mouth set in a stern line. She winced as she lifted the sling to her shoulders.

"This cold," she said. "The old one and I are kin. Two aching old fools." She picked up a small bowl.

"Drink this," she said. "We will not eat or drink till we are done walking." She shivered.

Talasi drained the bowl. It was only water, but it flooded her empty belly. Her bowels cramped. "No more," she said.

Pamosi stood over her, the little bowl in her hands.

"You must," she said. "You do not even remember this bowl. Look at it. Drink slowly. We have time." Talasi looked; she knew the bowl. In silence, she drank. Pamosi settled her sling on her back. "Our prayers," she said. They climbed the ladder. The light was terrible, thin and yellow, its shadows sickly. The two women scattered cornmeal. Talasi's lips did not move. Pamosi smiled to herself. That was good, that small defiance. Only Life fought. Death obeyed. If Taiwa could not hear that angry unspoken prayer, Taiwa could not hear any woman's prayer.

They kept clear of the trail. Their paint, their loosened hair were in violation. Women did not appear in public with those signs. They walked over the unmarked sand, between shrunken juniper and dying *naavu,* their pads black and wasted, so shrivelled that not even the starving pronghorns had touched them. Pamosi led her down into a burnt-orange *tupqa,* dead rabbitbrush and *øsvi* littering its sand.

"Our Mother is wounded." Pamosi said quietly. Talasi trudged in silence. It was nothing to her. She—who had drawn pictures in the black sand, dug in the cinders, planted and gathered; who was sister to raven and lizard and mouse; student to Toho, medicinewoman to her self and the Mother, who had known every use for every plant, from pine to smallest lichen—was gone from play and planting, kinship and knowledge. Wife to no one, mother to no one; she was nothing. Her Mother was nothing. She thought she would say the words to Pamosi, but they would not leave her heart, they spiralled there, moving in on themselves, tightening, strangling.

Pamosi beckoned her forward. Talasi stopped. The place was *lay'ta.* She wondered if they had crossed to the other side of time. Some could do that. Her aunt was very strong, very skilled.

"You know this place," Pamosi said.

Talasi set her hand on a small boulder. It was cold and real against her palm. She looked around. Her thoughts moved slowly, as sluggish as a starving creature. The place had changed. Where there had been seeps and young cottonwood, there was now blowing sand. Where there had been tracks, there was nothing. Where there had been rich earth, there were great gouges.

They climbed to the *tuukwi* edge. Far to the east, Talasi saw the familiar rooflines of Place of Water; they seemed ordinary, unchanged. Loneliness scratched at the boundaries of her heart; she stared at the empty sand and waited for numbness to return, its fog to enfold her.

"Put down your basket," Pamosi said gently. "You will spend the night here."

Talasi shrugged the basket from her shoulders and stood silent.

"You know this place," Pamosi said.

"No."

"Look down," Pamosi said firmly, set her hand square between Talasi's shoulders and moved her forward.

"No," Talasi mumbled. "I do not know this place." Pamosi saw her eyes close, felt the leap of in-drawn breath beneath her palm.

"Look," she said. "Open your eyes." Below them lay the narrow ledge, its surface pocked with perfect holes, and below the ledge, the death's fall to the bare sand. Talasi moved away from her aunt's touch. She saw the dancer, sun-bright, soaring, spinning out, casting his shadow on the desert floor . . .

. . . "Holy shit," Deena gasped.

"Mom-*my*," Deej whispered from the other bed.

"I'm sorry, honey," Deena mumbled. She sat up. The floor was ice under her bare feet. She pulled on her wool socks.

"That looks funny," Deej giggled. Deena glanced in the discount-store special, foot-wide, full-length mirror. There she was. Black satin and grey wool.

"It does," she said. "Come on, let's get moving. It's apple pancake day." She lit a cigarette and winced.

"Mom-*my*?" Deej said. "You promised."

Deena stubbed it out. All she wanted right that minute was semi-custody, a cup of coffee and the smoke curling up in front of her face while she figured out the dream. She picked up the phone.

"Liz," she said, "I dreamed about her. She's in deep shit."

"Mom-*my!*" Deej chimed.

"Shut up, darling child," Deena said. "Go get the apples and let Mommy finish talking."

That night, Liz turned the calendar to November, to a photograph of a sandstone arch; it seemed to hang in the blue air, burning in sunset, a great lens for the dark mountains miles away. They called it "Delicate" and it was that, a stone jewel, a miracle. On the floor, under the desk, lay scattered feathers and a tiny claw. She stuck one of the feathers up behind the calendar. It was iridescent in the lamp-light, dark green and without flaw. She swept the rest of the feathers out the door and wondered about omens. No one had taught her to read signs. She stopped sweeping and started to laugh. Her father's voice came back to her, her mother's, her dear dead aunt's: "Red sky at night, sailors' delight. Cows lying down mean rain. On Halloween, a quick girl can turn around and spy her true love in the mirror. Mist at night means a beautiful morning."

Sugar sauntered in and sniffed the broom. She batted the last feather into the corner and looked up at Liz with her gray eyes. Liz patted her.

"A silent cat is up to no good," she said. Sugar curled around her ankle. Liz poured her a dish of half-and-half and watched her tremble over the bowl. "A well-fed cat catches no mice," she said. Her bed was cold. She stretched herself out, piled on the quilts and watched the stars drift across the skylight . . .

. . . "Whether you hear or not," Pamosi said, "I leave you with this work." She took the medicine pouch from Talasi's basket and set it in her limp hands.

"There is *pale'na* within. One blossom brings vision, two, death." She emptied the contents of her basket. "Here is everything you need. Water, food, this blanket for warmth, these plants for smoke, sight-stones yours and mine. You have this earth, this rock, this light and sky." She felt her voice rise in an old chant. She had never sung it before. "You have your wisdom, your power, your courage, your thread that ties you to the Spirits, to Life." She unfolded the medicine pouch and touched the *pale'na*. "You have the means to death." She made a small fire, lit sage and waved its harsh smoke over everything, in a drifting, four-cornered pattern, weaving in Talasi, weaving in herself.

"You have my love," she said.

Talasi sank to the ground. She turned her head, closed her eyes and set her hands over her ears. Only the fog. Not life. Not death. Only the fog. Pamosi pulled her to her feet and slapped her once.

"Pay attention," she said. She held Talasi to her breast.

"I have one more thing to say. It is midday. I am leaving. I will return at sunrise." She saw her tears falling on Talasi's dusty hair. "I will find you here or gone. If you are here, I will know that you have decided to face the pain of living and we will go forward. Here or gone. You will choose . . . "

. . . Liz groped for the phone. There was a cold blue light over everything, snow hissing on the skylight, snow piled in the window corners.

"Lizzie," the voice said. Her heart jumped. She came full awake and pulled the quilts up to her chin.

"Lizzie, Lizzie," the voice said. "Are you there?"

"I am," she said. Something was missing; That ethereal, underwater, long-distance waver was not in the voice.

"It's Macleod," he said warmly. "I'm very drunk and I'm very lonesome."

She shook her head.

"Say something," he said.

"I'm not interested in the first, or the second," she said, "And I told you to never call me Lizzie."

"You're not interested in anything," he said. "You're not interested in commucashin . . . or fun . . . or facing facks. All you're inrested in is that punk who called you Lizzie. You thought I didn' know, but I did. I do."

"Macleod," she said. He cut her off.

"It takes two to screw up," he said, clear and cold, and hung up.

"You're right," she said to the silence, threw back the covers and stood. The clock glowed in the blue gloom; it was a little after 6:30. She heated up coffee, pulled on her boots and parka and walked out, the coffee kicking in.

At the road, she started to run . . . to the east, through the fog of first waking, past sullen heart and aching lungs; past the pale shapes of horses on the dark hillside, past gray houses, their windows warm with light, past gaunt pine, over the icy cattle guard and into the black tunnel that ran under the highway. She came out into the light and cut up into a grove of aspen and fir, under iced branches that glittered, under pink filaments of cloud, under a dawn that just kept rising.

In the silence of the trees, she stopped. Ahead lay a fallen ponderosa, its trunk split by lightning, its great roots twisted up into the icy air. Someone, long ago, had built a fire in its base; charred cans and flame-flogged bottles sparkled in the pine needles there.

"That punk who called you Lizzie." He had been right about that. And he had been right that she had made her half of the mess. From the beginning, she had said "Why not?" right up to the lukewarm end.

"Thank you, Macleod," she said. She looked around. Everything she saw was black or white, silver or gray, light or no-light. She bowed her head. Someone watching, maybe one of the lost guys off the main highway, maybe some drunk sleeping it off in the woods, maybe a wife jogging up from the little suburb, would have seen her lift her hands to the light and say something. To dawn. To the frosted velvet of the mullein. To scented pine. To blackened tin and splintered bottles.

She walked home in her own tracks, frosted grass crackling underfoot, faded yellow flowers trembling along the roadside like paper lanterns holding morning light. She thought of her other home, of storms and thaws, of the wild miracles of weather. One New Year's Eve, she had found violets growing under a dome of ice in the kids' long-abandoned sand box; another January midnight, she and Nick had melted ice in a banged-up enamel pan over a smoking woodstove in a shack in the white hills south of home. They had poured in rum and cloves and when they were thawed and goofy, he had pushed her back on the narrow bunk. As he had fumbled with the buttons on her jeans, he had said against her throat, "No matter what happens to us, Lizzie, no matter how far apart we get, if you ever really need me, I'll come to you." She had moved up around him and known that he was already planning to leave.

Thirty-three

"I'D LIKE TO BE A COUPLE HOURS LATE," Liz said. "Can you handle things? There's a full pot of soup from yesterday, cheese biscuits, a whole coffee-cake and a batch of cookies. I didn't sleep much and I need to take a run out to Qumovi."

"No problem," Artemis said. "But you *will* come in?"

"Of course. I just said so. I'll be maybe two hours late, at most. Artie, what's wrong? You sound lousy."

"Nothing really."

"Nothing?"

"Big-time mistake last night, woke up next to it. I almost didn't get out of the room." She paused. "Can you bring me some juniper from out there?"

"In two hours," Liz said. "I'll be there." She had a jug of spring water and a last stick of Eva's incense. Beyond that, she had her heart's gift, its treasure and debris; the two phone calls, the knowledge that Rose and Deena dreamed with her; and she knew that her sisters lay dreamless and dying. . . in a beige room, on a cold and barren mesa edge.

She took the north drive to Qumovi and found the place quickly, the mesa not so terribly high, the fall a killer. She stood back from the edge, half-expecting to see the charred remains of a small fire. There was nothing, not even sherds. She raised her arms to the morning light. A harsh breeze plucked at her jacket.

"Can*not* sing," she whispered and poured water in the four directions, east, south, west, north, whose ancient colors were unknown to her, whose minerals a mystery, whose animals a riddle.

"East," she said, "for old love; south, for new; west for last light; north, for wisdom." She marked a circle in the sand with her steps and left an opening. There she stood and began to pray. Not for love, not for wisdom, not even for life; only that she and her sisters could do the work. The eldest, Hatt's, was nearly done, Talasi's not finished. She and Rose and Deena—they had more than begun. For the second time in her life, she prayed and felt no shame.

Cloud shadows raced across the sand; above, the dawn was cool radiance. Washed in light, she knelt. She started to take Nick's bracelet from her wrist, to bury it in the black cinders in shining gratitude to the dreams; for surrender to the time and taboo that lay between her and Nick, for good good-bye and last farewell. She rested her palm on the cold earth and felt its refusal.

"Leave nothing here," it seemed to say. "That is gratitude enough."

She walked away slowly, the sun burning gently on her hair, and drove to a lone juniper on the western border of the park. She lit Eva's incense and circled the tree, silent, weaving smoke, the thin blue smoke of Asian cedar, the smoke that hung over wall-gazers, over those who sat, alone, rooted, helpless as the juniper. From each side of the tree, she took a sprig; to each side she gave thanks. She imagined Eva, she saw Artemis, faces rapt, eyes closed but open to what they saw and what they needed.

The kitchen was silent. Viv glanced up from the cutting board and nodded towards Artemis, who, oblivious, was pounding the daylights out of a mass of dough.

"Good," Artie snapped. "Smudge this place. Smudge me. That juniper will burn. Just hold it on the hot-plate a few minutes."

She glared at the bread dough.

"As my dear old dad is wont to say," Liz grinned. "Your eyes look like piss holes in the snow." She felt tears in hers, and gratitude. Artemis mad was Artemis alive; Suicide doesn't talk. It whines or whimpers or goes gray and silent. Artie picked up the dough and slammed it on the table.

"Go for it," Viv said. "Eahh, Art-ie! 'Ats roight, gel." She slid an Eggs Bernadette in the microwave. "Mastered the vernacular, I did," she said. "Brill-o, Artie, nail the barstards. Bollllllllocks!" She set the timer. "There, ya booger."

"My life is not a Cockney football match," Artie said tersely. Liz circled the kitchen, the juniper smoking richly in front of her.

"Certifiable," Viv grinned, "'ats wot we are."

"That's what Davie used to say," Liz said. She looked at Artemis, at her red eyes, her angry, puffy face, her set jaw; and she saw Davie. She could damn near smell him, the plant-withering, small animal-slaying reek of Jack Daniels and beer. "But he never admitted it," she said. "He never got mad."

"I bet," Artie said. "And he probably never woke up with a 52-year-old beer-gut hanging over his face." She closed her eyes.

"Coo," Viv said. "Nasty!"

"'Scuse me," Artie said. "I'll be right back." She walked with dignity out to the john and slammed the door. They could hear her in there.

"Good," Viv said. "I didn't know what to do. I was scared. I've never seen her look that bad." The timer dinged. "Christ," she said. "Certifiable, all of us."

Artie stomped back in. "I need to go home and take a shower," she said. "I came straight from that stinking motel."

Viv looked at her.

"Don't worry," she said. "I'll be back." She gathered up the juniper and sniffed the charred end. "That's so good," she said. "Once a Catholic always a Catholic. Smoke and light. Sin and confession. Right, Liz?"

"Are you sure you're okay?" Viv asked.

"I am fine," Artie said softly, "I'm glad you're here, I'm glad you ask me if I'm okay. I'm even gladder that neither of you give advice, because if you did, later, when I'm tired or scared or seeing things I'd rather not, I'll twist up what you said and use it to have that first, perfect, wonderful, smoke and honey J. D., straight up." She smoothed down her dull hair and wrapped her shawl around her shoulders. Viv was gone, running an order out to a spaced-out customer. Liz could hear her kicking the counter, sweetly calling the woman's name.

"Annette," she said. "Annette. Where are you? Annette?"

"My dad's a drunk," Artemis said. "Mom, my real mom was an acid head. She thought it was good for babies. Men aren't any of it. They bore me. That's the worst they do." She broke off a tiny sprig of juniper. "When Nick calls," she said, "have this nearby. Crush it in your fingers. Smell it."

"Christ," Viv snarled, back from the counter. "The bloody cow ran out. Couldn't wait five bloody minutes." She set the omelet in front of Liz. "Had breakfast? It's on the house. Spinach. Gruyere. Crois-bloody-sant. Lovely."

The evening was warm. Liz opened the door and windows to the sweet air and sat on the stoop, waiting for Deena, Nick's dad's crystal tumbler full of gin and ice and lime in her hand. Winter was holding off, the air almost summery. Vapor rose off the ice in her glass. Rose had called from Shungopavi.

"I'll be there with the two of you," she had said. "Even as I'm sleeping here."

She heard the phone and let the machine get it. The pine needles smelled like incense. Artie was right. Once a Catholic, always a Catholic. She had set a candle in the wet dirt; the little flame burned blue. The phone machine chattered and chimed.

"Lizzie," Nick said, "put down your book and pick up the phone." She was surprised that she was not surprised. She set her drink carefully on the pine needles and walked slowly into the house. He was silent. She saw herself as an acrobat, released from Macleod to the air, too quickly caught, by the voice, by the memories that made her hands tremble. She crushed Artie's juniper in her fingers and sniffed it. The scent was strong and green. It did no good.

She picked up the phone. "It was gin," she said.

"It'd be one or the other," he said.

"Or both." She remembered Saturday nights in his cabin, her gin beside her, her books; him, slouched in front of the television, watching reruns on some obscure station: *Leave it to Beaver, Rockford Files, The Avengers.* She'd watched him lip-synch perfectly with Ward and Rockford and Emma Peel.

"*My* Saturday nights are finally peaceful," he said.

"Then why call?"

"Too peaceful. I haven't heard from you in a long time. It's winter. You came to mind."

"You could be useful here," she said. She heard herself, voice as high as a girl's. He'd called her that. Girl. Lizzie. When she asked why, he had said, "Because nobody ever did. You were never one. Now you are."

"*You* could be useful *here*," he said and laughed. "It's been a long time."

"Still suffering from an over-abundance of social graces?" she asked. "Women pounding down the door?"

"Hey," he said. "I'm paying for this call."

"Small miracles," Liz said. "There's some work to do here. I think you'd find it a challenge. I'll write you the details." She felt the receiver rattling against her cheekbone. Her teeth were chattering. She'd longed for his voice, prayed for it, and she could hardly wait to hang up.

"What's your hurry?" he said. "I set the timer. We've got two more minutes." She remembered his friend Eddie, shaking his head and saying, "There's tight, there's cheap, then there's Nick Oliver."

"I don't know," she said "I'd rather write. It's a shock. Your voice. I always expect you're gone forever."

"Not yet," he said. "Maybe never."

It hung there, jittered on the air, "Maybe never good-bye, maybe never hello, maybe never never."

"Well," he said thoughtfully, "I haven't had a vacation in ten years. I guess it's time." He paused. "Lizzie, it's a visit."

"No!" she said. "God, my heart was going pitty-pat, my palms were sweaty. I was getting ready to figure out the invitations, bake the cake, fix me up a frilly blue garter."

"Write me what you need," he said. "When. Who else. I'll be there."

"I love you," she said.

"Ditto." he said. "Soon." The line went dead. Her face felt funny. She touched her lips. A goofy grin seemed to be stuck there. She looked in the mirror. Her eyes were shining, her cheeks pink. In the dim light, she could have been fourteen.

"You are a sorry excuse for an adult," she said to the reflection. It grinned back. She resumed the stoop, the gin and the waiting. By the time Deena arrived, she was immune to pain and ready to do battle. They brewed hot milk and molasses and built a fire. Night sucked up the warmth. The fire beat back the waves of cold. Deena rolled her sleeping bag out on the floor.

"I don't want to think about anything in *my* life," she said. "Tell me about this young impossible hero. Make me love him."

"That's the secret, isn't it," Liz said. "You can't make or unmake it."

She sat up in bed, her back propped against pillows, her cup clutched in her hands. She was still grinning.

"Never mind," Deena said. "One phone conversation makes you look like that. Whatever he's got, if we bottled it, we'd get rich."

"Only for women like me," Liz said. Deena wiggled down into the bag. She stared up at the ceiling, her face calm. The room smelled of woodsmoke and the fresh-split juniper drying next to the stove.

Deena said, "I wondered for a long time why you loved it so out here. I can feel it. It's like being on an island, isn't it?"

"A boat, I thought once, but an island is better. The pine branches, the wind, the snow when it drifts, the rain during the monsoons: they're like water. They move. They make sound. They're soothing. Sometimes they scare me. But this cabin stays steady." She set the cup on the bookshelf and slid under the quilts. "It's always hard for me to leave. I think an island would be like that."

"Indulge me," Deena said. Her voice was fuzzy. Liz leaned on her elbow and smiled down at her. Deena continued. "Well, we've been friends . . . what? . . . ten years? twenty?"

"So that's what friendship is . . . an island," Liz said.

"This one is." . . .

Talasi did not watch her aunt leave. She stared down at her own shadow. It grew longer and thinner on the sand, growing darker then fading away. When it was gone, she wrapped herself in her blanket and curled up, the medicine pouch under her head. She watched the sun; it was a cool disc in a gray sky. There were no clouds, only grayness; there was no horizon, only the gray land melting into the gray sky. She shivered and pulled Pamosi's blanket up over her. It was the one thing to die, but she'd had enough of cold.

The blanket did no good. It gave no warmth, nor did her body. The slow fog gathered in her. She remembered when fog had been friend, when clouds and rain and snow had been welcome. This fog, this fog she called on, was enemy and release. She was made of it, wrapped in it, surrounded by the earth and sky of it. The sun, fallen behind black *tuukwi*, or dark cloud: they were all the same, her bones, cloud, rock, mist and sand. She drew a breath and it seemed that night fell over her, without moon, without stars.

She waited for sleep. It did not come, The fog deepened. Her hands and feet began to numb, the bones, the meat, the skin, freezing, burning, going away. She had once held her hand in the black pool beneath Cottonwood Spring and felt the same burning, the freezing, then nothing. They had laughed, she and Rupi. It had been a game, like holding your breath till you saw stars, or dangling your feet off the *tuukwi* edge, or moving the little bone people across the sand, saying, "This is my husband, and this is my daughter and here's the son and here's the grandmother and here am I."

She studied the black air in front of her, saw the vapor of her breath, felt the vibration of something that arced in and away. She wondered what the sightless saw. She thought it might be this. A faint thread began to coil before her eyes, coiling luminous, coiling bright. She had seen it before, with Toho, and it had been beautiful, a moonbow, a jewelled snake, spiralling up, pale red and purple and soft green, the colors of dawn and cactus-flowers and new *sivahpi*. This thread was pale, the colors flickered and faded; the spiral was not steady. She knew she could make it burn; she knew she could snuff it out. She did not need the *pale'na* nor *tuukwi*. She need only let her life-thread fade, breath by breath, and then, airless, go out . . .

. . . "Oh no," Liz said. She threw off her warm quilts and saw, in the dark, Deena rising like a sleep-walker. The stove was bitter cold, the dry air worse.

"This is awful," Deena said numbly. "I'll make the fire." She crumpled newspapers and Liz's secret tabloids. She waved the last.

"God," she said, "I don't believe you read these. Aren't they great?"

"I think we're on our way to being a headline," Liz said. Deena shoved the paper in the stove, piled on pinecones and slivered juniper.

"Only juniper," she said. "Right?"

"Your guess is as good as mine." The fire roared up, a ragged circle of light and warmth spreading out from the old stove.

"Candles," Liz said. "No electricity." She tossed a box to Deena. "Stick 'em in cups," she said. "Put 'em everywhere. Especially on the sills." The windows were obsidian; in them the little flames reflected, and re-reflected, light on light, sequins on black mirrors.

Liz was muttering to herself. "Okay, okay," she said. "Smoke." She lit juniper incense and opened the door to the darkness, to the brittle air, the snow. She scooped up a handful and brought it into the cabin. They washed their faces with it. It went straight to vapor on their hot skin.

The room blazed. Deena looked at her.

"What now?"

"We go back to sleep," Liz said. "Back to work." They locked eyes. Deena started to giggle.

"We'll have memories," she said. "At least, we'll have that." She slid into the sleeping bag. Liz pulled the quilts up to her chin. She stretched out her left arm, wrist up.

"Do what I'm doing," she said.

"No," Deena said. "That's not quite it." She pulled herself over near the bed and reached up. Her fingertips touched Liz's. "I think that'll do it." she said. "Sweet dreams."

... Talasi slowed her breath. She might have been a sick and angry child, stubborn, lingering, barely flesh, not yet vapor. The life-thread began to waver; its light flared, was gone, and flared again. She stopped her breath. The thread began to fold in on itself. She choked on it and coughed. The thread brightened, curved out, steadily. She sighed and touched the medicine bag. It was hard work to Go Over. She was tired. She felt the pebbles beneath her hip and drew away. The effort drained her. She tugged at the medicine bag. She could not lift her head. Her throat tightened as though the fog had fingers, that wrapped around, that pressed, there, where the life-thread pulsed ...

... Liz felt the sweat break on her skin. It was a hard sweat, a stinking sweat. She could smell fear in it, despair, she could smell every night she had slept in that attic bedroom, resenting life. She felt Deena's fingertips; they were warm. She looked across the room and saw the ivory candle in the east window. The flame blurred and doubled and doubled again. She raised her arm, as though she could press her pulse upward, as though she could offer the pure rhythm of their linked hearts ...

... "No," Talasi whispered. "Leave me alone." ...

... "No more," Rose said. She sat upright against the rough wall of the old lady's house. There was a sweet, charred scent in the room. She saw the old lady's black eyes glittering in the firelight.

"You know what to do, granddaughter," the old woman said. "I will wait here for you. It's no work for an old lady." ...

. . . She heard whispers, not voices, but the hush-hush of passage through the frozen grass. Talasi turned her head. Three women sat at her side. Two *pahaanas*, one Parrot Clan. Their skin glistened as though it were harvest. They reached round arms out to her. She was too tired to move. She only watched as they pressed their wrists to her arm, to the places where life flowed under her skin, their heartbeats drumming, into the meat of her, into the blood, the old rhythm insistent, the old healing begun. Between the dreaming women, the life-thread began to thicken, to brighten, to spiral up in joy, in power, into its stubborn dance.

"No," Talasi said and heard her voice stronger. "No," she said to that and heard the beginning of a cry. The women did nothing. They only sat, side by side, holding their heart-drum to Talasi. "No!" Talasi cried and tried to twist away. The dance mocked her. She could not dance alone. She thought of Kihsi's body, the twist and spiral of their bodies in love, the tangle of that prayer. "No!" she screamed and knew she had no choice. If she surrendered, they won; if she fought them they won. She wondered in that instant, why women were not called warriors.

Her foot struck a rock. She felt the pain. Her throat scratched. She was thirsty. Something brushed her cheek. She breathed deep and smelled sage. Crushing it against her face, she breathed it in, felt tears cold on her skin. Above her, the mists cleared and she saw, bright as flame, Hotomqam's three stars. He was descending, toward morning, toward home. Above him, the Seven Sisters danced; below, Talasi lay alive, alone. She pulled the blankets tight.

"Choose," her aunt had said. Chosen, she thought and felt ashamed. In her palm, the pathstone lay like warm rain. She closed her fingers over it and curled on her side, waiting for the dawn . . .

Thirty-four

LIZ WOKE. She opened the window. Snow muted the ravens' scrawk, the faint roar of the highway. She heard Deena turn in her sleep. Sugar flounced off the bed and twined around her ankles, Bob butted the front door with his great head. She let him out, started water for coffee and sat, half-dazed, thinking how gracious Deena was, to sleep and let her wake up alone. Those first few minutes, of dawn, of solitude, of moving slow, of silence, were medicine. Outside, the snow tossed back light.

Deena opened one eye.

"We won," she said. She scrambled out of the sleeping bag and grabbed Liz around the waist. "I finally won something," she said. She pulled up a stool. "And no one will ever know but us and Rose."

Not unless we want to be tucked away somewhere for our own safety," Liz said. "Coffee?" Deena nodded.

"I wish Rose were here," she said. "I want to celebrate."

"Me, too."

Deena raised her cup. "Here's to us. Here's to whatever lies ahead."

Liz called in early evening; She'd started to write, but her longing to hear his voice won out. His phone machine took the call, the recording close enough, cool, husky; he wasn't in, but he sure would get back to you. She kept the message simple, hung up and started a letter. As she wrote, she saw his crazy house, the stuffed peacock, the full bookcases and empty refrigerator, the stack of dead six-packs, the chainsaw parts on the dining-room table, if indeed there still was a dining-room table. He'd been known to use furniture as firewood. She wondered if he still had the aqua lava-lamp and the beautifully drafted design for roach clips, using real roaches. She wondered if Sock still lived there and if he was any kinder to him than he had been. She wondered how he'd travel to her. He was too cheap to fly, too edgy to take the bus. She saw him driving straight through, exalted on speed, hydrated on beer, intent as a samurai behind the wheel.

She sealed the letter and addressed it. It was absurd, the joy she took in writing his name on the envelope. In the years after the break-up, she had written it a hundred times, always with hope, always with shame, always with the sense that she sent, as the Japanese float burning poems out on rivers, love to a ghost.

She called the cats in and went to bed. They fought for space on her legs, settled down and began washing each other, their fur shining in the blue snow light. She pulled up the quilts and went cautiously to the dreams . . .

. . . It was the most beautiful smoke Pamosi had ever seen, the slender curl of blue that rose from the *tuukwi* against the cool dawn. Talasi turned from the fire. She stood unsteadily and bowed.

"I am done with it," she said, "but not by my choice."

"Thank You," Pamosi said. "Thank You for living in us." She began to laugh and took Talasi in her arms.

"Welcome home," she said. She sniffed Talasi's hair. "It is time for you to wash that smell of death from you. We *will* spare the water."

Talasi bent and offered her the path bowl. "I would have smashed this," Pamosi said, and drank. "I would have broken your grinding stones and torn your robes." She shook her niece. "Sit," she said. "You have only begun healing. Tell me how, if not by your choice."

"I have helpers," Talasi said. "Two *pahaana*, one woman of our clan. They came to me and made me live. They pressed their heart-lines to mine. I had no choice. Even in fighting them was life. Alone, I would have died."

"They were *your* vision," Pamosi said. "We forget too easily that we are all children of one Mother and Father. It does not matter how you chose life. For once, Owl, it matters *why*. She has work for us . . ."

. . . Work, Liz thought. She watched the far highway lights on the ceiling, the stars through the skylight, the clouds. She could have been a fish, underwater, light from far mysteries. There was work beyond restoring Hatt's treasures. There was the work she had come to the rock and light to do, the work within, the work without, the work alone, the work in partnership, in community. She smiled and touched her face. She knew if she sat up and looked in the obsidian window she would see something beautiful, something seen for the first time. She rolled on her side and returned to sleep . . .

. . . "The men have lost the way," Pamosi said. She brushed sand over the dying fire and began to gather up their blankets and bowls. "There are a few, Toho, Kihsi, some younger men, the old *kikmongwi* at Far House; that is all."

"And the women?" Talasi asked. It was hard to talk, but with each word, she felt her strength grow. The tea was warm in her belly; her morning prayers were wrapped around her, like a plain, well-made shawl. She still carried Kihsi. He would be with her always, but he seemed far away, beyond a shield of her making, a clear shield of love, through which she saw him as small and distinct as a tree on the long eastern slope of Two-Color Mountain.

"Some of the women wander with the gamblers," Pamosi said. "Tsohtsona is lost in the games, your mother snared in your father's madness; Kunya's wife moved on; other women have put their husbands' things outside their doors. A few of us talk of walling off a pathway to the fields, so we do not have to see the gambling." She stared out fiercely at the village. "Some have turned their men away from their sleeping mats, but others take the fools in.

"The old stories are coming true. The fools do not sing, do not pray, do not work. In their hurry to return to the game, they have stripped the Sacred Trees for firewood. The roots lie naked, exposed. When there is rain, it is not held, it tears away the soil. The fields are dying.

"Your uncle and Toho tried to talk with the fools, but they only laugh and say, over and over again, 'Do not worry. Everything is as it should be.' It is said that Kunya approached the *kikmongwi's* wife and she let him walk out with her."

Talasi rose and steadied herself on Pamosi's shoulder.

"I am ready to go back," she said. She ran her fingers through her stringy hair. "I will clean myself, and then we will bring the women together and talk. I need only simple things for a while. Food and work will mend me." She smiled. "Look at me. I'm shaking. But I can feel—the numbness is gone."

"There has not been a medicinewoman for our people for a long time," Pamosi said. "Her first work will be to teach the people that power is not only in the kivas. I hope they can hear. The lost ones hear nothing but the dice, some of the others are deafened by fear. Some of them have come to believe that things can keep them safe, *tsorposi* and shells and piles of corn."

"The old stories," Talasi said. "We can re-tell them."

. . . "Liz, it's me, Rose. Wake up." Liz pulled the quilts over her head and dragged the phone under with her.

"My God, Rose," she said, "it's a hundred and forty-seven degrees below zero. Is it morning?"

"Early. I just got back from the old lady's. She gets up about three, puts on the television and that's it. There's never one minute of silence in that house from three in the morning till seven at night, when she goes to bed. The morning after we helped Talasi, I woke up to 'Sesame Street.' She made it, didn't she?"

"You don't know?"

"I lost the dream when she stubbed her toe. Last night, all I dreamed about was quiz shows."

"She made it. She knows about us. We're her vision."

"Oh my goodness," Rose said. "How'd Deena take it?"

"She's a softball player," Liz said. "Our team won. She loved it!"

"I hope the next one is this easy," Rose said. "Connie and Joe can come in tonight. Can you call Katz and meet us at the home? I talked to Annie a few minutes ago and she'll join us."

"We'll be there," Liz said.

"Nine. We'll have everybody tucked in. Rich'll cover the station for me." Liz stuck her nose out of the covers. Frost lupine sparkled on the cracked window. There was a fine sifting of snow across the quilt. Sugar's green eyes peered through the frost. She opened her pink mouth in a silent, indignant mew.

"Are you still there?" Rose asked.

"There's a furry vision nagging me." Liz said. "Somehow, somewhere, I've got to find the courage to get out of these warm covers and start the fire and feed the cats."

"That's not so easy," Rose laughed. "The old lady says it's the daily stuff that's hard. 'That other stuff,' she says, 'that magic stuff. That ain't no different than television.'"

"All right," Liz said. "I'm doing it. I'm getting up. I'll see you tonight."

Katz dumped a bag of cheese and crackers out on the ping-pong table. Joe Yazzie set two quarts of Crown Royal near the paddles and pulled up a chair; Connie bought soda from the machine.

"Mixers," she said. "If anybody wants 'em."

"Let's get going," Katz said. "I've got a late date."

"I can tell," Liz said sweetly.

"What do you mean?"

"You're all dressed up."

Joe grinned and opened the whisky. "Maybe you better have some of this, man," he said.

"Why?" Katz said. "What's wrong?"

Rose walked in and stopped in front of him. She studied him from head to foot and shook her head.

"Nothing," she said. Liz looked away.

"Come on," Katz said. "What's so funny? The rest of my life could depend on tonight."

"It's a first date?" Liz asked.

"More or less."

"How's that?" Joe asked. "It either is or isn't." He set a plastic tumbler next to Katz. "You do it or you don't."

"Shut up, Joe," Connie said and whacked him. She narrowed her eyes at Katz. "You know," she said, "I think that scorpion bolo tie might spook the lady. You know?"

"Is it real?" Rose asked. She leaned over to get a closer look."Katz, what are you wearing? You smell like a preacher."

"And you permed your hair?" Liz asked.

"I got it styled," he said. "That's all. But it keeps frizzing out." He patted it down. "I don't know," he pulled off the tie and looked lovingly at it. "My ex-wife gave it to me. We were in Vegas. It was sort of a honeymoon."

"Just for tonight, take it off," Liz said. "Once she gets to know you, it'll drive her wild. Trust me."

"I don't. I don't trust anybody."

"Me neither." Annie Tewa dropped her pack on the far end of the table, poured herself a shot and flopped down next to Liz. She tossed a sheaf of papers on the table.

"Paul sent this. It's a copy of the official report of the most recent vandalizing up near that uranium mine site. Backhoe job. Messy, the fifth in two months on both rims. The suckers cleaned out a ten-room dwelling up near those new exploratory holes near Tuweep. The BLM guys that went in found a baby's skull. They'd used it for batting practice."

Joe turned his head.

"They're fools," he said. "Don't say nothing else."

"Just this," Annie said. "Once we finish this, we keep working. Every time they upgrade those roads for mining, the vampires strike." She looked around their circle, eye to eye. Even Joe held her gaze. "I want to propose something. Anything we can't save, we burn." They nodded. She took a handful of crackers and glanced at Rose.

"Out the window," Rose said. "There's a flower patch right underneath." Annie broke off a scrap of cracker, opened the window and tossed the cracker to the ground.

"For thanks," Rose whispered to Liz. Annie sat down.

"I'm Annie Tewa, Fire Clan," she said.

"Rose Willard, Bearstrap." She blushed.

"Joe Yazzie, Bitter Water."

"Connie Marquez, Bearstrap."

"Bob Katz, Ashkenazy."

"Liz Morrigan, at large."

"I've just got one question," Annie said. She sipped her whisky and looked at Katz over the edge of the glass. "What happened to your hair?"

The Plan emerged around midnight. It was as solid as a plan could be, as anything could be that depended on women and men and timing and

the possibility of clear roads in a mountain town in late December. Joe
Yazzie had a cousin who had worked with the guy who had installed the
security system. One of Katz's former clients, an unlucky but discrete
hooker, gave him a gizmo that could de-bug anything; she'd worked an
aero-space convention at a local hotel. Annie's great-aunt had a spare
room up on First Mesa for long-term storage. She'd been living in the
1920s for so long that no one would believe her if she spilled the beans.
Paul had requisitioned a set of walkie-talkies. He'd forget to return them.
Nick was the last link.

"He'll criticize everything," Liz said, "and he'll be right about half
the time."

"A team player," Katz said mildly. He shook his head. "This is
hopeless—we're amateurs. Worse, we're enthusiastic amateurs."

"Not me," Joe said. "I am a relocation expert. Back when my people and
them Hopis were going through all that Big Mountain stuff, I was going
to offer to help them." He grinned. "I love to relocate. I love to re-name.
We're going to call this Small Mountain."

Driving home, the sky was black water, holding Orion and the crescent moon in its depths, clouds scudding across their light.

"Slow down," she whispered, as she fell into bed. Time was moving too
fast; she wasn't ready for Christmas or Small Mountain or Nick. She was
thinking of him constantly, thinking of the frozen path to the cabin, and
him, walking towards her, walking away . . .

. . . Talasi rose from the dry sand. The little spring was gone, ferns and
flowers dried and gone to dust. The cottonwood rattled in the Powamuya wind. She walked toward the broken drawings. They were her
work, to sleep under them, live with them till they gave up their message. She
did not fear them; she was like them, incomplete. In the long moons of healing
she had come to see that she must live with that. As must her people.

Few babies lived to be born, and those that did were weak and sad-eyed.
There had been little snow. Already, the fields were cracked, the earth as
withered as an old grandmother. Even the eagles, it was said, were few, starved
out, some taken heedlessly by strangers, for gambling, for trade. She thought
of the naked skies near Place of Eagles, of the empty rooms in Nest House;
the Peoples' world was drawing in on itself, shrivelling from lack of rain,
lack of song. The Sacred Mountains seemed smaller, more distant, the Kachinas far, far away.

The drawings were as blurred as the beginning of a vision. She set her
belongings below them and sat on a near boulder, grateful that Kihsi's memory
remained as small and flat as a girl's first Kachina doll.

She thought of the women, how they had built the walled path, how they had asked for blessings as they mixed the *tsǿqa* and set the pale red stones in place. The walls had been built true. They held and the women knew they had done the right thing. Every day they sang their gratitude, walking, one woman at a time, through the narrow passageway, shielded from the sight of the fools crouched like ghosts in the barren plaza.

The women had built nothing but the wall for many winters; no houses, no field markers, no dams. Fewer and fewer children ran the alleyways and played on the slopes behind the village. Some of the older ones had grown to adults without initiation. The line of Kachinas at the dances dwindled, spirit by spirit. Sometimes a dancer would falter, a chant fade away, garbled and indistinct in the dry air. So many violations occurred that the elders were no longer shocked when people chattered during the silences and broken *pahos* were found far from the Parrot shrines.

"There is no rest," Pamosi said. "No sign from which we might take hope. It is hard to pray when we are thirsty. It is impossible to see beauty when we are hungry. And to heal the fools, the wounded ones, we need more voices. I am afraid that we are damaged beyond our power to heal ourselves." She bowed her head and rubbed her thin, twisted arms. "I think, so often, of the Sacred Trees. Gone. Gone forever."

The setting sun warmed Talasi's shoulders. She was cold with hunger. She turned her face to the sun. As she moved, a jackrabbit exploded from the sage. Hunger forgotten, cold left behind, Talasi leaped up and ran with the rabbit. She felt the doe's heart pound, felt the hot blood flooding her strong legs. They ran together, then the rabbit leaped high, twisted like a dancer in the air and doubled back. Its black eyes met Talasi's. The *tupqa* walls flared in light for an instant, then began to darken, red to gray, gray to black, as coals die, as ashes are born.

She stood at First Dawn on the third day and cast her thanks to Taiwa, to His children, to His painters who had once stood on the same sand and let His message emerge on the cliff-face. She gathered her medicines into the dog-skin bag, scattered the last drops of water to the Four Directions and to her sore heart and began the walk home.

The message had been clear. Her woman's work . . . within . . . without . . . that was all she had . . .

. . . the days blurred. Liz became a genius at work. She couldn't make a mistake. Soups fell together in a wash of cream and broth and spices. Her hands moved on the dough as though she had baked for centuries. Her thoughts danced above the work, cataloguing, listing: rent a wreck, calm Katz, calm Deena, calm herself, clear any evidence from Hatt's room, set up an alibi with Viv, stand with Artemis at the foot of the Peaks and hear the words she spoke.

"It's in your hands. You have everything you need." She blessed Liz and hung a strand of tiny garnets around her neck.

"Wear them till it's over," she said. "They give heart." Liz held them to the light. They were burning, translucent, light pouring through them, fire in their hearts.

"They're on loan," Artemis said. "They have more power that way."

Late that afternoon, Liz sat in Hatt's room and ran her finger over the stones. They were round and smooth and cool. The silver on her wrist was the same, the turquoise, encircling. She remembered Talasi's bracelet pressing into her skin, their heartbeats pulsing together. She set her wrist to Hatt's, to that faint, steady rhythm, a beat that did not alter, did not change. "I'm sorry," she said and opened the top dresser drawer. Rose had wrapped the album in an old shawl; Hatt's diaries were tucked in as well. Liz turned the album pages till she came to Kwaayo's picture. She peeled it carefully away. A few sage leaves had been tucked behind it, still soft, still pale green. She set the photo and sage on Hatt's breast, wrapped the diaries in the shawl and stuffed them in her purse. She left the album for the children.

"When I come back," she said, "you'll have your bracelet." She slipped Kwaayo's photo and the sage into her pocket, aware of the silence, the rose light, aware of every movement she made. She felt bouyant and graceful. She could bake, she could listen, she could take revenge and she could say good-bye, with grace, with love. She touched Hatt's wrist.

"Good-bye," she said. "It will be finished."

"Christmas cookies?" Deena asked. "A buswoman's holiday? Friday night, provided Daddy lets the child out of the house?"

Her voice was tight over the phone.

"I'd love it. I finished all my chores. Boxes have been sent, cards mailed, cars rented, Katz de-fused. I'm ready for Christmas at Small Mountain. The only thing that's missing is my brood."

"I've wondered about that," Deena said. "You never say much."

"I miss 'em," Liz said. "And I'm glad they're where they are. I'll take the loneliness. I'll take the freedom . . . mine and theirs."

"I wonder if I'll ever feel that way."

"I used to think I was a monster for feeling that way."

"Who knows? Who knows anything? You let go, you take back, that's the best I've figured out. Both of 'em hurt . . . So," Liz could see her straightening her shoulders, slitting open a cigarette pack with her thumbnail, "so, Friday night. Six."

"In my infinite wisdom," Liz said, "I packed my cookie cutters when I moved. I've got a rabbit, a star, a camel and an amorphous blob. Shall I bring 'em?"

"Perfect. Deej'll love the blob. She'll make monster cookies. Blue ones."

Liz stretched out under the quilts and watched Orion laze along the eastern sky, his shoulders just visible through the skylight. She felt like the hunter, her dreams the prey. She was still-hunting in the old way, the quiet way. She could hear Hatt.

"The hunter finds a game-trail, prepares himself, and waits. The deer who has chosen the hunter appears."

She thought of Nick, his shoulders above her, his back under her hands. She ran her palms along her thighs. The thirst built. She let it be. She wanted more than release; she wanted his tranced face above her, his body like night in her bones. For this night alone, she wanted to wait, silent, prepared . . .

. . . for the first time, Toho did not greet her on the trail. It had been four winters since they had last met, four winters of work, in company, in solitude, grinding, planting, walking the walled path, singing, witnessing the births, the namings, the deaths. She passed the second snake. Toho was not by the gray boulder. She looked toward Place of Eagles, the empty trails, the empty skies. She could have been the last one left, the only woman in the world.

"Sister," she heard. "Welcome." He stood above her, as humpbacked and intent as the Flute-Player, the Ancient One. She bowed to him and began the climb home . . .

Liz picked up the phone. "It's five," she said. "The world is a block of ice."

"It's seven here," Nick said. "I'm already an hour late. Wake up, Lizzie. Time's money. I'll be there on the twenty-seventh," he said. "The old man needs me here for Christ-awful-mas. Flight 147. American. Eleven AM in Phoenix. Do *not* get me any presents!"

She grinned. "No problem," she said, "no money. We go Dutch on everything while you're here. I've got some Burger King coupons. We can celebrate."

"Sky Harbor," he said, "eleven, the twenty-seventh."

"Check, Cap'n," she said. "I'd salute, but it's too cold to take my arm out of the covers."

"I can see you now," he said. "I can hardly wait."

Christmas dawned warm and clear. She lit candles, ate blue monster cookies for breakfast, called her kids and got through. She and Deena and Deej shopped at a convenience store for Christmas dinner and cooked together: sour cream chicken enchiladas, mulled V-8 juice, Liz's killer nachos and an entire pan of Sara Lee brownies with a full pint of Haagen-Daaz double nut ice cream on top. Deena had torn up Deej's wish list. "There's nothing on it without a television show attached," she said and gave her a kitten. It climbed on the table while they were opening the presents, finished off the enchiladas, staggered into the living-room and curled up in Deej's lap, its belly like a tennis ball.

"It's my best present," Deej said firmly. "I hope it doesn't throw up."

Liz and Deena had given each other earrings, and slithery nightgowns, Deena's black satin with black lace, Liz's lavender, a cool column of silk.

"We're psychic," Deena said. She handed Liz a bulky package. She'd wrapped it in newspaper and tied it with a shoelace.

"Functional," she said. "I hope you can use it."

Liz folded back the paper. There was a box of strike-anywhere matches and a can of charcoal fire starter.

"Ashes to ashes," she said. "I love you very much."

And then, less than overnight it seemed, she was sitting in the idling car, Phoenix warm and filthy outside, and Nick was walking toward her, not in blue, but in a three-piece pale grey suit, his gold star glittering in his left ear, his mustache intact, his hair a mess, and she was tugging at the door handle, crying, forgetting and not giving a damn that he hated public scenes.

"You know I hate public scenes," he said and took her in his arms and sighed. She felt the breath leave his body. He slumped against her for a second, took a deep breath and pulled her tight. He kissed her forehead. Sequins of light danced in front of her eyes.

"I always forget to breathe when I'm with you," she said against his shoulder. He ran his finger from the pulse in her throat to the opening of her work-shirt.

"Breathe," he said. "I need you warm and alive." He stepped back.

"Lizzie," he said. "Lizzie, Elizabeth, let's go. Let's get out of here. Let's go where we can do everything I've been thinking about for the last however long." He tossed his pack in the backseat and climbed in the driver's side. Liz waited. He reached across their seats and unlocked the door.

"You're in charge," she said. "Something tells me these things."

He nodded. Her throat was dry. She closed the door and leaned back in the seat. There was something about being on the passenger side, something luxurious and scary. She looked over at his beautiful, banged-up hands on the steering wheel. She watched him float the car through the airport bedlam and she felt herself move aside, imperceptibly, within, to give him room.

"Turn left up here," she said.

"Good," he said. "You finally learned to navigate."

"You finally learn to fly?" she asked.

"I'm older," he said. "It could be useful." She didn't expect him to say more. You didn't talk with Nick. You fit together puzzles and sometimes you just had to wait for the next piece to fall. They hit the highway and headed north.

"How're the police out here?" he asked.

"Speed limit's sixty-five. They go for you about seventy-one. Once we hit the North Country, no big deal. I've got Arizona plates. Makes me a good old girl."

"You *are* a good old girl," he said. "Arizona plates sounds permanent."

"Yes."

"Liz," he said. She stopped him with her fingers on his lips.

"Not now," she said. "Not now about how this is just a visit and I shouldn't get any ideas and besides you need to have a wife and make babies. Not now!"

"Check," he said and pulled off onto the shoulder. In the rear-view mirror, Phoenix was almost pretty, wrapped in opal haze, sky azure, the saguaro flat and artsy in the noon light.

"I love you just as much as I ever did," he said. He cupped her face in his big hands and kissed her forehead again.

"Meaning not quite enough," Liz said.

"As much as I can," he said.

She tilted up his glasses. "Close your eyes." She kissed his closed lids. "You are about to see some of the most beautiful, heedless, inhuman glory you have ever seen. I give it to you."

"I accept," he said. "Let's get on with this big adventure."

"You're water for me," he said. It had been so easy, no kisses, their clothes Gothic Romance-melting off, his body gliding over hers, their perfect, perfect fit. Neither of them mentioned the long thirst. She didn't come, as solid as he was inside her, as wonderfully as his lips moved. He sighed into her and stayed, braced on his elbows above her, his face relaxed. "We are so good at that," he said. "Maybe that's what it is." She would not be angry about his saying that till later, when he was gone, when she was returned to sleeping with memories. For the moment, she pulled the sheet up over them and held him by his rough hair.

"I *love* you," she said. He grinned.

"Pretty good," she said. "You didn't flinch."

"I was raw material," he said. "Sorry I jerked you around so bad."

"Takes two," she said, slid her hand down between their bellies and laughed. He moved up over her. His face was tranced, his back warm muscle and motion under her hands. "Takes two," she said and arched up to meet him.

Afterwards, he said, "You never come with me, do you? You used to fool me."

"You've learned some things," she said. "So have I."

"I learned when a woman avoids an answer," he grinned.

"No," she said. "I can't. There's too much emotion. I come with strangers or men I don't much like. The best sex I ever had with Lazar was at the end when I hated him." Artemis's words came back to her. "Use him," she had said. "Use him."

"I can't use you," Liz said. "I think it's a gift." She propped herself up on the pillows and looked down at him. "You look scrawnier," she said. "You still living on one meal a day and cigarettes?"

"Don't mother me," he said. "I don't sleep with my mother." She rubbed his shoulder.

"Any analyst worth her salt would *pay* you to be a patient," she said. "You're pure unconscious." She pinched him. "When is your gender going to catch on that people other than mothers care about their friends, actually have feelings in relation to them?"

"Don't start, Lizzie," he said and went silent. The conversation was over, the puzzle piece withheld. He lit a cigarette and they both watched the smoke drift up past the east window. Day had faded away, as it always had when they were in bed together. She remembered the first weeks of loving him and how she'd had to wear a watch to bed, to keep a clock nearby, because she was afraid they'd go to sleep or love, and wake up a thousand years old.

"I'm hungry," she said. "Let's go eat."

"All right!" he said, the puzzle piece dropping into place. "You didn't ask me if *I* was hungry." He bit her shoulder. "Where's to eat. Cheap. Close. I'm jet-lagged." He kissed her cheek. "And wiped out, thanks to you."

"You'll live," she said. "I have a master's degree in mental health and I know how to restore those precious bodily fluids." She bent her head and slowly kissed his body.

"Mistress," he said. "Don't ever get a Ph.D." He turned slowly, never losing contact with her. He kissed the inside of her thigh, and then she was startled to feel him tug away. He rested her cheek against his belly.

"It's your turn, Lizzie," he said. "You can use me. You can come with me. No more strangers. It's too dangerous." He held her against his skin.

"Use me," he murmured. "Use me." She felt the slow sweet ache build and pulse and, startled, trembled and tumbled over, crying and laughing into his salt skin. He waited for her, then moved up, stretched out next to her, and held her to him, riffling her hair. "I love to be used," he said.

"No food," he said. "Just a beer. I'm too tired to do anything but swallow." Folded in his arms, in the great peace of that, she rubbed her cheek against his smooth chest. "I like this best," she said. "This is what I missed."

"Ditto," he murmured and was asleep. She held him warm and fast, her body a blanket. She thought about dying then and there and remembered she hadn't seen Grand Gulch or run Crystal Rapid or slipped Hatt's bracelet on her wrist. Nick nuzzled her damp hair. "Beer," he whispered. "Please."

She slipped out from under his arm and walked out to the icy kitchen. The cabin seemed different. She wandered around, putting things to rights, his pack under the desk, her scattered clothes in a neat pile. She took out milk and beer, poured herself a glass of milk, put the beer back and remembered he wanted it. She built a fire and climbed into bed next to him. They were a close fit on the narrow mattress. The stove threw orange light on their faces.

"Sweet fire," he said. "There's a present in my pack for you." He burrowed into her shoulder.

"Tomorrow," she said. Before sleep claimed her, she played the bittersweet game she had always played with his sleeping body. She had never told him about it. It was her only secret from him. She slid her leg next to his and felt him move away. Then, and she knew dead certain what he would do, she moved away and felt his leg cross over hers, hooking her, pulling her close. In the dark, she smiled.

Thirty-five

THEY HAD PRAYED AND TALKED FOR TWO DAYS; they had slept little, enough to keep their thoughts clear, little enough to blur their own wills, to let the teaching come through. Toho was a husk, his bones rattling in his skin, his voice barely his own. Standing at *tuukwi* edge at dawn, Talasi saw morning shine in him, as though the sun dwelt inside his wrinkled bag of skin.

"I have gone to the leaders," he said. "They are frightened into forgetfulness. They have forgotten to pray. They say the words, but their hearts are silent. They have forgotten to be silent. They have forgotten to share. They hoard corn and other things. They forget their kinship."

"I know how it is," Talasi said, "to have terror close the heart. For a long time I could not make even the gestures of prayer. I had no voice, no song. Perhaps they are closed-in, as I was."

Toho nodded. "Well said. I am growing bitter, and there are too many enemies. Those from without: the knife-winds, the raiders, sickness, more accidents than we have ever known, the fire at Water-Holding House, Pavemsi's death when the wall collapsed."

"And those from within?"

"Deep within. The ones we brought with us. I do not want to name them. To name them gives them power."

"Terror. Hopelessness. To name them is to conquer them," Talasi said.

"Perhaps," Toho said. "I do not think as clearly as I once did. More and more, I feel like an old seed pod rattling in these new winds."

"If the People could name the enemies within," Talasi said, "if they could call them out and know we all carry them, if they could bring them to Taiwa and let him burn them dry, to Spider Grandmother so she could weave them out, might we feel less shame? It is shame that is choking us. Might the naming open our throats, our hearts?"

"And free us to pray," Toho said. He bowed his head. "And to dream." . . .

. . . Ravens screamed them awake. The windows were etched from top to bottom with frost. Nick opened one eye and laughed.

"All that heavy breathing," he said. He reached across her and scratched a spot clear on the glass.

"How do you stand it?" he said and kissed her hair. "How do you stand leaving this place for one minute?" She looked out the little lens. Dawn shimmered along the icy trunk of the great pine.

"Chemicals," she said. She started to climb over him to start their breakfast, remembered how he hated to be held down and slid naked from the quilts and the fine creature-heat of their bodies. He pulled her back.

"Forget chemicals," he said. "Lizzie, you remember everything, what I like, what I hate, how I like my coffee, every word I ever said to you. You shouldn't do that. I don't want it."

"It's a rough job," she said, "but somebody's gotta do it."

He laughed. "But for now, I'll take it," he said against her throat. "All of it. Everything you remember, especially the part about each and every nerve ending I own . . . "

"Not yet," she said. She climbed out of bed and set kindling on the coals of last night's fire. When she looked back at him, he was grinning at her. She had never held him off, even for a second. The kindling caught. She felt the quick heat on her face and she wished, for *that* second, to be alone. She set juniper on the blaze.

"Hey," he said. "Turn around." Slowly, she closed the stove and turned around.

"You look the same," he said. She smiled down at him.

"Look," she said. "It's been almost six years. See. The gray. The lines." She cupped her breasts in her hands. "The droop."

"So what?" he said and ran his fingers up her thigh. "Tell me what to do." He threw the quilts away from his body.

"Oh Lord," she said.

"Tell me what you want."

Forever, she thought, and said, "Everything. Everything you've ever imagined. Everything I've missed so much. Right now." She moved up over him and down, so he filled her, so she enclosed him. As she ran her fingers through his thick hair and felt his hungry mouth, she thought of Macleod, how simple it had been, how easy. Then she closed her mind and drifted down into her body, calling with every cell on that which would never change in her, on that joy and terror and worship. Offering it up, using Nick, using herself for the prayer.

By evening, they had managed to stay vertical long enough to walk the bitter-cold, dazzling meadows below the mountain, buy groceries and cook supper for the Small Mountain band.

"If I chop wood for the fire that heats the cabin while you cook, that counts," Nick said. "That makes me a New Man."

"I agree, and I have never forgotten your cooking," Liz said.

"I have never forgotten your axe-work," he said, and closed the door.

She was chopping green onions to sprinkle on the curry when she heard voices outside. Rose came in with two bags of corn.

"Where did you get that?" Liz asked.

"Where did you get *that*?" Rose answered. "The lumberjack?"

"Prayer," Liz said.

"Joe Yazzie's last weekend in Vegas," Rose said. "He gave me fifty bucks and said to find a luxury for tonight." She poked through the cupboard and brought out the stewpot. "How you doing?"

Liz scraped the onions into a flat blue bowl and began to dice hard-boiled eggs. "Sistuh," she said, "I love this man so much and I hate half of what happens to me when he's around."

"How so?" Rose said. She was shucking corn faster than anybody Liz had ever seen. She grinned at Liz. "It's hereditary," she said. "Me and my cousins used to have contests. Answer the question."

"He asked me earlier if I wanted to go for coffee. Now, this man is the cheapest sucker you ever met. I have *never* known him to pay for anything he could get me to fix him. So he asked me and I couldn't say anything. What did he want? What did he mean? Was he bored? Didn't he want to be alone with me? What was the secret behind it? Where did it fit? I ended up making a pot of coffee myself."

"He does have that way about him," Rose said. "He seems as though he knows some secret, as though he has something valuable he might give, if you just got the riddle right. It's not you. I think it's him." She piled the corn on the counter. "The old lady is helping me see. It's no magic. It's doing what I already know how to do. I see him. I see what you love."

Liz took a deep breath.

"That's the first full breath I've taken since he got here, except when he was asleep and I was watching the fire die."

Rose took the stone fetish from its dish and pressed it into Liz's hand. "Hold that," she said. She tapped Liz's closed fist sharply. "He is big and there is darkness in him," she said, "and he is beautiful in an old, old way, but he is more afraid than you, less experienced. That is why he takes up so much room."

Nick came in through the door, followed by Katz, Yazzie, Paul and Annie.

"These people are looking for a party," he said. He glanced at Liz, who was scooping pilaf into a huge bowl, and moved to her side. "You all right?" he asked. She looked over at Rose.

"Woman talk," she said. He kissed the top of her head.

"You know I hate public scenes," she said and patted his butt.

Joe unfolded the diagram on the cleared table and traced the circuitry with his finger.

"My friend says it can go one of two ways. If we jam it here, we either kill the system and it's dead, or we kill the system only in the garage and that can be detected at some central security office. We have no way of knowing until the cops are reading us our rights. We've got five minutes or we've got Grandfather Time. It's like those metallic strips people stick on their windows. They might be hot, they might be plastic."

"Can we post somebody at the end of the block? Get some two-way radios?" Nick asked.

"Done," Paul said. He pulled an NPS walkie-talkie from his NPS pack.

"That's how I like to see my taxes used," Nick said. He looked up at Yazzie. "You're no amateur," he said. "What are you getting out of this?"

"Vengeance," Joe said. "I lost my friend, the old lady's boy, to the Jesus Way." He scooped himself more ice cream. "He was a good man. He got scared. He's nothin' now."

"Okay," Katz said, "worst case: we're caught. Breaking and entering. Intent to commit robbery." He looked at all of them. "Nothing on any of you, swear to it? Not even a Boy Scout knife. Armed robbery is mandatory life sentence."

"This ain't party . . ." Liz said.

"Right," Katz said. "This ain't no Ed Abbey book, either. Rose and the Mystery Woman have the most to lose. Kids, unfit mother stuff."

"It's not that bad," Rose said. "Manny and I are tight, we're okay. Nobody's going after my kids."

"Okay, I can be disbarred. Paul? Annie?"

"They'll take my nice uniform," Annie said. "Kick me out of my ancestral home. Cut off my supply of bad coffee."

"Ditto," Paul said.

"Ain't no never-mind to me," Joe said. "I got lawyers."

Nick turned to Liz. "Nothing as bad as losing kids," he said, "but we could get locked up for a while." He pressed his thigh against hers. "Have you thought about that? Really?"

"I have been," she said. "Locked up."

"Listen, Ms. Shrink," Katz snapped. "We are talking LOCKED UP. We are not talking about some psychic state. We are talking no sun, no air, no mountains, no cats, no meadow. Maybe medication if you get too uppity, nasty-mean ladies who aren't too tightly wrapped and that doesn't include the other prisoners. We are talking JAIL."

"I promised," she said.

"Me too," Rose said. Paul and Annie nodded. "I can't back out," Rose said. "Those are my peoples' things. My promise isn't to Hatt. It's to something else. My grandma. My kids."

"I'm vowed to fun," Joe said. "Hozhoni any way I gotta do it."

"Well then," Katz said cheerfully, "there's nothing to do but get on with this mess." He raised his beer. "To the New Moon."

"To Paamiyaw, the Play Moon," Annie said grimly.

"To trouble," Nick said.

"To fun," Joe grinned.

"To friends," Paul said, "old and new."

"To Spider Grandmother," Rose said, "all of us."

"To Hatt," Liz said, "I wish she were here."

"You found yourself some good friends," Nick said. "I'm glad." He pulled her close. She kissed him, tasting the sweat of good love, tasting herself on his skin.

"Damn it," she said. "This is so good."

"Don't think," he said. "No thinking."

"Right," she said. "I love you."

"Me too," he whispered, his voice, his long body gentled by exhaustion and tenderness. "I wish I didn't." . . .

. . . Talasi dreamed and knew she dreamed. She stood at the base of a narrow slab of firerock. Long ago, it had broken from the *tuukwi*-side and sunk itself firmly in the talus. In its shadow curled a lizard, the color of pale sand and nearly as still, around its neck a dull black collar. Dreaming, Talasi saw an *old* dream, the *pahaana;* the metal stake, *lay'ta.* She made herself crouch over the lizard. Not metal, not terrible, the collar was only a band of dark scales, a false shadow to help the lizard hide.

The lizard coiled in on itself, its slender body wound to the west, its tail and snout aligned, a barely breathing journey sign. Its eyelids flickered. She stepped back and steadied herself on the firerock. Beneath her fingers, the slab began to hum, the sound a fine itch in her body, a leaping in her blood, from fingers to arm to shoulders to the bones of her breast. She sang with it; her heart sang the drone, the rise and fall. It was a song of making, a song of praise. She traced on the rock-face the coiled body of the lizard. And woke . . .

. . . Liz moved away from Nick. She thought of jail, of the sun, of her children cold miles away, of how she loved them and could not keep them safe. She thought of love and real work. His leg crossed hers, his arm drew her close . . .

. . . "Here," Talasi said. Toho nodded.

"It is near the kiva," he said. "It will be safe. The lizard?"

"There," she said and looked down. There was nothing in the sand, not even a faint ripple.

"Show me where you will work," Toho said.

"Here," she traced the stone. "And here, where there are these two holes . . . for eyes . . . this is the head." Toho bent and picked a pebble from the sand. His face tightened.

"Ah," he said in a small voice, "the world circles around me." He leaned lightly on her shoulder. "Take this," he said and handed her the stone. "You will need more of them. It is an older stone than the firerock, harder. You use it so." He struck once on the *tuukwi* behind the slab and stepped back.

"This work is yours alone to do."

She held the stone to Father Sun. His light poured into her hand; the stone caught cold fire and shaped itself to fit her fingers. She struck. The firerock rang.

"It sings," Toho said. "I have never heard this." She struck again and again, the rock ringing at each blow, the sound echoing off the *tuukwi* face.

"Because it stands separate," he said, "it rings." He turned and began to climb the trail to his house, each step burning in his hips and knees. He thought of his age. He thought of the endless winters he had seen, the harvests, the dry times and wet. This dry time would not end. As he looked out over the withered fields, he became them. He felt the sun on his soil, the useless warmth under his bones, the twisted, dead roots of old hope within him.

Below, Talasi worked, and as he heard the ringing of her dream, he heard the rain's song, as though the clouds had opened, as though they poured down.

. . . Nick leaned back in the rocker and rested his heels on the wood-stove's base. Liz was propped against the pillows in the devastated bed. She wore her grandfather's bathrobe over Deena's Christmas gown and she was silent, watching the coffee vapor drift upward in the morning light.

"You never used to do that," he said.

"Drink coffee?" she said. "You're wrong. I was weaned on it."

"No," he said, "just sit. Do nothing. You were always talking, always planning, always headed somewhere."

"I was the sole support for three kids," she said. "You don't suppose that had something to do with it?" She stretched out her legs and balanced the coffee cup on her knees. "And you, my sweet?" she asked. "Always on the hustle, an hour late, a dollar short?"

"You know why," he said. "I told you. You dragged it out of me."

"Sure," she said. "So we've got two, maybe three full days to spend together, which is something else we never used to do. Makes me nervous."

"Me, too. We could spend it in bed, but I ought to have some pictures to take back, something for the old man."

"They've got these lovely little burro salt-and-pepper shakers up in the gift shop at the Canyon. You know how he is. He'd love that."

Nick snorted. "Let's go be tourists," he said. "You the guide; I'm the innocent greenhorn. I'm in your hands."

"I notice," she said and drew him down to her body. He pulled the nightgown up above her hips. She opened the bathrobe and he fit himself against her flesh.

"I love it like this," he said. "Half-naked." He grabbed her hair and held her still. "Like I found you here. Like we're strangers."

"But we're not," she said. "We never were."

They stood at every viewpoint on the U.S. Department of the Interior, Grand Canyon National Park map, from Hermit's Rest to Desert View. "If I've got to pay this much to get in," he had said, "I'm gonna get my money's worth." They stood apart, silent, and it was perfect. At Lipan Point, he turned to her, took her by the shoulders and faced her down toward the green twist and lace of Unkar Rapids.

"Lizzie," he said, "you're making me offers I can barely refuse." She looked at him, at what was visible, his big, pirate face, his rough, dark hair, his eyes that made him useless at poker, his carpenter's hands. He wore a torn blue parka and he looked young and determined, like the hikers and husbands and dads they'd met on the West Rim Trail. She saw, too, that which was invisible, his kaleidoscope mind, his rage, his terror, the part of him that wanted to curl up with a safe woman and safe kids and watch re-runs of *Leave it to Beaver*, while the money rolled in and the memories of his childhood faded away. She lifted her eyes and looked beyond him, beyond Nick seen and unseen, beyond the impossibility and saw, to the east, the Painted Desert, like a great, broken slab of agate, lavender and rose and blue-gray, as solid as stone, as shifting.

"It's not me," she said. "It's this place."

Without a word, he walked away and disappeared into the juniper beyond the parking lot. She sat on the stone wall. From a side canyon far below, a black dot began to move up in sweeping circles, spiralling, gaining mass and shape, soaring, drifting, playing on a thermal, till it hung at eye-level, rose up, hovered higher and screamed its raven scream. From behind her, she heard the answering cry.

"Well, I can't stand this," she said to the space that hung in front of her and was grateful that it did not answer back.

Nick touched her shoulder.

"Did you see that?" he said. "I was taking a leak back there and they screamed and sailed off."

He buried his face in her curls. "You still smell like hashish," he said.

"Those days are long-gone," she said. "It's rosemary shampoo and juniper rinse."

"You'll never be a man-killer," he said. "You haven't got a mysterious bone in your body."

She stood next to him at a turning in the South Kaibab Trail, watching the sun set through a veil of dry snow. She watched it hard, watched it flare blood-orange and vanish below the black line of the far mesas, watched, as pure emerald blazed along the horizon. She turned to take Nick's hand and could not see him. Where he stood, looking down at her, she saw only the fiery after-image of the setting sun.

"I can't see you either," he said. He reached out and touched her face with his icy hands. "Make a public scene," he said. "There's nobody here but us."

They set up her tent in the pine forest a little south of the mine site. She wanted him to see it. The cold under the tall pines was astonishing. They built a fire, broiled steaks, dumped them on plates and crawled into the double sleeping bag. Nick tilted up his beer.

"It's frozen," he said.

"Put it between us," she said. "We'll thaw it." She tried to spread butter on a hard roll and watched everything crumble in her hands.

"Forget the food," he said. He pulled a chocolate bar out of his parka pocket and they ate it, taking bites of the brittle sweetness, feeling it melt and run down their throats. They drank rum with it and finished with oranges, icy and clean.

"Sleep," he said. He wrapped his arms around her and full-clothed, they fell instantly asleep. She woke once. The cold had deepened; she lay awake. Nick jolted up, once, twice, his eyes blind open. She held his head to her breast and listened to his breathing; he eased back to sleep. She had once believed she could live by that sound. She had been sure that if she could come to that every night, to his breathing, to the pulse of him, the strong beat of blood in his wrists, his throat, she could survive anything. She freed her arm from the sleeping bag and touched him lightly on the brow, at the place near his eye, where the blood beat against his pale skin. He moved under her touch, turning his head from side to side. She cupped his face in her palms, kissed his forehead and watched him sink back into sleep . . .

. . . "Where is the grinding stone?" Talasi asked. "I am done with the other work. The message was clear. It is time for the People to take their stand and sing. If they will not do that, it is time for Them to move on. In the grinding I will find the words to tell them."

Toho stirred the fire. "I will warm some food," he said. "Then you will grind. I will bake *piki*. Together, we will carry it to the kiva at Place of Water."

"You will bake *piki*," she said and smiled. "Pamosi once told me that age makes women like men, and men like women."

"Healing," he said, "not age."

"Your stone is under the old robes," he said. "There is corn where it has always been. Use the white. Use it up." . . .

. . . "We're gonna dieeeee!" Liz whispered. Nick had undone her jeans and his. Every time he moved, the terrible cold air trailed down her sides. "This is like making love in outer space," she said.

"Oh yes," he said. "Yes, yes yes."

She felt him shudder. He pulled himself from her body, trying to hold back. She pulled him down and kissed his icy mouth and felt him explode against her. He kissed her face, her eyes, then coiled down and kissed her belly.

"I want it all," he whispered against her skin. "I want to be here and home. I want a family and I want you. I want to be no more than a hundred miles from your brain and body for the rest of my life and I never want to see you again."

"I know," she said, moved him from her body and buttoned up her jeans. They crawled out of the tent into the bright cold.

"I'll be back," she said. There was a faint trail between the juniper, a slight shimmer in the dried grass. She saw deer, three of them, filing slowly ahead, white mist threading from their black muzzles.

"Thank you," she said, and crouched over frosted pebbles. Steam rose, and mica glittered in the black stones.

"Coffee!" Nick bellowed. "Food! Civilization!" In the silence that rang in after his voice, she heard the sigh of the wind and the whine of a helicopter somewhere near the Canyon.

"They want to put a uranium mine here," she said quietly, "at least one, maybe many." As she scanned the sky for the chopper, a raven dropped out of the trees and glided past. A trick of the wind carried away the chopper's whine, and she heard the whisper of the real bird's wings.

"Bring on the Ice Age," Nick said. "Wipe us humans out. It's okay with me."

"Till then," Liz said, "let's go northeast. We'll eat, stop at Desert View and climb the tower, then drive up to Mexican Hat. There's a motel on the San Juan and a restaurant with the best Navajo taco you ever ate. I want to eat supper. I want to sit on the cliffs above the Goosenecks and look down at the river and have you hold me and keep me warm while I tell you a dream. Then, I want to sleep with you in that San Juan motel and forget that we ever have to go home."

"You're the guide," Nick said. "I'm yours."

From the tower's curved windows, they looked down at the snow-etched Canyon, at the silver-green snake of the Colorado River.

"I'd like to be on that someday," he said.

Liz pointed East. "We're going *there*," she said. "We'd better hit the road so we can catch as much light as possible." He took her face in his hands and turned her to the soft winter light.

"You really are the same," he said, "and you're completely different. I didn't know you cared about the light. I never noticed."

"I didn't. All I cared about was making the pain go away. And the joke is, the light does just that."

"You aren't going to believe this," he said. "I want to spend money on you. I want to give you something good. To keep. From here. Now."

"Promises, promises," she said. "Let's go."

As they drove away, down easy curves, past the blocky brown canyon of the Little Colorado, out into the olive desert, she slipped the tiny studs Nick had bought for her in her earlobes. They had once been Navajo buttons, silver, set with dots of turquoise; embossed with thunderclouds, one for each sacred direction.

"They're good," he said, "with your gypsy skin."

"Thank you," she said. He slowed the car. They approached the narrow bridge at Cameron.

"Look at that," he said reverently. He pointed to the old iron bridge that spanned the gorge a few hundred feet to the west of the highway. A spider might have spun it, an Iron Age spider, a spider with perfect balance and a forge in its belly. "That's the kind of work I wish I'd done," he said. She remembered his smudged face above the iron's hellish light, his naked chest shining with sweat, his big hands light and sure on the glowing metal. She wanted to beg him to stay.

"I wish I'd been here then," he said fiercely. "You, too. Do you think of that?"

"All the time. When Hatt talked, she gave it to me. It was hot, dirty, lonesome and I'd give anything to go back there."

"No can do," he said. "Not to then, not to any other time."

"Thank you, Dad," she said and they headed on up to Tuba City. She drove the next long stretch to Kayenta, past Peabody Coal's railroad line, those tracks like surgical clips in the curving land. At Tsegi, she pulled off the road and gestured to Nick to get out. They'd been travelling in easy silence; she didn't want to break it. They stood on the roadside and watched indigo clouds scudding over voluptuous sandstone hills.

"That's the most womanly rock I've ever seen," Nick said. "I'd like to dive in there and disappear for as long as it takes."

"There're ruins in here. They were no fools. They knew where to go, those Old Ones." She glanced down at the cinders brilliant with broken glass, beer bottles, whisky bottles, wine bottles, pop, anything that would throw hard and smash good.

"I want to eat this place," she said. "I want it to eat me. It's gorgeous, busted glass and all."

"You want, you want," Nick said. "You're a greedy, greedy Lizzie." He held her by the hips and traced the line of her throat with his warm lips. When he leaned back, she closed her eyes and felt the breeze mimic his kisses, as though cold silver trickled down her throat to the cleft between her breasts.

The motel was half-empty, the restaurant quiet and sweetly gloomy, a few semi-cowboys and full-tilt Navajos shooting pool by the little bar. Nick brought their beers to the table and they sipped them peacefully, talking, waiting for their Navajo tacos.

"This is just right," he said. "I'm so comfortable with you. Why can't . . ."

"Please don't," she said. "I want to pretend this is the last night of the world, okay?"

"No," he said, "I can't do that. I won't leave you hurting again. I want to talk."

"I walked into this clear-hearted," she said, "and I'm not some '80s woman. I hate the word 'communication.' You don't 'communicate' away pain or love or anything."

The waitress slid their plates on the table.

"Look," he said, "it isn't personal. I just want kids, that's all. The lady doesn't even matter." He reached for her hand. She swatted his arm.

"She better matter!" Liz said. "I'm your last on-the-way-to-the-real-thing woman. She better matter or I'll curse you. And I can do it 'cause I carry rats and razors in my pockets."

"You remember that," he said flatly.

"I remember everything," she said. "And I know it *is* personal. The French say 'the *baiser* and *baisé*,' the kisser and the kissed. You're the kissed;

I'm the kisser. That's how it's been, that's how it is, and that's how it will always be. There's nothing either of us can do to change that."

He cut into his taco. "Could be," he said. "What you are for me is like looking in a mirror looking in a mirror."

"You can paralyze yourself doing that," she said, "and I mustn't go on being a reflection." He looked at her. She turned her head. He reached across the table. It seemed to her a much longer way than just arm's length.

"Let's get out of here," he said. "Let's go look at rocks."

She led him to the edge. Below them, the San Juan River threaded silver through the three dark curves of the Goosenecks. Nick lowered himself carefully to the rim and sat, his legs dangling into space.

"I never did tell you about height, did I?" he asked. She settled down beside him, and he pulled her close.

"No," she said, "but I can guess, brother." She laughed. Without letting go of her, he let a cigarette. Orion blazed over the far canyon rim. The scent of crushed sage surrounded them. She stretched out on the cold sand and pillowed her head in his lap.

"You okay?" he asked.

"I am. I've been having these dreams."

He stroked her hair. "Tell me," he said. "We've got all night."

He leaned naked against the bathroom door; his earring caught the light.

"*Hotomqam*," she said. "Show-off."

"Dreamer," he said. "For tonight, till morning, don't wear anything but my gifts."

She'd draped a scarf over the bedside lamp; the light was warm, pink and purple and rose on her skin, shining off her silver earrings. "I am," she said.

He smiled. "There's more. You forgot." He walked toward the bed, his body shadowed, and took a package from the dresser and set it on her belly.

"Go ahead. I told you I brought you something."

It was wrapped with newspaper, bound with rubber bands. "Festive," Liz commented.

"Merry Christmas," he said. "Happy New Year, Happy Birthday, Samhain, Candlemas, and Summer Solstice."

She unfolded the paper. "It's not blue and frilly," she said, and held the black lace garter to the light.

"I'm not asking you to marry me," he said. A silver star, cool twin to his, glinted against the garter.

"You don't look good in gold," he said. He touched his earring. "It's for kinship," he said, "it's forever." He took the garter from her hands, separated the earring from it, and fit the star through the second hole in her right ear. Then he bent and slipped the garter up her leg. His hand rested a second on her thigh and moved on.

She did not dream till early morning, First Dawn gray in the motel window, Nick warm beside her . . .

. . . After sunset on the fourth evening, her grinding was done. She carried the meal to the old man and walked out to the *tuukwi* edge. He had brewed juniper tea. She sat and sipped it, watching across the valley to House of Eagles. Few fires burned there. Most of the windows were dark. The People were not meant to live in such solitude. They were meant to live in neighborliness and joy. Family after family had left; There were only four clans left in all of Black Sands. With each farewell, the fools had huddled in the plaza, watching the worn dice fall, playing for the possessions their neighbors left behind. Talasi shivered.

She remembered the last time she had seen Rupi, on a hilltop back of Place of Water. Unseen, she had quietly watched her break pot after pot on the sand and cinders. As she walked to her, Rupi had looked up.

"They will not play for these," she had said. "These were my sister's." She had stepped away from her work and they had embraced.

"How I hate our village!" Rupi had whispered. "Three baby girls, gone. Ugliness where the Sacred Trees once grew. Look at us! We are old women too soon." She kicked the rocks away from her feet.

"You are leaving?"

"Yes." Her voice was bitter. "Come with us. There is food. Enough water. In the new home, babies will come. You will be my sister." She touched Talasi's thin back. "Remember? Our promise?"

"Thank you," Talasi said. "If I could leave, I would go with you. I must stay here." She had paused. "And Kihsi? Will he leave?"

"I do not know," Rupi had said. "He and the men bring so little back from hunting. He and Poliw; their children still live. He must feed them." She shook her head. "You have not seen him?"

"No. Not because I am good," Talasi said. "I think of him always. I want him still. But to see him would be to live in a dream. I must be awake."

Rupi had touched Talasi's coiled hair. "I think of that old Home Dance and the little squirrel; your Hé-e-e doll." She smiled. "You should wear only one coil, like Her. I think of your hand in mine, the sound of water at the spring that night. We have lost so much." They had looked out over the village; below the ball-court gleamed in the noon sun, like bad water, like the eye of something gone mad.

She set her empty bowl on the ground. Smoke curled from Toho's roof. She thought of him bent over the baking stone. She thought of the day ahead and the she prayed that his old hands were steady . . .

. . . Liz sent Nick around the last corner of the trail. She waited in the shadow of the rock wall. Nothing broke the silence but the knife-wind. She pulled her collar up, her wool cap down and imagined him in that keening wind, looking up, at the dark mountains framed in the soar of the arch; at the blackbirds darting through the keystone curve, and the bright nothing of the sky. She heard his boots click slowly across the rock shelf and fade into silence. The sun was apricot through her closed lids.

"Lizzie," he said, "get out here."

She turned the corner and stepped onto the sandstone bench that sloped down to the arch. Nick was gone. There was only rock and light and sky. She sat on the warm sandstone and listened to the wind whistle in the great boulders to the east.

He emerged there and walked slowly to the arch, his face turned from her, his dark hair wild. She watched him across that cold dazzling air. He did not step into the center of the space between the great columns of sandstone. He stood just outside and turned to face her. She felt the sun burn down into her hair.

Thirty-six

"WHERE *ARE* THEY?" Katz muttered into his ski mask. A wicked cold had settled over the town, icing the pines, glazing the night sky, turning the January thaw into dangerous filigree.

"At least we look normal in these ski-masks," Deena whispered.

"I don't think hiding under burlap sacks in a suburban cul-de-sac is normal," Katz said grimly. They were in the back of a battered Ford pick-up, its license plate blurred with frozen mud, a clutch of meadowlark feathers hanging from the rear-view mirror. Paul sat in the driver's seat, doing paperwork by flashlight. Two blocks away, at the entrance into the maze of suburban streets, Annie Tewa lay under a sleeping bag in the back of a rusting, sway-back station wagon. She glanced up over the rim of frost on the back window.

Move it, she thought. Two hunched people hustled down the street. "About time," she muttered. A pebble clattered against the side of the wagon. She nodded. Fifteen minutes, maybe twenty till she needed to start watching. She looked up at the houses, the size of them; their garages, as big as most of the houses in her village. From deep in the sleeping bag, the walkie-talkie crackled.

"Where *are* they?" Katz snapped.

"Within a block."

The line went dead.

"You're welcome," she said and pulled the sleeping bag up to her chin. She wondered if there were *pahaana* in Nepal and if there were none, she wished urgently to be there.

"You okay?" Nick mumbled.

344

"I'm terrified," Liz said.

"Good," he said. A car crunched over the frozen slush.

"Come here," he said and pulled her into a hug. "They'll think we're a couple of teen-agers." Liz pressed against him. "Yes?" she whispered. He bit her lip. She glanced up and saw his earring glittering in the streetlight.

"Fag-*gots!*" a kid yelled out the car window. The driver honked and slowed. She could hear young male voices, high and excited, with that crazy-dog snarl, that low whine of out-for-blood. "Fag-*gots!*" they roared. Liz stepped back and pulled off the ski-cap.

"Awwww, it's just some chick," a kid yelled. "Hope you get lucky!" The car roared, careened around the corner and was gone. She heard a bottle explode on the sidewalk.

"Let's go," Nick said hoarsely. She tucked her hair back up and patted the solid bulge of the charcoal starter in her pocket. They walked past the green pick-up, separated and disappeared into the line of juniper at the edge of the Latham yard. The garage light glared off black ice. Nick hoisted her up and the light was gone. He slipped Katz's client's friend's lockcard between the door and the doorframe. They held their breath and heard the sweet click of the bolt released. Behind them, the pick-up hissed in over the ice. Deena and Katz slipped in the door and waited. Joe melted into the flat darkness. They saw his shadow rise up in the back window.

"This is like dancin'," Deena said.

"I don't dance," Nick said and grinned. "I'm Nick."

"Miss Kitty." They shook hands.

Liz's feet had gone numb with cold. Joe waved them forward.

"We go." He turned away from the window. Liz saw him fumble over something. Juniper smoke rose in the air.

"For the Old Ones," he said. "We ask your blessing." He tossed a silver dollar in the air. "For the New Ones," he said. "Stay outta the way."

Rose stepped into the room, a big NPS emergency flashlamp in her hands. She threw the switch and the garage blazed with light. It was packed, floor to ceiling, wall to wall, with cartons, rugs, tattered baskets, old trunks, a plain gray jug as tall as a child. A tasseled bag hung next to the security master box.

Liz closed her eyes and breathed in the smoke. "Please," she whispered, "if you're there, guide us."

"Move!" Nick snapped. She looked over her shoulder and saw Katz huddled in the back of the pick-up. Nick wrestled two rugs to his shoulders.

"No," she said. "The trunks. The black one, the green."

He looked at her. She stared back.

"Okay," he said. Together, they eased the top trunk off the pile. Deena stepped between them and they swung the trunk up to Katz and ran back.

"You *do* dance," Deena said. She and Liz loaded the remaining two trunks into the truck and went back for baskets. Nick and Paul cradled the huge jug in an old saddle blanket and carried it out.

"The black-and-white pots," Rose said "All of them need to go." Joe was bent over the tangle of wires, his shoulders bunched in concentration. Liz patted his back.

"How much time?" she asked.

"I wish I knew," he said. She reached up for the tasselled bag.

"What's this?"

He shook his head. "I'm a long time away from these things . . . arrow case, maybe? It's lion. That's the tail."

She lifted it down. Dust flew up and blurred her vision. Joe was a big shadow next to her. Cold white light blazed in the window and blinked out. She saw her face, her eyes the black slits of a mask. Something buzzed.

"Rattler," Joe whispered. He laughed.

"Out!" Annie hissed over the walkie-talkie.

"Too soon," Joe muttered. "Sons-a-bitches!" Liz passed the arrow case to him. She turned. Everyone was gone. She heard the pick-up roll out over the ice. Nick's shadow slipped past the window. The room was dark. She picked her way between the piles of treasure and stood in the doorway. Her throat ached. Her hands were cramped with fear. She pulled the charcoal starter out and circled the room, spraying everything she could, then stepped outside and lit the matchbook.

"*Antsa*," she said and tossed the flame into a stack of faded baskets. They caught instantly, went up in pale blue flame. She looked over her shoulder. An unmarked Cherokee, lights low, cruised slowly up to the house.

"Go home," she said, crumpled Kwaayo's picture and threw it into the fire's heart. It curled once and was smoke. A car door closed softly. She backed into the juniper, cut across a side-yard and slid into the passenger seat of Joe Yazzie's black Bronco. He pulled out onto the main street.

"Look back," he said. The garage windows glowed bright orange. "You know what those Jesus Way people say." She shook her head.

"The fire next time."

He left her in the Tenderhome back parking lot.

"Good to meet you," he said. He jutted his chin at the door. "We don't go in these places. Too many bad things."

"You're smart," she said. "Give my best to Connie."

"Oh, I do," he said. "Every chance I get." She stepped out into the cold and she could hear his big laugh every step of the way across the dark lot. She opened the door to the home and walked into Nick's arms. His eyes were red-rimmed and peaceful.

"Richard?" she asked.

"I'll never tell," he said. "He also made a big pot of coffee."

"I wonder if he does windows," she said sweetly.

"Not till I'm gone."

"Truly," she said, "I'm done for a long time with all of that. I need a real break." He kissed the top of her head.

"You do," he said. "You gotta look in the mirror and see Liz."

They'd left the Christmas tree up in the solarium and the place almost smelled good. Rose handed her a chocolate-chip cookie.

"Richard has great instincts," she said.

Annie was stretched out on the couch. "If my grandma saw me now with you hoodlums," she said, "she'd make me grind corn for a year."

"Where's Deena and Katz and Paul?" Liz asked.

"Downstairs, unloading," Nick said. "I gotta get back." She followed him down the stairs into a basement room. It was a mausoleum for things, for oak dressers and mildewed cartons, gilded ornate mirrors, and racks of winter coats reeking of camphor. The place was spotless. Katz was gray under the strips of fluorescent lights. He and Deena swung the last trunk into place.

"I need to go through that," Liz said.

"A friend taught me the secret of locks," Katz said. "Shall I?"

"By all means."

He fiddled with the combination and grunted in satisfaction.

"You open it," he said.

She swung back the lid. Under the chill light lay all the desert's color, all the patterns of the Colorado Plateau, worked in leather, worked in silver, worked in wool. There were saddle blankets and a leather bridle studded with conchos, the turquoise the old kind, veined, darkened by the sweat of horse and rider. A cigar box was tucked under leather thongs. Liz knelt and opened it. She could smell the dark scent of tobacco. When she looked up, Katz and Deena were gone. Nick watched her from the doorway's shadow.

Hatt's stone box rested in a tangle of turquoise and heishi and silver rings and Zuni stone fetish: tiny coral birds, jasper bears, a jet cougar with a shining crystal heart-line. She set the little creatures aside and opened the lid.

"This is it," she whispered.

The box was green and gray, the stone unremarkable, dull, the perfect setting for the wine-red velvet that lay within. Liz unfolded the cloth. She felt Nick lean over her shoulder; she could smell him, his work-sweat, the good animal scent of his hair. He lifted the bracelet out of the cloth and held it out to her. She sank back on her heels. She was tired, her bones liquid, her muscles supple as the old cloth. She could hear Katz and Deena in the hall, their soft voices, Katz's fingers drumming against the wall.

"Here," Nick said. "I wish it was mine to give."

He slipped it around her wrist. He did it well, found the soft spot between the bones, pushed gently, kissed her skin where her heartbeat pulsed, where the silver circle did not close.

"I'd better go," she said.

She paused at Hatt's door. The same old sounds murmured in the hallway, a cough, a whimper, a sigh, the midnight drone of a radio turned low. She stepped in and heard the rasp of Hatt's breath. A car pulled into the back parking lot; its headlights shone through the curtains, and washed Hatt's hair in light. Liz stood over her. Under her fingers, Hatt's skin was warm and dry.

"On the heart-line," Liz whispered. She leaned across the blanket, across Changing Woman and Monster Slayer and Born for Water, across the long mound of bone and flesh, and lifted Hatt's left arm. She tugged the bracelet from her wrist and slipped it around Hatt's, found the soft place, kissed the pulse.

"You can go now," she said. "Go home." She wanted one final illicit act, to bundle Hatt in her blanket and carry her safely north, to Tsegi, to one of the perfect caves that pock those mesas where the warm sandstone flows back and back, into that red canyon, into that place where the bones of the Old Ones lie. She pulled the blanket to Hatt's throat and kissed her forehead.

"Another time," she said. And left.

"I'm almost sorry it's over," Katz said. Liz nodded. Annie sat up slowly. She grinned at Paul.

"I'm your boss," she said, "so I can tell you this. Remember that slogan in ranger training: 'Fire, our friend and our enemy'?" He laughed. "Well, once," she said, "I burned a sandal that washed out of that one-room place near Box Canyon."

"I saw you," Paul said. She nodded.

"We've got a lot of work to do."

Paul grinned. "You're the boss."

Rose finished her coffee and looked around at all of them. "I've got to go," she said. "Manny's got a new job; he's got to be there by six-thirty. I want to fix him breakfast, talk, you know?" Deena nodded. Rose touched Nick's shoulder.

"When are you leaving?" she asked.

"Tomorrow."

"I'm sorry," Rose said. Nick stood and hugged her carefully. "So am I," he said. They all cleared away the cups and crumbs and ash trays. Rich walked in and flipped on the television. It did not surprise Liz that she did not want to leave.

"It's as though you're already gone," Liz said. "Don't let me feel that way." Nick uncoiled from around her and leaned back against the pillows. "You hate good-byes," he said. "You always have." He pulled her head down to his chest. "Listen. That's a heartbeat. I'm here. I'm no dream."

She kissed their sweat from his skin.

"I know," she said, "I was just trying to tell you that I'm going to miss you. That I already miss you. Because this good-bye is for good." She laughed. The tears were running down her face. "I'm a mess," she said. "Good-bye for *good?* For lousy, that's what good-bye is for."

"Yes," he said quietly. "Lousy. I'll miss you, too. For a long, long time." She moved up beside him, curved her body against his, skin to skin, muscle to muscle, pulse to pulse. He fell asleep. She stayed awake as long as she could. Through the night, she woke again and again, and played the old game, moving her leg away, moving it close. Each time, no matter what she did, from the immeasurable distance of sleep, he moved closer . . .

. . . They were twins, sisters, the old man in the one-shouldered robe of the Kachina Mana, his hair caught on one side in the coil of Hé-e-e Wuhti; Talasi the same. He carried a flat basket piled high with white *piki.* She held his arm, stopping as he stopped, feeling his small weight as he struggled for breath. The village streets were empty except for a bony dog, her teats withered and useless. Her pups had been eaten, whether by wild dog or human no one knew.

They had not sent word of their visit. The old Priest had moved on with most of the people of Antelope House. The new leader was young. The old women said he was frightened of the old ways, and ignorant. They said he was pitiful and dangerous, cold to his wife. They said he loved power more than the hunt, more than his children, more than his own mother. He had forbidden the dice. The fools had simply crept away to a hidden place, drawn the game's circle in the cracked earth and tumbled down their kernels of stunted corn.

At the full moon, Pamosi had sent two cousins, strong young men, to bring Toho to East-Rising House. Though she was bent near double with twisting sickness, she had fed them all. She had told them the gossip and more.

"We are gone past the time when anything can be forbidden," she said. "Rules are smoke. All that is left are our songs, our circle."

Talasi and Toho reached the kiva as dawn washed up from the East. They offered cornmeal and prayed, Toho's head trembling like a cottonwood leaf. Talasi turned to him and bowed.

"Thank you," she said. They walked to the roof-hole and began their descent, stepping down into the smoky air, the whispers of the men rising up, like the whirr of raven's wings over the dying fields.

"Forgive us," Toho said. "I am dying. This woman, your cousin Talasi, is my helper. It may be that we bring messages from our Creator."

The new priest nodded. He was handsome. He had the sharp black eyes and high cheekbones of the People from the South. Green feathers and discs of *tsorposi* hung from his ears; on his wrist a woodstone bird's head was set in a band of shell chips. He and the others had been making *pahos.* Within their circle lay neat piles of sticks and cotton and small clouds of eagle down. Talasi looked away.

"Welcome," the new priest said. He was graceful, his voice low and musical. She realized she did not know his name, or how he sang, or danced, or if he had ever stood, shivering, under Crow Mother's great wings.

Toho leaned against her. She could hear his harsh breathing.

"Please join us," the new priest said. The others nodded politely. Toho settled slowly to the floor, Talasi behind him, her back straight, her hands on his shoulders. He set the tray of *piki* at the edge of the circle.

"Two women," the new priest said. "Or men dressed as women, or woman and man."

"Two teachers," Toho said, "not by our will."

The new priest nodded. Talasi saw that he was no fool.

"We have prayed," Toho said. "We sang over our long troubles. It may be that Masau'u will use us now."

"It may be," the new priest said smoothly.

Talasi pressed her palms against Toho's forehead. In the last instant before the work took her, she looked around the circle of men and saw only strangers. The room began to fade. She saw, as she had once seen, only the flickering pulse of a life-thread. It was many colors, the red of the heart-line, the mottled brown of the great snake, the burning yellow of the old lion's eyes . . .

. . . The skylight was black. Liz burrowed into Nick's shoulder away from that cold, starless dark. It seemed to fall over them. She struggled up. The icy air cleared her head.

"Hey," Nick murmured, "are you crazy? Get back in here." He snagged her back into his warmth. "What's wrong?" he whispered into her hair. "You smell scared."

"Nightmare," she said.

"Use me," he said sleepily.

She shivered. "Hold me," she said. "Press your hand against my back . . . there, between my shoulder blades. Stay awake. Don't move your hand away till I wake up." As his palm settled square against her spine, she felt his warmth, his strength, his old, old skill and she drew all of it in, as though he were an ancient ocean and she the shoreline. His touch washed over her, from her back to her shoulders to the base of her skull to her dreams, each wave cresting in on itself, carrying her safely, in perfect harmony, forward, steadily into the kiva. She reached out into the dream . . .

... Talasi leaned back into an unknown touch and watched the thread of the old man's life begin to glow, to redden, till scarlet mist drifted all around them. His voice thundered out, singing, the song floating on the waves of blood-heat pouring through her back and hands.

"Beware," the voice rang out. "Beware. These are not stories. Your houses will tumble in, your weaving will be torn from your looms unfinished. There will be sleep without dreams, creatures gone to vapor even as they leave their mothers. The dying will be trapped between life and Going Over. Our children will see their Mother Earth pierced and dying, their Father Sky fouled and dying. Our children will kill the deer, the rabbit, the turkey without thanks. They will smile and kill each other. They will fall on their women's bodies and bring only disease.

"We will rip from Mother Earth a glowing curse, that which is hidden, that which is never to be loosed. Even now, we have felled the Sacred Trees and let the earth wash away from our Mother's body, we have lost our home. We have lost all but our singing."

His voice died away, no more than the whisper of spring rain, the whisper of too little, too late and twisted in on itself. The mist of his breathing darkened. Storm-red, dust-devil, it spiralled up. Words, not the People's, harsh and guttural, filled the light.

Through the blood-black air, Talasi saw the polite faces of the men. She saw their eyes close. One by one, each stranger turned away, man by un-named man, till they sat in a blind circle, each one turned away from his kin, each one staring politely into the dark.

Toho slumped against her. A dry wind poured down through the roof-hole and spun around the mute circle. It caught the *paho* sticks, the string, the clouds of eagle down and whirled them, round and round, faster and faster, till all that remained was a snarled, heartless mess ...

... Liz opened her eyes. Dust motes shimmered in the golden light. She could hear icicles melting outside the window. Nick's hand was still pressed flat against her, his arm curved round her waist. She felt hollow and fragile. Her shoulders ached. He slid his hand from her belly to her breasts and stroked her. His breath was warm at the base of her skull.

"Now?" he whispered into her hair.

She turned and pressed against him, breast to breast, and went quietly into the dark peace of his body.

Moving On

"I TOLD HIM I WANTED TO SAY GOOD-BYE," Liz said, "as though we'd be seeing each other again in a week or two." Deena shaded her eyes against the sun pouring through the cafe window, and nodded.

"And?"

"I took him to the shuttle. We both said we couldn't have stood that drive to Phoenix. He leaned over, kissed me, climbed out, and walked away." She stabbed at her coffeecake. "We never even held each other one last time."

"But you did," Deena said. "Whenever you did. That's how I always say good-bye to Deej. Like it's no big deal."

"But the truth is, it's finally over, all of it. Nick. Small Mountain."

"Yes."

"You know what hurts the most?" Liz asked. Deena shook her head. "We'll never know if Hatt's bracelet gets buried with her. That's what eats at me. She's going to die. Her kids will do the right thing and, someday, I'll wander out here and see that bracelet on somebody's wrist."

"A skinny tan wrist . . . or a fat hairy one, right next to one of those watchbands with forty-three turquoise."

"That's it. That's what's gonna haunt me."

As they left the cafe, a wet snow began to fall. Deena zipped out of the parking lot and headed north, her taillights pastel in that thick white air. Liz stocked up on coffee and chocolate and three tabloids. A cow had knocked a flying saucer out of the sky. A farmer had been tripped into a watering trough by a vicious rabbit. A man had eaten his wife. She was grateful someone was on top of the real news.

The road home faded in and out, carlights floating in the snow like Japanese lanterns, the pines rising like dark islands in a pale northern sea.

The cabin was still warm. She set juniper on the coals and waited for it to flare up, to release its warmth, to melt her tears. The snow became dry and vicious. It blasted the north wall of the cabin and sifted in through the leaks in the stove-pipe, hissing, sending up plumes of steam.

"White-out," she whispered. "Me too." Her bones felt hollow, her mind as blank as the cabin's windows. "Nothing moving out there," she said to Sugar, who ignored her thoroughly. "Nothing in here."

"You wait," she said. "You wait till you feel like this." She'd seen a cat in pain, moving, stopping, moving, stopping, no move the right one, no place free from pain, all places cursed. She poked through the refrigerator, saw nothing even remotely appealing, closed the door, started to write Jen, gave up, picked up a book, set it down, picked up the paper, set it down, poured a glass of milk and left it half-empty on the counter. Sugar lapped it up.

"Thanks, sister," she said, piled juniper on the fire and crawled, fully clothed, into bed. She didn't think she could sleep, didn't really care, she just knew that she couldn't outrun this one, this lousy, good, good-bye. There might be a kind of wisdom in just going flat with it. A cat would. A woman would, with any other awful but distinctly non-fatal misery. The stove blasted, the pipe glowed red. The heat worked on her. She started to sweat, hard. She could smell the fear. She pulled the sleeping bag over the quilts and went into it. . . .

. . . The men were gone. Talasi held Toho's body in her arms. A clean breeze drifted in and out of the roof-hole, spinning the tangled feathers in ever-widening circles, till the earth floor was empty of all but foot-prints. She sang to Toho, of her love for him, of the Peoples' undying thanks for his work. She sang her promises: that she would find the few people left and carry him into the Mother; that she would care for his new charge, a wounded she-hawk; that she would make sure his sacred place, his tools, were not defiled, in the days to come, the seasons to come, in the unknown worlds ahead.

The roof-hole went dark. Kihsi climbed down the ladder and crouched next to her. He stroked the old man's hair. He set his hand in the center of her back and smiled as she leaned back against his touch.

"I am very tired," she said. Kihsi poured some water from the great *wikoro* near the fire-pit and carried it to her. She drank deeply.

"Are you strong enough to help me carry him?" Kihsi asked.

She nodded.

"We can take him to my mother's house and prepare him for the journey home," Kihsi said. He watched her. She was older, her face lined, her hair no longer sleek. Beneath the heavy robe, the sweet curve of her body had been sharpened by too little food. She looked up at him. The depth of her eyes frightened him. If he looked too long, he could be lost. There was a coolness in her gaze, a calm, the look of a grandmother. He ached to touch her.

"I can do that," she said. "I can come to your mother's house."

"Poliw has taken the children to my cousin's," he said. "She will return to help us."

Talasi turned her eyes from Toho's face and looked straight at Kihsi. "You are still most beautiful to me," she said quietly. "I am jealous of Poliw, of the children. Too often, I have prayed that it all could be undone, that we had fled, that we had taken the time we were not given. These next four days of mourning for the Old One; those are all we have."

He nodded. "We are leaving."

"You and your children and your wife," she said.

"Not my wife," he said.

"The children's mother, then," Talasi said. "Your friend. She is strong. She left her village to come here. The gossip about us still goes on and I see how she looks at you . . . with trust."

He nodded.

She stared into the empty circle. There was no charm there, no seeing, no spirit voice to speak what she must say.

"I am glad for you," she said, "and sad."

He stroked her hair. "It is the same for me," he said. "How else could it be?"

He stood. "Set him down. We will take him to be washed. We will fast." He laughed bitterly. "How do you fast when there is no food?"

She folded her shawl and set it under Toho's head. "I have asked myself that question," she said. "There has been no answer."

. . . The blizzard had broken. Her eyes glazed with sleep, Liz watched the darkness beyond the snow-piled windowsill. In the skylight, Orion drifted down, toward the white world, toward the morning light . . .

 . . . They kept Hotomqam behind them as they trudged the last steps to Toho's house. The waning Kelmuya moon was a slim crescent, tilted and empty.

By the time they began their slow climb to the *tuukwi* edge, Hotomqam was gone, only the pale moon left shining . . .

. . . Liz woke, wrapped herself in a quilt and hauled the rocker out to the front stoop. Dawn crept across the fresh snow and quickened. Shadows faded and were gone, the glazed grasses opal in the shifting light. There was pure beauty in that place; pure absence and good-bye, at last. She could live with both. As the first sun-sherd cleared the horizon, she said her prayer of thanks and went back to bed . . .

. . . "I sent for Pamosi," Poliw said, "Thought I am sure gossip travelled faster than my messenger."

They had laid Toho on a new reed mat, his hair washed, his old body clean. Talasi had baked *piki* from the last pile of corn. They had water for their guests, a few dried berries. They had not eaten for two days.

An old man climbed slowly down the ladder. They knew him. He was Kwingvi. He had carved wonderful things from the dark-leafed trees that grew near Two-Color Mountain. When his hands had grown too weak for that work, he had taught himself to make other things, regalia, pitch-smeared baskets studded with precious shells and stones. He set a gift at Toho's side, a bottomless basket covered with perfectly matched chips of *tsorposi*, edged with shining beaver teeth and slivers of red pipestone.

"For the old lion's journey," Kwingvi said.

"We thank you," he said to Toho. "May your spirit hear us."

As day moved into evening, more people came, the few who remembered, the few who sang.

They all left gifts, those who wove, those who made sandals, those who carved, those who wound the soft strips of rabbit fur into his last sleeping robe.

As early evening filled the roof-hole, Pamosi crept down the ladder. Her great eyes, black with the medicine she had taken to help her travel, burned with pain. From her carrying sling, she took a bundle of pure white cotton, unspun and raw. They made Toho a mask and secured it with a braided cord woven with four turkey feathers.

"He could journey without the mask," Pamosi said. "His work was pure. He needs nothing to declare the goodness of his life."

She unwrapped a bowl and set it by Kwingvi's basket. A single lion was painted in black against the bone white of its perfect shape.

"I learned from a woman from the East," Pamosi said, "to paint from dreams, for the Gone-Over, for their journey."

Talasi set the drained shampoo roots aside to be buried with him. They unwrapped him and dressed him in an unworn kilt, its hem hung with shells. They adorned him with strings of *tsorposi*, and his beaded cap, black and white, beaded in the spirals old as memory. Later, they would pack his tools: his staffs, his rattle, the pouches of paints and minerals, the string of snake fangs, his digging stick, his atalatl, the bird snare woven from his young wife's hair . . .

. . .Liz woke and dressed for work, the dream singing in her. She climbed through knee-high snow to the car, anxious to be on the road, out of the gray light. The snow had fallen thick. Ravens fluttered up from the pines, circled slowly and dropped back, shaking down glittering clouds of snow.

She took it slow on the glazed highway, as though she travelled on dreams and waking mattered very much. The sun was frozen, a silvery hole in the flat sky. She thought of Toho's warning, of terrible skies, of the dying suspended between life and death and new beginning. She prayed for Hatt's release and her own. She prayed to continue moving on.

The cafe kitchen was warm and sweet. Artemis was glorious again, shining black-and-purple silk wound through her hair, her wrists shimmering with bangles. Liz stood near the big oven, stretching, bending, letting the heat flow over her throat and shoulders. Artemis brought her a cup of cinnamon tea.

"Shall I help?" she asked.

"The tea is perfect. I just need to get to work."

"We need bread and soup buns and bagels," Artie said. "Lots of kneading." She set her hand on Liz's shoulders. "You're very tight there," she said. She did something that hurt, then felt wonderful.

"I'm just scared," Liz said. "That's all."

Artie unclasped the garnets from Liz's throat.

"You don't need these anymore," she said. "You're on your own."

The storm blasted back in, with rain, with ice, with all the power the Hopi had danced for in the early summer. Artie left. Viv called the boss and told him they were closing early. "Enough's enough," she said fiercely, and turned to Liz. "Have you got a place to stay in town?"

"I'll go to Deena's." Liz said. "I'll be fine."

She packed a bag of brownies, muffins and a half-pound of coffee beans and closed up the place. Driving was impossible. The walk was just what she needed, into a wall of wind under a furious sky; she had to concentrate on every step. By the time she got to Deena's door, she was sweating and exhausted and mildly jubilant.

"Give me a real challenge," she said. "No more ghosts, no more banshees, no more phantom-romance hanging 'round."

"Sounds like a hit," Denna said glumly.

"You look terrible." Liz said.

Deena brought the coffee pot into the woodstove and they settled in.

"A friend in need brings brownies," she said. "Some things never change." She shook her head. "Yes. Some. Things. Never. Change."

"I think I get the point. Continue."

Deena leaned forward, coffee mug clasped in her right hand, cigarette dangling from the left. She stared at the floor. Cigarette smoke curled past her. She was barefooted and she dug her strong toes into the carpet.

Liz thought of a snow leopard she'd seen pawing at the concrete in an eastern zoo.

"It's Deej," Deena said. "Or more like it's *not* Deej. She was supposed to be here this weekend. I made plans. She wanted a pajama party. Look," she waved toward the kitchen, "chips and popcorn and ice-cream cake in the freezer and fruit pops I made myself and I rented a video, that one about the crystal, and called her best friend. It was all set, all ready and so was I and no Deej." She looked up. Her eyes were dry, her jaw set so hard the bone burned white under her skin. "Here's the killer. Jack didn't call it off. It was Deej. 'I choose to stay at Daddy's,' she said in this prissy little voice," She stood up. "I will now pace," she said. "She knew, Liz. She knew she was hurting me. It was a conspiracy. Jack got on the phone. He said, in *his* prissy little voice, 'I think we should honor Deej's choices.' Hell, he never honored anybody else's choices in his life." She shook her head.

"What did you do?"

Deena stopped and planted her fists on her hips. "I asked him to put her back on. Oh, he was so gracious; he was just Mr. Mom. I reminded her that Amanda was coming over. I told her about the ice-cream cake. I didn't want to bribe her. I did. I don't know. She just said it again, about choosing, and she hung up!"

"He's been working on her."

"I know. And, there's nothing I can do. Divorce is war and kids are territory." She disappeared into the kitchen. When she reappeared her arms were full. She balanced the cake, the popcorn, the chips. She held the video in her teeth. Liz plucked it out. "No television, please," she said. "I never told you this: I hate television. So, now, in real life?"

"So, I do my two least favorite things. I wait and I let it be." She tilted the popcorn and chips onto the coffee table.

"Why are we so tediously honorable?" Liz laughed.

"Because," Deena said as she ripped open the chips, "there's something about being able to live with myself. Something about not wanting anything I didn't get fair and square."

They watched the fire dim. The little aspen rattled in the wind. Liz could hear clumps of snow thunder off the neighbor's pines. Deena rolled out the sleeping mat.

"Early?" she said.

"Six. Artie's on early bake. I'm not due till seven-thirty, but I'd better give myself enough time to walk." She stretched under the blankets. Deena kissed her on the forehead.

"We'll just save that cake for your birthday," she said.

"Then that's breakfast," Liz said. "I'm forty-six tomorrow."

"No fooling," Deena said. Liz heard her click off the kitchen light and pad down the hall. She stretched again. Her back felt fine. Summer was long gone. She remembered the streetlight through the spindly aspen.

She remembered Macleod's heavy heat. She almost missed him. She thought about waking up unashamed and Deena wanting only what she got fair and square and that seemed right . . .

... They carried Toho to his old kiva and dug a shallow grave in the center of the hard-packed floor. They were weak with hunger. They took turns. Pamosi carrying smoking juniper slowly around the small circle of the room. In the circle's heart, behind the pure white cotton, Toho faced the roof-hole. Pamosi watched him, knew his spirit walked toward the light, that the air moved easily in his breast; that he saw, without pain, that the People's stay was over, that it had been no more than an intake of the Spirit's breath. The medicine was wearing off. She felt the dull pain creeping in her bones.

"Goodbye," she whispered, "may we meet soon." . . .

... Thunder shook the house. Liz woke, saw lightning, the silhouette of the little aspen, then nothing but a shimmering curtain of snow. She turned on her side. Beyond the railroad tracks, the thunder faded to a low growl. She could hear Deena move in her sleep. She thought of her children, of her mother and father and brother, of the great magic of their lives passing through her; she thought of Deena and Deej, of Rose and Manny, of Hatt, of the old family, the new, the ancient one she'd found in sleep. She gauged the trickster light. It was possibly the first morning of her forty-sixth year. It was the year an old dream-maker had called the Turning Year, the year upon which one's life pivoted. She guessed that Toho had been only a little older when he died. And then she thought of Macleod and Nick, that joy, and Joe Yazzie's huge laughter and she prayed for the dream to go on . . .

... They buried him with his tools, his signs of power, his last gifts. They were afraid as they touched the wands, the lion's yellowed teeth, the pouch of black crystals. They worked quickly, putting everything in its place, covering everything deep with sifted earth. Pamosi smoothed the surface with a parrot wing, and traced the nesting circles of the old migrations. Footsteps echoed on the roof. A stranger tapped on the ladder-pole and, at their welcome, climbed down.

Pamosi scattered sage on the burning juniper coals. The stranger washed the smoke down over his body. He was short, and darker than sandstone. "Thank you, Grandmother," he said. "I am from the South, once a trader to your people. I knew this old man. I bring these."

He opened a cotton sack and drew out two birds, their tails spilling like colored light over his arms.

"These are not for the game," he said harshly. "I will help you close in this burial, as we have learned to do. The fools live with us, too. We have left them. We will travel north when your people next leave."

He helped them dig a shallow pit near Toho's left hand. Poliw untied her last *tsorposi* strand and draped it over the birds. Their feathers caught the firelight and were gone in a shower of dark sand. They finished the work. The fire burned down, flickering on their faces, on the prayer feathers that shimmered at the four directions. Pamosi set the firebowl, still glowing, in the kiva's western curve. Evening after evening, far into time, far into the new worlds, the sun would melt down into the earth, over the ashes of Toho's last fire. Climbing the ladder, Talasi looked back. The coals glowed like a burning eye, as though Masau'u stood there, watching over the old lion's empty hide.

They worked through the night, prying loose the rough black stones, tumbling them down, sealing the old man in. By dawn, the kiva was rubble. They prayed in the cold purple light, and walked the broken circle of stones, setting *pahos* in the sand, between the boulders, wherever the twigs would hold steady. Their hands trembled, their good-byes rang out softly. Toho was nearly home; their home was gone.

Talasi felt a touch on her aching shoulders and turned. Pamosi held out the little path bowl. "Drink this," she said.

Talasi held the bowl to her lips. The burial mound shone in the cool gray light, the *pahos* flowers of light. She drank carefully. The tea was warm. Her aching throat opened. She swallowed and took a deep breath. Kihsi and Poliw were gone.

"We will leave the old one some *piki*," Pamosi said, "and then we will go." Her helpers moved towards them on the trail from House of Eagles. "Live with me," she said. "I will not leave for a while."

"I will," Talasi said. "I will be grateful to do that."

. . . "Happy Birthday." Deena knelt by the sleeping mat with a pot of coffee. Curtains open, the room was filled with snowlight, delicate as white jade. Liz sat up and waited for Deena to fill the empty mug.

"I'm afraid the dream is ending," she said.

Deena poured. "Drink," she said. "It's too early for deep meaning." She held out the half-and-half. "Luxury," she said.

"Thank you." Liz crossed her legs and rested her arms on her knees. "What time is it?"

"Early. Rose just called and asked us if we were going to be lazy and let the sun drag us out of bed. That's what the old lady says whenever she stays up there. She's gonna be unbearable if this keeps up."

"Was it Hatt?" Deena carried the coffee and cream back into the kitchen.

"No. Rose is at Paul and Claire's with her family. They went out for dinner last night and got stranded by the storm. They want us to come out."

"Sounds fishy. It being my birthday and all." She heard Deena fiddling around in the kitchen running water, opening jars, closing cupboard doors.

"Come on." Liz said. "Show your face. I want you to look me in the eye. Besides, I can't go. I have to work."

"No. Phil called. The highway's blocked from the south; he can't get in. You have a full day off without pay."

"Well," Liz said "How about that! Here's to coincidence." She raised the cup. "Let me jolt my brain back to this century and we'll hit the road. I suppose we'll have to skip the cake for breakfast because we might as well take it out to Paul and Claire's."

"My thought exactly."

They inched their way north on the slick highway.

"Do you mind driving?" Liz asked.

"Nope," Deena said. She tapped the brake and slid elegantly away from a stalled pick-up. "I almost enjoy this." She glided into the fast lane, accelerated and began the long, slow climb up the last hill out of town.

The heater purred. Liz felt cradled in warmth, held safe in Deena's good hands on the wheel. Wisps of vapor drifted between them and the sharp sun. The pines were blurred with snow, the mountains glistening.

"Katz's cat is buried out there somewhere," she said fuzzily and waved toward the far cinder cones.

"Take a nap," Deena said. "You want to be awake for the casual gathering of friends we're meeting for breakfast."

"I knew it," Liz said. "Viv was all giggly yesterday." She watched the moiré ribbon of highway ahead. They crested the hill and began to drop down; in the distance, the Painted Desert was pastel with snow. Liz closed her eyes.

"Sleep," Deena said. "I'll wake you when we get there."

"I don't want to miss anything," Liz said . . .

. . . The little hawk hopped on its good leg and screamed. Talasi rolled her mat and set it against the wall. Her fresh-washed hair felt heavy. She tossed it back from her face. There was no reason to wind it in coils. There was no one to see her. No one to gossip. The hawk screamed again.

"Be patient," she said. She bent to take dried meat from the bowl near the firepit and winced. As Kelmuya's cold moon approached, her bones had begun to ache. She sighed. It was in the blood. They had carried Pamosi, her body hunched and twisted, on a litter for the the journey north. She had taken Talasi's hands in hers and wept.

"I miss our work," she'd said. "Remember."

The hawk screamed again; she was always hungry, and she had spied the meat. Talasi tucked the scraps in a pouch, untethered the hawk, set her on her shoulder and climbed the ladder. The old white dog was at the roof-hole. She sniffed carefully at Talasi's feet and took the strip of meat she offered.

It was long past Third Dawn. The sun hung in perfect balance overhead. There were no shadows. She thought, as she always did, sun or shadow, of her last sight of Kihsi, his dark body growing smaller, his family steady behind him, all of them lost at last in the bright northern light. House of Eagles was empty, Place of Water nearly so. The burial mound was overgrown with *pale'na* and rabbitbrush. Only the faded *piki* basket remained. The spirit-trail feathers were gone, blown away in the harsh winds. The gamblers had been the last to leave, drifting north from all the ruined places, their arms filled with what had been left behind, their heads bowed in shame. None had come near her, nor close to Toho's grave. Stories had been told. She knew the gossips feared her. *"Pow-aqa,"* they said. "Woman of dark power. Øqala Wuhti."

She sat on the warm rock and let the heat drift into her sore bones. There was little time to rest. She laughed. "Woman of dark power." Had she the power, she would not have worked so hard, gathering, planting, hovering over the young corn, she and the white dog scaring away the ravens; grinding, rationing out the gruel and rabbit and dried bitter berries. Had she the power, her bones would not mutter with that dull ache. She thought of Pamosi, of her courage, of how the twisting illness broke her body and left her mind whole.

"That was not such a blessing," she said to the hawk. The white dog pricked its ears. "No more meat," she said. "Chase a rabbit. Bring me one." She thought of the days ahead and wondered if *her* courage would hold. In the basket near the firepit, there were powders and dried flowers. "One for vision, two for death." She shook her head. That path was closed. If she took it, the stubborn *pahaanas* and her Parrot cousin would just return and make her live.

The little hawk fluttered its good right wing and screamed. To the south, over the great hollow in the earth, flew a huge eagle, its feathers shining. It circled down, again and again, swooped low over the dried grasses and rose, something struggling in its talons. The hawk hopped wildly on her shoulder.

"There is grinding to be done," Talasi said. "I will work on the roof and you can scream to your friend." The bird blinked its golden eyes and settled firmly on her wrist. She began the climb home, through purple beeweed and the pale folded blossoms of three-flower, past the tumbled kiva, past the stone snakes, invisible in the bright sun, up the twisting trail, the white dog grinning at her heels.

She stopped at the firerock slab. The spiral was in shadow, the lizard's eyes flat, her tail curled delicately into the unseen hole from which she emerged. Talasi tapped the outer curve of the spiral and the rock rang. She sang with it, the dog curling round her ankle, the hawk peacefully prodding its feathers. She sang to them, to the clouds, to the mountains, to the stories and memories and unknown gift of the last of her life.

The rocks are ringing,
the rocks are ringing,
they are ringing, in this light,
they are ringing toward the mountains,
they are ringing in the people,
they are ringing in the clouds.

We shall live again,
we shall live again . . .

SPIRIT TRAIL

The Oldest Man speaks:
"That was a good one, old woman. Lots of loving, old ones dying right, babies getting born. Only part I didn't get was those pictures of colored light. You made that up. That would mean no more stories would be told. That could never be."